D0906073

The Broken Vase

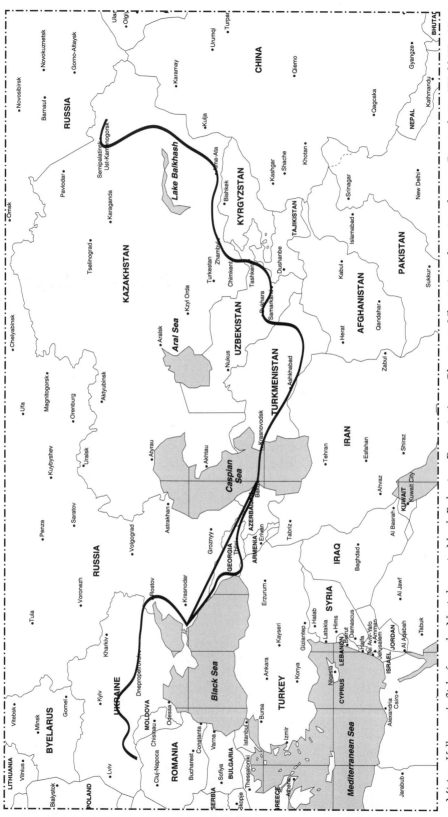

Miriam Kellerman's flight from the Nazis began in North Bukovina, Romania (now Chernivtsi, Ukraine), and continued across Russia during World War II.

The Broken Vase

A novel based on the life
of Penina Krupitsky, a Holocaust survivor

Phillip H. McMath
and Emily Matson Lewis

Butler
Center
Books

LITTLE ROCK, ARKANSAS

Butler Center Books

The Butler Center for Arkansas Studies
Central Arkansas Library System
100 Rock Street
Little Rock, Arkansas 72201

First Edition: September 2010

ISBN 978-1-935106-20-3 (10-digit ISBN 1-935106-20-1)

12 11 10 9 8 7 6 5 4 3 2 1

Copyeditor: Dawn Nahlen
Proofreader: Ali Welky
Book and cover design: H. K. Stewart

All images contained in this book were provided courtesy of Penina
Krupitsky unless otherwise noted.

Library of Congress Cataloging-in-Publication Data

McMath, Phillip H., 1945-
  The broken vase : a novel based on the life of Penina Krupitsky, a Holocaust
survivor : / Phillip H. McMath and Emily Matson Lewis. -- 1st ed.
     p. cm.
  Includes bibliographical references.
  ISBN 978-1-935106-20-3 (alk. paper)
  1. Krupitsky, Penina, 1924---Fiction. 2. Holocaust, Jewish (1939-1945)--Fiction. I.
Lewis, Emily Matson. II. Title.

PS3563.C3865B76 2010
813'.54--dc22
                              2010021222

Printed in the United States of America

This book is printed on archival-quality paper that meets requirements of the American
National Standard for Information Sciences, Permanence of Paper, Printed Library Materials,
ANSI Z39.48-1984.

Dedicated to the memory of Max and Deborah Geller

"A piece of bread when you are hungry is more important than a piece of cake when you are full."

Deborah Geller

.

Table of Contents

Preface

As a student I had the good fortune of studying European literature under Dr. Ben Kimpel, one of the most impressive men I have ever known. Ben introduced me to the Russian greats, which was an experience from which I have never quite recovered. This in turn led to an interest in Russian history and language.

Isolated language study is difficult, so I found a Russian teacher, Penina Krupitsky, "Miriam Kellerman" in our book, who was superb. Even though I was something of an indifferent student, I did make a wonderful friend.

Along the way I gradually learned a little of her personal story: that she was Jewish, had been born in what then was northern Romania in a place called Czernowitz—a town I had never heard of—and that she had survived the Holocaust by fleeing into the Soviet Union. I also knew that she, her husband, and children had emigrated in the 1980s to the United States, where they now live. I knew little else.

We lost contact briefly, but then one day she wanted to meet. Over lunch, she asked me to write a historical novel based on her life. I declined, explaining that I was too busy writing something else and didn't have time. She then said, "When will you finish?" My response was that it would be a couple of years. "I'll wait," she replied.

Two years later I began. It turned out that a local writer, Emily Matson Lewis, in concert with Penina, had researched Penina's life. Emily graciously allowed me to use her marvelous notes. Armed with these, and in close collaboration with Penina, I have fashioned a *roman à clef*.

This has been a very great honor. Particularly gratifying has been the privilege of working with Penina, a truly extraordinary human being of indomitable courage, will, and character. The more I have written, the more I have realized the importance of her story as a symbol of that sublime something we can only call the greatness of the human spirit.

Why a novel? Penina said she wanted something unique, artistic, to memorialize her parents, not just another straightforward memoir, of which there have been so many. It must be said that, while permitting certain artistic liberties, she insisted on scrupulous attention to the facts. In that respect, it is a "true story" in the common use of that term. No significant event has been invented or altered.

Since I have found that fiction frequently offers intimacy without context and history the opposite, I have attempted to provide both. In this regard I have added footnotes to frame the individual narrative as standing in the foreground of a much larger canvas—the tragedy of Miriam Kellerman, our heroine trapped in a world at war.

It is conventional to think that a great "Dark Age" was averted in Hitler's defeat. In large measure this is true. But in a sense, it seems to me, this view is too narrow.

From the increasing perspective of time, we can see now a little clearer picture: that Europe—and with it the world—has been really at war with itself since 1914. This titanic struggle certainly continued after 1918 in Russia and Eastern Europe in the form of revolution, civil war, and Stalinist terror—followed hard upon with the rise of Hitler, the Spanish Civil War, and the invasion of Poland in 1939. This global war did not really finish in 1945, as has been supposed, but has spread under different names and forms throughout the world with the subsequent Maoist revolution in China and spin-off wars in Korea, Vietnam, and the Middle East.

To be sure, it is too soon to assess this opinion completely, except to say that we now can see it more as one monumental event spilling out of the failures and illusions of the 19th century into the 20th and 21st, not as isolated struggles labeled the First, Second, and Cold Wars, etc., which I suggest are little more than convenient, but in some ways useless, subcategories. In a word, what has evolved is one Great World War that, for better or worse, will be midwife to a new phase in the human drama that simply lies beyond the limits of our immediate historical vision.

Be that as it may, one consequence is beyond doubt: the permanent and perhaps fatal damage to the West, what Stefan Zweig in despair called a kind of European "suicide." Like Miriam Kellerman, is the West now a "broken vase," and can it ever be mended? In a sense, the particularity of her story is but a microcosm of the bigger tragedy.

As for acknowledgments and sources for this novel, the principal historical ones have been Alexander Werth's superb *Russia at War* (Carroll and Graf, 1964) and Martin Gilbert's essential *The Holocaust* (Owl Books, 1985).

I would like to thank my very dear friends Eddie Back and Ronnie Cameron for their encouragement and support, without which this book never would have been published. Likewise, I would like to acknowledge my debt to my outstanding secretary, Shelia Murberger, for suffering through the numerous rewrites in her spare time with efficiency and dedication.

But of greater importance, I have relied upon the forbearance and patience of my dear friend Penina and the love, support, and invaluable editing of my beloved wife, Carol.

Phillip H. McMath
2010

Foreword

I was born on July 13, 1924, in Czernowitz (now Chernivtsi, Ukraine), North Bukovina, Romania. This part of Romania belonged to the Austrian-Hungarian Empire until World War I. Czernowitz, called the Jewel of Bukovina because of its architectural gems, sits on the Prut River at the foot of the Carpathian Mountains. Its population consisted mainly of Ukrainians, Romanians, and Jews, many of them graduates of Vienna University, as was my father, Menasche Geller, a lawyer. My hometown was so beautiful that I was not surprised in my first year at school to find out that it was sometimes called "Little Vienna."

My father, Max (as we all called him), was a highly intelligent, well-read, honest, and kind person. We didn't see much of him during the week because of his job, but on the weekend he would play with us and sometimes take us out of town to the mountains. My mother, Deborah (Dora Schapiro-Geller), was beautiful, intelligent, well-read, warm-hearted, and a reasonable disciplinarian. She always liked to help people and encouraged us to do the same.

My brother, Joseph Geller, became a well-known building engineer. Later in his career, he built "intercontinental" hotels in Europe, Africa, and other places. Joseph lived in Tel-Aviv. Sadly, he died two years ago.

My mother instilled in us honesty, integrity, and kindness. She taught us the way to deal with people, how to respect our friends and others. She worked at a private lycée, teaching French. When I was a baby, she stopped working and devoted her life to the family. Of course, she did not forget to visit the beauty salon every Friday and to meet her friends once a week for lunch or a cup of tea or a shopping spree. However, she preferred to buy clothes for the family in Bucharest or Vienna, the two cities my parents went to rather often.

In summer, my mother would take us to the Carpathians (in June and July) and to the Black Sea (in August). September was my parents' vacation. They usually spent it in Switzerland, Czechoslovakia, and Austria. We stayed at home with our maid, Stefana. She was considered to be Mother's assistant and a member of the family. I don't remember ever hearing the word "maid" or "servant" used in reference to her.

In 1937, my father was fired because of his religion. Our beautiful life was in danger. My poor mama became the "bread finder."

In July 1940, the Soviets "freed" us from the capitalist yoke, thus liberating us from a normal life, by invading Bukovina. Then on June 22, 1941, Germany attacked the Soviet Union. Though we did not know exactly what was going on with the European Jews in the Nazi-occupied territories, we knew what happened in Germany. We realized that our very existence was in jeopardy. My father, an admirer of German culture, would not believe all the rumors. My mother, a more practical person, started packing. A few days later, she told me to leave on foot with a group of students. The elderly people would be taken care of.

I was against this plan, but my mother insisted. Late on the eve of my departure, she came to my room. My bags were packed. She looked lost, pale; her eyes were sad and tears rolled down her face. "We might see each other for the last time, my dear," she said and started sobbing. Then, regaining composure, she continued, "Put into practice whatever I taught you. Be respectful to people, help others whenever you can, divide the last piece of bread when you see another hungry person. Be always appreciative for everything people are doing for you. With time, you will learn that a piece of bread when you are hungry is more important than a piece of cake when you are full. Always respect people for what they are, but not for who they are." She started crying again and left the room.

My parents were taken "good" care of. They were among the first to be deported to "Bershad," Transnistria, a vast territory in Western Ukraine, and the first deportees from Bukovina and Bessarabia (a province on the eastern border of Romania) were the most unfortunate. A great number of them died from starvation, complete exhaustion, and sickness.

Bershad held first place among the other ghettoes in Transnistria for the number of victims brutalized by the German and Romanian officials, whose sadism was exercised the most there. Their victims went through all the terrors of hunger, cold, homelessness, forced labor, sickness, epidemics, and death.

One eyewitness, Mr. Joseph Löwy, wrote: "We, the exiled from Bukovina, exhausted because of days of walking in pouring, cold autumn rain and snowstorms, were driven by Romanian guards over muddy fields and through forests. We sank in clinging mud, with blows from their rifle stocks; the gendarmes drove us away from dying parents and children."

And this exactly happened to my dear Deborah. She collapsed, and nobody was allowed to help her. They shot my mother and started ripping her golden crowns out of her mouth while she was still breathing. My father died or was killed soon after.

They, as well as millions of others, were silenced and left in the death valleys of ghettos and camps during the Holocaust. They cannot speak and raise their voices. We who are alive are obliged to speak to everyone about the Holocaust, about the hatred that can cripple people and lead them to murder others.

I hope my book, *The Broken Vase*, will help young people and become an inspiration to them. It will teach them how to build a world of love and not of hatred.

Penina Krupitsky
2009

I

Barbarossa

They pitched camp in the small evergreen forest near the Czernowitz[1] airport. By dark they had built a great fire, singing songs and telling funny stories about anything but the Occupation. At last, the cold June air forced them reluctantly into their sleeping bags, but sleep held no interest. There was so much to think about, and it was too wonderful to lose such precious moments in mere sleep, so they fought against their friend sleep, trying to hold time, freeze it, and savor it in the illusion of a final escape from the eternal ticking of the clock.

This was June 21, 1941. The clock did not rest but ticked on as millions of men were waiting, watching their own clocks tick inexorably toward midnight and a new day dawning under the aegis of the Nordic King Barbarossa.[2] On it ticked.

Tick. Tick. Tick. Till the last second touched 12. One more tick and it was June 22; one more tick and they were into the new day.

Tick. Tick. Tick.

History's clock had ticked billions of times to get to this moment, it had been patient, and the final tick at last had come.

Tick. Tick. Tick.

Every tick was watched by a million pairs of German eyes, waiting many miles from Miriam Kellerman's camp as she now looked at her watch, seeing its second hand sweep away another day, then turning off the lamp and lying back. Someone said something in the dark, a pause, a joke, everyone giggled. Another pause, another joke, not as good, a weaker giggle. She could not remember if she slept or not, could not remember the exact interval between the ticks or the hour, but she did remember an explosion.

She sat up. Someone screamed. Miriam found herself outside, where she saw a young man, illuminated by distant fires, pointing to a sky filled with flame and flares. The airport was burning! Had a plane crashed? Yes, that was it, another explosion, the sound of aircraft, more explosions.

"We're being bombed!" someone yelled.

Miriam watched in shocked fascination. Yes, that was it. They were being bombed. The flames danced in shadows across her face as she listened to aircraft moaning above, then watched as red tracers arched lazily, too graceful to hurt anyone she remembered thinking, lifting languidly from the airport like a stream of liquid fire softly entering the belly of the clouds.

Barump. Barump. Barump. They went in bursts. How strangely beautiful, she recalled thinking.

Another heavy explosion, then two more, much closer, as she felt the shock waves caress her face. Someone shoved her; she fell, got up, and raced to her tent. It was a chaos of yelling and stumbling, a ragged mob of schoolchildren who shoved things in packs and ran herd-like over the same ground that, only the day before, they had crossed in such orderly and happy anticipation.

With explosions echoing and planes droning, they were force-marched back toward Czernowitz, crying, trembling, muttering, till they ran upon a roadblock strung like a hastily spun spider web across their path. Their teacher shouted the great question to a Russian officer. The answer shot back quickly: "It's war! Hitler has attacked us! Germany and the Soviet Union are at war!"

Miriam got home in time to hear the radio crackle out the admission that the Nazi army was advancing. Then there was the music of patriotic songs, praise of the heroic Soviet army, and at last a short pause, followed by instructions that seemed disjointed and hasty: Children were to flee on foot eastward, while adults were to await transportation. When more patriotic music scratched out as filler, Deborah Kellerman clicked it off.

David Kellerman slumped into his chair, mumbling like a man in a delirium, "I've lost too much. I am too old, too old to run. I'm never leaving."

"Dream if you wish," snapped Deborah, standing over him, "but I'm going to pack!" Then to Miriam, "Dear, please leave us, just for a moment. Stay in your room; I'll be there shortly."

Miriam sat on her bed, waiting, gently rubbing her little dog Hans. After what seemed a very long time, Deborah came in and said, "You must get ready, Miriam. I'll go find out who's leaving, when, where, and by what route. Then, there's no choice, you must go with them. Meantime you must pack…must be ready, there'll not be a moment to lose. The German army is advancing rapidly, and you must be gone when they arrive."

"But Mother, what will…?"

Deborah interrupted. "You must leave, you must leave at once! There is no alternative," she cried, adding more softly, "We'll meet you in Kiev, don't worry…there'll be transportation for us all. There's nothing to worry about, my dear! The arrangements are already being made as we speak; it's all planned out and very well organized. We'll see you in Kiev."

"But Mother," sobbed Miriam, "Kiev is such a long way!"

Deborah interrupted again, saying, "Isaac has returned. You will go together; you won't have to wait any longer. I know this will please you."

Miriam fell silent, indeed pleased but feeling vaguely guilty all the same. In less than an hour she had taken up her school pack again, used only a little before in the make-believe of the camp-out but filled now with blankets, sandwiches, and a thermos of tea. Then she rummaged to find an old black valise into which she stuffed blouses, skirts, two dresses, and some lingerie. Gently she draped her jacket over the bag and sat on her bed waiting. She was ready. But she didn't leave. Instead, she simply waited, packed yet uncertain.

Two days later, Deborah said solemnly, "Everything is prepared. You'll leave tomorrow."

"Tomorrow, Mama?"

"Yes, tomorrow, there's no doubt, tomorrow."

One more night at home, and then what? She saw Isaac, who was of the opinion that they could leave at any moment and should be constantly ready. She lay on her bed staring at the curtains, wrapping herself again mentally in their beautiful texture, remembering the safety of her childhood imaginings. The little princess, she realized with a shock, the little lady was on the verge of becoming, of all things, a little soldier retreating eastward with the Red Army.

That last night Deborah came and sat by her for the final time, her face broken with sorrow. She stroked Miriam gently, then managed to say: "Miriam, Miriam, it's possible, dear, that we will never see each other again. There's so much I should say. But I want you to remember everything that I have taught you. I want you always to be honest and compassionate, help others whenever you can. Treat everyone with decency and respect; be loyal to your friends. Always appreciate what people are doing for you."

She stopped, choked up, not quite able to go on. Then she remained very quiet for a very long time, softly stroking Miriam's head, hands, and face, kissing them insatiably, then embracing her. Miriam felt Deborah's tears caressing her cheeks, then her lips, and finally her eyes. Her heart broke, never to mend. She had always known her mother's love, yes to be sure, she had always known that but never really felt its fathomless depths till now. This farewell, with its exquisitely joyous pain, was seared in her memory by this long, silent embrace, till at last Deborah stood wearily, lingered, and was gone.

Miriam unsuccessfully tried to will herself to sleep, but when she gave up, sleep surprised her, took her away to a place where Deborah's agony consumed her in a turmoil of dream-like grief till she awoke in exhaustion. She lay staring upward, fearful of moving, listening to her mother's voice: "Be thankful, Miriam, for a piece of bread when you are hungry; you'll find that it is much better than a piece of cake when you are full."

But she did not want any bread, nor any cake, only her mother again, whom she knew now she might be losing forever. Only Deborah could assuage her hunger. Nothing else would ever do.

Some bombing startled her, but she flinched without moving her head or changing her expression. Instead, she concentrated on the sounds of Deborah in the kitchen, her voice mingling stridently with Isaac's, which was saying, "Mrs. Kellerman, please, Mrs. Kellerman, you must listen! My parents want you to move in with them. You'll be safe there, completely safe, please!"

But Deborah was refusing, saying "no" over and over. "No! No! No!" she said hysterically.

"But," Isaac said, "physicians are critical, valuable. Father won't be bothered. He'll have influence, can protect you as part of his family, see? Please! I beg you!"

"No," Deborah said. "David will never leave, never, it's impossible, useless to ask, so please don't. We thank you, of course, but please, please don't mention it anymore." Then she added, tears gracing her eyes, "Isaac, I want to speak to you of Miriam. Promise me that you will take care of her."

Miriam walked in slowly before Isaac could answer, just in time to catch his eye as he delivered his promise, almost like a wedding vow: "Yes, I will." Then to Miriam, he said, "I promise that with all my soul, Mrs. Kellerman."

Seeing Miriam, Deborah wept, held them both, her arms melding them for a moment, three-as-one. Now David Kellerman shuffled in but said nothing, standing aside silently like an intruder.

The Germans were drawing nearer. Miriam could wait no longer. A group left in the early afternoon, with Isaac and Miriam among them, trudging east.

2

The Dniester[3]

Miriam, a month shy of 17, was almost as frightened by the older age of her group as she was by the retreat itself. They were mostly her older brother Karl's contemporaries, young people, to be sure, but six or seven years beyond her age. Yet no one felt quite old enough to face what was coming. They were seized by a new kind of fear that none could describe; not even in the Soviet Occupation had there been anything like this. It was like being taken at the throat by some great beast that kept choking and squeezing, forcing one to gasp for air, as Miriam hurried along to a frantic, internal drumbeat in her chest, stepping, stumbling, and sometimes running to the shuffling cadence of the group.

She had not understood before, but now it was very clear that her parents could never have kept up. This is what they knew and simply couldn't bring themselves to say. The flight was too much; it cast the weak aside and, in the end, favored only the strong. But one step at a time, one moment at a time, Miriam resolved that she could do it that way; otherwise she was lost.

She now fixed her eye upon the backpack of the girl trudging just in front, a stout youth named Becky. Miriam's thoughts quickly raced back to her parents. This parting memory kept intruding against her will. Like a recording it would be played again and again, over and over, those last haunting hours, those last goodbyes: Deborah's tearful face and David's abject, pitiful, silent defeat.

"Miriam, please," her mother had begged, the soft words screaming in Miriam's mental ear: "Miriam, be thankful for a piece of bread; it's better than cake when you're full. Be honest, be compassionate, help others. Isaac, promise you'll take care of her; you must promise. You may freeze; here, take some warm clothes!"

"But, Mama, it's not even fall! I'll be fine. This will be a summer adventure. I'll be back well before winter!" Miriam had said with a smile. But her mother knew better and desperately stuffed everything that would fit into her valise.

"We'll come later, don't worry, there'll be transportation," Deborah had said. "We'll meet you soon, in Kiev. Don't worry, my dear, it is already arranged."

They had stood in the hallway, next to the small hill of baggage. It was time to leave and join the group. Knowing that time had at last slipped away from them, Deborah's stoicism fell from her as a shield at last too heavy to carry, and she clung to Miriam like a child, sobbing, finally turning from her as Miriam pulled away and handed Deborah to her father. Miriam would see forever her mother's face buried in David's chest as suddenly, unexpectedly, he was strong and Deborah weak, broken, and exhausted, with nothing left. He held her up with one arm, preventing her from slumping to the floor; with the other arm he waved Miriam away.

"Go away now, quickly, you must go, you can stay no longer," he had said with that little motion of the arm—and she saw they were no more, were gone. Just a little movement of a hand, that's all it took, and it was finished. *How frail life is! How very fragile! How suddenly it all changes!* she thought. *What fantasies are all notions of permanence. Why had we ever been so stupid as to believe in them?! At the root of it all is a great nothingness! Nothingness! What fools we are not to see it!*

Now Becky's green backpack bulged ahead, each pocket of it filled to bursting, while Miriam's little pack felt ominously light. She gripped her valise tighter and strove ahead one step at a time; that was all she could do. Already she was tired, but she was equally determined to survive. Survival would be a vindication, a victory for Deborah and David Kellerman. She would survive for them! Her survival would defeat Hitler! Anything else would be a betrayal of her parents, who wanted her to flee and survive.

As they reached the eastern edge of town, another bombardment began. Miriam ran for a ditch, hid, and watched as a cloud of German Stukas[4] swarmed over her like malicious black insects. They buzzed so close that she could almost see the pilots' leering faces as they stooped downward in an eerie whistling, screaming, angular dive, then pulled up, releasing their bombs behind like small explosive eggs. Then they lingered and dipped down again to drop more dollops of fire on the columns behind and ahead.

The planes zigzagged away just before some Russian soldiers, in ragged formation, shuffled past. A few days before, Miriam would have laughed at these shabby, frightened boys carrying guns, but today she could not. For the first time, she felt a pang of sympathy. Now, falling in behind them, her own tiny clump somehow adhered together, a smaller mass within a much larger one, pressing tightly but still separate, till at last they reached the river to find soldiers spread out on either side.

It was the Dniester, flowing broadly and swiftly before them. They all had to cross at the same narrow spot, crowd forward into one ever larger glob, moving out of Bukovina. Here their relationship to the soldiers really changed. They were no longer foes, occupiers, but friends struggling against the same pursuing wolf. They all were its prey now, and they knew it lurked behind and around their herd with hungry, panting delight.

It was late afternoon when this exodus at last touched the river. This was at Khatin, about 35 kilometers from Czernowitz, where a line of linked pontoons had been hastily thrown across and the soldiers regulated people in a thin but urgent stream to the other side. Yet this tide swelled and swelled, exerting ever-greater pressure from behind itself, till it grew into a great, quivering, surging, mindless creature trying to press through a hole that was much too small. As she was pushed, punched, and pulled in a screaming current toward the river, she lost sight of Isaac. She yelled his name, reached for him, grabbed someone in front, grabbed another, but he had vanished. He had had her by the hand, held as tight as ever he could, but she was pulled away, out of his grasp and, worse, out of sight. "Isaac!" she screamed, but the din was now so great that she hardly heard her own voice. Everyone was screaming someone's name, it seemed, and "Isaac" had no special place on the bridge that day.

Once over the water, Miriam gripped Becky's pack, hanging on, fearing to fall, to be knocked away, drown, or be trampled, while they pressed forward, forward, ever onward. She held on and side-stepped, careful not to cross her legs, as onward they went, till at last, halfway, she could see ahead some uniforms with shoulder-boards, officers on the other side, she realized, who were checking papers, verifying everyone. It was ridiculous! It was madness! Papers?! Checking papers! Miriam saw an old man pushed back because he had no papers. She recognized him as a Communist, imprisoned by the Romanians but released by the Russians. But now he had no papers and was cast aside. He was nothing and was only just allowed to squeeze through—doomed—returning to find his own special bullet from the Nazi *Einsatzgruppen*.[5]

"Isaac!" she cried, looking ahead again, seeing him at last on the far bank, stretching out to her hopelessly with a queer look. "Isaac!" she screamed. He started to worm back toward her but was stopped by rapid shots fired in the air. The line also stopped. There were shouts in Russian as Miriam found herself frozen, gently rocking up and down, with a strong current gurgling just below her feet. A gruff Russian voice shouted, filling what had passed for a kind of silence, "You must go back! Go back to the other side! You will be permitted to cross momentarily!"

There was a roar of protest, followed by more shots and shouts. "Where will you go? Will you go back if you can't cross?" Isaac yelled.

"No! I will drown before I return," Miriam cried. "I will not go back! Never! Wait! I'll get across! Wait! I'm coming!"

Isaac smiled bitterly. Miriam was startled that he could smile at all. He knew she couldn't swim.

Isaac yelled again, "I'll wait, take your time; slide in behind the crowd, around them the other way!" he said, motioning.

But the line started stuttering backward, stupidly, as against everyone's will, against all logic, Miriam found herself shuffling back to where she had begun. "You must wait!" yelled the officer. "The army must cross first!" he said, striding up and down. "Anyone trying to cross will be shot! Wait until you are ordered!"

So they waited, huddled sullenly along the road like beaten animals until dusk deepened into near darkness. Then a long brown line of stern-faced infantry came to cross. As the last soldier shuffled by, the officer motioned. The mob rose as one, not as humans but as something else, lunging madly toward the bridge, knocking him into the Dniester. Miriam did not see the officer come up and didn't care. She raced with this surge onto the planks, everyone screaming, pushing, watching others falling into the water, splashing, sinking.

Crushing ahead over the pontoons that bobbed up and down under this weight, as if they wanted to side at last with the current and have done with them all, Miriam saw a little girl fall and disappear, while her mother pushed on, not seeing, not even looking down as the child drowned. Miriam heard the child scream, saw her lifted above the waves by means of some hidden force, and then vanish.

In front an old woman stumbled and grabbed the sleeve of a man who reached for her, but she fell into the river. As she was carried away, Miriam saw her skirt billow out like an umbrella that bore her up, then close as she rolled to swim but sank instead.

Miriam began to sob, great body-wracking sobs that she could not hear because of the noise, but still she kept moving. Hands and elbows jabbed and struck her. She was shoved. She was poked. She was cursed. Feet nipped her heels like yapping dogs, but she kept her balance by leaning on someone in front. To trip was to die—there was no rail or guard, one slip was to perish—so she pushed and shouted she knew not what and held she knew not what as she slowly shuffled toward the other side.

Then, as if they had waited for the sun to sink, the Stukas stooped yet again, sending bullets into the bridge with a sound like rocks striking wood. They strafed down in a graceful, whining, sliding arc, shooting and pulling up, wagging their wings as they sailed away. Now Miriam heard a completely new sound, a great collective groan. There was no real discernable speech, only this deep bestial moan, just as she came upon a bleeding woman lying across a pontoon, her feet almost touching the water as she stared up at Miriam with a look of resignation—then her eyes softly shut, closing off the world with all the indifference of the dead.

Miriam stopped. "The Germans are going to blow up the bridge!" was the first clear sentence she heard above the pain of the increasing pressure and the pandemonium of the ever-expanding groan. Miriam had managed to stagger her way to the middle of the bridge, but flames now leapt before her higher and higher.

"The Russians are burning the bridge, we cannot pass! They are burning it! They are burning it! We will all burn to death!" was the next clear thing she heard. "Go on! Go on! Run through it!" someone shouted from behind.

She felt a push, tried to step over the woman, lost her balance and nearly fell, not into the river but into the flames, yet the mass pressed her through it until she was nearly across. But Isaac was not there. She forced her way around a set of elbows, fixing her gaze upon the people in front, pushed and pushed, and for the first time in her life, cursed as she finally tumbled to the other side, miraculously stumbling onto solid ground.

"Isaac!" she cried out over and over. "Isaac! Where are you?! Isaac! Wait, Isaac! Wait! I'm across! Isaac, I'm coming!"

Now the mass opened up, spreading itself to the right and left, as Miriam marveled at the dirt beneath her feet, real dirt—the other side! She was out of Bukovina and across the Dniester! But the Stukas reappeared, bombing and rattling the bridge once more. Miriam jumped into a crater, landing on top of others, and then someone fell on top of her. The bodies were piled in layers like sacks of flour as the explosions and bullets popped through people with a dull thud, entering one and sometimes going into the next and out again.

With an arm, a leg, a kick from somewhere, another great weight falling on her, Miriam lay suffocating, sandwiched between the dead and dying. But still she held her valise, just pulling it over her the instant another body fell on top of it, nearly blinding her. Half conscious, she was crushed downward, smothering her heart to near bursting. There was another great explosion, then something struck her very hard, harder than ever, and she blacked out.

It was dark when she awoke. She could see nothing, nor could she move. Then she noticed something wet dripping on her, trickling down her nose, cheek, and onto her lips. It tasted strange. God! Oh, God, it's blood! It was not hers, she knew. Blood everywhere! She could smell it, it was in her mouth, its salty bitterness was on her tongue. She was soaked—she was covered in blood! She screamed until she thought she would faint, and then she shoved and squirmed through the bodies. Emerging from this collective tomb, she pushed aside corpses, heads, loose arms and legs, then at last a dead woman whom she lifted up by the hair and shoved away as she crawled out in a kind of resurrection.

There were people everywhere, wandering about the riverbank, moaning and mumbling in a mad, stumbling, circling herd of lost souls, as if abandoned now to roam freely in the inferno that the bridge, road, and field had become. Indeed, they had crossed not into salvation at all but into hell.

Her bags! She turned and like an animal digging in the ground for food, she rummaged through the bodies till she found her valise and pack and pulled them free. Standing up, she could see someone there, barely visible, standing in the dark. "We're alive!" a male voice shouted.

It was Isaac. "Miriam, we're alive! We crossed the river!" he said, embracing her. "We're across! What happened to you?! I've looked everywhere! Have you come out of the ground?"

"Yes, Isaac, I have just come out of the ground, out of a grave," she cried, falling into his arms.

They began trudging eastward again, shambling slowly through the night with shadowy shapes darting around like ghosts till they happened upon a roadblock of hard faces illuminated by headlights—soldiers asking yet again for papers.

"Your papers!" they said with rude, fear-tinged voices. "Show us your papers!"

Mechanically, with trembling fingers, Miriam and Isaac produced them. Mechanically, they were waved on. Mechanically, they walked. Like zombies, they trudged into Eurasia, staggering their way ahead of Hitler's Blitzkrieging army.

"They are savages," Miriam muttered as she walked along, her valise and pack growing heavier with every step. "Their culture, the vaunted German culture, means nothing at all, prevents nothing at all, has been swept aside by the Nazis like a cobweb," she said through clenched teeth, then louder to Isaac: "The Germans are barbarians! All of them! Barbarians! Isaac, I tell you, I hate them! Hate them all!"

"Hush, dear, be as quiet as possible. There, there just ahead, is a little group; let's fall in behind, come on, hurry and catch them."

Silently they merged into the rear of the little group, but soon they came upon yet another checkpoint. The Soviets, they realized, were obsessed with infiltrators. But this took far too long, this endless checking of documents. Isaac suggested they divide into three smaller segments so each might stand in sight of the other two, then pass more quickly through the checkpoints. Miriam, of course, stayed with him, and Becky, who they were pleased to find again, and another girl became part of their little subgroup. They moved quickly this way until they saw the sky growing light, gradually diluting the darkness from the east.

Isaac, always in the lead, halted. "The others are straggling behind," he said, looking back. "Let's wait till they catch up."

"I'm exhausted," Becky said dropping her pack with a thud. "Let's sleep for a time. I must have some sleep."

"Yes," pleaded her friend, likewise dumping her pack. "Let's sleep, Isaac, can't we? Just for at least an hour or so. I just can't go on anymore; I must have some sleep."

"OK," sighed Isaac, glancing around, pointing to the left. "Looks like a field of some kind over there. Let's go in it a ways. We can hide there pretty good, I think, lie down for a short time."

"Good," Becky said, lifting her pack with a grunt. "I'll find us a spot," she added, as she walked off and soon found herself stumbling through rows of head-high corn. They formed a well-hidden circle among the stalks and slept a sleep not of fatigue but of near annihilation. From this extinction they awoke in a dreaded instant to the world of war, Isaac first nudging Miriam, then everyone else. He ordered them in an urgent whisper to get up and resume walking.

"Don't speak German!" he warned in a louder voice while they were saddling their packs in weary silence. "Only Russian, or you will be shot. The Russians are jumpy, shooting at everything and everyone; they don't care, anything strange will get shot at, any strange sound, especially German. So whatever you do, don't speak German."

For several days they made good progress, stayed together, got through the checkpoints, and slept in hidden circles for a few hours before starting to walk again, walking into the endless space of the steppe. Then their food ran out. They tried begging from other refugees without success. Miriam traded away her watch for some stale bread, hard cheese, and cucumbers from a sly old man pulling a wagon with a horse—enough food to fill their stomachs once but no more.

"Forget about food!" Isaac snapped when someone complained. "It's a luxury. You're young and can go without it. Think of the old people who can't keep up! We're lucky! We're strong! We're going to survive and kill Nazis! Don't let them defeat you! Don't give them that pleasure! Eat your anger! It will keep you alive! It'll keep you walking. The Germans are just behind us, remember? But we're not going to let the bastards catch us! So forget it! Forget eating! Just keep walking! Keep moving!"

"Don't speak German, Miriam, you keep speaking German!" he continued. "Always speak Russian! You must learn it now, really learn it! No more schoolbook Russian but the real thing! It's your new language, like it or not."

Hand over your papers! Keep moving! Sleep a little! Get up! Don't speak German! Keep moving! Don't ever give up! Get angry! Eat anger! Keep moving! Speak Russian! Hand over your papers!

The next town was Proskurov.[6] They had to reach it. The last soldiers had promised they would find trains there; then they could ride deeper into the Soviet Union. Escape! They were now hearing guns in the west as planes flew over in droning waves, heavy bombers. "German Heinkels," Isaac said. The front was catching them, but at Proskurov, it was said, they could get some rest and then ride quickly away to safety. It was there they would be reunited with their friends; it was there they would find food, fresh water, and maybe—hope-on-hope, please God!—news of their parents! "Arrangements have been made," they had been told.

So they kept walking, thinking now only of Proskurov. As before, they had thought only of the bridge, like a new lover, now it was Proskurov! *Dear Proskurov! I no longer think of the Dniester and its wretched bridge, only of my dearest Proskurov! Please embrace me, Proskurov! My love! My hope! My salvation!*

Their escape had taken them more than 150 kilometers, and as they approached the town, they sensed something odd, something not quite right. They moved ever closer with their eyes fixed on that ill-defined region of horizon and sky until they saw a light in the east that was not the morning sun at all, but a false brightness haloing over Proskurov.

"It's on fire," Isaac said quietly, as much to himself as the others. Coming to a halt, setting down his bag, he said somewhat louder, "Proskurov is burning."

"They're bombing it," Becky said matter-of-factly, now coming up beside him. Everyone knew this long before it was said, so there was little comment as they stood and watched in mesmerized disappointment.

"Isaac, what do we do now?" Becky asked finally, turning toward him slightly.

"Keep walking," he said, picking up his bag and moving forward. "We have no choice but to keep going. Come on, let's go."

So they pressed on toward the flames. Soon there was an acrid smell burning cruelly into their nostrils. "Smoke," someone said, as to herself. "I smell smoke."

Gradually the sky glowed larger, brighter, until it seemed as if they were nearing the very edge of a netherworld. People slowly appeared in front of them, specters, as from nowhere, then behind, emerging from the fields like sleepwalkers, moving as one mass toward the blood-red edge of Proskurov's horizon. Finally they reached the station only to find that the trains were burning; cattle cars, charred and glowing, seemed to be kneeling or lying on their sides like dead or dying elephants someone had set alight.

It had all been a lie. Proskurov was a whore. They could only keep walking.

Keep walking! Walk! Find another town! Forget Proskurov! We'll find another one! Keep moving!

Isaac said they must now get past Proskurov as quickly as possible.

"We'll just go around it. Come on, we'll find a bombed-out area on the other side and hide there. Once a place is bombed, the Germans won't bomb it again. There we'll be safe," he said. "Don't look at the bodies. It's war, people're killed, their problems are over. Don't look at them; it'll do no good, that's what the Nazis want. Just keep walking; we'll find a place to hide soon. Come on!" he said in something like a low shout.

But there was a buzz, a plane—a whistle and an explosion. Miriam ran to a ruin and dove under it. Time raced and yet seemed to stop as the ground jumped under her. She was unhurt. *Isaac, as always, is right, the Nazis would not bomb something they had destroyed. They were good, efficient Germans. They loved to destroy new things; rubble held no allure. It is the place of salvation, the rubble—always hide there from a German; hide from him in the destruction he has made! There is safety in the ruins! Blessed are the ruins; they will make you free!*

More Heinkels roared over, more bombs fell somewhere in the distance, and then all was quiet. *I can't go out. I will stay here until it's completely safe,* Miriam remembered thinking. Then she began to freeze in the chill of the night, shivering until her teeth rattled. Finally, wrapped in the arms of darkness, she slept against her pack.

3

The Vase

"It's time for me to play, Mama!" said Miriam. Deborah sighed. They had just returned from the mountains, and now this precocious 3-year-old was already asking for something else to do—she was never satisfied. Her mother thought a moment and then called to Stefana, the maid, asking her to manage a lunch for the "July Girls."

"Yes, yes! The July Girls! That would be wonderful!" Miriam said, looking at her mother and clapping her hands.

Mama and Stefana set her to coloring luncheon invitations for her two friends, all three of them born within a week in the summer of 1924. The mamas had all immediately seen the advantages. Bianca had a brother who was no more useful for play than Miriam's brother, Karl, and although Dora was an only child, so were they all in a way. Anticipating great fun, Miriam began coloring the invitations with three stick-figure girls of her imagination, all with beautiful curly hair. The curls were especially fun to draw, and Miriam loved them, even though such tresses on the pictures were pure fiction. Inside the invitations, she and Stefana drew three tiny figures that would be the dolls belonging to the three girls. It might be a lunch invitation, but they couldn't get together without their dolls. They would make it a very special lunch, indeed. Bianca and Dora would want it that way.

On the back of each invitation, Miriam began to draw a door and put her name over it in large letters. "Anyone can read my name," she said to no one in particular. "I've been practicing writing and have explained the invitations to Stefana, who will deliver them. See, my name is on the door, so the girls will come to my house this time to play."

It wasn't long before Bianca and Dora knocked, arriving with their dolls and their smiling mamas. When Miriam opened the door, her friends were holding their invitations in such a particular and beautiful way, and this pleased her. They stood shyly, waiting, not entering. Then

Stefana interrupted, taking charge, taking them in hand to the study, where she set three large cushions on the rug.

Gesturing toward the cushions, she said proudly, "These are your dolls' beds, ladies. Now you should get your babies fed and ready for their naps."

The July Girls plopped down with a giggle for their luncheon. Feeling very grown up, they all were excited by the prospect of "coming of age" at 4 the next month.

After the year had turned to 1929, Miriam sent out invitations again for another lunch with her friends, but this time no one came. Everyone was away. Papa was at work doing whatever he did, which was an enigma to Miriam, while Mama was out shopping and older brother Karl was at school. Stefana was busy in the kitchen. Miriam heard the plinking and clanking of washing and cooking that Stefana seemed to do unceasingly throughout almost all the mornings of Miriam's earliest life, when she was lonely in the apartment and not yet promoted to being that great thing called a schoolgirl.

Now Miriam went casually to the window. It was cold and raw and impossible to play outside in the re-frozen slush on such a winter morning. Her mother had told her to amuse herself in her room, but although she loved to read, this morning she was weary of her own books. So she sat down among others, the adult books lining the wall of the study that were read mostly by her mother. Here were the French and German novels, poetry, and plays with which her mother spent her leisure hours. Miriam sat on the floor, flipping idly through the pages of an old book, looking for the letters in her name, naming the letters she knew, pronouncing them in German. But no story came with the letters today. Nothing came at all, so Miriam put it away and wandered aimlessly into the dining room in search of something else to do.

Unexpectedly, the sun broke through the clouds and poured into the room, catching the facets cut into the crystal vase in the center of the dining table, making little rainbows dance around the intricate carvings. The vase sparkled like the diamond Miriam had seen on her mother's finger. Fascinated, she waved her hands through the light, setting the motes of dust into delicate motion, scattering the rainbows while playing the light beam up and down, causing the little diamond images to disappear and reappear like magic.

Twinkling ice diamonds and rainbows came before her memory's eye. There had been a large bush outside covered with very dry, powdery snow before the slush had come. Then the snow had been pretty; now it was dirty and ugly. But then the sun had played over the snowflakes piled upon the branches of the bush in a wonderful display of dancing light and dazzling snow that had entranced Miriam. *Would the vase do the same as the snow? Would it be more beautiful in little pieces like lots of tiny diamonds?* In a moment she found herself opening the door to the balcony and pulling a footstool from the study. She shoved the footstool to the railing, climbed up, and peered over, seeing the sunshine now brighter than ever bathing the carefully shoveled sidewalk. The snow had been pushed into dingy clumps, with all the sparkle vanished and beauty gone.

Miriam returned to the table, slid the vase to the edge, nonchalantly watching as the light moved away from the crystal. Tugging the vase to her chest, she had not imagined how heavy it would be, but she brought it to the balcony anyway, struggled onto the footstool, and worked the vase up to the railing edge. It was a relief to push it over. There was a wonderful crash, and a thrilling, shattering sound came up to her as she looked down, standing on her tiptoes and leaning over the balcony.

"I was right!" she yelled. "I was right!" she screamed louder.

The vase was indeed a scattered wash of diamonds on the walk, thousands of crystals with the glint of sunshine in each piece, the light dancing over them like jewels on the bottom of a stream. "How beautiful! How spectacular!" she yelled and then giggled. It seemed even more beautiful than when the vase had been on the table.

Or was it? she wondered, and now was not so sure and began to feel a vague wave of regret for what she had done.

As the clouds overcame the sun, her guilt and remorse crept just as smoothly like a dark shadow over the sun of her joy. Miriam knew that her mother would not like the diamonds on the walk, however beautiful they were in the sunlight. She turned and went inside. It had grown colder in the room through the open door, so she closed it quietly and carefully put the stool back in the study. Picking up her books again, she decided then and there that she would learn French.

Miriam was punished, to be sure. There were tears and an unforgettable spanking, followed by lectures, but they didn't matter because she had already drawn her own conclusions from breaking the vase. She had become convinced of the fragility of all such beautiful things, as well as seeing that the other things in the house, after all, did not really belong to her but to adult people, even to people she didn't know or couldn't see. The house was hers but not quite hers; the things were hers but not quite hers—except for the dolls and the invitations and a few small books—but nothing else was ever quite hers. She had decided she would have to walk more carefully through this house than she ever had, she would have to ask more questions until they were answered by much wiser people, and she would have to bear her frustration of being unable to read the forbidden books, reading instead the lessons that were thrust before her in the same lecturing tones that had been voiced after the spanking.

The next winter was harder, colder, and darker. But the fact that she was 5 gave Miriam an ever-increasing sense of confidence. Surely, she reasoned, sitting alone again much as she had done before, with Stefana in the kitchen again plinking and clanking and everyone else gone, things are possible for me at 5 that were just not possible for me at 4. "I'm 5, and I can appreciate beautiful things," she said out loud.

I wouldn't think of touching any of Mother's crystal now, and I know which books I'm to read and to study, whether French or German, and I'm never under any circumstances to read Balzac or the German poets that Mother reads so often, saying that some day she will share them when I'm older and "no longer a child…," and, of course, I know I am not ever to enter my parents' bedroom uninvited.

Miriam arose, stood for a moment, then, as in approaching the crystal vase, she walked almost unconsciously into her mother's room and began to finger through her dresses. *My own dress feels too small, too small for me, and my shoes are drab. I need a change,* she thought, thumbing through her mother's closet. She soon found the plum-colored *fais de chine* dress with matching shoes. She looked closely at the silk with the brilliancy of satin and thought of her mother, remembering the night her parents had dressed for an evening with friends and the sight of Deborah wearing the dress, with its long train hanging down onto the floor. Miriam struggled to slip off her dress and kick her shoes into the corner, so she could put on her mother's long, heavy gown. Then she stuck her feet into the high-heeled shoes and shuffled over to the floor-length mirror.

"Ah, yes," she said proudly, smoothing the satin, "but where is the train?"

She looked behind to see it clumped on the floor at her feet, despite the heels. Of course, she needed to be several feet taller, and so she pushed a stool in front of the mirror and climbed up, planting the wobbly heels in the soft surface of the stool while turning to look down at the train. *Beautiful! So very beautiful!* she thought.

"How elegant," she said, using that word out loud for the first time, a new one she had heard her mother use only the day before. She never forgot a new word, always filing it away like a miser hoarding nuggets of purest gold.

Now she was startled by the sound of unexpected giggling and laughter in the kitchen. Miriam had forgotten she wasn't entirely alone, and she realized, too, that it was not a good idea to be preening in front of her mama's mirror. There would be another spanking, yet another lecture. She began to step from the stool gingerly but lost her balance, tangling herself in the fabric and falling as a heel gave way, then ripping the train as she rolled onto the floor. She hesitated, staring at the ceiling before laboriously standing up, ashen, dressed in a torn gown, holding a broken heel in her hand. She quickly changed into her own clothes, grabbed the gown and shoes, deciding that she would take her mother's things to the summer linens to hide.

She slipped noiselessly past the kitchen, quietly opened the door, and tiptoed all the way up the apartment stairs to the attic. There she found a huge trunk for the out-of-season bed linens, almost full with her mother's pretty eyelet batiste sheets. She leaned over and pulled the top part of the pile aside, stuffed in the dress, hid it with sheets, then stuck in the shoes and covered them. Miriam returned to her book with the hope that all would be well and nothing would happen after all, not like the broken vase with spankings and lectures and beautiful but false diamonds scattered in the snow.

Within a few days Deborah looked for the dress and searched for the shoes. Vexed, she called Maria, the laundress; then Karl and Miriam were interrogated, but Miriam said that she knew nothing, nothing at all.

Finally, Deborah said to Papa, "I don't think Maria could have taken them, and Stefana wouldn't have done it, that's for sure. So how could they have disappeared? We shall have to confront Maria again, there's no other choice."

As always, Papa agreed quietly. So the next month a new woman came to wash the linens for Passover. When Mama and the woman came down from the attic, with the ripped dress in her mother's hand and the shoes in the laundress's, they held them out so that Miriam could see them clearly but in silence.

There were no tears or spanking. Miriam was treated instead with a kind of shunning, with the implicit knowledge that she had known yet said nothing, had allowed blame to fall on Maria and had permitted her to be unjustly accused. It was a moral failure that Miriam sensed as her censure, and it was the worst of all.

"You let someone suffer because of you, Miriam. An innocent person was accused unjustly…and you did not have the courage to tell the truth," was what she saw in her mother's eyes and, worse, what her own conscience whispered to her. She vowed never to do such an unjust thing again no matter what the cost. Never again!

A surprised Maria found herself summoned to the house to hear the confession of a 5-year-old who, under coercion and with choking throat and teary eyes, spoke in a cracking voice to confess and ask forgiveness. Maria gave her a long hug and left.

Such little-girl dramas were played out every day in the quaint town of Czernowitz, a picturesque place in the Romanian province of Bukovina. As provincial cities went, it was quite civilized, largely because it had repeatedly changed hands in the unending melodramatic country-stealing of Central Eastern Europe. A great cultural variety had been deposited by these imperial shiftings, like different plates of land crashing together from political earthquakes.

Before Hitler's war, Czernowitz was a satellite of some importance in northern Romania. It had a university, an Orthodox seminary, an ancient synagogue, a quaint central park, a good orchestra, a few theaters, some cinemas, and the usual coffeehouses filled with chess-playing newspaper addicts. It even rejoiced in a modest art gallery. Of course the Kellermans enjoyed these things, and being affluent, they sometimes vacationed south to Bucharest but more often entrained for Vienna—where Deborah and David had been educated, met, and romanced—or went with the children to the Black Sea for the summer sun and beach. Too, David, an Austro-Hungarian cavalry officer who had compromised his health in the First World War, habitually took Deborah with him to a Czech spa for a September rest.

In a word, Czernowitz was something of a diamond in a crown of European gems; in fact, it was the finest jewel of Bukovina and northern Romania. But, of course, such fine things are often stolen and re-stolen, and it had been a subject of dispute between the Moldavian Principality and the Polish Kingdom until the Ottoman Turks settled the matter in 1541. Then they were driven out by the Russians, who in turn allowed it to be pinched away by the Austrian Habsburgs in 1775, only to be lost again when the Great War at long last killed off all the Habsburgs and Romanovs, and Bukovina was bartered back to Romania in the great Wilsonian estate sale of Versailles. Eventually, through all of the goings and comings and crossings and exchangings, Czernowitz became a polyglot of Romanians, Moldavians, Germans, Russians, Hungarians, Ukrainians, Poles, and Jews.

Miriam Kellerman's family spoke German, Romanian, French, and, as Jews, were, of course, familiar with Yiddish. David and Deborah Kellerman observed the religious holidays without being orthodox or very devout, yet they circulated freely among all aspects of society, regardless of ethnicity.

In Miriam's tiny world there was their Romanian maid, Stefana, and Stanislav, a large, red-faced Pole who brought dairy products with a smile and inevitable good jokes. Then there were Irina Jubash, Miriam's good friend and daughter of a Gentile Hungarian doctor, and Marcella Argintaru, another of Miriam's best friends, whose father was an Orthodox Christian priest.

Karl, her brother, as she would often say, "was little use to me." Four years older, he intimidated when not ignoring her, and certainly he never played with her. She therefore frequently found herself alone, reading and thinking on the floor of her little room, companioned only by her literature, dreams, and newfound words.

Miriam's very best friend, in fact, was Stefana, and it was with her dear, sweet Stefana that much of her preschool time was spent. Stefana was part of an adventure that became one of Miriam's favorite childhood memories. It had happened the year they had gone to the mountains, on a day that Stefana had taken her to the park. As they walked along, they found what seemed to be an unattended pram. Stefana bent over it to discover a baby tucked away among a great pile of blankets. "I wonder who this baby belongs to?" she had asked.

When she lifted Miriam up, she could see the little infant's pink bonnet that fit snugly around her head, with curls peeking from under the edge. Miriam cried out, "Stefana, I want a baby, too!"

Stefana laughed with quiet embarrassment.

Miriam repeated the demand, adding, "How will I get one?"

"Ask your mother, dear," she said, turning away from the question.

Miriam, at home, did just that. "Mama," she said, running into the kitchen. "Mama, how do I get a baby? I need one with curls, you know, a real live baby with real hair."

Her mother studied the dough on the counter a moment, then turned to Miriam with a nervous laugh. "A baby? A real baby, you mean? Why? We have a real baby, Miriam. You are your mama's baby."

"Ah, Mama! But I'm not a baby anymore, and I need a little baby of my own, with pretty curls. Tell me how I can get one," Miriam demanded, stamping her foot.

Deborah turned and sat down at the table, setting Miriam upon her lap. "Well, Miriam, babies grow the way flowers do, from…from a seed," she said tenderly, rocking her a little, like an infant.

"Then I want a seed. Where do I get one?"

"Where? Well, let's see," Deborah said. "The seed you buy from the pharmacy; the seed is a pill that you take."

That was fine, but there was another problem. "I don't want a baby boy just now, Mama, only a baby girl. What kind of pill is there for a baby girl?"

"Oh, let's see…it's a pink one for a girl and a blue for a boy. Yes, of course, that's the way it works—pink for a little girl and blue for a little boy. You have to do it that way," she said with a very nervous, red-faced laugh.

"Oh, thank you kindly, Mama."

The next day, with Stefana enticed out for another walk, and while a friend diverted her, Miriam renewed her campaign for a daughter by crossing the street to the pharmacy. It belonged to a family friend with the happy nickname of "Uncle Obengruber."

Miriam stepped up to the door, opened it, and slipped inside, causing a small bell to ring out. "Who's there?" gruffed out Uncle Obengruber from somewhere in the back.

"It's me," Miriam squeaked.

She heard Uncle Obengruber grunt, then she heard several quick, very heavy steps as he shuffled up to the corner of a counter and looked down at her. "Miriam, my little one! Where is your mama?" Uncle Obengruber asked.

Himself a Gentile, he was married to one of Deborah's friends, a beautiful Jewess.

Miriam shrugged.

"Where's Stefana?"

Miriam pointed across the street to Stefana, still in animated conversation with her woman friend.

Uncle Obengruber stepped out and called to Stefana, motioning to her. She entered grimly, panting out, "Miriam, what are you doing here? Why did you leave me? What do you want from Uncle Obengruber?"

"Please," Miriam said, "Uncle Obengruber, I need a pill to get a baby…a pink one, a pink pill, please, for a baby girl. I'd like to have a baby girl with little curls."

Miriam studied Uncle Obengruber's face. It had quite suddenly changed. She saw that it was squeezing itself and changing color before laughter burst out under pressure like an exploding ball. It took a moment for him to gather himself, but when he did, he replied, "A pink pill, you say, and why not a blue one? You don't have anything against boys, do you? Blue ones make boys, don't you know?"

Miriam nodded politely. Stefana laughed with mild embarrassment.

Then Uncle Obengruber said, "But, first, I have to take care of a customer. Wait here."

When he returned, another man shuffled close behind. "Fritz, this is Miss Miriam Kellerman and her good friend, Miss Stefana. I wanted you to meet Miss Miriam."

The assistant nodded politely but withheld his right hand, which was busy wiping the left with a towel.

"See, you must know to whom we are giving these precious pills," said Uncle Obengruber with exaggerated seriousness. Now Fritz put the towel away and smiled, so Miriam smiled back.

"Here, Miriam," said Uncle Obengruber, pouring two pills—one pink and one blue—from a small packet into her little, sweaty open hand. "Now, Miriam, dear, please be very, very careful with these. Remember it takes quite a long time for a baby to grow. I'm sure you will have plenty of time to prepare. Please let us know which pill you take, and thank you. Please come again. Give your parents my very best regards," he said with a wave.

Miriam put the pills in her pocket, thanked him, bowed, and leaned over to shake his big hand, but she received a sweet kiss instead. This made her feel warm, and strangely she felt like the baby in the pram with everyone looking at her. Happy that her pocket held her pills packed tightly away, she looked up proudly at Stefana.

"Come," Stefana said officially in her deepest voice as they held hands and walked out.

Uncle Obengruber followed them to the threshold, holding the door. "Now, Miriam, whatever Miss Stefana says, you believe her, my little one. She's absolutely correct," he said a little too loudly, shaking his fat forefinger.

At home there was the usual lecture about not running away or crossing the street without a parent or Stefana, how it was, of course, "very dangerous" and that Miriam should work on obedience and be less self-willed. But, unlike the lecture about the broken vase or the torn dress, this all was said with a forced anger that Miriam saw through easily.

Then they asked her where she would keep the pills and what would she do with them. She did not answer but looked up with a certain stubborn silence. She would make that decision later, as always, alone; it was private, so she did not wish to speak of it to anyone.

"Well, let's just put them in this very special place in your bureau drawer, Miriam. If you still want one on your birthday, you can take it then, but not until. How would that be, dear, all right?" Deborah asked.

Miriam smiled a slight assent. Deborah's voice told her this was how it was to be. Her mother's small victory meant Miriam would have to wait a little longer for her marvelous baby girl with the curly tresses. Of course, Miriam never imagined that the baby would not be born in Romania at all, but in Russia, in deepest winter, east of the German advance.

4

Passover and the Bear

Miriam sat munching her morning croissant, watching her mother. "Stefana," Mama said, "this will be a very busy day with Passover just two weeks away."

Miriam's mother's brown eyes searched Stefana's for signs of understanding. To get everything done, Mama and Stefana would have to be partners, work together. Stefana knew this, smiled, and nodded.

"Now, help Miriam get ready. Marta will want to measure her for the Passover dress, so make sure Miriam wears the proper undergarments—you know, stockings and so on."

Miriam groaned quietly and continued to eat the croissant. Her mind drifted back to the summer before the spanking when they had gone to the mountains. Frequently, her mother and Stefana spoke of the Carpathians[7] of North Bukovina as a captivating place—lovely, cool, and very mysterious. Everyone in the family remembered that summer and hoped to return soon to those enchanting mountains. So Miriam's mind traveled back there, while her mother and Stefana chattered on and on about all that needed to be done for Passover. Miriam thought about what she would do in the Carpathians and how she would run and grow bigger and stronger than ever because soon she would start school. In fact, she dreamed of growing as large and strong as her brother Karl. She could not wait.

That summer when she had gone by rail with her family and Stefana, she had felt the youthful enthusiasm for all change. Miriam remembered the crowded train, with sparks flying from its iron wheels, while she sat watching the passing countryside—villages, forests, streams winding underneath bridges, and roads that slipped past like a dream. When she leaned forward, there, rounding a curve, were the black engines like faithful giants pulling them to the Carpathians standing on the horizon.

"It's only two hours, Miriam, until we arrive in the town of Vizhnitza," her mother had said, adding, "The landlord will meet us, and we'll take a wonderful wagon ride up to the village of Vizhenka. There, at the very top, you'll see our little cottage."

Miriam had asked lots of questions, so many that her mother grew irritated. "Look out the window or amuse yourself with your doll and books," she said, leaning back. "I'm tired."

But Miriam could not entertain herself with such things, not like Karl was doing with a science book just now, not with the Carpathians looming out the window. She was simply mesmerized by the world passing by her. In fact, it seemed like a great illusion, until, in a flash, they arrived at the little town. Here, true to her mother's word, they were met by the wagon.

The landlord lifted her onto the seat for an exciting and bumpy ride along a two-rut lane that rose ever upward. Soon it swung them around a very sharp turn and into a clearing, where a fairytale house perched itself on a steep slope before them. They stopped. The landlord helped Miriam out, lifting her again to set her ever so gingerly on the ground like a poppet he was afraid to break. "This way, please," he said. "You are in the front room...the one with the adjoining screened porch. Since you're our first guests this season, you'll be the very first to use the kitchen and the shower in the yard. I can already tell it will be a delight having you here."

This pleased Deborah greatly. She thanked the landlord profusely and graciously began inquiring of him about the vegetable garden, the fruit trees, and the other details of Alpine living.

Meanwhile, Miriam ran into the house to explore every corner. In the front room she found a cot, and, depositing her doll and books, she curled up on it, quietly watching Deborah and Stefana unpack. Miriam had even more than the usual 1001 questions she had asked on the train, but she avoided asking because she knew this was really not quite the time. She did not want her mother's sharp words or Stefana's irritated looks, so she sat by an act of will very quietly, observing, hoping the two women would not realize that it was her naptime. But she became drowsy watching them go back and forth, organizing, arranging, and performing the endless details of unpacking.

Deborah said with a clap of her hands, "It's time to wash up, my dear. Come on...let's look at the shower outside! Come on. Stefana, please finish the unpacking."

Outside, her mother pointed to all the outbuildings for the animals, then to a place on the other side.

"Who lives there?" Miriam asked.

"Oh, that's the landlord's cottage," Deborah said as they explored the garden, walking past the berry bushes, smelling now a fragrance that mixed the warm-cool sunshine into an invigorating elixir of health and freedom.

"Here's the shower," Deborah announced with the pride of one unveiling a great discovery. "There," she added, pointing through a fence at a fat cistern extruding a showerhead from its bottom like a deformed appendage.

After she undressed, Miriam pulled the chain, laughed, clapped, and danced with pleasure as Deborah washed her with cold soapy water, then pulled the chain again for a rinse.

"Do I look stronger now, Mama?" Miriam asked, as the air chilled her into a goose-bump shiver.

"Yes, my angel," her mother said, smiling warmly, "you look stronger…yes, indeed, and in two weeks, you'll be stronger still…"

As the days wore on, Miriam's chronic bronchitis retreated before the onslaught of fresh air sufficiently that she was soon indulged long morning walks and even longer hours of play. "This is the way life is supposed to be," she announced on one such walk.

"Yes, dear," Deborah said, a little startled. "You're right, it's supposed to be like this. But if it were this way always, you wouldn't appreciate it."

"Why not?" asked Miriam, dropping her mother's hand and looking up, a little bewildered.

"Well, dear, you just wouldn't. You would simply take it for granted; it's the contrast that makes it so sweet…and bitter; the two go together, I'm afraid."

"No, no, I don't need 'contrast' at all! I want life like this all the time, and I would love it as much as ever I could. Each day I would love as much as the day before. No, I don't need contrast," she added with a determined look, taking her mother's hand and leading her along the path as if, for a moment at least, their roles had switched.

The next day Miriam was introduced to Teresa, the landlord's daughter, who was twice her age. They played together, rarely speaking but not really needing to, and when they did speak, Teresa's words sounded rather odd and unfamiliar, given in a strange accent. Since Teresa was also a little deaf, they communicated with as many signs as words, a system they soon perfected. And it wasn't long before Teresa taught Miriam the true joys of running, hiding under berry bushes, and playing games in the valley behind the house.

Miriam noticed that, while Deborah would watch from the front porch, her smile would sometimes droop into something like a frown.

"Why are you frowning, Mother?" Miriam finally had the courage to ask.

"Oh," Deborah answered with awkward surprise, "was I frowning? No, dear, I was not frowning…I was smiling."

"Are we doing anything wrong?"

"Of course not. You know very well I'd tell you."

Then Miriam caught her again.

"There, I caught you frowning again, Mother, don't deny it."

"Oh," said Deborah embarrassed. "Was I?"

"Yes, you were."

"I didn't mean to…you and Teresa are a great joy to watch."

"Yes, when you look at us, you smile, but when you look into the mountains you don't. I've noticed that. Karl is there…you're worried about Karl, aren't you, Mama?"

"Yes, I confess it, I worry about Karl."

"Why?"

"I worry he may get lost or fall, and then there're bears there, and, I am told, wolves. He's a young boy, alone, so, I worry."

"Yes, he told me there were bears, and he growled like one and raised his hands in the air like claws and said they'd eat me."

"He shouldn't tease you that way."

"Yes, but you're worried they'll eat him."

Deborah laughed nervously. "No, really, I worry more that he'll get lost or take a tumble, but there's no containing him, he's stubborn and wants to hike. We can't hold him back like a child forever; he must be allowed to grow up."

"How about me, Mama? Will I be allowed to grow up?"

"Yes, of course, Miriam, don't be silly, but you're much younger."

"And I'm a girl and he's a boy," interrupted Miriam, laughing a more relaxed laugh.

"Yes, you're right, but you'll still be allowed to grow up."

"But Karl says that because I'm so small and a little girl that the bears'll eat me if I go into the mountains."

"No, dear, that's ridiculous. Karl was wrong to say such things. He just did that to keep you from going with him; you know how he likes to be alone."

"But you said yourself you worried that the bears might eat Karl. If they might get him, then they might get me, too?"

"No, no, don't be silly. We should've never mentioned bears. They're probably extinct anyway."

"Extinct?" asked Miriam, always pouncing on a new word.

"Gone forever, eliminated as a species…no longer living."

Miriam thought for a moment, rolling "extinct" around in her head like a puppy with a new ball, then adding, "Will we be extinct someday?"

"We? Extinct?" Deborah exclaimed in shock.

"Yes, the Kellermans? The Jews? All of humanity?" Miriam said, raising her hands up in an expansive gesture to the heavens. "Will we all disappear someday, vanish, become extinct?"

Deborah was now determined to erase Miriam's anxieties, and her own, with a trip up the mountain, so the next day they went on a berry-picking expedition. Miriam was quietly frightened, and she kept following her mother's eyes upward, borrowing from her a certain worried squint as together they scanned the peaks for Karl, who had gone ahead. But there were no bears, wolves, or animals of any sort, just a few broad-winged birds soaring above in an absolute freedom that Miriam found herself envying.

Teresa was with them, fearless and confidently climbing, yet waiting faithfully ahead like their guide. She would pause to look at the view or to examine a flower, ever sharp-eyed for blueberries that she plopped in her bucket, and soon she began to help Miriam fill hers with great handfuls.

They had climbed for about half an hour, and Miriam was quite proud of herself for keeping up and not complaining. As she walked upward, she was pleased at her strength, growing day by day. Soon she found herself looking across an immense valley at a dark green forest, then downward at a sliver of a stream stretching like a silver thread beneath them.

"Children, do you see? Here're lots more berries. Just look," Deborah said. "Let's finish filling our buckets, all the way to the top."

They could not resist eating berries, but still the little buckets overfilled and spilled the berries upon the ground, making tiny blue spots on the green grass.

"That's enough, let's go now, children." She added, "Teresa, watch Miriam, hold her hand, be careful, don't spill any more."

Seeing Teresa take Miriam's hand, Deborah turned to go down the mountain. Miriam took a few steps but then pulled away, wanting more. She sat to pick again, proudly imagining her mother's pleasure at the sight of berries mounding over the top of her bucket. Teresa went on, calling back, but Miriam, affecting not to hear, remained.

Teresa vanished, turning every few steps to call, attempting to lure Miriam into following, but Miriam kept picking berries. "Miriam, you can't see me, can you?" called Teresa, from down the slope, now just out of sight.

Miriam looked up. Teresa was right. She couldn't see her, and neither could she see nor hear Deborah. Not waiting any longer, she stuffed some berries in her pockets, then rose and started to run down the path. "Mama!" she cried, the sound of her feet thumping almost as loudly as her heart. Now she was running too fast. *Will I fall into the valley, where the thread of water will embrace and sweep me away?* she wondered as panic forced its way into her throat as a scream and her legs ran faster and faster toward Teresa, looming ahead on the trail.

"Miriam!" Teresa said, holding out her hand, but the child flew past, plunging down the mountain. The wind was sucking away her breath and blowing away the tears as the scream transformed itself into a repeated word, "Mama! Mama! Mama!"

She crashed into her mother's arms—with Deborah falling, rolling them into a ball near the cliff while hugging and whispering soft assurances. "Say something, Miriam," Deborah gasped. But Miriam couldn't; she stared down the cliff, then laid back and stared at the sky, caught her breath and got up.

For an hour she was silent, her fear touching everyone, even Karl, who, always brave, reticent, and cold, seemed oddly affected. He studied her curiously, as if he had never actually seen her before, as if he were seeing her for the very first time. "Who is this person?" he asked by his look. "Who are you? Will I ever really know who you are?"

The scream soon returned. "Mama! Mama!" she sobbed, sitting up in bed. "A bear was chasing me…making me run faster and faster, sending me flying off the mountain into the silver stream, where I was drowning."

The next day Miriam was taken into Vizhnitza. Though she was not told the name of the place, it was called "the sanatorium." The doctor examined her, pronouncing very solemnly, in the way that doctors have of undermining what they are saying, that she was "well and not to worry."

"What should I do?" Deborah asked, sensing this contradiction.

"She needs to relax; give her the baths for her nerves."

In a flash it seemed Miriam found herself sitting in hot water, her loose garments floating around like soft clouds as she gazed up into her mother's face, rosy in the heat, with the little wisps of slightly wet hair curling away from her braided coils. Even though there were others there, the baths were quite private and reserved for visitors and the very rich.

"How do you feel, dear?" Deborah asked softly, bathing her.

"Better…much better, Mama."

"There never was a bear, you know."

"Oh, yes there was, Mama; there's always a bear somewhere."

"But he's gone, my dear, gone forever," she said, gently massaging her shoulders.

Miriam felt too good to argue, though her heart said that, even in the beauty of the mountains, there would always be a beast of some kind to watch out for, but she, for the moment at least, felt happy again and a little sleepy.

As their time wound away, Miriam, even though healthier and stronger, grew even more taciturn in anticipation of the end. Of course it came much too soon, the final days racing ever faster till it was time to leave at last. She watched Teresa wave until she and the fantastic gingerbread house evaporated in the trees and the wagon turned gradually into a downward curve, the horse switching his tail seemingly as a means of keeping his balance as he pulled them into the valley.

Miriam's heart hurt; she put her hand over it, but still it throbbed with a longing that merged with a worse pain rising in her throat. But the air, the delicious air, she would never forget, nor would she ever forget Teresa, the fabulous house, the mountains—nor the bear.

But those memories seemed little more than a dream now as she sat in the kitchen. Taking in two deep gulps of air, as if to recapture the Carpathians, she contented herself with munching and watching Mama prepare for Passover.

"What are you thinking about?" Deborah asked after a time, looking at Miriam with that way she always had when she knew her daughter's mind was wandering off to some unknown place. "You must tell me what you are thinking about, my dear," she insisted softly.

"I was thinking about our summer in the Carpathians with my friend, Teresa," Miriam said quietly, without mentioning the bear. "And the fairytale house…"

Her mother smiled. "Oh, yes, that was a wonderful time, a wonderful summer, indeed. Now, help us get ready for Marta's visit."

Miriam felt like one of her mother's chickens about to be trussed for baking. Deborah stared down at her again, waiting for a reaction. Miriam watched closely as Deborah's pale complexion was transformed by two spots of blood burning their way to the surface of her cheeks by some hidden flame. There was no doubt of their significance; Miriam would have to be a willing chicken now, for sure, but she affected nonchalance by taking another casual bite, chewing slowly, swallowing, and spreading her charming baby smile without evincing the slightest inclination to speak.

Ignoring the slaughtered bird lying on the table, Deborah turned away and muttered to Stefana as they bent worriedly over a long list of things yet to be done. While Miriam studied her even more closely, the morning light shone on Deborah's blue-black hair, making the heavy waves shimmer. She gasped.

Deborah seemed a queen wearing a shiny coronet—resplendent, dazzling—with a sheen hers would never have. She tried to visualize curls of yellow circling the head of a tall, regal young lady that she always knew she would be, but the image slipped the grasp of her mind; she could never be the queen's daughter; she could never quite be the beauty of her imagining.

She slid down with a sigh and moved to her mother's side. *I need finery,* she thought almost out loud. *That's it, I need finery from Marta to make everything just right.*

Deborah patted her rather absent-mindedly without looking up from her list. "Go to your room, Miriam," she said. "Stefana will be there in a minute to help Marta measure you."

Their white furball of a dog, Hans, jumped up. "Race you, Hans!" Miriam shouted, clapping her hands and running to her room. But Hans had his own rules, so he won as he always did, by a step, just to keep it interesting.

Marta, the expert dressmaker, and Deborah were really good friends, so hot chocolate was always waiting. They spent lots of time visiting and going over sewing projects. There were so many, and, to complicate things, Karl had ruined his jacket playing sports, of course— something he did with ever-greater concentration.

He was a paradox: a sports-loving intellectual. Miriam would never understand him.

Now Miriam strained to listen as she slid into her chemise, but she didn't hear her name in the kitchen murmurings; apparently, for once, she was not in trouble. All she had done was grow a little larger—a soon-to-be schoolgirl, then a grand lady, that was her plan.

When Marta came to her room, her hands, which Miriam expected to be cold, were warm from holding the cup of hot chocolate. *Oh,* she thought as she raised her own hands to let the measuring tape tickle its way around her middle, *I need to shoo from my mind all the trussed-up chickens and stand like a proper princess being fitted for a royal gown.*

The next day, Stefana was unusually quiet, and Deborah's smile vanished as they sent Hans and Miriam scuttling out of the busy kitchen. Despite the early morning frowns, the cold of yesterday had given way to a most glorious day, and soon the smiles were seen again.

"You can go out, it's so pretty, you and Hans," Deborah allowed. But Miriam found herself waiting for Deborah, who would certainly order Karl to take them for a walk. He would complain and walk too fast or not speak, but Hans and Miriam would run and play despite all his studied indifference.

Still Karl delayed, so Miriam curled under a shawl on the ottoman like a cat sleeping in the study. Quickly bored, she reached for a picture book and flipped the pages. Hans, who stared at her with his adoringly sad eyes, waited for any movement toward the door.

Of course, Karl didn't want to take them out. His friends were waiting, and he was embarrassed. But Miriam had been waiting, too, patiently petting Hans and reading. She said, "Your friends like me, and everybody but Mr. Shumakher loves Hans!"

"That's not the point!" Karl growled. "I'm almost 4 years older, and you're, you're, you're just a child!"

Humiliation rose hotly to her cheeks. She turned to Stefana, saying, "Would you please help me with my coat? I'm gong for a walk with my dear friend, Mister Hans."

Perhaps Karl, the boy prince, who obviously wants to be a king, simply does not recognize the girl princess without her finery, she declared to an inner self. *That must be it.*

But Karl was soon spoken to, and shortly they were on their walk. Karl followed, stomping defiantly along like a Prussian soldier. His friends waved, but Karl only stamped harder, angrier, saying nothing, not even waving.

"You'll ruin your boots, Karl. Mother'll have to ask Mr. Shumakher to make new ones," Miriam said quietly.

Karl frowned an even deeper frown. Miriam had more to say but didn't. A nine-year-old brother could turn into a monster—or become a bear.

She turned to Hans. He was on a sniffing mission. Miriam envied his inner joy; dogs knew how to play. She wondered why Karl didn't bother to play at least with Hans, who always enjoyed the moment. *Hans is very wise,* she mused, *wiser than Karl, who thinks he's smarter than everyone else. I shall try harder to be like Hans, no matter what happens to me. It's better to be happy than smart. What good is it if all it does is make you unhappy?*

Passover had a bumpy start. For breakfast Miriam was allowed fruit, hot chocolate, matzah, and a special Passover pastry.

Deborah asked Miriam, "Why are you so sour and grumpy? It's Passover! You should be happy! Cheer up!"

"Oh, yes, I know, it's just that my tummy is crying for bread. But see! I'm smiling now. Look!" she said, forcing a broad but unconvincing grin.

Displeased, Deborah turned away, helping Stefana arrange pretty fruit slices neatly around Miriam's plate, with little pieces of matzah shaped into crude animals at the center.

Sweet, sweet Stefana, thought Miriam, watching her, *How I do love her so.*

Miriam's special spoon lay beside her favorite mug, ready to stir cream into the hot chocolate. Everyone wanted her to be happy, so she resolved to be so. Her mother was right; it was a special day, and she should be very happy, indeed.

"Now you must help in the kitchen," Deborah said, tying a big apron around Miriam's middle.

Stefana took her by the hand, then plopped her down in front of a large bowl at the table.

"I want a scarf," demanded Miriam. "A princess must wear a scarf if she's to help servants cook."

"Princess?" Stefana asked, astonished.

"Yes, I'm a princess during Passover, and I must have a scarf."

Stefana found a scarf and tied it around her head with a neat bow under her chin.

"There you are, your ladyship!" she said, playing along. "A princess in a scarf."

"This is shredded coconut," Deborah intruded, handing Miriam a large fork. "You do remember it, don't you, dear? Your task is to make the coconut all fluffy...like this," she said, demonstrating. "All fluffy..."

Miriam made the coconut fly out in great snow-like fluffs.

"Enough," Stefana said much too soon for Miriam. "That's good," she added, taking away the fork. "Now you must make the cookies with a maraschino cherry on top. Here, take them from the jar, like so," she said. "Fifty." Then she lined up five spoons, telling Miriam to put 10 cherries in a line each-by-each.

"You can eat two, if you wish," Stefana said, "but only two."

Miriam ate two. Still she really did not feel like a young lady at all, much less a princess. She probably could have counted to 48, but since she liked cherries, she began to do her job, remembering not to lick her fingers. "One, two, three, four," she counted out loudly.

Her mother had been right. The baking cookies smelled irresistible. She remembered Aunt Ruchelle complimenting her mother on them last Passover. "So beautiful your macaroons are, Deborah!" Aunt Ruchelle had said, speaking her Hebrew name. Though Christians often called her Diane, her Jewish friends simply called her Dora. Her full name was Deborah Ruth—it seemed awfully complicated.

Miriam wondered about that as she was counting and thinking, *What does Papa call Mama when they are alone? Someday I'll ask,* she resolved, *not now, but I will ask. I mean, he can't call her 'your mother' when they are alone, can he?*

She thought again about why her parents were such a mystery. The bedroom door was kept closed when they were there, guarding a kind of inner sanctum, a perpetual unknown that perplexed her. *Why?* she wondered while counting cherries, *why is it such a secret? My father is a great puzzle...and he and Mother together are even greater.*

The task of baking cookies intruded on her thoughts as she realized that they were now, indeed, ready. They were quite beautiful, puffy and golden, with the cherries darkened and heavy from the heat. Stefana told her to be patient and wait for them to cool.

Stefana and her mother re-checked the hampers filled with baked goods for the poor Christians. *I'm going on a journey with my marvelous mother, what a delight!* Miriam thought as Stefana handed her a small basket filled with cheese croissants. *Oh, oh, no, no, let's not give away these, something so delicious! But that's very wrong of me, of course we must give them away,* Miriam admonished herself, striding along between the two women, her face set in what she determined to be a very grown-up expression. It was as adult as she could make it, with her eyes staring straight ahead, affecting a pleasantly serious look.

While they strolled along, the houses grew closer, the flowers vanished, and puddles of filthy water had to be navigated while dirty children stopped their play to watch in silence. *Is something wrong?* she wondered. Miriam glanced up first at Deborah, then at Stefana, but they seemed not to notice. A moment ago there had been squeals of playing children, but their ensuing quietude was far worse.

"What's that smell?" Miriam asked.

"Cabbages," Deborah said gravely.

Miriam's nose wrinkled.

"Cabbages? Why do they eat cabbages?" she asked, just above a whisper.

"Because it's cheap," Stefana answered with surprising sharpness.

Now they stepped tentatively into a building that reeked of cabbage. There was a hall, echoing noises, more odors, a blinding darkness. Miriam's fingers tightened around the basket. Deborah's voice intruded. A woman appeared in a half-lit doorway; behind her a child looked around, staring right at Miriam, trying to say something while fearfully gripping the woman's skirt. Deborah's voice came again, urging Miriam to offer the basket. She hesitated, but Deborah nudged harder. Miriam felt the strange woman's fingers touch hers—she jerked them away as if burnt, and the exchange was made. The woman laughed, hiding the basket behind her. Deborah smiled sternly and said something that Miriam could not understand.

Her head was dizzy, she couldn't remember anything; but by then she was outside, and the air, though still filled with the stench of cabbage, seemed refreshing. She was breathing again in the cool out-of-doors, reminding her of that time in the mountains once more—lying heaving with relief in her mother's arms. For a moment she felt the surge of life flowing back into her, evoking that Carpathian summer—the air, the water, the flowers, the berries, the bath—a kind of arcadia she wished to return to and wasn't sure she would ever regain.

On the walk home, she imagined her mother asking her again to go to another dark apartment. But she resolved not to. *Never!* she decided. She saw herself stamping her foot and refusing. No one would be able to force her—it was too horrible.

"Why did we do that?" Miriam found herself asking.

"Because it was the right thing to do," Deborah said after she recovered from the shock of the question. "It was our duty to help others less fortunate than ourselves."

"Why?" asked Miriam. "Why is it our duty to help others less fortunate than ourselves?"

"Well…," Deborah stumbled over her answer, starting to say God requires it or something like that, but instead said, "It's our duty to help our fellow human beings. You must always be compassionate, Miriam. I thought I'd taught you that."

"Yes, but I think they hate us."

"Hate us!" Deborah said stopping and staring down at Miriam.

"Yes, I saw it in their eyes; they hated us for helping them."

Deborah was trying to respond when Miriam added, "I won't do that ever again, not ever. You can't make me. It's too painful. I'll help people in other ways, Mama."

Once home, Miriam quickly cleansed herself of the awful cabbages by donning her new dress. Now she forced her mind into a sense of pleasant anticipation; wonderful people were coming. The Persian rugs were rolled away to make space for dining; the long, heavy leaves of the big table were slid in, pushed, and finally manipulated into place. Her mother's pride reflected itself in each piece of polished silver and every china plate, all placed in their very precise and proper spot, arranged and waiting—things as they should be in a world as it should be, far from the horror of cabbage smells, dark halls, dirty children, and muddy streets.

Best of all, with the rugs gone, Miriam had more parquet squares on which to play a hopping game she loved. Soon she was jumping from one stone to another across a treacherous river, like the silver one that threaded along the floor of the Carpathian valley, reaching for the safety of the princess's castle. Even though Karl stuck out a newly polished boot to trip her, the princess was much too agile and deftly shifted away.

But the game ended quickly when Deborah said, "Miriam, please, go to your room! Wait there for the guests and your aunt and uncle. You'll see them from your window as they arrive. Go now!" she said sternly, defending Karl as she always seemed to.

Miriam banged a few dissonant keys on the piano, *en passant*, before exiting, protesting that one very special princess was not in the least bit pleased. Her tiny room, no bigger than the length of the couch fronting the bay window on one side and bookshelves on the other, was her haven. It was a relief, but still, she thought, it should have been her choice to come. It had once been a porch, and one wall was a collage of small windows with a sliding glass door in the center. It was deliciously isolated and, she realized to her great delight, afforded her the advantage of seeing the approaching guests without herself being seen.

But it was early, so she wrapped herself in one of the ivory-colored curtains adorned with pink roses, hiding her like the ottoman's shawl. The roses looked very real, and they mingled wonderfully with the background to suggest castle walls. The guests would have to pay homage to the romantic lady immured in the tower, that was for sure, a princess chained against the stone, with flowers entwining her gorgeous face, hiding her from the vulgar, prying eyes of all but her most faithful friends.

She was supposed to stand watch, be a kind of sentinel and alert those in the great hall of the guests' approach. But no one came, and she grew uncomfortably hot, so she untwisted and sat, slumping down by her desk. Alas, this wonderful sanctuary was "straightened up"—all her drawings had vanished and all her books had been banished to their shelves, where they now stood at attention like dutiful soldiers. She liberated one and started to read.

Oh! There was a sound! The front door! Voices! She jumped up, bounded away and down the hall at a run. She had missed them! Missed the guests! Entering, she found her radiant mother greeting everyone. As Deborah and Mrs. Kovalsky embraced, her husband handed Miriam a bouquet.

"Ah, Fraulein Miriam, these are for you! A very joyous holiday to you and your family," he said proudly but stiffly, as if rehearsed.

Miriam gathered the flowers gently to her chest, touched by this chivalry, but realizing that Mr. Kovalsky had exhausted his lines, smiled and turned away in mild disappointment.

Now Aunt Ruchelle ambled up, striding arm-in-arm with her silent husband, trudging right up to David, who greeted them in a maundering, understated way as if he wanted to say something and could not.

Everyone had arrived but Karl.

"Miriam, go get your brother; tell him everyone is here!"

Miriam sighed and went to serve the summons. She found him holed up, as usual, with his science books. She did her duty. He said nothing, paused, laid the book aside in quiet irritation, then walked sullenly past. She waited, knowing how it would be—he would enter with that look of superior boredom he so loved, like wearing a frown in an otherwise happy play.

Haughtily he emerged into the main room, was spoken to by everyone, then Miriam came in quietly behind and was ignored, and the celebration began.

5

Moses

"Don't worry, school will be wonderful!" Deborah had said, waking Miriam that morning from a sleep fitful in its anticipation of the glory of this day.

September 1, 1930, had dawned perfectly, brilliantly warm and clear. The sky's blueness drew Miriam's eyes inexorably upward, where she saw a plane pass with a low drone, silver and shiny across the sun. *Only heaven could make such a day! I'm going to school at last!* she thought, looking down to gaze upon Deborah's smiling face as, leading Miriam by the hand, she weaved them along and through people ambling in crowded clumps and singles in every direction. The great moment had indeed arrived! She thanked God for it and squeezed her mother's hand a little tighter, lowering her eyes to cross the street busy with buses, cars, trucks, and the pedestrians who, like themselves, were hurrying to catch the approaching tram.

Stepping aboard and worming her way inside, she caught the eye of another little girl sitting nervously nearby with her mother. Miriam yelled, "School will be wonderful, my parents told me!" But the little girl looked away shyly.

They got off at the school stop and worked their way into a stream of families herding toward the building. Deborah urged her into the classroom and introduced her to the teacher. Miriam peered up at the amiable young lady with long, wavy hair, who stared down with a sweet smile.

"Come," said the woman, taking her hand. "I'll show you where to sit."

Miriam sat primly and proudly, consciously willing that her legs not move or kick so as not to look silly, but her restless eyes wandered, darting from child to child until they finally settled on a shelf sagging under the weight of some well-worn books. *What were they?* she marveled, as she tried to read the titles with a squint. But now the teacher stepped boldly forward, scribbled some notes, then with a sharp clap commanded, "Your attention, please! Please!"

There was a great hush, a pause, and then she welcomed them and announced that they would take a tour. They lined up noisily but quieted under the shock of yet another loud clap and the first frown of the day.

Soon their shoes clattered over the wooden floor as the classrooms unfolded along the way, till at last they came to the library. Miriam had already heard about it. She was so excited to be there, and her breathing, as in a first passion, heaved with longing to touch the books, but the teacher took everyone to the far wall and sat them at a very long table. Miriam tried not to look infantile sitting in a chair made for an adult, her foot just touching the floor.

Now the teacher read a poem.
Come into the quiet room, the room that has no walls;
Come into the silent room where timeless wisdom calls.
Come into the empty room so friendly, so full of friendly faces;
Spend your life in this room in strange and foreign places.

Miriam tried to memorize this as she heard it, then saw it printed on the wall and decided to write it down. The teacher caught her breath and recited another verse about a little boy whose mother put two pieces of cake on a dish.
Papa, you think you see two pieces of cake on the dish.
Now I will prove them three!
First, this is one, and that is two,
As plain as plain can be.
I add the one onto the two;
And two and one make three!
And the father said, "You will take number 3."

No one laughed. Miriam, along with the others, gazed solemnly, soaking up the lesson. Trying hard to be modest about her knowledge, she vowed never to appear too clever, never to show off, trick or embarrass others—it was to be a virtue of value years later when, to her Russian comrades, she had to pretend not to know German quite so well.

But, alas, her schoolgirl bliss was soon vitiated by a bad cough. She was to miss school—worse, to be held back. "I must not be held back!" she cried. "I must keep up; teach me, Mother, teach me everything! Everything! Please!"

58

Deborah tried to teach her everything she knew about nature, history, language, and every other topic Miriam could possibly grasp until the spring found her in school again. She did well, as always, but somehow the magic had vanished. The new teachers were not as good, and her old friends were lost forever.

Then, at 11, she found herself pushed ahead a grade and, without being consulted, placed in a private lycée—what her parents referred to ad nauseam as a "privileged education." She liked everything, especially French, and, as they always did, words saved her.

She studied with Mrs. Greenspan, strict, dour, but an immensely effective language teacher of some renown. *I can try Balzac now,* Miriam reflected with pride, *and all the other forbidden books in Mother's library.*

But Miriam noticed something else. There was another private lycée in Czernowitz for Christian Orthodox girls. *What really is a Jew?* she wondered, *and why must there be a special school just for Gentiles?*

She wanted to ask her "religion teacher," Mr. Mehler, but to her horror she learned he was not even a rabbi. "Oh, he's only a substitute," a friend said, as they strolled along the hall, "with a degree in geography, of all things."

"Geography?!" Miriam blurted out, coming to a full stop.

"Yes," said the friend, turning to her, "he's really sort of stupid. I don't know why they keep him. He was supposed to be temporary but stays on for some reason. I guess they don't have anyone else."

"Why is he teaching religion? We should have a rabbi for something as important as religion."

"I agree," said her friend. "All he does is drone on and on about Old Testament stories."

"Which he knows nothing about," Miriam added with a huff.

"Exactly," said her friend, turning away, "nothing at all."

The next day the class listened quietly as Mr. Mehler tried his hand at Exodus.

"Moses," he droned in a low, just audible voice, "tapped the sea with his rod and the water divided, leaving dry land for all the people to cross to freedom—you know, to escape from the army trying to catch and kill them because they were Jews."

Miriam's hand shot up, butting in: "This can't be!" she shouted. "The moon causes the tides, not a stick! It must have been the spring tides."

The geographer's voice intruded into the silence: "Please, ask that question again, if you would be so kind, Miss Kellerman. I very much need to be enlightened on this point, if you please, repeat that again. We all need benefit of your great knowledge of scriptures."

Miriam recalled little after that except the very long face of the principal, her lips moving slowly, sternly, asking questions, but they seemed someone else's questions, not hers at all, coming from some other place, not at or about Miriam, but as in a nightmare or a vision, while she seemed to stand outside herself, saying nothing but watching herself and the principal from a great distance.

"You must tell your parents," she remembered the woman saying at last.

"Yes, Ma'am," she whispered, "I will tell them. I'm very sorry, it won't happen again."

"How could you have behaved in such a way?" Deborah asked, pacing about, then stopping in front of her, wagging her finger. "Have all of our lessons about respect fallen upon deaf ears?! Do you want to be thrown out of the lycée?"

Uncharacteristically, David interrupted his marching up and down, a step behind Deborah, to say in a near shout, "Don't you know how fortunate you are? How expensive it is? That you've risked everything with your impertinence, your insolence? It's a wonder they don't expel you. You have willfully risked a privileged education...do you know that, Miriam?! Willfully risked everything!"

Miriam remembered her vow never to show others up or embarrass them and saw what the violation of that self-promise now cost. It was an important lesson, but she also knew she could save herself by simply saying all the right things. Mr. Mehler was a fool, a waste of her time and her parents' precious money, but there it was—he was giving her a "privileged education" and that was that. Besides, there was always French—she was secretly enraptured by the early stages of a Balzac novel—and she always had Mrs. Greenspan; that at least was something.

She patiently waited for the pacing and lecturing to run its course, drew her breath, and proceeded to say all the right things. Now she had learned another great thing—that she must play the game. She did not say this, of course, but she now knew it. Mr. Mehler had taught her that much; he was a better teacher than his reputation. They would all, everyone, henceforth, see this in her actions, see that Miriam Kellerman had learned never, never to question authority or to risk dishonoring herself or her family again.

In a word, she was resolved to become exactly what Deborah and David Kellerman wanted her to be, what they had worked so hard to have—a well-read, cultured, very disciplined young lady, appreciative of beauty and order, believing in social codes, traditions, and morality—a good and virtuous debtor who must gradually repay everything given at such great cost, not with money, to be sure, but with success. Only this would be enough. And, yes, this they would have. Miriam was determined not to disappoint; she would be a very great success, indeed.

6

The Relatives

Deborah, with her bearing, beauty, and abundant, very dark hair, always attracted a certain attention in Czernowitz. Once, to Miriam's great embarrassment, a teacher even spoke openly to her of this. But Deborah's charm always made the family, especially David, uncomfortable. *It can't be helped,* Miriam decided. Her mother's allure was simply a fact, like breathing, and it was as unconscious as it was natural.

As is often the case, rather like poetry in translation, this ineffable something was not quite replicated in the offspring. But there were things the children did inherit: from David, with his fair complexion and blue eyes, they easily passed for Gentiles; and, from Deborah, they received the legacy of language, native fluency in German with a slightly sophisticated Viennese accent.

If a person ever troubled to consider David Kellerman, he would have seen a rather diminutive man of medium height, only slightly taller than Deborah, but physically very much in her shadow. As he was calm, quiet, compassionate, and always the European gentleman, his kind of charm was purchased only at the cost of long acquaintance. Because of this mildness, his children (as children frequently do) took him for granted, and Deborah was the more imposing figure, the disciplinarian and the family's center of gravity.

Miriam was shocked to realize that she knew so little about her father. It was never quite clear what he actually did. Oh, she knew he was a lawyer who worked for a successful German-Romanian company, but what did he really do for them? *He's obviously very clever, cultured, and curious and has a very studious and analytical mind, but why doesn't he tell us more about the details of his work?*

It was something she ruminated a lot about. Yet he was content to be vague and leave his children to guess. He disappeared each morning into a very imposing building, seemed to work hard there for long hours, returned, and picked up the strands of his private life without any comment whatsoever. There were no colleagues or references or business socials. He was responsible, to be sure. That is, he could be depended upon to support his family, notice his children, and stay quietly even-tempered. They assumed he had a high position in this mysterious business because by Czernowitz's standards, though not wealthy, they lived very well.

Then, in 1937 there was a shift of fortune; his work, for some secret reason, was jeopardized. He was not yet discharged, but he clearly hung over an abyss. The strain showed: he grew pale, pensive, and painfully thin. Then one day, Deborah announced they needed "a change of scenery," as she put it. So they packed for a two-day trip to the village "to see your father's family."

Previously there had always been a certain excitement about going to visit the relatives in the country, but there was something very different about this trip. Before, David had exuded a quiet excitement, but now he wore a mute grimness of manner like an ill-fitting suit. This, Miriam realized rather quickly, was not so much a holiday as a project— a mission to save David Kellerman.

It was a very dreary journey, indeed, mercifully broken only by their arrival at what was referred to a little portentously as "the relatives' store."

A sad little bell tinkled out their arrival. Miriam quietly slipped from Deborah's hand to escape among the goods, sneaking along, smelling the spices, scooping up the flour and sugar in handfuls like sand on a beach. She toyed with some long-stemmed matches, kerosene, and lanterns, as if she might start a great conflagration that would relieve the relatives of their obvious misery by destroying this place, end everything maybe, end the world with all its absurdity—its bears, wolves, cabbages, poor dirty children, and penurious relatives. As Deborah and David were heard to greet Aunt Rosa and her fat husband, Uncle Mendel, David's older brother, with the predictable prattle, Miriam sank ever deeper into boredom and ennui.

"Dear Deborah, how wonderful to see you!" Aunt Ruchelle gushed with awkward amiability as the two husbands vanished to some secret lair in the back. Deborah struggled valiantly to chitchat with Aunt Rosa and Aunt Esther, who had stepped in, but it was all stiff and painful, as Miriam, watching from a distance, noted that the counter formed a kind of barrier between them. *Why?* she wondered. *Aren't we relatives? Why must there always be a barrier between people?*

There were no customers. Miriam thought she might find one or two in the back, but there was none.

Aunt Rosa showed Deborah around in the obvious hope that she would make a sale, but Deborah always brought food—rolls, pastries, fruits, nuts, and sweets, enough for all—and very carefully selected gifts. Miriam listened to the chatter about the weather, flowers, the improvements in the place, and so on, then she slinked away, retreating deeper among the shelves, scanning them for something new. It was secure there, free of all such barriers and the implicit pain in her mother's artificially cheerful voice, trying to jolly their relatives, whose desperation seemed to be as bad or worse than their own.

Suddenly her overly large Aunt Esther, with an overly loud manner, as if lying in ambush, spotted Miriam and, in her overly happy but threatening way, waddled out from behind the counter like some immense creature intent on capturing and consuming her. Miriam wheeled away but was seized in an instant and pulled into the arms of this great maw-like flesh. Miriam pushed back a bit, surfaced, uttered a little cry, but was jerked in again as if to be munched and munched.

"Oh, dear Miriam, I'm your Aunt Esther, remember me? Oh, of course you do. My, how you've grown, my dear; such a pretty little girl you've become, so grown up," she gushed, as Miriam pulled away again. "Why, Miriam, dear, is there anything wrong?! I'm still your favorite aunt, aren't I?" Esther cried, clapping her hands as if to catch the answer in the air.

Miriam slid away to the right, nearly falling.

"Oh, dearest," Aunt Esther said, turning to the sounding of the bell, "why, here're your dear Uncle Dov and Aunt Ruchelle!"

"Oh, my God!" Miriam exclaimed, running away and hiding, not to be found for almost half an hour of assiduous searching.

David drove onward to Uncle Dov's, but while they rolled through the countryside where animals (cows, horses, and goats) grazed along the river, the air gradually took on that heavy, acrid, almost burning odor of the barnyard, which, in mingling with the water smell, was the first real pleasure of the trip for Miriam, and she yearned for more. As they pulled up to the small farm, Miriam, almost before they stopped, jumped out, gleefully uncertain whether to run to the goat pasture or search for her cousins in the house. She chose the pasture—there would be animals there—and as the evening was touched up by the brightness of a dying sun, she ran in her old shoes that had no need of staying mudless or out of the damp grass or whatever else she might step into; she ran and ran, ran until her eyes streamed tears, flying over the field like a bird searching for a cloud. She yelled gleefully down the goat path, rejoicing like the circling falcons of the Carpathians. *I shall keep running and running, until I run away forever! I shall never stop, until I am free of them all, free of everything! I shall run and they shall never catch me, not ever!*

Olga's voice soon cried out, "Miriam! Miriam! Come back! Where are you going? Come back!"

Miriam raced over to find Olga sitting on the back porch, the sun's rays stroking her attractive pale face as she held an open book, waiting for Miriam to return.

"What're you reading?" Miriam asked breathlessly, plopping down beside her.

Olga spent the next hour reviewing everything she had read and studied that spring. Her eyes sparkled as they shared the silly gossip of schoolgirls: their stuffy lady instructors and the handsome gentleman teachers. While they talked, like at a literary soirée, they were blithely unaware of the goats, trotting to the barn not a hundred yards away. The sun set, brightening everything into a soft glow, then gently faded into the half darkness of evening.

"What a beautiful sunset!" Miriam said quietly as they chatted the sun down. Then, just as it sank, she added, "What a wonderful family!"

At that moment a night chill crept over them, and Olga rose to gather her shawl more tightly around her shoulders.

"Show me your room, Olga," Miriam asked, rising to stand beside her in the blackness.

"Come on, this way," Olga said, laying her book facedown in the chair and open so as not to lose her place, then led the way to a back room with a low door, through which the girls had to duck. In the winter, it served as a supply space, but today it reflected Olga's delicate touch: a pile of soft shawls and throws graced the little bed, books rested on the rough table, and a fresh bouquet of meadow flowers adorned the bureau. Miriam admired these, wondered who had picked them and from where.

"Were these saved from the goats?" Miriam asked, pointing to them.

"You know more about the country than I thought," Olga said with a quiet laugh.

Now these are nice relatives, Miriam thought. *Attractive, simple but sophisticated, well-read and curious, with an eye for beauty. The little bouquet is arranged in the manner of their lives: casual, neat, with a subdued but striking grace.*

Olga noticed her admiration of the flowers.

"Perfect aren't they?" she said, touching them gently.

"Yes, perfect," Miriam agreed quietly, "absolutely perfect."

In the end, the visit was little more than a slice of bliss amid the bleakness of David Kellerman's slow dissolution. Courageously, he affected a certain devil-may-care confidence, but it was an effort. Still, they managed to squeeze out a few delightful days and the family mood lifted briefly.

"Make the best of things, my dear," Aunt Ruchelle was a little too fond of saying, and Miriam resolved very hard to try. Somehow the little room with its perfect bouquet remained an ideal; literature, a friend, flowers, fresh water and air (always that), and a bit of countryside with some hills to hide a sun sinking behind a pasture in soft light—little else was needed for a good mind and a better heart, she decided, as her ambitions contemplated repose, quietude, and peace, rather than action, noise, and war.

As always these delicious days fell away, and she left the village buoyed by the illusion that a strong family could defeat anything, except maybe time itself. In the terrible days to come, this little country trip would remain as a kind of Elysium lost, searched for but never quite regained, lost to everything but a vague memory, like a pleasant dream destroyed by the disappointment of awakening.

7

Boarders!

The fall of '37 saw the family decline accelerate. First, Stefana disappeared, and although she had married, no one took her place. Second, there were other, more subtle changes. Deborah refused acceptable invitations, and David came home less and less.

Dinner was always a silent meal. Conversation was so awkward it was eventually dropped; they ate without words. Miriam found the clinking of silverware on china so irritating she had to resist a scream. Mercifully, the eating grew faster, until like animals, everyone wolfed it down and escaped to their lairs.

Miriam wondered even more what Deborah and David said behind those closed doors. Even Hans, who seemed to know everything, pricked up his ears at any change. Miriam found him to be the best conversationalist in the house. She would banter with him in dog-talk, explaining that she simply did not understand. She also told him something she wouldn't tell anyone: that she was afraid but didn't quite know of what. Her parents refused to say anything. It seemed there was some malicious force controlling their fate that no one dared mention.

Soon Deborah lost her appetite, growing ashen, thin, and withdrawn, and she, who always seemed master of everything, increasingly seemed master of nothing. Miriam tried talking to Karl, but he merely scoffed and walked away. "She's just ill," he said, talking over his shoulder with an affected nonchalance. "She'll be all right, it'll pass."

By 1937 things had clarified. David's company, like so many others jointly owned by Germans and Romanians, began to purge Jews. "Jews have to go! Jews must leave! No more Jews!" The parents' reactions differed. David gambled while Deborah saved. Not touching what she squirreled away in a Swiss bank, now Deborah literally did it all: wife, mother, cook, housekeeper, dressmaker, laundress, shopper, and, as always, decision-maker.

One day their former dressmaker appeared with some old dresses she had turned into "new." Then the shoemaker did the same before Passover with "new" shoes for the family. Gifts like this were touching but hardly enough, and worse, they were humiliating. Miriam remembered the woman with the child hiding behind her dress, and now she began to understand that look of desperation mingled with embarrassment and rage.

The life they had known was gradually being pared away, inexorably inched off in a kind of destruction by fractions. Then, after the shoes and dresses, Miriam was stung by a far worse degradation, an empty space in place of the piano. Instead of music there was now to be an anguishing silence, a void, a mute symbol of the Kellermans' almost invisible disintegration.

The next winter, Miriam noticed that her mother never wore her sealskin, so she slipped into the sanctum of her parents' bedroom to find that all the expensive coats were gone. Then the worst debasement of all occurred.

"Miriam? Miriam? Are you all right, dear?" Deborah asked, seeing the grimace of horror after she said they were to have three boarders.

"Boarders?!" Miriam swallowed and asked, "Who are they, Mama? And when will they come?"

Miriam had seen only one "boarder." He was the son of a friend who needed a place to study. That was in '29 when things had been normal. Miriam was 5 and the boy was a very interesting and handsome 19. After a few days admiring his curly blond hair, she asked if they could switch, with scissors and paste. An alarmed Deborah caught them and, after realizing the innocence of it, still felt constrained to lecture, saying, "Miriam, dear, you have straight hair, and you must be satisfied with it. When you're older, we'll take you to a hairdresser and you'll get pretty new waves. But for now, my pet, please, no more scissors and glue."

Now there were to be other boarders, older, less intriguing, even disturbing. How were they going to manage? Where would these intruders live? One was to live with them; the others were to be known officially as "dinner guests."

"Mother's meals are delicious, of course," she said to Hans one lonely evening in her room, scratching behind his ears, "but it is so humiliating for her to scurry around like a servant, never sitting at the table, fretting from one chore to the next. Where is Papa, you ask? Well, he's busy losing our money gambling; that's why he's never here, he does nothing for us. Mother has to do it all, but I worry about her, Hans. She is getting thinner by the day, and she never eats anything. Papa comes home late, and they go to bed. Of course, I have no idea what they talk about, but then he leaves very early, and I don't see him again."

She continued, "I don't know if he works at all, but I do know he gambles. I heard them talking when they didn't know it. Hans, he must lose a lot because mother sold her expensive fur coats, coats she cherished, and now the piano! My God, our piano! And most of the jewelry gone, too! Pretty soon we won't have anything, Hans, nothing at all—then we'll be in the streets like those awful beggars, worse even than that woman in the cabbage place with that wretched child. We'll be just like them; it's too terrible to think about. But, don't worry, I'll never sell you, sweet little wonderful Hans, because you're the most precious thing in the world to me. I love you so much. In fact, you are my very best friend, now that I have lost my dear Stefana."

Hans looked up in gratitude as Miriam started to weep. After a time, she dried her eyes and said quietly, "My part, I realize, my job is to act as if nothing's wrong. Oh, I'll always be the pampered, loved, special child whose studies and health come first. I know that. I mean I'm not even permitted to help around the house; Mother would be hurt if I did. But it's too horrible to watch, Hans, horrible—mother being a slave, I mean, and getting thinner and paler. I worry she won't last much longer; then what'll happen, I don't know."

Hans closed his eyes, enjoying the ear rub.

"You know what it's like, dear sweet Hans? It's like we're all in a big boat, rocking along, plowing through an ever-rising sea, with Mother doing all the rowing and steering, trying to sail us away from some great, black, terrible thing on the western horizon, blowing out of Germany. That's what it's like. But she's not strong enough, and I don't think it'll be very long before it catches us. Then we'll need a miracle to save us, just like Moses."

8

Love among the Dead

In that increasingly troubled fall of '37, Miriam, now 13, had been enrolled in yet another, less expensive lycée. Still she strove mightily to live as before. One day, Deborah walked in and asked, "How would you like a blue skating costume this year, Miriam?"

Miriam answered, "Yes, Mama. Oh, please, yes! Blue, blue! That would be wonderful!"

Deborah smiled a hard smile, bent over and then said, "Could the costume be cream, with blue trim, matching hat and mittens? Would that do, dear?"

Miriam nodded.

Deborah straightened, saying, "I think we can manage; yes, we can do that," turning her head away slightly, looking down as if there were something on the floor she hadn't seen before.

What a wonderful mother I have, Miriam thought, *to do this in the midst of all our troubles.*

At the rink, Karl raced past with his loud friends. He always was ahead, impatient, and oblivious of Miriam. But after a few turns, she felt she might skate past, even though never really believing she could keep up with him in anything, except maybe French.

I love this! she said, turning into a backward glide. *And I'm going to be good at it! I'm going to race like the wind and dance like a queen, graceful, stylish, and admired!* she yelled as a squeal echoed with the other children's voices in the great barn of ice.

This was her first season, skating twice a week from November through February, with costume balls, friends, and dance routines. She even found herself even more at the "Maccabee Gym," doing additional calisthenics and gymnastics *to get stronger,* she told herself.

"I guess I need to apologize to Karl, though I never really said anything—about sports, I mean," she told Hans one day. "I think I understand why he loves it so; life is more exciting now. Oh, did I tell you that at the Skater Ball I'm going to wear my new costume? You know, the organdy one with silk and feathers that mother made. We're going to skate the Legend of the Snow Queen, right in the middle of the ice rink in front of everyone. It'll be fantastic, Hans, just fantastic! I can't wait!"

Tree decorations were set out as a "deep dark woods" in which the story was set. The Snow Queen, the geese, and the suitors gracefully turned and slid over the ice to the beat of music, which pulsated a little too loudly. This gave Miriam an even more elaborate notion.

"What's that, dear?" Deborah asked.

"You remember Olga, the girl I skated with at the party last year?"

"Yes, I remember her."

"Well, Olga and I were acting silly the other day, and, well, we thought of pairing up—you know, doing a comic number together for the Winter Ball. It'll be lots and lots of fun."

"Pairing up?" Deborah asked quietly.

"Well, it seems there's a song about a cock's courtship of a hen; it's really funny. Olga recited it and had us in hysterics. Here, see, I wrote down the words," she said, handing Deborah a sliver of paper.

Deborah looked down at the scribble and laughed. "That's absolutely awful, but it does sound like fun!"

They sat quietly for a moment, exchanging smiles. Then Deborah ventured, "I suppose, Miriam, you'll be the cock, and Olga'll be the hen? Am I right about that, my dear?"

Miriam giggled. "Mama!" she said. "Why? How did you know?"

"Well, I just did. Let's begin at once."

Over the next month, the new costume took shape. Soon Miriam stood before the mirror in the changing room, completely disguised; her organdy dress was colored in the very bright red of the cock; her cap had a cock's comb; her mask was of the same organdy as the dress. The sleeves were diaphanous and had little sections layered with feathers that covered her hands. The same fabric was used for her legs down to the feet; then a darker, wrinkled fabric covered her cute little boots with curled-up toes like a fairy's. Olga's costume was less bright but equally feathered and in a curious, bird-like way, much more feminine.

When Miriam slid over the ice for the final pose, kneeling and pleading with the hen to take her as her cock, applause mingled with laughter. It was even better than they hoped; the ball was so bewitching. As a finale the seniors performed the "*Scène d'amour*" from Berlioz's *Roméo et Juliette*. Here the lovely, tragic young lover, longing for her hero, spun on the ice in such a sadly exquisite way that many wept. Miriam had made them laugh, then they had cried, and now they came to smile again.

"Come, Miriam, let's go to the reception," Deborah said, taking her hand and leading her off. "I want to see if everyone's enjoying the food I brought. You must need some tea. I'm so proud of you," she added, squeezing her hand as an afterthought.

One day a decree came down that tutoring bright children in the home might be another way "to economize." Karl had graduated in 1936 at age 16, two years early. Of course, university was next, but, as always, there were problems: first, money, and second, age—university students had to be 18. So Karl spent that summer tutoring. To his chagrin, one of his pupils was Miriam.

"The plan is simple," Deborah explained. "When Miriam is safely arrived at one level, you'll begin pushing her up to the next."

This meant Miriam could barely swallow one slice of math before having to chew the next. It made her ill, tired, and worse, bored. She hated numbers, loved words. Why couldn't she do one and Karl the other?

That summer Miriam moiled her way through math. She was slow, and by fall she was desperate.

"She's not ready!" Karl proclaimed with loud condescension. "She's a dunce! You'll have to get an extension."

"Extension?!" cried Deborah, turning pale.

"Yes, an extension, or she'll fail the exam."

"Fail?!"

"Yes, fail."

"But how do I get an extension?"

"I don't know, but you better get one somehow, Mother; it's her only hope. Try bronchitis; it should do the trick."

"Bronchitis?"

"Sure, take it off the shelf, Mother. It's gotta be good for something."

They were saved—bronchitis bought Miriam a "low pass."

Now all was well: Karl went off to vanquish academic Bucharest, while Miriam blissfully unburdened her brain of algebra by tutoring German.

At the new lycée the students, wearing distinctive uniforms, were watched constantly and knew it. Freud was all the rage and, like most with new ideas, was more admired than read. The "new science" had proven that "one cannot be too careful with one's children."

Of course, the children had a different take on the good doctor— they wanted, indeed needed, to be with the other sex. But how? A movie would never do; teachers would be there. Neither could they go on the promenade; that was conspicuous.

The restrictions, as they often do, had the opposite effect. "Walls cannot keep love out," a boy quoted with stiff pride.

"How about the park?" another suggested.

"No, we go there too much; there'll be teachers around for sure," Miriam said.

"How about the woods nearby?" someone else ventured.

"No, it's too dangerous; adults lurk in the shadows," someone said.

One bright-eyed boy came up with the solution—the Christian cemetery.

"The Christian cemetery!?" everyone exclaimed at once. "My God!"

Czernowitz had a beautiful Gentile burial ground. Entering its rusty, ornate iron gate, one could stroll among the markers, stones, and crosses, pastoral and serene, or mosey up a hill and, on the other side, be invisible from the street.

"What could be more pious or innocent?" said the boy who had quoted Shakespeare.

"Certainly, no teacher'll be there," Miriam added, coming around. "Let's go look."

The setting had everything—privacy, quietude, and even some wonderfully uncomfortable stone benches.

"Look, benches!" a girl squealed, sitting with a giggle.

So once or twice a week the children gathered for love among the dead, and, to be sure, Miriam refused to be left out. After school, she stepped over to the phone box. "I'm going to Sarah's house, Mama, to study. I'll be back for supper," she said, hanging up while Deborah was still squawking out questions.

"How wonderful!" she shouted as she skipped among the graves like the spirit who once frolicked in a goat pasture.

Then she stopped, shivered, and glanced around at all these dead people sleeping in utter indifference to the children treading over them. *Is this a sacrilege?* admonished an inner voice that she was never comfortable hearing.

Her misgivings were quickly vanquished by distant laughter. She fled up the hill and down to a meadow where there were no graves, ran on to the voices, past couples singing and some even beginning to dance. She plopped down on a stone bench near a friend. Others came, squeezing in. Her heart pounded. She laughed. She said unthinking things no one heard. She clapped her hands and sang a silly song. Everyone chattered at once—about people, parents, movies, and music.

The difficulty of these trysts was exceeded only by their delight—Fridays were out because of the Shabbat dinner, Saturdays had morning school, and on Sundays Christians always came to shamble mournfully among the graves.

Weekday afternoons were best. Of course, these children thought themselves exceedingly clever in their victory over all adults and the good Dr. Freud, but Miriam, remembering it later, said, "I think he would've smiled at our coming so unwittingly toward him, our incipient love larking among the dead."

9

First Love

The Garfunkels lived in a nearby apartment building, just a few yards away from their wholesale flour store. They had two sons, Abraham and Daniel, longtime playmates of Karl and Miriam.

Daniel was certainly the more playful, three years younger than Karl, while Abraham was more thoughtful and two years older than Karl. Daniel was not interested in dating, but Miriam, nevertheless, was interested in him—he was fun, good looking, and bright. On the other hand, Abraham was tall, uncommonly handsome, with a fascinating, intriguing, and, at times, frightening intellect.

One day Abraham and Karl decided they were much too intellectual to be interested in playing anymore; they should concentrate on discussing and debating seriously. Miriam was considered a hanger-on, superfluous, even made to feel silly. Unknown to the boys, Miriam continued to read voraciously. She abandoned Balzac for Freud and soon was introduced to Stefan Zweig.[8] When she finished his short stories, she plunged headlong into Tolstoy, sadly finishing *War and Peace*. *My favorite novel of all time*, she thought, turning the last page with a lump in her throat.

"Zweig is famous for subsuming Freudian insight into the lives and psyche of his characters," Deborah pronounced rather sententiously when she came upon Miriam reading Zweig's "The Burning Secret" one rainy afternoon.

"Yes, and Tolstoy understood the same thing without so much as reading a single page of Freud," Miriam shot back with a hint of pride.

"Yes, yes," Deborah said after a half-instant's pause, "you're quite right my dear. You are very percipient about literature, you know."

Miriam ignored the compliment because she knew it was true. "Mother, how many betrayals do you count in "The Burning Secret"? Huh?'"

"Betrayals? Well, dear, to tell you the truth, I have never thought of it."

"I keep finding new ones."

"How many?"

"Yes, well, there's the baron's betrayal of the little boy, the mother's betrayal of her husband with the baron…"

"And the mother's betrayal of her son," offered Deborah.

"Right, that's three."

"Are there any more?"

"The little boy's betrayal of his father, that's four," Miriam said, counting on her fingers.

"How is that?"

"He doesn't tell him of his mother's betrayal, his wife, with the baron at the end."

"And so doesn't betray his mother, keeps her 'burning secret.'"

"Yes, in the end he had to betray someone, his mother or his father," Miriam said. "Why did he not betray his mother? She'd failed him, hadn't she? She was in the wrong, the father had done nothing; his wife had been unfaithful."

"Yes, but that's it, he loved her the most, and so he forgave her the double life. It's a story of forgiveness."

"Yes, it is, indeed," Deborah said a little wistfully, "a story of forgiveness."

"But why did he love her the most, do you think, Mama?"

"His mother?"

"Yes, loved her more than the father."

"Well, dear, we're not told why, are we?"

"No, but I think Zweig thinks you must know."

"Well, Miriam, that's where Freud comes in, I'm afraid, isn't it?"

By her fourteenth year Miriam noticed that Karl's and Abraham's world had expanded from Freud to Marx, from the private to political. For her part, she much preferred the subject over the object, art to argument, solitude to strife, her own room and mind to the eternal combat of politics.

She watched with amazement as Karl and Abraham became leaders of a circle of Jewish youth so obsessed with Socialism and Zionism that they put together a clandestine group they called "the organization." Of course, there arose a problem of dominance, and Karl and Abraham, while still friends, soon found themselves rivals.

To Miriam's eye, Abraham, while smooth and good-looking, also seemed somewhat threatening, even a little sinister. "He's like a sleek cat with only just-retracted claws," she told a friend. "Karl, on the other hand, is too open and honest, too incapable of flattery to be a politician. You always know where you stand with him, there's no pretense, no dissimulation." *Dissimulation* was her latest new word, and she used it at every opportunity. "Of course, for Karl, I'm still a pest—you know, to be ignored as much as possible."

But what she didn't tell her friend was that for Abraham she had become another matter entirely, a challenge and a goal. He had resolved to do something Karl had failed, or not even tried, to do—to make Karl's little sister into a committed Zionist.

In the summer of 1938, Abraham made a point of explaining "the organization's" theories to Miriam. It was his opening salvo in his great campaign. He said to her with an unintended didactic air: "We're not on the right of Zionism, Miriam, not like Weizmann. We're all good socialists, except we think Jews should be able to express their identity fully everywhere, particularly in our own land. Of course, this also means being able to fulfill, in a healthy way, all aspects of one's personality."

He smiled at the word "all" for some reason, which struck Miriam as a little frightening.

"People are a paradox, complex and simple," he continued. "Sure, we need ideas to feed our intellects." Here he hesitated, then said, "We need and want everything, really—good food, ideas, sex," lifting an eyebrow, "you know, like Dr. Freud says, to satisfy our basic impulses, or we'll become repressed and neurotic. There're many different forms of starvation; bourgeois society starves us with its repressive morality."

He hesitated again but, in the face of Miriam's reticence, offered in a preachy tone, "It's society's place—no, *duty*—to feed us, including, as I have said, our sexual appetites." Seeing her quiet alarm rising in the form of a blush, he added, "You understand, don't you, Miriam? I mean, you've read a little Freud, haven't you?"

She watched in mild shock as he smiled in that half malefic manner he had when he was most pleased. Still she said nothing, only grimaced and turned away.

Then Abraham went on to great lengths to explain that living together prior to marriage was "acceptable." "One shouldn't be restricted by bourgeois prejudices anymore; it's not healthy. To be a good Zionist, and I know you want to be a good Zionist, Miriam, you have to adopt the new value-structure, untrammeled by outdated conventions of our essentially shallow and hypocritical past. Forgive me for saying so, Miriam, but you are too much influenced on an unconscious level by the reactionary attitudes of your parents. To find fulfillment, both physically and sexually, you need to cast these off, become part of the great new world we are building. As a Jew you must become a Zionist, but you cannot be a Zionist until you liberate yourself from the worn-out dogmas that have clearly failed and must now be replaced."

Still too amazed to respond, she heard an internal voice saying that, rather like her attitude about Freud, it was not necessary for her to agree with all of Abraham's ideas in order to agree with some. After a pause, she looked up and said quietly, "Interesting ideas. But I don't find them entirely acceptable. For example, you don't trouble to define what you mean by 'healthy sex.' I'm not sure promiscuity is healthy, but never mind. Perhaps we'll discuss these in greater detail someday," abruptly standing up before he could reply. "For the moment, however, I'm afraid I've got to be going. I'm expected home shortly. Bye, for now," she said with a slight wave and hurried away.

Shaken, she raced home, frantically and unsuccessfully attempting homework, but there was a noise. She lifted her head to listen. Deborah was in the kitchen. *My God!* she wondered, staring at the wall blankly. *What would she say?!*

Then she was terrified by the shocking realization that she wanted very much to see Abraham again. To her chagrin she was depressed when the days inched past and she heard nothing. *Why?* she thought. *It's crazy! Mad! I should never want to see him anymore, but I do. Why doesn't he call me?* Miriam knew that she would of course see him again. Something about Abraham was much too powerful for her. *I must prepare, be ready to meet his arguments. I'll reread Zweig and even some more of Freud. They'll tell me what to do.*

She even tried to talk to Deborah again about Freud and Zweig, but the conversation ended almost as soon as it had begun. Deborah appeared uncomfortable despite her professed interest in Freud, which now seemed perhaps more fashionable than real.

Maybe he's right after all! Maybe we have to overcome the hypocrisy of the worn-out bourgeois morality of our parents. She won't even talk to me about it; she either lectures or avoids the subject, how can that be right? She reads about it, I read about it, but we can't talk about it?! Not really! It's all so silly! My God, maybe Abraham is right after all!

Then she remembered Deborah's explanation of why she had selected the chairs and beds for the apartment: "Our beds and chairs are uniformly hard, very firm surfaces, because...," she had said, not wanting to go on, "because softness incurs too much sensuality."

Oh, what nonsense! What utter tripe! Miriam had wanted to respond but then thought: *I too prefer firm beds and chairs. But isn't it only because I've grown accustomed to them, consider them natural? Maybe it's a mistake always reading complexity into simple things. Perhaps this is the mistake Abraham and Karl are making, and Mother too—maybe they all are wrong, going too far in either direction.*

But sooner than expected she found herself in Abraham's room, alone. She came, she said, "to continue our debate." He looked up, smiled, asked her to sit, then nudged very close while Miriam chattered on about Zweig and his "relationship to Freud"; of how he "subsumed Freud's theories of the subconscious." He gently set her book aside and reached for her hand, held it, then put his arm around her and pulled her limply toward him. Zweig fluttered to the floor.

Unexpectedly, a young man, without knocking, poked his head through the door. Miriam jerked away, retrieved the book, stood up, and stepped back. "Abrasha, Abrasha? Oh, gosh! Sorry, I didn't know you had a guest!" he laughed, his head poking through, staring with an uncomfortable smile.

She eyed him. He was tall and thin, with intense, very clever-looking eyes. He retreated a bit, saying that he would return later.

"Don't be absurd, Isaac! Come on in!" Abraham said without any hint of irritation, motioning to enter.

Isaac came in tentatively. Abraham introduced Miriam as "Karl's little sister," adding, "Miriam, this is Isaac Blumenthal; he's a very good friend."

She nodded but did not offer her hand. Isaac stepped closer, almost bowed.

"Isaac, we were just discussing Freud's theory of sexual fixations," said Abraham with a sardonic laugh.

"In what context?" asked Isaac, raising an eyebrow.

Miriam's embarrassment was now total, but Abraham affected to ignore this, saying, "In the context of Stefan Zweig. Miriam was explaining to me how Freud runs as a thematic leitmotif throughout all of Zweig's fiction, that it is in essence an artistic expression of Freud."

"Is that so?" said Isaac, turning to Miriam. Seeing her flushed face, he added, "Well, that's very perspicacious of you. I know you must be very bright to be Karl Kellerman's sister. I'm a great fan of Zweig myself; he's brilliant, though I have to say that it's clear that Freud is not as original as he seems at first glance. Few really are. Most of his ideas of the subconscious are stolen, if you will, from Schopenhauer. Have you read Schopenhauer, Miriam?"

"Not yet. I prefer poetry to philosophy," she managed to say somewhat stiffly before slowly relaxing under Isaac's charm and obvious brilliance. In fact, she didn't know what "perspicacious" meant, but she could sense its definition and would certainly look it up as soon as a dictionary came to hand. But worse, she had never heard of Schopenhauer.

"Really? Which ones? Do you like Heine?" Isaac asked with gentle condescension.

Miriam now was on much surer ground, scrupled to say that every German-speaking youth loved Heinrich Heine, saying instead, "Oh, yes, indeed, he's one of my favorites. And, of course, there's Schiller, a true genius, don't you agree?"

Abraham said nothing during this exchange; rather, he looked back and forth, as if following a tennis match. He marveled at how Miriam's discomfort gradually melted under Isaac's natural attraction.

The discussion on German poets continued till Abraham, feeling a little bored, at last broke in. "I thought we were going to discuss Freud, Zweig, and Schopenhauer, but now you two literati have diverted us into the much overplowed ground of school-book poets."

Miriam's embarrassment switched to irritation, and she said a little archly, "And what insight would you grace us with, Abrasha? Please, don't be shy!"

"Oh, that all great artists have always intuitively known what Freud states overtly: his great merit is to state consciously what unconsciously was always there." Turning to Isaac, he added with an unintended hint of anger, "But I like very much what you said about Schopenhauer; frankly, I had not thought of it. It's indeed 'perspicacious' of you, Isaac. So Freud stole it all from our dear, sweet, happy friend Arthur!?"

Both laughed out loud, but Miriam did not. In an instant she resented Abraham, found him egotistical, and was shocked at her own previous infatuation, feeling rescued by Isaac. "This is all very grand," she said, borrowing a phrase she had recently heard in a movie, "but I have to get home," she added, putting away Zweig and collecting her little jacket.

Sensing her displeasure, Abraham said as she stepped toward the door, "You really must read Schopenhauer, Miriam. I think he'll help you overcome your stale, unworkable middle-class prejudices. Maybe we can talk about him next time, would you like that, huh?"

Miriam hesitated, matched his unpleasant grin, and exited.

Gaining the street, she broke into a run. She wasn't sure why but was hoping that running would relieve her anxiety, not about Abraham, she realized with a start, but Isaac. *What must Isaac have thought? I am not one of Abraham's silly girls to be toyed with, used,* her inner voice cried out, as she ran ever faster, quickly reaching her front step, breathless. She paused, sat down, gathered herself, and walked in as calmly as she could.

The next day Abraham appeared, standing on the same front step where Miriam had labored so hard to gather herself.

"Miriam, I came to ask you over to our house for a talk. I have something very interesting to chat with you about."

Miriam begged off, claiming homework, but she invited him in for a few minutes. He declined. "OK, tell me now, what's on your mind?" she asked with a thin smile.

Abraham refused, insisting that she had to come to the Garfunkels'.

Miriam told him she would see him later, "after I've finished my work, before dinner." Then she politely closed the door, pleased with herself. But his visit was disturbing. Nervously she finished her lessons and paced about. *Perhaps I'll just go over to the Garfunkels', just for a few minutes; it won't hurt anything.*

She entered the Garfunkels' house and, seeing Abraham, said rather self-consciously, "Now, please, tell me whatever it was you wanted to say."

He smiled his cat-like smile. "The young man who came in yesterday during our little talk—what do you know of him? Huh?"

Miriam stood cold and mute, so Abraham continued, "He's a good friend of mine, as I said. His father's a doctor, very highly thought of. As for Isaac, he is very smart, a year ahead of me in school. He's already doing quite well in his studies." In the teeth of her silence he added, "Miriam, it's obvious he's interested in you."

What had they said behind my back?! she wondered almost out loud and wished very much to put tongue to. *Have I been exchanged like a horse or something? One moment I belong to one, then another?!*

"I suppose I disappointed you," she said instead.

"No, it's not that at all."

"What is it then? I mean, for weeks I have been the object of your attention, someone to educate, enlighten, and convert to Zionism; the conversion of Karl's little sister seemed a great goal of yours. You even tried to kiss me. I've never been kissed, and you were determined to be the first."

He smiled weakly. "It was innocent, entirely honorable, I assure you, Miriam," adding, "I was not serious."

"Weren't you? You toyed with me then, is that it?"

"That's not what I meant."

"What did you mean?"

Abraham was unusually silent, even chastened.

"You know what I think, Abrasha? I think that I was the object of a power struggle between you and Karl, that and nothing more."

"Don't be ridiculous."

"What else am I to think?"

"I'm sorry if that's your impression."

A pause. "Well, maybe, but you're right about one thing. Isaac is very impressive. In fact, Abrasha, while there're some things about you I really admire, he's much the better man," she said, striding out, closing the door with something less than a slam.

She walked slowly home, thinking. She was angry but intrigued. It had not been what she expected, but somehow she knew it would not end here. She must wait and see.

Two months later, however, in October, Abraham dropped by unannounced. He seemed to favor the element of surprise. "Miriam, we—my date and I—and Isaac, you remember him? We are going to a film today." He then told her about it. "Why don't you join us? Afterwards, we'll go to a café, you know, chat about it," he said, with that distressing smile slowly broadening into a rare grin.

Miriam thought and then said, "That's a film I would love to see! I heard Karl talking about it. I'll have to ask Mama. I am not sure she'll let me. But thank you, Abraham."

To Miriam's surprise, Deborah agreed, but then she admonished, "Come straight home after it's over."

Why should I come home early? she wondered. *Mama never said that before. She's always trusted me, and Czernowitz is safe, at least where we're going.*

The film was short and somewhat interesting, with Czernowitz's native son, Joseph Smith, as the star. There were a few fun tunes and everyone sang along, but it was no work of art. On that, everyone agreed. Abraham, always the leader, took them to a crowded café in the City Center, where they managed to find a small corner table. The conversation, predictably, focused on the film, its ideas, its cinematography, and the possibility that Joseph Smith would become an "even more influential and famous actor in movies," as Abraham put it. They had just about exhausted everyone's thoughts about film's influence on modern culture, that "it was the great artistic innovation of our time," as someone ventured, "along with jazz," another corrected, when Abraham, sensing things had run their course, suggested they stroll along the promenade.

"I really must be going," Miriam said standing up rather abruptly, not wanting to admit her concern about her mother but saying, "I've got some work to look over." There was a mild protest, but Miriam insisted.

"Isaac, be a good friend, will you see Miriam home?" Abraham said, turning to him. "Anya and I have something we really need to discuss. We're going on ahead."

Isaac nodded as Abraham went away without waiting for an answer. The others smiled their goodbyes, and Isaac and Miriam found themselves walking together, Miriam feeling a mixture of pleasure and apprehension as they strolled quietly. Then Isaac gently held her elbow and bent toward her.

"Miriam, I am a gentleman, you know?" he pronounced rather self-consciously. "You needn't be concerned."

Miriam remained silent, but she listened intently as Isaac tried to chat first about the film again, then failing that, about a novel she had never heard of. They crossed the Central Plaza and into the "new street," as everyone still called it, with its ornate and expensive houses on either side and the Orthodox Seminary at the other end. It was always very quiet here, especially at night. In fact, they found themselves quite alone.

Isaac stopped and, looking directly into her eyes, said, "Are you afraid of me, Miriam? Don't be. Let's talk about something you like. Do you like Heinrich Heine?"

Miriam laughed. "You have already asked me that. Really Isaac, are there any German-speaking students anywhere who don't like Heinrich Heine?"

Undaunted, Isaac recited some of Heine's poetry. But he did it sincerely, unselfconsciously, without showing off. Miriam was touched, and tears graced her eyes.

Part of her remained unconvinced, stood outside the scene. The incident with Abraham had done something; her guard was still up. Isaac went on a little too long, and now Miriam felt oddly embarrassed. She rubbed away the tear and said, "It's late. I must be going; Mama'll be waiting. She'll be upset if I'm much later. I was supposed to go straight home."

Isaac hesitated, then steered her along the walk without speaking. "It'll be quicker this way," he said turning her unexpectedly down a side street.

A few steps from her door, he held her arm, looked at her intensely and said, "If you have some time, I'd like to see you again, Miriam." Without waiting for a response, very tenderly he kissed her hand, smiled slightly, took her to the door, and just as quickly was gone.

She thought she had mumbled something but was too stunned to remember exactly what as she stood watching until he was swallowed by the darkness.

Inside, Deborah looked up from a book with a questioning glance. Miriam sat down near her, not knowing how she would answer the inevitable questions. But they did not come. Instead, the evening passed in light chatter. It was as if Miriam was at last being given her own private space. Deborah seemed so wise, Miriam decided in that instant, forming this inalterable opinion for the first time.

But strangely, unexpectedly, several months passed before Miriam saw Isaac again. One day, during the winter, he stopped by the rink. Miriam noticed him watching her. She waited a respectable moment before gliding gracefully over.

"Hi, are you going skating today?"

"No, I don't think so," he said quietly.

In the short following pause, Miriam looked at Isaac with pleasure.

"I've come to see you," he said.

"Let's skate together," she insisted cheerfully.

"I'll just watch. Your skating is so beautiful, like a ballet."

Miriam slipped easily back on the ice, sliding smoothly up to a friend. Her cheeks flushed and eyes sparkling, she said, "Let's try a *pas de deux*."

The two girls embraced and turned, executing the maneuver in a gliding, near perfect hand-in-hand circle. Each time they twisted around, she cast an eye at Isaac, who never stopped smiling. It was one of the happiest moments in Miriam Kellerman's life.

10

Winter

While Bukovina's lease on winter was so long, Miriam still loved it best. It meant friends, skating, sledding, and parties. But the snows of 1937, with their particularly biting frost, came upon her with an unanticipated, even foreboding, heaviness.

On one of those cold days, although she had finished her other work, she was still left with a math problem set before her like a great enemy; she loathed it with all her heart. Was there an escape? How, as she had often mused, could one possibly prefer numbers to words? It would forever remain a mystery.

A few minutes later, she intruded upon Deborah in the kitchen, sitting in a corner, tired, thoughtful, and sad. Her father was out, as always it seemed, which Miriam tried very hard to accept as his way of assuaging the unassuagable. As for her mother, what relief was there for her? Miriam sighed, turned, and without ever being seen, crept silently back to her room to study, as much for Deborah as herself. It was all that she could do, all that was in her power to give happiness to her mother and to escape from the despair that dogged them all.

To be sure, she loved studying, yet there seemed no end. *One would spend one's life studying or to study at all was pointless*, she decided. Education was a process, like life, with no resting point, and one must go on to the end without ever quite knowing why. Miriam had had so many wonderful things she had taken for granted, but now, in the midst of their troubles, they seemed to be slipping from her, and more and more she found herself sitting at her desk, day after day, sadly wondering what to do besides homework and what was to become of them.

Then one day, coming home from the lycée, she bumped into her mother's young cousin whom everyone called "Peppi."

"Peppi! I'm sorry! I didn't see you! How are you? What have you been doing for fun?" gushed Miriam.

Trying not to appear pleased, Peppi brushed this off with a condescending nod. Miriam rattled on and on with unanswered questions. Finally, Peppi interrupted, explaining that she had been wanting to see her to ask a favor. It appeared, she quietly confessed, that her heretofore happy life, like Miriam's, was falling apart.

"What's wrong, Peppi?" Miriam asked, the joy draining from her face.

"What *isn't* wrong, Miriam? What's wrong with you, I may ask...what's wrong with everyone? But right now what's right is the better question, isn't it?!" she said, raising her voice, almost to a cry.

In fact, Peppi's situation was not so bad. Her parents enjoyed a rich apartment—old, ornate, and long in the family. Miriam remembered Deborah saying this alone made them well-to-do.

"Remember my good friend, Zelda?"

"Yes, of course."

"Well, Zelda's always going to parties—she's very social, you know—and occasionally I'm asked, too."

"Yes?" said Miriam with a quiet inquisitiveness.

"Well, Zelda's getting introduced to society next month, 'coming out' as they say. There'll be an enormous ball with two orchestras, two ballrooms, and a reception, lovely gowns, everything you can imagine. It'll be wonderful, and I'm invited," she said, clapping her hands. "What's more, I can select my own escort."

"Oh?" Miriam said quietly.

"Yes, indeed, and, Miriam," she said, leaning forward, trying to show off her French, "*entre nous*, what do you say, huh?"

"What do I say to what?"

"I need an escort, dear."

"Escort? Of course; who's he to be?"

Peppi laughed. "Don't be silly; the idea is to meet all the young gentlemen, that's why I'm going. But I can't go alone. I must have an escort, and there're only two that'll do: an old woman or a good friend."

"An old woman?" Miriam asked in confusion.

"Miriam!" Peppi growled. "Don't be obtuse. It's you I mean, my dear, a good friend. Will you be my escort? Will you?" Peppi said, applauding with a little jump.

After a slight pause Miriam said, "I don't know, I'll have to ask Mama."

"Oh, good, wonderful, you'll do it! I knew you would!" she said, hopping again. "It'll be such fun!"

"But what'll I wear? I really don't have anything, Peppi, nothing at all. Really, I don't have a thing."

Peppi giggled hysterically but found enough breath to say, "Oh, Miriam, your mother'll be so excited she'll find something, you know she will. She's so resourceful; you know how much she loves such things. She'll come up with something wonderful," she said clasping her hands quickly, as if to hold this wonder long enough to show to Miriam.

Peppi was right—Deborah's face brightened as Miriam told her. Deborah thought for just a moment, then said, "Miriam, of course, you'll need a new dress. Let's see, I think," she reflected again, dressing her in the details of her mind by staring off into space.

"Miriam, you think your mother might use this?" Peppi asked, appearing two days later with a handful of new blue satin.

"Oh, yes, I think so, Peppi. How delightful!" laughed Miriam, taking it. "Thank you ever so much. You know, Peppi, I think I dreamed about this last night," she said excitedly, "your coming with this fabric. I just knew you'd be here soon—how wonderful!"

Deborah was indeed pleased. In fact she even asked Marta, their former dressmaker, to make a very special design, so Marta cut and pinned while Deborah sewed.

Shortly Miriam found herself studying her image in the mirror, her slender white throat rising gracefully from the scooped neckline. *Fourteen, I'm almost a woman. Marta has made a new me,* she thought as her hand inspected her waist and hip, pulled a wrinkle straight, turning side-to-side, checking every possible view of herself.

On the evening of the ball Deborah gushed, "My darling, you're going to have such fun! You look exquisite! Now remember what I told you. Stay close to Peppi, and make note of everything so we can all enjoy it, together, will you, please? Don't forget? We want to hear all about it."

Miriam giggled with pleasure as her eye followed the coyly smiling young ladies gliding along in their new gowns while, with gloved hands, they endlessly smoothed the fabric of dresses or patted the coils of delicate coiffured hair. The young gentlemen were the most delectable of all as they shuffled swiftly past to take their station like new soldiers on parade—erect, proud, yet very uncertain.

The latest swing music played brashly as Miriam, sitting enthralled, tried to listen politely to Peppi's nervous prattling as she squirmed beside her. Peppi could stand it no more, was neglected too long, and finally cried out hysterically, "Oh, Miriam! Why, oh, why did I say I'd do this? Why? It's terrible…no one will ever dance with me! No one! What will I do?!"

In an instant, as if overhearing her, she was whisked off by a gawky boy who danced her away like something out of a romantic American movie. Then Peppi whispered something in her partner's ear, and soon Miriam was circling like a *pas de deux*, smooth as ice.

"I'm grown up at last!" she mused, whirling in the young man's arms. "No longer a child. I will never be the same."

The first ball was prelude to the next, and Miriam, thinking of little else, readied herself with ever-greater anticipation. Peppi had said she'd come, but instead there was an adolescent but masculine voice saying, "I'm here to pick up Fraulein Miriam."

My God! A boy! Who can it be?!

Miriam found Deborah interrogating a tall, strikingly handsome, and very well dressed young man. "How did you get here? In a sledge? A fiacre? A taxi?" Without waiting for an answer Deborah demanded, "When is the ball over exactly? Do you have warm robes for the ride?"

The young man answered politely, then smiled past Deborah at Miriam.

"Do you know what happened then?" Miriam asked Hans the next night, sitting on her bed with the dog in her arms. "Well, we danced every dance, me and that wonderful boy. Frederick was his name, the son of a well-to-do Gentile, and gosh was he a charmer and wonderful dancer. Gee, Hans, we danced every dance. People were even watching us, we were so good. I have to confess that I was a little too proud. Ha! And Peppi? Well, she was there of course, but I could tell she was green, I mean positively green with jealousy. See, she had arranged for the boy to come, as a surprise, to pick me up, but I could tell she regretted it. Without realizing it, she had given me the very best dancer!"

Miriam gave a little chuckle, shifting, moving Hans to a more comfortable spot in her lap. "Then, Hans, the next thing that happened was the worst thing that ever happened in my whole, entire life. You won't believe this, but Mother comes in with a notepad! Yes, a notepad, comes in and starts taking notes! Scribbling away the names of everyone there! My God! I was so embarrassed! Frederick, the dear, was a real sport, but I could tell he was upset for me. I mean, it ruined the evening. It really did. It was over. That was that. The bubble burst, and I who had been so enchantingly happy could only ask Frederick to take me home, which he, ever the gentleman, did immediately."

She continued, "I mean I hardly spoke to her, Hans, just told her I was going home and walked out. I could tell it made her really mad, but apparently she stayed to finish her little investigation. In the cab, on the way home, Frederick, the sweetie, tried to console me, but of course I cried all the way. There was nothing the poor boy could say, nothing at all.

"Mother came in a little later; I heard her come in. I was in my room, but it didn't matter that I was lying on my bed crying; she got me up and began to grill me with a thousand crazy questions, Hans. Who was I dancing with? Did I like Frederick? Who were his parents? What did we talk about? Did he try to kiss me?! My God! She wrote all this stuff down in her little pad like some sort of police inspector or something!

"Hans, I couldn't believe it. I mean I went from being upset to being concerned about Mama. I just stopped crying and stared at her in amazement. There she was, asking her thousand questions, pacing around and scribbling away. It was quite mad, my dearest, quite mad, indeed. I am truly worried about her. I love her more than anything. You and Mother are the most important people to me—of course you are a people too, Hans, but she's under a lot of strain. That is what is happening. She was excited by the balls at first, but then they seemed to upset her."

Here Miriam reflected, scratching Hans behind the ears, then lifted him to her breast and gave him a kiss before saying, "I'm afraid my precious mother is coming apart, Hans. I just don't know what is going to happen to us. I must find a way to help her. I really must."

Within a few short days Miriam was set down for another grilling. "Miriam, I'm quite sure Peppi's going to arrange things for the next ball, like before, but there're important things we must discuss first."

"I approve of most of the young men," she said, trying to smile, "but not all, yes, to be sure," she fretted, "you must always be well mannered, considerate, but there're young men you must never, ever, dance with, you understand? Decline them diplomatically. You must always be very proper and polite but also careful. Very careful, do you understand me? Do you!!? We simply can't afford a scandal of any kind. Do you hear? You'd be ruined, ruined!" she said, striding about talking as much to herself as to Miriam. "You absolutely must make a good marriage, Miriam, you must. A lot depends on this, on your making a good marriage, I mean. Do you understand?" she said pausing, wagging a finger. "Miriam, no scandal!"

Miriam nodded.

She had no intention of a scandal, but what could she say? And marriage? Who had said anything about that?

"Marriage, Mother? I'm much too young," she said wearily.

"Absolutely, my dear, absolutely, much too young, absolutely, you're quite right, but someday, sooner that you know, you will think about it, and if you are ruined now, your prospects will also be ruined. People don't forget scandals so easily."

"I have no intention of causing any scandal, Mother, none," Miriam said.

"Good, I'm glad to hear it, but one can't be too careful."

"Mother, you have nothing to worry about."

"Good, now here's the list," she said, thrusting it into her hand. "You must have nothing to do with anyone whose name is not on it! Nothing! You understand? Nothing at all!"

Frederick was missing.

"Where is Frederick, Mother? Why isn't he on here?"

"You are not to go out with Frederick anymore."

"But I like Frederick. He's charming, a wonderful dancer, fun, and a gentleman."

"You are not to go out with Frederick again! Is that clear? Not ever!"

"Why not? Because he is a Gentile?"

"No! That's not fair, Miriam! You know that has absolutely nothing to do with it."

"Then why? He comes from a good family and is a gentleman and I like him."

"That's just it, Miriam, dear, you like him too much. I can tell. I saw it from the very first. You are too young to be serious about anyone, understand? You will dance only with those on the list and no one else."

At the third ball Miriam went with Peppi again and tried to dance only with the boys on the sacred list, but it was no fun, so she found Frederick and asked him. But it was not the same. He was uncomfortable, proper but uncomfortable. Clearly he wanted nothing to do with her. Deborah had ruined it. In fact, Deborah had ruined it all. Miriam's mind came quickly to the right word, *spontaneity*. It was gone forever from dancing, killed with Deborah's horrid little inquisition, list, and wagging finger.

Later, Peppi said she would take her also for ball number four, so Miriam was delighted to find Isaac, who had not been at any of the dances, standing on the top step. Affecting a certain calm she invited him in, but her chat floundered before Isaac's icy reserve. It was only then that she noticed his clothes.

"Where's Peppi?" Miriam asked.

"I don't know."

"But you're not dressed!" she stammered, pointing.

"Balls are stupid, frivolous, and bourgeois," he pronounced solemnly. "Intelligent people shouldn't waste their time with such nonsense."

"You're not going?"

"Do I look like it? Of course not. I'm never going to a ball again as long as I live, and I suggest that you do the same, Miriam."

"You don't want me to go?"

"No."

"But I have to tonight, Isaac. I told Peppi I would, and I am already dressed."

"Fine, go if you must, but never again."

"OK, I won't."

"Good. Now, if you'll excuse me, I must be off."

"You came to tell me this? Not to go to the ball?'

"Yes, but now I must leave. I have things to do."

She followed him to the door.

"But, but, Isaac," she muttered, then implored, "When will I see you again?"

He bowed slightly, saying with something of a mysterious air, "Don't worry, I'll see you soon. Goodnight, Miriam," and quietly left.

Had he seen something in her face? Heard something in her voice? He always seemed to read her perfectly! It was pleasing but also a little disconcerting. Isaac clearly had some strange power over her, seemed to know her very soul. She was disturbed in a new and exciting way yet was delighted and determined to keep this a secret from everyone, especially him, if she could.

Knock! Knock!

Peppi was at the door. "There was nothing particularly bad about the ball that evening," Miriam told Hans later, but she was distracted, thinking only of Isaac. Now seeing it all through his eyes, it was indeed "a silly, bourgeois affair" that had lost its glamour irretrievably. "Hans, I shan't go to another ball as long as I live. Isaac is right, and I will do as he asks."

"I'm saying goodbye to Peppi and Zelda and all the rest of Czernowitz's 'high society,'" she proclaimed the next morning at breakfast.

"What are you talking about?" Deborah asked, looking up, holding her fork.

"You can put away your notebook; it has done its work—no one wants to have anything to do with me, Mother. You have driven them all away."

"Don't be impertinent, Miriam!" Deborah said, dropping the fork.

"I'm sorry, but balls are all silly, bourgeois affairs, Mother. Intelligent people shouldn't waste their time with them."

Miriam was sure the only thing that could possibly make her happy now was Isaac. But so far he had an infernal habit of coming and going in and out of her life in the most perplexing way, and it seemed the agony of his going was relieved only by the happiness of his return. Still worse, far worse, she realized that the pain was only increasing with each transition, as if he knew precisely what he was doing and this was all part of some great plan! But she didn't care. He must come and stay. He was worth the waiting! Deborah might as well tear out all the pages of her stupid book, erase all the useless words and notes, and write down only one name in their place: ISAAC! ISAAC! Miriam said out loud as she paced and wondered when he would return and relieve her suffering. *Isaac, please, come and take me away! All I want now is for you to come and take me away forever!*

II

Zionism

Miriam and her friends had developed the amusing habit of riding the tram from stop to stop, collecting companions, chatting, laughing, hopping on and off, off and on, and walking two more blocks to the main promenade, strolling past the shops under the pretense of seeing what was what, while really wanting to see who was who—the university boys who happened along after class.

All the girls wished more than anything to be sophisticated, worldly, and attractive, but, of course, on the first point, they were always in the deepest despair. Their cute school uniforms betrayed them and proclaimed to all the world that they were simply the silly children of the lycée, nothing more or less.

Miriam, like all young girls of a certain sensibility, had a good idea of what it meant to be beautiful, but she was even more convinced that it would forever elude her, somehow remain just out of reach. But she also had an idea of what was worldly, and she tried to avoid the watchful eyes of roaming teachers by ducking through shop doors and hiding under the harmless subterfuge of ordering something like lemonade or sweets. She definitely knew that she wasn't acting very worldly, and she certainly had no illusions about being beautiful in that childish uniform, much less sophisticated. Her teenage situation, fluctuating as it did between fun and frustration, was as gleeful as it was glum, as adult as it was adolescent, and so her moods swung between these pairs of opposites like the pendulum of an emotional clock.

But it had to happen. At last, on one lovely September afternoon, newly fresh from such an excursion with her friends, she ran into Isaac. He was emerging suavely from a café, and he greeted her with a knowing smile as she stood by a group of girls, staring helplessly at him. Miriam first went stiff, then dizzy, struggling to recover her balance while trying not to act either surprised or pleased. She was also too transfixed to notice that the other girls had the exact same thought: A handsome man! A college man! Noticing them! They giggled in a collective wave of squirming delight, but Isaac, his eyes solidly fixed upon Miriam, studiously ignored them. As this became uncomfortably obvious, the girls turned in amazement from him to her.

Finally, one of the bravest dared to extend a hand, and the rest quickly followed. Isaac greeted each with an even-handed but polite indifference, then asked if he could speak to Miriam alone. Alone? Miriam stammered, "No, I'm sorry, thank you. I have to take the tram home," and, not waiting for an answer, turned and fled without quite breaking into a run.

Mercifully, the tram, as if on cue, arrived in time for her to hop to safety, where she found a seat only to see Isaac standing grinning just outside her window. She waved shyly as the car jerked forward, pulling him from view as she leaned back, caught her breath, and settled in nervously.

"Is this seat taken, Miss?" Isaac asked, standing over her with a mischievous grin, then, without waiting for an answer, sitting beside her. Miriam looked away, staring blankly out the window. In that instant, feeling his leg pressing against hers, she sensed the surging current of some indefinable change. She felt as if Isaac had laid claimed to her forever, irrevocably, and she knew in that instant that, whatever might happen, he was the love of her life.

Her chest fluttered as she caught her breath and tried to speak, but words, her old friends, for once would not ride across her tongue to her rescue. Her heart turned over and she turned back to stare at him in speechless, breathless panic.

Isaac saved her, saying quietly, "I'll walk you home."

It was if he intuitively knew that his "laying claim" had to be solemnized and sealed on the altar of her doorstep. For some reason she relaxed and found herself growing strangely calm; her heart stopped tumbling, slowed, and she at last caught her breath. Suddenly, it felt so right to be seated with Isaac. Now the words rose up in a flood, and the two began to talk incessantly. The tram stop came much too soon, and in an instant they were at her door.

Deborah appeared as if by magic, with an unconvincing smile. Isaac was the first to speak, explaining how he had run into Miriam on the promenade, and he asked if he might take her to a lecture that very evening.

There was a pause, and then Deborah asked, "A lecture?"

Isaac nodded, explaining the details.

Deborah shocked Miriam by saying, "Yes, of course, that would be very kind of you, Isaac. Thank you."

In that instant it seemed some great Thing had come to Miriam's aid, sweeping even Deborah's power away. This Thing, for good or ill, had in that moment taken control and would decide everything for her now.

Isaac turned and waved and was back within a few hours. He took her outside. "I suppose you want to know what the lecture is about?" he asked a little too seriously.

Miriam laughed. She didn't care.

"Well, I'm not exactly sure," he said. "I thought we'd start by dropping by a group having a discussion on Zionism."

"It's a good thing Mother didn't ask. She's always so thorough; she might not have let me go. I'm not sure she and Father really approve of Zionism, even though Karl talks about it a lot."

"Oh, it'll be very interesting, I think, and if it's a bore, well, we'll walk over to the university. There's a very quiet café I've found nearby. We'll be alone; we won't run into a teacher or anyone like that, they never go there," he said knowingly.

Miriam said, "Yes, I'd love to," so softly she couldn't hear herself, but Isaac did hear her or read her lips, and that was enough.

It turned out the door to Zionism was locked. It was the wrong night for the lecture. Isaac laughed, "I swear I didn't know! Come on, let's go to the café. I'll deliver the lecture myself, on anything you wish. You choose the subject," he said with a pride that somehow escaped sounding egotistical.

Miriam was maddeningly self-conscious again and had been since he had come for her, but she summoned her courage as they walked to ask, "Are you a Zionist, Isaac?"

"Not really," he said casually, "but it's important to know about, to understand. I have a certain sympathy with their ideas, and as a Jew, you can't not know about Zionism, Miriam."

This response relaxed her, and soon she found herself sitting in a delightfully out-of-the-way café, chattering on and on about poetry, literature, politics, religion, and, of course, Zionism. But the moments evaporated, were transformed from learning to returning to the apartment door. Here Isaac hesitated and then pulled her close, kissing her delicately on the forehead.

In a soft voice he answered the question in her eyes. "I've had a wonderful time, Miriam. Your folks'd better resign themselves to seeing me around. I plan to see you lots more."

To Miriam's great surprise, Deborah let her go out with him as much as she wished, but still she was interrogated: "What did you do? How did it go? What did you discuss? Did he try to kiss you?"

Yet Deborah, for once, evinced a certain hesitation—indecision, even. Indecision?! Isaac had such miraculous powers! Indecisive was one word that Miriam thought she would never use to describe Deborah Kellerman!

However, Isaac, the law student, was frequently gone, his place taken by letters that arrived in a flood. Still these treasures were just letters and not the flesh and blood of the man without whom Miriam's life seemed a desert.

With the hot romance safely contained, Miriam Kellerman's education became the object of Deborah's obsessive energy. She was her old self once more, lecturing and ordering. With Isaac, Miriam was strong, grown-up, and confident, but without him, she was just a dippy schoolgirl again, weak, and thrown back into dependence. How could she ever be free, ever break away?

"When will he come back and take me off for good?" she wondered out loud to Hans. "Of course, you'll go, too, don't worry. I'll never leave you, my dearest Hans, but I must be with Isaac forever," she said, wistfully rubbing Hans's neck, "forever...to the very end of my days."

12

The Road to Kiev

In a moment it seemed she was awake. She did not know the time as she crawled out, stood up, and scanned the darkly glowing horizon of early morning. "Isaac! Isaac!" she yelled. "Where are you? It's me, Miriam! Isaac! Isaac!" she shouted as loudly as she could. But there was no answer. She called for the others, but there was no response. The sun pushed up its ugly forehead just enough to show her the ruins, the smoldering station, the trains, and the bodies and to reveal that she was alone. *Alone! You see! You are now alone!* it seemed to rejoice in saying. But she remembered Isaac repeating over and over, heard his voice admonishing, *Keep moving, Miriam! Don't let them defeat us! Keep walking!*

She shouldered her pack and picked up her valise. *They will be on the other side of Proskurov*, she decided. *I'll go there; I'll find them waiting for me on the other side.*

Soon she passed the station and began to wander down the tracks. Then the planes came again with more bombs, and she found herself lying in a ditch. When they were gone, she got up and began to walk again.

But there was an odd noise, a loud moan, a horrid shriek, and a burned man came running toward her. He was screaming, holding two tiny bodies, limp in his arms. His children's bloody heads bobbed as the man ran past with this double-offering, sobbing like a godless Abraham who had sacrificed his everything to a great nothing, making no attempt to hide, showing the world what had been done. This was his gift! His sacrifice to history! *Let history find a meaning for itself now!* he seemed to say. *Show this to Kant, Hegel, Marx, Lenin, God, and all the rest! Show them this! What can they say to these children? Make sense of this, if you dare!*

The man disappeared as quickly as he had come, went by her like something out of a nightmare that frightened one awake for an instant before the relief of it being just a dream. But it was real, and Miriam could not go on, could not move forward or backward or sit or run. She just stood there gripping her valise—she was frozen.

Then a thought seized her, shook her from her stupor. *You must find Isaac!* it screamed at her. *Get hold of yourself and find Isaac! Go find Isaac and the others! Do it now!* She found herself running down the track calling his name; then she ran over to the road where there were people, ran from one group to another, calling.

She kept running and screaming, calling and calling until she found one cluster that seemed to notice her. She ran behind them, searching, asking, searching and calling, running and running: "Have you seen Isaac? I'm looking for Isaac Blumenthal! Have you seen him?! I must find him, you understand! Please tell me if you have seen him!"

Then she realized she was speaking German. *No, no,* Isaac's voice said to her, *you must speak Russian, Miriam! Russian is your new tongue! Always speak Russian!* She tried as best she could to speak it, but still no one answered; she was alone among crowds of unknown people. They were not of her kind at all, not human—she was the only real human in the whole world now. The only one left.

The road was filled with these desperate, strange, unearthly creatures, walking bodies driven only by the great fear-beast and the illusion of hope that there was safety *somewhere*. A great mass of flesh that was pushing, pushing on and on toward *Kiev!* Someone at last said to her the only answer she understood in Russian, said confidentially, as if revealing a great secret, "Go to Kiev! It's safe there! Our army is going to hold Kiev! Go there!"

Miriam realized she was just a microbe in this great new body. She would embed herself and go with it to Kiev, where perhaps her parents were waiting. She still hoped but it was becoming a thin one. *Perhaps I have lost them and Isaac forever, yet I'll go on, survive, not just for myself, but for Mother, Father, and for Isaac,* she found herself thinking. *It's impossible! They are lost to me, I know it! But I'll survive just for them! I have lost everyone and everything but my memories; there'll be no more illusions or false ambitions!*

Henceforth she was free of any ambition for a future to call her own; only the past had meaning, only her life for her dear missing ones could be her true possession. She would own nothing else now, hope for no one else. It was very clear: her duty was to live, to survive for their sake, all else was dross. Now she could march to Kiev. Kiev was her new future; she would live only for it. Kiev would be her new love and her new hope!

99

The road to Kiev presented a new kind of chaos of brown and red dust, people, animals, and machines. Miriam walked along it with little rest and less food. One day she fell asleep walking, then awoke only to find herself lying in a slowly moving cart. She continued to think or dream of the bridge and listen to the tramping feet, explosions, and the cries, over and over. *But still,* she assured herself, *I have escaped! I am alive! I have escaped! I am alive!* This became a kind of mantra and, though she was not really given to it, her prayer.

There was someone else in the cart, a mother with a child. The woman began to mutter to a man slogging beside her, then he grabbed Miriam, and the woman kicked her until she rolled out onto the road. Painfully Miriam got up and resumed her stumbling, dream-like walk, walking and sleeping but somehow still standing. The valise was gone, she knew not where or when it was taken or dropped or forgotten, and she had nothing now but her half-empty pack. She possessed only what she could stand up with empty-handed or carry on her back; she could no longer hold anything in her hands for very long—it would only fall away.

Then she saw a platform with railroad flat cars in the middle of a large field. The Soviets had organized trains to carry their citizens away, and everyone rushed toward them. Miriam, against her will, was forced along toward the edge of one. Seemingly, without any effort on her part, unexpectedly, some force emerged—a mysterious power or fate, it seemed—that came to her rescue, effortlessly pushed and then lifted her on top, along the floor, away from the edge. This Thing must have saved her before, she realized, and now it was saving her again. She could not have gotten on the car herself, could not have walked very much farther toward Kiev.

Tightly packed together, they huddled like cattle, wondering with the top of their dumb minds what would become of them. Pause. Voices, commands, another pause. Then they jerked and banged, jerked again and began to roll forward, the wheels clicking slowly, then faster and faster—*click, click, click*—until Miriam fell asleep to the rhythm. Soon she was awakened by something, she knew not what. They were stopped. Then they started forward again, just as before, moving smoothly for a time, until they stopped once again as something was connected and they lurched forward gradually to go faster and faster over the open and very flat countryside.

Miriam remembered hearing a strange, pitiful cry of joy. Someone told her that they were on their way to Kiev. Hours went by in a blurred, dull fashion, and Miriam slept soundly as she was rocked gently to and fro by the rails.

Then she awoke again to new explosions. Stukas! There could be no mistake; Stukas she knew well. The car jolted to a hard stop. The people jumped off and spread into a large field like ants fleeing a rolling flow of flaming gasoline. Miriam did not remember getting off the train; she only knew she was running, running, running, running as fast as ever she could through a field as in a slow-motion dream, then falling, pressing close to the earth, hugging it, smelling and tasting the dirt as the heaviness of the bombs smothered her screams and sucked the air from her lungs while she crawled deeper into the new spring wheat and hid in stalks that waved gracefully in a soft breeze over her.

Then it was oddly quiet. The planes were gone. She rolled over and looked up. It was actually a very pretty summer's day—warm, almost cloudless with puffs of white sailing serenely over a sky of brightest blue. It was clear of everything, everything but a low, very dark billow of smoke that drifted over, masking the sun in black. She dared not get up, waited for a long time, lying on her back.

Rolling over, hugging the earth, she crawled farther away until the smoke was no longer above her.

Finally, shaking, she slowly stood up. But there was no one. The rear cars of the train were burning, bodies were burning. The people who had cried with such joy were now burning along the track like rag dolls set alight by some malicious child. There was no living person to be seen. The engine had gone, scurrying forward with a few cars like a lizard fleeing its broken tail.

She did not know where Kiev was or how to get there, so she returned to the tracks. *There will be another train soon,* she consoled herself, looking up and down the empty rails in either direction as they disappeared in an eternity of distance. Then she looked again at the sky. There were no Stukas. It was mercifully silent. *The Germans would not bother with a lone little girl walking to Kiev,* she thought, *alone in the great space of the steppe where there is no train and no people.*

Still sensing the enemy drawing near, closer than ever, she kept moving east, as Isaac had always said. Hearing his voice, *Keep going, Miriam, don't stop, walk on,* she walked and walked, stepping along the fine line between the rails and the gravel. She was numb. She wanted to close her eyes and seemed to sleep again as she trudged down the tracks.

Then something struck her. She fell. It was not a dream, some unfamiliar part of her mind told her, it was a blow, and she really was on the ground. A German stood above her in camouflage uniform, yelling harshly in an accent she did not recognize. He slapped her face as she tried to get up, threw her back down, and rolled her in a ditch. She was pulled into the stalks of grain that were fresh, green, and unripe for harvesting. She screamed, kicked, and spoke German, telling him she was an Aryan and not a Slav or, worse, a Jew. He paid this no heed but beat her until she was still, pulling her by her legs facedown through the wheat.

There was this fear, a fear that lay on her heavier than any she had ever known, heavier even than at the bridge or under any air attack by bombs and bullets. She was rolled over; now she stared into the German's steel gray-blue eyes. He was not like any man she had ever seen. She watched him in disbelief as he ripped her clothes away. His hat fell off stupidly, as he spread her legs apart and forced himself into her with several brutal heaves, all the while pulling her hair until she screamed, biting and kicking, as he pinned her arms into silence. Finally, his great humping weight snuffed out her will, and she lay limp until he exhausted himself hotly inside her. Then, strangely, he was still, his bulk crushing her as he breathed in a heavy, half-suffocated quietness, motionless, like a panting, near-dead animal.

There was pain—sharp—inside. She was bleeding. She knew she was no longer her mother's innocent little girl, no longer a sweet lycée student, nor was she Isaac's fiancée or a skating princess, twirling in a graceful *pas de deux* on the ice. She was meat—*treif*—torn away for a moment's satiation, nothing more.

She lay staring at the sun, expecting it to fall or to weep for her, but it did not. She waited, hearing his breathing, watching the indifferent clouds floating past and listening to the insects buzzing happily among the spring stalks, as if nothing at all had happened to Miriam Kellerman.

"I didn't hurt you," he said gruffly. "You're all right," he added impatiently, sitting up, as if some creature other than himself had done the deed. Mumbling in irritation about something she had done, as if it were somehow all her doing and not his, he stood up.

Who was speaking? Miriam wondered. *Him? Is he speaking to me? Why is he addressing me at all?*

"Run along now, you'll catch another train," he yelled. "We can't bomb them all," and disappeared as quickly as he had arrived.

Miriam lay wishing the earth would swallow her, take her away. But it refused. She looked up at the sun again. *Why, oh why, will it not fall from shame?* she wondered. *It was a great mistake, God making such a fine sun in such a world, in such a time. Why would He have need of such a world? He should make only the moons of darkness; only they should reign in such a world as this.* But the sun remained; it did not move or disappear or go out or fall from God's sky. The insects never stopped buzzing, and one, a fly, even lit on her face. With her first movement, she weakly brushed it away and got up.

She put on her skirt and found her underpants. She picked up her pack and moved tentatively through the field, the blood trickling down her legs onto the broken green stalks, trailing tiny red flecks of herself behind. At last, she found the tracks and staggered along their blackish gray lines, hiding in bushes, moving silently, weeping, bleeding slowly like a wounded rabbit. Then she crouched in the grass and cleaned the blood as best she could. She put on her soiled panties as a bandage to both her wound and her humiliation. While of little use for either, they were all she had.

Exhausted, she even slept a little, then roused herself and walked again. She ambled along in a kind of sluggish madness through the afternoon. At last, as before, a station appeared, breaking the horizon's straight, slightly curving mark with its outline of roof. She spotted people waiting like all the others, waiting and hoping for yet another hopeless train, crowding into another desperate mob. For the first time she felt contempt for this stupid herd on an unknown platform in the awful, endless space of the Ukraine, waiting in a quiet panic for yet another doomed deliverance.

Maybe it would just be better if we all died here and now, extinguished ourselves, everyone, and end the suffering, she thought, as she stumbled upon the station platform and stood like a machine pretending to be human but expressionless, mute, stolid, and alone in the slowly milling crowd.

People stared before averting their eyes as if they had not seen, but she knew otherwise. *They see the blood, know everything,* she concluded and was ashamed.

The infernal train did at last come. More flat cars. Again the Thing lifted her onto one, and in silence she spent the night sleeping lightly, moving her sore limbs along its rough floor until at last the morning came, shining across desperate faces, as if to illuminate their sadness, hunger, fear, and pitiful illusions, its early light brightening the false expectation of another fitful day.

Then there came on schedule—the Germans being punctual—the morning bombardment. Almost mechanically now, Miriam scrambled into the field and hid again but not too far. This time she stayed where she could see the tracks. A routine had developed. She knew what to do. She waited. She watched. She was patient. She did not panic. She was no longer the innocent schoolgirl stumbling across the Dniester or running from group to group calling out names or screaming out of control when a few bombs fell; she wasn't that at all. Now she was somebody else entirely.

A blonde woman with a nursing baby found her, crouched down, and peered blindly at her. The woman touched her, offered a damp cloth, shifted the baby to her hip, and delicately wiped Miriam's legs. Then she gently rinsed the cloth with water she carried for herself and her child. Miriam took the cloth into her shaking hands, hesitated, and then, with a shudder, began to clean herself, not caring who saw. The woman looked away, tending her baby. When she turned back, she saw Miriam staring toward the tracks again, touched her arm without looking back, and pointed without speaking. They climbed a small hill and ambled down in time to catch the next freight, this time a boxcar.

Several women helped her up, but Miriam did not look at them, could not bear knowing another human being or learning another name or even a face. She wanted no one and quickly found a corner to fall asleep, hoping to slip backward into time, escape into the delicious grace of true sleep. Later, an hour or more, she wasn't certain, a woman tapped her softly and pointed. They were approaching another stop. Miriam saw the big sign KAZATIN[9] written in Cyrillic.

Peasants with buckets stood waiting on the platform. The passengers emerged from the car as from a cave, filthy, thirsty, hungry, and haunted. One peasant woman stood with a large bucket and threw water over her. Others did the same. Wordlessly, all of them lined up for a long drink. Then they were shown the toilets—meager, dirty, and needed.

"Come, now!" a woman yelled at her. "Come this way!" she growled. Miriam followed her like a docile child. The woman shoved her back into the cattle car. Miriam crawled again to her corner and huddled with her head buried on her knees.

Don't touch me! Don't come near me! she was screaming inwardly without uttering a sound. *No one touch me! I never want to be touched again! Never, ever again!* She tried to regain control but found great clumps of hair in her hands, so she sat hard upon her hands as firmly as she could. *Please, God, don't let me go mad! Please! Not that! Please!*

Then she found her hands pulling her hair again and so closed her fists and crossed them in her lap so she could watch them, but the hands opened once more, so she gripped her elbows as tightly as she could and hung on to herself with all her might. *I must hang on and not let go! I must hang on!* she repeated over and over.

It seemed she did this till they stopped with a great lurch. Once more she saw a sign, FASTOV.[10] Once more, peasants waited. A younger woman, her head encircled by two long, blonde plaits, offered up cups of cream-of-wheat. Miriam tasted it, crying gratefully for the first hot food since Czernowitz. She ate, wept, and thanked her. This woman watched with steady eyes, pulled the knot from her neckerchief, brushed soot off her apron, and gently washed Miriam with the scarf. Then she looked closely at Miriam, made a little cry, turned, and hurried away. Miriam was amazed. *Why had she gone? What did she see? Why?*

A crone hurriedly lifted loaves from a basket, then turned on her heels and quickly moved off from her like the girl had done. Miriam clutched her bread, murmuring a thanks that no one heard. Suddenly, she realized the image of herself in their eyes. She was a beaten thing, a hungry, abused, dying creature. They were appalled. That's why they had fled.

She looked around to see if others were frightened, too, and saw that she was not alone. Hungry eyes were all watching her, darting covetous looks at the bread she clutched to her breast like a child. Her eyes met theirs. She looked down and extended her arms, holding out the bread, steadying herself as hands tore her little loaf into pieces. *They're beasts, everyone, beasts!*

Miriam returned to the car and retreated again into her little warren. She was an animal, too, she decided, but now these people would not kill her; she had given them all she had. The German had taken part of her, and what was left they would not want. She would save what was left, the part no one wanted, that was hers to keep. It was all she really needed; it was all that remained to her to have as her very own.

13

The Kolkhoz"

Miriam and the others were crowded into a "Great Hall" that announced itself by an overly large red sign with gold letters as the "Central Committee of the Ukraine Communist Party." It was a vast place with a crush of evacuees soiling the expensive rugs with muddy boots and bare feet. Gradually more people sandwiched into one half of this Great Hall until Miriam could hardly move or even fall, barely breathing in the crush. Then somehow some dirty pallets appeared on the few remaining patches of rug, and a few old people and children were able to lie down.

This done, some uniformed women began to move among the people, bringing hot food. Hot food? "What's that?!" Miriam asked to no one in particular. She could only dream of such a thing. She felt like a beggar as she reached for a tin cup full of borscht. Its taste and another glop of very hot creamed wheat unwound the tension in her body. It was the first thing that might be described as pleasure since she left home.

But while her body relaxed, her mind did not. It, like an ever-alert brute, thought only of the next threat. Now it readily noticed the Communist officials checking documents, categorizing them in a babble of Russian, Ukrainian, Romanian, and Yiddish. Then, out of nowhere it seemed, a brown uniform stood stiffly before her, asking for something in a business-like but almost kindly voice. No Soviet official had ever spoken to her in anything approaching amiability. With a hint of impatience, the voice repeated itself in very swallowed, rapid-fire Russian, as her ear gratefully sorted out "passport." She fumbled and handed it to him. "Is there a problem?" she said with a smile, as cordially as she could manage while contriving to pull herself up taller and glancing around in feigned nonchalance.

Looking back, she smiled at the officer as he studied her picture with silent concentration. Then he looked up, down again, up, checking the photo with her face, then back down. In that eternity between the glance up and the glance down, between the shorter upward look and the much longer downward one, the finger-flipping of one's papers in a totalitarian world, Miriam knew that her fate hung in the decision of an eye. Then the young man stared one more time at her, scribbled a quick note in her passport, closed it with a snap, handed it back with a thin smile, and moved on.

What category did he give me? she wondered, studying his note but not making out so much as a single word. Then she was told to wait. She heard more Russian from a buxom, uniformed woman in charge, and the Russian word for "*kolkhoz*" struck her ear. "Farm! Not a farm!" she cried. "Please, no, no, please—can't I go to a factory? Please!? A factory!? Not a collective farm, please! Send me to a factory!" she shouted in German.

The Jews nearby were being sent to collectives, too, and Miriam heard them complaining loudly in Yiddish. "Oh, please, don't send me to a *kolkhoz!*" she pleaded in very bad Russian to this woman, who walked off with rather a wicked laugh. Miriam had seen the collectives along the tracks. They were dilapidated peasant huts and hovels squatting in the heat near fields without a single man. Instead, women and children struggled alone, laboring as only peasants can.

She simply could not do farm work. It horrified her. *I'm not a peasant! I'm bred for the city!* she thought, as these fears found a voice in, "Not a *kolkhoz!* Please, send me to a factory!" she shouted again to no one in particular.

Another frumpy peasant woman walked over and threw a pallet at her, screeching out like a great predatory bird, "You! Lie down! Be quiet until you're summoned! No more from you, you understand! You'll go where you are sent!"

Miriam's old friend, fatigue, came to embrace her on this smelly, mildewed pallet into a deep sleep. Surprisingly, the decision of where to send her didn't matter; farm or factory, it meant nothing in the delicious closing of her eyes.

"Wake up!" the old woman squawked, shoving her shoulder rudely. "Get up! Follow me!"

Light was filtering into the Great Hall much more softly than before. She must have slept a very long time, Miriam decided as she stood up, shouldering her pack to stumble along behind the woman through a large door and onto the street. Here she huddled in a sullen group, saying nothing, standing among them in a near stupor.

Then the young man who had checked her passport emerged, spoke to her in unintelligible Russian, and motioned her over to another crowd. She searched in vain for any familiar faces, so stood silently waiting alone. Her future was once again in this official's grasp, and there was nothing she could do but wait. She tried to smile, but he, like everyone else, simply ignored her, avoiding her eyes, always looking away.

At last, unexpectedly, he directed her group down several streets toward the station. She marveled that her legs were able to move, but she found that her mind had developed of late the surprising ability to switch-off without her consent, and now it did just that, forcing her into a kind of torpor until she found herself standing before the now familiar iron wheels of a waiting freight. Then the Thing came to her aid, as it always seemed to in such moments, and lifted her through the entrance, pushing her forward and back to her familiar far corner. No one ever took her corner, it was always there, empty and waiting. Here she sat pulling her skirt tightly around her, hugging her knees, looking beyond, trying to search out the faces. Yet no one really had any faces. She needed to learn that, she decided. *There are no faces,* she told herself. *Forget looking for them; there are no faces anymore, so don't bother looking for them; there aren't any and never will be again.*

There was a long wait after the last people loaded, then voices, shouts, a whistle, and the car lurched once, twice, three times, till it jerked out of the station. She heard a child crying and looked up and saw the mother patting its head, a tear rolling down the woman's cheek. Miriam stared with what she imagined to be an expressionless look. *What, after all, was another tear on another mother's face? What could it matter now?*

She turned away, peering through a crack at the flat Ukrainian steppe, slowly unwinding beneath the sun like the flattest sea of green as they clicked along for an hour before slowing for a squat, shabby station looking very much like all the others. The bodies inside braced for the train's braking motion while it came to the now predictably abrupt halt. There was a long moment of heavy silence, followed by the rasping of the doors, revealing the shock of bright and sharply painful sunlight. Then, without being told, everyone stood up. The woman stooped to pick up the baby, but no one spoke; not even the baby whimpered. The woman's tears had long since dried, and she waited silently like the others, holding the child next to her breast, motionless—all of them now like trained animals awaiting a familiar command. Clearly they were learning. No one moved or made a sound; they simply waited. The war had been a harsh teacher for these survivors. Even horror has its routine, its habits.

Then a *muzhik* appeared, proudly displaying gold teeth and wearing a red official's cap. He paused, stared at them like a farmer sizing up his newly bought stock, before gesturing them toward a cluster of buildings beyond the tracks. Not waiting, he rudely began to jerk them out, pulling them violently to the ground, but Miriam jumped away to the dirt, falling behind a very broad-hipped woman clutching a child and a small, dirty bag, shuffling ahead ponderously like a great ox. Miriam glued her eyes to the woman's skirt. The sheer docile motion of her fat hips trudging ahead was somehow comforting and kept her moving.

The sunlight grew weaker and a faint breeze taunted Miriam, whispering a promise of a cooler night. *Maybe, too, there would be food! Rest! Quiet! Be mum, inconspicuous, and patient. Be very, very patient. Wait and say nothing*, she reflected, finding herself standing in a kind of central square. Strangely, some resilient part of her mind conjured an image of Deborah in this place, rearranging the flower plants, putting them here and there, demanding, fixing, and setting things right. This revelry was interrupted by what she took to be the *kolkhoz* director shouting at four stout peasant women standing in the front doorway of the office. These creatures ambled forward in slow obedience and began to divide everyone into roughly equal groups. Soon these were moving in different directions, splitting up, each bunch following one of the women like a newly purchased coffle of slaves.

Miriam's crone led them for about a mile down a very dusty road, then stopped and turned to push and shout them into a ragged line. She paused, barked out some more instructions to no one in particular, before she came up to Miriam and pushed her rudely toward a tall, bony, somewhat morose-looking woman who had been waiting, standing there in front of a hut with three filthy children—two boys and a very small, sad little girl of 6 or so.

This woman mumbled and motioned to her to follow. Miriam soon found herself in a squalid little hovel of a house—an *izba*. She looked around, noticing a broken mirror on a nearby wall. She turned, stepped closer, and stared into it. Reflected behind her she saw the tall woman peering over the shoulder of another person she did not recognize. *Who is that? Whose old woman eyes are those?* She choked out a little cry. She was transfixed by these dark mirror-eyes; she was looking at a dead person, someone she didn't know.

Her mind tried to memorize this face to know who she really was—no, what she had become. How had this happened to her? When was it ever to end? When could she go home? How could she make the nightmare stop so she could wake up in her wonderful room next to her sweet little Hans, with the comforting smell and sound of Deborah cooking in the kitchen?! She wanted to kiss her mother in the morning and put on her sweet schoolgirl dress and go to the lycée and see her friends, to study French, be silly, and talk about boys. Where had all of that gone, and who is this wretched creature studying her in the mirror?

She averted her gaze and would have run away if she could have, run like the others had done. Now she understood why they had, since no sane person would ever want to look at that pathetic creature in that reflection for very long.

Miriam turned to catch the old woman and the three children staring at her.

Embarrassed, Miriam bowed slightly and gazed at the dirty floor. The woman spoke in Russian and motioned toward a rough bench where Miriam could put her pack. Confused, she stood for a moment. Solicitously, the woman handed her a cup half-full of water. Accepting it, Miriam tried to form a smile.

"Thank you," she said as graciously as she could, but the woman looked away without speaking. The bite of cream-of-wheat and a swallow of borscht were now more than a day away. She could remember a little food and water before that—there had been some, no doubt, but she could not recall when.

The woman whispered to the eldest child, a girl with dirty, torn trousers. This urchin moved toward her, shyly took her hand and pulled her outside to a rough building a few yards off. The smell told Miriam everything. Then the girl dropped her hand, laughed, and ran away.

Miriam swallowed hard, trying to keep her stomach down. The door hung partially open. She creaked it fully open and peered inside. In the half-light, her eyes gradually took in a wad of filthy papers and rags lying in a corner. A dirty towel hung limply from a peg, lorded over by buzzing black flies. Despite this dim horror, there was a certain pleasure in at least being alone, even in this place. Still she hesitated before she stepped in, turned, and sat.

As she did so, Deborah—smiling, sweet-faced Deborah—came, taking Miriam's hand and walking her through fresh evergreens toward two small buildings like the chalet in the Carpathians where the bear had chased her. Here, doors revealed vines and flowers curling over smiling wooden faces, and, inside, a table offered baskets of sweet-smelling soap, clean towels, and lotions. An unbroken gilt mirror hung above the porcelain washstand. Deborah pointed to the smaller of the two seats, and Miriam stared down before covering the abyss of a dark hole by turning and sitting. She gazed up, questioning Deborah's smile until she gently made Miriam doze, then left like any mother leaving a sleeping child.

Miriam awoke to find her mother gone; she waited but Deborah did not return. She seemed to come only when she wished and to vanish as strangely as she had appeared. Still Miriam waited, hoping she would be conjured by her lingering in the welcome but awful solitude of this place. But she refused, so Miriam returned to find the children crawling upon a musty pallet set upon the floor. The woman was staring into the broken mirror as she removed her scarf to free her braid; she turned, smiled shyly, and motioned Miriam over to a bench, where she curled up, face to the wall, and fell asleep.

14

A New Assignment

The next day, Miriam was taken back to the collective's office, where she was interviewed for her new assignment. She was too emaciated for any "real work," the director said. Her job instead would be caring for children. Miriam Kellerman would be a babysitter.

She was too tired to care, said nothing, and returned to the *izba*, where the woman tried to teach her to cook. She pointed to a big black stove in the middle of the room, opened the oven door, then took some rather large tongs and pulled a pot forward, slid open the lid, and dropped several meat patties into the boiling water.

"You know what to do next, don't you?" the woman asked with a cruel smile.

Miriam pretended to. Then a neighbor came, depositing her son, a malnourished lad of 3 and his sickly looking sister of 4; shortly a Tartar-faced toddler arrived. Miriam took the baby in her arms as the women hurried off for the fields.

Miriam stared at the filthy cubs, then reluctantly placed the toddler on the floor and tried very hard to smile the others into submission, but only succeeded in frightening them into a good cry. Now, desperate, she looked around. On the nearby table a basket contained a wad of cloths and rags, and Miriam sorted through these and pulled out the cleanest. With this she cleaned the children's faces. Finally, she took the older boy by the hand, picked up the toddler, motioned the girl to follow, went through the door, and wandered down the dusty road toward where she had been told there was a small river.

Seeing some trees, she headed for them. Everyone seemed to brighten at the sight and smell of water. Three more children joined them along the way, and they were too dirty not to wash, so, despite her fear of water, Miriam herded them all toward the warm brown stream. It was broad but not swift, so she stepped gingerly into its edge. Then she dampened the rag and let the children clean themselves as she washed her own face before trying to clean the children again. She scrubbed vigorously the faces of each until finally, winning their trust, the older ones offered up their hands to be scrubbed as well.

Miriam then noticed a strange odor, not just from the children but also from herself. She had not bathed since Czernowitz. After cleaning each child, she waded up to her knees and bathed as best she could. Then she took off the children's shoes, and soon they all dangled their feet playfully in the water. Their spirits rose as they had what could only be described as fun. Miriam joined in for a time and then sat on the bank, watching them frolic in the shallows. It was a bright day, and she relaxed as the hot sun dried her into a blissful half-snooze. For the first time she felt utterly free of the war. She savored this but, of course, knew it could not last.

They had to return, so she rounded everyone up and took them along. At the door a strong cooking smell greeted them. Miriam opened the oven door, thrust the tongs through the big pot's handle, and tried to lift it, but it lurched and fell onto the oven with a clatter. Sweating, her heart racing, she maneuvered it forward, crying with frustration and fear, almost in a panic. She quickly grabbed some rags and pulled up the hot handle yet again, when a spark burst from the fire and burned her hand. Ignoring the stinging pain, and with all her remaining strength, she lifted the pot, scraping it over to the edge of the oven. She managed with her leg to pull a chair toward it, dropped some of the rags onto the chair, and then gave a mighty heave and pulled the pot out, letting it drop with a crash onto the seat. She patted the oven door closed and quickly slid the chair across the earthen floor, hoping the rags, already scorched, would not catch fire.

Watching until this was done, the children sidled up to find a bowl and spoon to eat the stew. She poured tin cups of milk for the youngest, but since there was not enough, she gave only water to the older. None of the children protested or smiled and no one talked; they just watched and waited patiently for their turn.

This eating could not truthfully be described as pleasurable. It was strictly business. Miriam ate a little bit but put down her spoon, unable to swallow the meat, forcing a smile that was not returned. Too, the food had an unpleasant effect and, feeling an urge, she excused herself in German and walked quickly to the outhouse.

Returning, she noticed for the first time a low branch of an apple tree, picked a somewhat green one, and began to eat. The first bite was beyond marvelous. But at the second bite, oddly, she began to feel sick again. Still, she forced herself to finish the apple. There was some protest, but it stayed down.

Since there were no toys, the children began to scream and romp with each other on the floor. Miriam needed something to do, so she spent the afternoon cleaning. She swept and swept until nearly exhausted, then she folded and stacked the two thin blankets. This small pile proved irresistible to the boys, and they began jumping on it like a trampoline. The girls played with the dirty bowls, which the little girl had found and was trying to stack. Then the boys began poking, fighting, and chasing in circles. Things were out of hand, but Miriam did not know their names, and so little Russian came to mind that she could not admonish them well enough to make them stop.

The afternoon wore on as the chaos continued, until the toddler fell exhausted into a very deep sleep. Miriam covered her up and prayed for the other children to fall asleep, too. They didn't but kept stomping around, making a racket, screaming, and willfully doing as they wished.

Finally, Miriam heard the women's rattling return from the field, but not one child ran out to meet them. The women shuffled in tiredly, chatting and putting down their things. The neighbor woman examined first the children and the room and lastly stared at Miriam. But she turned away, saying nothing, as the mistress of the house looked around with a frown. Though she also said nothing, Miriam sensed her displeasure. It was clear that the women had not been particularly bothered by the dirty floor, so perhaps it was the loss of control that annoyed them—or maybe her assiduous cleaning was taken as an implied criticism. She didn't know.

However, nothing was said. Dinner consisted of leftovers with bread and milk, and Miriam felt better. Still, she could eat little and managed only a bite of bread and a few sips of milk. This was not unnoticed, and Miriam was made to understand that she was not to get such a "large portion" again. From then on, it was just bread and milk, nothing more.

The next morning came rather too early, with the woman brusquely shaking Miriam awake. But "today'll be different," she was told. "You're going to cook mamaliga," a hot Moldavian cornmeal. Once again, Miriam found herself stuck hotly at the oven door as the woman threw in fuel. Then the woman showed her how to maneuver the pot correctly. This peasant obviously had strength that Miriam did not, but the woman didn't seem to realize or, if she did, to care. No matter; Miriam simply had to do it. In fact, she had little choice in anything except going to the outhouse.

Next, she was taken out and handed a hoe to dig potatoes. (She asked for a cabbage, but it was forbidden, a rare treat not to be had for the asking.) Her duties were expanding. *These peasants fill their days with work and little else, laboring from sun-to-sun.* It was numbing. *How do they do it?* she repeatedly asked herself as she hoed and dug in the garden.

That evening in the *izba*, the woman wiped off the potatoes and popped them into the oven. Soon Miriam, to her surprise, realized that their skins were nutritious. Eventually, again to her surprise, she even grew to like them. However, the first time, to everyone's shock, she spit out the skin before realizing she was supposed to eat it. She never did that again.

"Eat the skin!" the woman shouted, then added more calmly, "It's good for you, so don't waste it, understand?!!"

Miriam felt herself an outsider, a stranger, that she would never be accepted no matter how hard she tried. Despite all of her efforts, the children were forever dirty, the pot heavier, and the weeds continued to elude her. Of course, the outhouse remained a horror, but since she was living on stolen apples, green plums, a little milk, small bites of bread and potatoes, and little else, she was a constant *habituée* of the privy. Indeed, besides trips to the river, her life alternated between that horrible hut of a house, the garden, and the wretched toilet.

Then, at the beginning of the second week, the woman surprised her with a sliver of very dirty soap. Soap! Now Miriam was given the luxury of washing not only herself but also the children with soap! Anxious that she would never get another piece, she hoarded it in her pack like a precious stone.

Despite the river soap-baths, she always felt terribly dirty. She rinsed her short hair every day and began to fret about lice as she braided the little girl's hair. She remembered with sadness the long, thick braid she had when fleeing from home. She had asked a woman to cut it, she forgot just where, but now she felt naked as she imagined the plait coiled pathetically somewhere, perhaps along the railroad tracks, as a kind of remnant of her lost self.

Every life, she mused, *has a turning point, a moment after which things are never quite the same. Mine has already happened, and that braid of hair is its symbol. My hair will never be so beautiful again. Once a young man I loved touched it in great love and tenderness. Now I'm shorn like a lamb and am little more than a dirty peasant in a wretched izba on a kolkhoz somewhere in the vastness of the Ukraine. Would Isaac, if he ever saw me, even recognize me? Could he ever really love me again? Will anyone really know me? Am I lost forever? Do I even know myself any longer?*

As she plaited the little girl's golden locks, she closed her eyes and imagined the new identity papers and the new photograph of this sad, unsmiling, Romanian girl with the dead eyes and the short-cropped hair. In her mind's eye she stared at the imaginary papers filed away somewhere, wondering about what they might say, where she had gone, or what she had become. Those papers became like a darkened mirror in the disheveled hovel of her mind. Miriam could not envision what they said anymore than she could countenance the unhappy face in the broken glass hanging crookedly across the wall. She was simply not Miriam Kellerman—that person was gone, never to be found. The reflection there was no longer the childlike Romanian princess, but a poor, sad peasant girl whose innocence had been cruelly stolen and lay discarded somewhere under buzzing flies, warmed by an insouciant sun that would not bother to weep or come to her rescue, much less call her name.

15

Rostov[12]

The food remained always the same. Occasionally, the woman, as a treat, would hand Miriam an onion, a precious leaf of cabbage, or a scorched cucumber. Miriam would wash this treasure to share with the children at lunch. There was also goat's milk, and sometimes cheese or butter might make an appearance. Miriam took a small amount for her bread but continued to eat very little. From time to time, the children would get some fried pork fat, but Miriam could not tolerate it, and it was no longer offered.

It wasn't long before the meals grew still smaller, until at last the food simply ran out. The woman explained as best she could (Miriam's Russian was improving but still inadequate), pointing to the depleted garden and to the empty food basket. She then directed her up the dirt road to the collective's office and said, "Go there and ask them for help, or you'll starve. I can do nothing for you."

So Miriam found herself once again a vagabond upon the path to nowhere. As she wandered along, she reflected upon the past two months. Her weight, always slight, had almost certainly dropped by half. Now, with nothing but a glass of water and a green plum to keep her stomach company, she set her stick-like legs upon the dusty road, trudging slowly with her pack hanging loosely from her back.

Within a mile or so she was overtaken with dizziness, and the morning light seemed to become increasingly peculiar and strange. The *izbas* were passing in a blur, drifting by with an odd unreality, until her belly turned over and she had to stop. There was no privy, only a bush, but it didn't matter, and at least it didn't smell. Here she squatted.

She was weak and alone. No one came or went, no wagons or traffic of any kind, nothing. Since her time as a fugitive, her life had fluctuated between being herded and kept like an animal or utterly deserted, desolate, and desperate. She couldn't decide which was worse. She turned back.

To the old woman's great surprise, she found Miriam huddled in the outhouse, sick and delirious.

Miriam's next to last memory was the privy; her last, the collective's office, a tawdry little room that also doubled as the dispensary. The Germans were advancing again, and the *muzhiki* were as fearful of harboring refugees as they were of having them die on their hands.

Miriam found herself lying supine on a cold metal table. She felt like a corpse with the power of thought as she stared upward into a blindingly bright ceiling light. Then she noticed a pain in her arm and lifted it to see a primitive IV by which glucose and water needled its way into her flesh in a steady flow.

I am dying, she thought, *and they won't be able to save me. It's hopeless; death is beside me. I can feel it, patiently waiting to take me away.* But death demurred. Days passed in a delirium of distorted time as Miriam, in that mortal hesitation, gathered strength, and death, for reasons beyond her understanding, stepped back but not quite away.

Eventually a dish of very watery creamed wheat appeared. A spoonful was ladled on her tongue. It was difficult to swallow; her belly was swollen like a melon, and she was dehydrated. She was urged to eat, gently spoken to by someone in a quiet, feminine voice.

"You must, if you are to survive," the voice said softly. She ate it all, but it took nearly an hour.

Things were bleary until the days slowly came back into focus. Why she yet lived, she did not know, but she did. Then she remembered that she had promised herself to survive and wondered if that was why she had done it, to keep that promise.

About 10 days or so passed; she grew stronger, enough to hear women's voices hovering around her. *Who are they?* she wondered. *What are they saying? What's wrong with me?* She looked at her belly. It was not as bad as before. She looked at her legs, still there but small and thin.

"The Germans are coming! The Germans are coming!" she remembered someone shouting. It was time to run again, to get back on the road or rail on the way east. *But how? I'm too weak.* Her heart sped up and fluttered. *They'll leave me and I'll die,* she decided. *The Germans will come and find the emaciated corpse of a little dead Jew on a slab or thrown in a corner. It won't matter. No one will care. And I'll be forgotten as if I had never existed.*

Then a girl about her own age rolled up a wheelchair. She sat Miriam gently in it and wheeled her into the corridor, where other patients stood in confused huddles, as in the unspeaking dumbness of a madhouse. Miriam's mind, like a turtle pulling back into a shell, retreated again. She did not sleep, but she did not quite see or think either. She was in a stupor until a green truck appeared, and she, along with the others, was loaded and driven to a railroad station, where, like so many times before, they all were crowded into a string of freight cars.

Another train! The Thing had been patiently waiting at the station like a friend to see her properly loaded in another fleeing freight. She never understood how, but it always happened, each time the same, each time she took no part—it remains a mystery.

Then she passed out, only to awaken to the familiar rocking. She did not know where they were going and did not care. They would go where the train took them, stop where it stopped, do as they were told, then do it all over again and again, as long as Death stepped back and refused to take her. The Thing would take her if Death would not. It was as simple as that. She no longer had to worry or be afraid. *Whatever happens, however it ends, nothing matters. It will all happen that way, and that's it. It will end as it will end.* In the comfort of this despair, she turned and slept against the wall.

At long last someone said, "Rostov," casually, routinely, like she was riding a trolley with a grown-up who bought the ticket and told her where to sit and when to get off.

"Rostov," Miriam thought, without really thinking what it meant. She knew nothing of Rostov and did not care.

If she had bothered to lift her head, she could have read the sign between the cracks, ROSTOV in large Cyrillic capitals. They halted. There were shouts. A whistle. A jolt. Steam was released under pressure, and they were diverted onto a side track.

The door slid open. Orders yelled out. Miriam found herself outside walking slowly. Everyone else went ahead, but she who could not run could only walk a little faster. She finally found a crude toilet behind the stationhouse. There were several holes in it, but no doors, and everything was open. But there was a line, so she wandered off and squatted by a bush, turned on a hydrant, washed her face and hands. Revived, she thought of running away but decided it was too much trouble. *They would just bomb me again, catch me again, put me on another train to nowhere.*

She wandered back, noticed a familiar-looking woman with a baby. They had been in the same car. The woman was gesturing to her frantically, yelling, "It's time to go back! Come on! It's time to go back to the train! It'll leave us! Hurry! Hurry! The Germans are coming!" she shouted. "The Germans are coming!"

But Miriam could not hurry, and feeling the urge again, she ambled over to the toilet, hoping perhaps it would be empty. It was. Everyone was back at the train. She sat, enjoying the quietude. Finally, she sauntered back to the car. Still it went nowhere. "Why aren't we going?" she heard a man ask.

"We have to wait; another train is coming through, a military one; we have to let it pass," someone said who seemed to know. They waited for what seemed a very long time. Miriam found a bench and sat with a group of fat women who left just enough room for her bony hips to find a hard perch at the end.

Then the buzz of talk was silenced by a distant down-the-track whistle. "Here it comes!" a man shouted.

Miriam, who had not cared, got up and stepped near the track. It was a very great, camouflaged train, flying red hammer-and-sickle flags, roaring past, armored, filled with soldiers and guns, rushing, blowing its horn, whistling and surging like an iron creature that made Miriam recoil in a shudder as its hot wind touched her cheeks like the breath of a beast. It had more power and speed than she had ever imagined. She remembered hearing that Trotsky[13] had such a train in the Revolution, but he was in exile, so she asked whose it was.

"It must belong to a field marshal or maybe a very great Communist commissar," a woman standing beside her said with a hint of pride. But it was only a few cars and quickly gone, its illusion of power vanishing as if it had never been.

Still their train did not move. Another long freight rolled in slowly and stopped beside it. "What the hell are we waiting on?" someone asked.

"For the Germans," someone else said. Some few laughed.

If Miriam had heard laughter since the children played in the water, she could not remember it. It made her feel better. She tried to return to her bench seat, but it was taken, so she sat elsewhere and watched as thousands milled about like ants around empty sandboxes. From time to time she instinctively looked up for planes, but the sky was a limpid blue and blessedly free of machines—no Heinkels or Stukas marred the clouds that day.

"There's no fire falling on us from God's heaven," she said out loud.

"Not yet," another retorted.

Miriam looked around for the woman with the baby or anyone familiar. *Even the cry of a baby would be a comfort.* Now she saw several mothers with children standing close to the rails, reluctant to board until the very last moment. They stood watching their children and chatting. Miriam walked over to them, feeling comfortable as with old friends simply because she recognized them. She stood slightly to the side of this small group, and, though not speaking, she felt secure.

Then someone called out a name for the train that had just pulled in as from the Odessa Polytechnic Institute. That was Karl's college! He had been at the OPI on June 22, the opening of Barbarossa.

Deftly Miriam pulled herself over the coupling and bounced down on the other side. "Karl! Karl!" she yelled. But no one answered. She called again and again, as she hurried along the pretty green passenger cars. A boy leaned out a window. Miriam questioned him, but he shrugged and disappeared inside. She continued along, calling. Then a familiar voice shouted from somewhere. Miriam looked around to behold a young man in a clean white shirt, standing in the doorway.

"I'm Friedlander," he said, smiling broadly, "and you're Miriam Kellerman," he added, hopping down and coming over.

"Friedlander?! My God!" she cried, clapping her hands. His father was a Czernowitz lawyer. "Friedlander!" she said again, surprising herself by falling into his arms.

Laughingly, he pushed her back gently.

"I'm sorry. Your first name is Hans, isn't it?"

"Ernst."

"Forgive me, Ernst, but I haven't seen anyone I know since, since I lost Isaac."

"Isaac Blumenthal?"

"Yes, we got separated."

"I see."

"Where is Karl? My brother, Karl Kellerman. Ernst, he was at the Institute. Is he with you? Have you seen him?! Is he well?"

"Oh yes, Karl's very well. He just stepped out."

"He's with you? On this train?! Karl is on this train?!"

"Yes, he'll be back in a minute. He'll be right back! Just wait here, he won't be long."

"Where? Where did he go?! I must find him now, where is he, Ernst?! I must find him! Please tell me! Where is Karl?! Please tell me, where's my brother?!" she said, clasping him by his clean shirt with both hands.

"I don't know," he said, freeing himself in a kindly way. "He went to the station, I guess, but, Miriam, you have only to wait, he'll return in a moment, he must. Our train'll be here just a short while, a few minutes they said. So you wait, he'll be here in no time."

"But Ernst, I can't, I can't wait, our train is leaving any second. I must see him, I must!"

A whistle blew. Miriam flinched. "Oh, God! There, it's our train! We're leaving!"

"But..."

"Karl!" she screamed. "Karl! Karl! Where are you?! Karl! It's me, Miriam!"

The whistle blew again.

"Miriam, come with us!" Friedlander said with a concerned look. "Just go with us!"

A group of young men began to return to the Odessa train, but Karl was not among them. She thought she had never seen so many young men together like that. There were no women anywhere, none at all on Karl's train, just men. Miriam began to shake.

"I don't know, I mean I can't," she sobbed. "I can't!"

"Why on earth not?!"

"Karl!" she screamed again, shaking, walking up and down, back and forth, sobbing and nervously running her hands through her hair.

The whistle blew a third time. Then, without speaking to Friedlander, Miriam turned and, crawling over the couplings, disappeared.

Miriam leaned against the wall of her boxcar and peeked through a slat as the OPI car slid from view. Then she lay back against the wall and wept, horrified at what she had done. *But at least I've stopped shaking; now maybe I can sleep,* she thought, but she could not.

Instead, she spent an hour against the wall in silence. The Rostov region was retreating into the distance, and with it perhaps her last family was slipping away. Gradually, by conscious effort, she tried to shift her thoughts to the future. "Where're we going?" she asked someone, sitting up and speaking for the first time in an hour. There was no immediate answer.

At last someone spoke into the silence, saying in a subdued voice, "Krasnodarsky."[14]

"Krasnodarsky," someone else repeated.

"Yes, Krasnodarsky," another added, as the name was passed around like a curiosity everyone wanted to examine. There were nods and murmurs and comments. Then a gentleman turned and said gently, "Krasnodar."

Miriam didn't know which was correct, Krasnodar or Krasnodarsky. She only knew that the train was going east away from the Germans again, away from Karl, away from Czernowitz and ever deeper into Eurasia.

Then they stopped. Surprisingly, people came on board and a small bag tied with a rope fell into her lap. Other such bags quickly dropped into the laps of everyone. The women behind her opened theirs greedily: bread, fruit, boiled eggs, and milk. *What can I do with such a feast?* she thought, as her belly turned over. The fear of vomiting quickly gave way to another dread. Nearby a mother eyed Miriam's package, while fondling two sickly infants who would not stop crying. *She wants mine,* Miriam thought. *She'll steal it when I'm asleep or, if I die, take it from my cold hands. Perhaps somebody'll even kill me for it.*

Slowly she opened the paper, and item by item—bread, fruit, eggs—parceled out the food to people who did not comment or thank her. But Miriam also saved a part of it, took these remaining crumbs, soaked them in an inch of milk and ate a little. She gave the rest to the woman, who pulled one infant from her nipple, urging it to suckle a balled-up handkerchief she had wrapped around some of the milk-soaked bread like a crude breast. Miriam watched as the child worked hard to drain the handkerchief.

Why? Why does life fight on? Miriam wondered as she watched the baby struggle to suck it dry. *Why? What sustains us? Is it the same Thing that saves me? If not that, what is it?*

Now she leaned back, retreated yet again into herself, her own private world, remembering the earrings she had once given for a small loaf of bread, cheese, and cucumbers. But she was feeling neither joy nor self-congratulation. *It's better to have nothing that others might envy*, she decided, pulling her mind back into its own hard carapace of inner-consciousness. *It's best to own nothing*, she repeated over and over, eventually falling asleep, secure that she had nothing anyone would want, nothing they could take, steal, or kill her for. Then, with nothing in her hand or lap, she slept soundly for a very long time.

16

A New and Unusual Friend

In normal times the difference between Rostov and Krasnodar would have come as a shock. Krasnodar was beautiful, with vast fields of various grains and thriving collectives unscarred by war. But, not being normal times, this distinction did not register with Miriam. Her inner world was much too insular. It was safer inside than out, and so there she remained, in her interior world, until the car door slid open at the station. Her eyes lit upon the station sign: BELORECHENSKAYA.[15]

Someone spoke to her, and out she came to be led into the station for an interview by a stout party boss, who singled her out with the crook of his short thick finger as if he had been waiting just for her. Miriam searched his eyes and, noting a certain reluctant kindness, decided she was safe, at least for the moment. He mumbled something and then motioned to a *muzhik*, who shoved her into a wagon, where she promptly fell into a doze until, hearing his voice from the front, she awoke.

Something else was said, and she reluctantly gathered her pack and set herself upon the ground of yet another *kolkhoz*. Then his grim-faced wife, Maria, waddled from a farmhouse. Miriam's Russian was now good enough to understand something of what the husband said—that she should be permitted to sleepwalk to a small bed. This she did, falling into a death-like peace until morning.

As always, she was too soon shoved awake, this time by Maria, and given the now all too familiar hard bread and goat's milk. Quickly, after a few gulps, Maria showed her the bathhouse. A sauna! For the first time since Czernowitz, she could really wash. Wash! She slipped into the steaming water and let it seep through and around her hair and body with a sensual, warming pleasure. She lingered, scrubbing, even splashing, and relaxing for the first time since playing in the river with the children.

Maria returned, helped her out, and surveyed her nakedness. Miriam's thinning flesh and frame seemed to frighten her. "Here," she said, throwing her an old dress that fit like a sack on a post, then handing her rags and soap while telling her in almost incomprehensible Russian to start hauling water and washing clothes. Miriam did this till lunch, when she was indulged thin soup and more rock-hard bread.

The afternoon was filled with unending house chores and even more difficult outside work. Maria and Miriam soon found themselves communicating through a series of gestures and staccato Russian from which Miriam could rescue only an occasional word. Increasingly, she was loaded down like a donkey—her efforts at pleasing Maria were futile—and any uncertainty or hesitation ignited an explosion of incoherence from her new mistress.

But Miriam was grateful because, for the first in a very long time, she had enough to eat. So she still struggled to please Maria, while knowing full well that it was the husband, Ivan, who had saved her. *Without him I'd be lost, he's my only ally. But it'll never work; Maria is jealous; she's no longer young or pretty, and she hates me for it. She wants to work me to death or drive me away. It's only because of Ivan that I am still here; he has pitied me, and the witch knows it. I am doomed if I stay; she will win in the end. There's only so much he can do, and she'll break me.*

A few weeks later Maria awoke Miriam with a shove, threw some breakfast at her, and turned away ranting and cursing. Then Ivan appeared and said with not an unkindly tone, "Gather your things; you're going away."

He loaded Miriam up, once again like a chattel going to market, and drove her through town, down the road a few miles leading back to the river. Here they crossed at a small bridge near a cluster of official-looking buildings set in an open field surrounded by a high barbed-wire fence and some guards. The place was depressing, bare, and uncared for. Inside everything was gray, and there was even a faint smell of chloroform.

A uniformed nurse emerged, greeted them warmly, and led them to another area. It was a clinic. The medicinal smells made Miriam fear she might wretch. "Why am I here?" she asked after catching her breath.

Ivan ignored her, turned, and chatted with the nurse instead. Then he was gone. A goodbye, a sad smile, and he was no more.

"Your home is here, in the infirmary," said the nurse, showing her around and to a small corner bed.

"But I don't need to be in an infirmary," Miriam said.

"Oh, my dear," said the nurse, "you're not a patient at all, but a worker, a nurse's orderly."

"A nurse's orderly?!"

"Yes, a helper."

"But I don't know how to help…"

"Don't worry, you'll learn."

Miriam looked around. "Who's here?" she asked.

"Juveniles, it's a place for them, juveniles."

"Juveniles?" she repeated, not knowing the Russian word.

"Boys," said the nurse, "it's a colony for boys."

Ivan had given her to a penal colony!

He's rescued me twice, I know very well, and I never even thanked him. I shall never see him again, and I owe him so much. How odd can life be? she thought, unpacking her things and stuffing them carefully under her little bed in the corner.

Miriam soon discovered the juvenile inmates were of the very worst sort. To get out of work, many wounded themselves and demanded to be treated. Then there were the endless infections and childhood diseases: impetigo, mumps, measles, and chickenpox—enough to destroy what little remained of her appetite, and so she began to starve again.

Worse, the boys were insolent and demanding. Her job, she came to understand, was to wash sores! She asked for gloves, but was told there were "none to spare." Her "patients" would laugh and disrobe unnecessarily, and then they would howl like hyenas, titillated by her humiliation.

Her phobia of men increased. At night she was tossed and beaten in the arms of the rape nightmare, repeatedly attacked by these boys with their sick, sore-covered bodies, muscled hard and naked against her flesh. Each night she suffered a worse horror than before and could no longer find solace in her fantasies and remembrances. Miriam tried thinking of Deborah, but she would not come again.

She felt she had been abandoned, and without Deborah, Miriam feared she would go mad.

The nurses were sympathetic, but they had problems of their own, they said. "Make do, just make do," they repeated. A few tried to help, but having their own duties, did nothing. Miriam was alone, alone with the boys and trapped in her bad dreams. She did not know if she could last. Her private shell, so hard for so long, now seemed to be cracking.

Then, to her great surprise, one good thing was occurring: she was learning Russian. The nurses spoke to her slowly and carefully, and she began to detect more and more words and to separate and combine them into sentences and the handy everyday phrases that people rely on. She began connecting the nurses' words and their motherly tone, gradually putting together the puzzle of that great language. Each day she concentrated on putting new pieces in place. In a way each new word was like sticky mud. She would throw it against the wall of her memory, and it would fall away into forgetfulness. But she'd throw it again, until it would stick for a while, fall, then be thrown again, and stick at last, never to fall away.

One nurse was particularly kind, and her slow words came carefully like the best teacher. She would smile at Miriam's attempts, nod encouragingly, and help with mistakes. Quickly, Miriam regained her old schoolgirl pride in learning; she was the successful lycée student again, the bright, eager Miriam Kellerman who would go to the very top of the language class.

Soon, Miriam, the new nurse's assistant, was achieving a certain status, and the Russian language became the new box where she could hide, her salvation. She hid in its grammar, found safety in its syntax and its innate poetry. Perhaps, she wondered, there was something about the Russians she didn't understand. This, after all, was the language of Pushkin, Turgenev, Dostoyevsky, and Tolstoy. She chose to place them side by side with Goethe, Schiller, Heine, and Zweig, but the Russians more than held their own.

Gradually, armed with Russian, she began to steel herself against the hooligans and to fight back in their own idiom.

Then one day, a lad stood before her she had never seen before. He was about 17. He stared very critically, without the slightest hint of kindness. His eyes seemed to survey her thinness, her patched clothes, and her swollen starvation belly, and then he demanded to be washed and his sores treated. But his rough speech was not really frightening, not any longer, for Miriam had become inured and stared back with an equally hard expression.

Dramatically, he thrust his arm toward her but with none of the insolence she had seen in the others. He seemed a little different somehow. She instantly became curious.

A nurse interrupted. She hurriedly scolded him in rapid-fire Russian. Miriam realized she was telling him to be polite. The boy nodded slightly. "I am Tkachenko," he said proudly, ignoring the nurse and concentrating his gaze on Miriam. He announced this as if he had a position of great importance. Miriam smiled without speaking and began to examine his skin. He watched her closely, as she gently washed his sores and applied first the ointment, then the bandages.

Realizing her Russian was bad, he spoke slowly, very simply, as if she were a child. "I am Tkachenko," he repeated. "What's your name?"

Miriam did not answer.

"How old are you?"

Still she was silent.

"Where do you live?" he insisted.

Miriam mumbled a reply, then left the room. But Tkachenko returned for treatment every day for a week. At the end of his work, he came to her, and each time he brought new questions.

Gradually, Miriam warmed to Tkachenko, practicing her Russian in a way that she couldn't do with the others. She found in discussing things with him that she improved rapidly. She even told him a little bit of her story. To be sure, she never said she was a Jew. She never told anyone that; it was her deepest secret. She always said she was Romanian, which, of course, was true.

Sometimes he would supply a word that she needed to help her explain her thoughts or frame her questions. They were never together more than a few minutes, and their conversations were always of the most basic kind. Still, something significant had occurred. Miriam had won Tkachenko's respect and, she realized with a bit of a shock, his protection. He was very curious about this strange Romanian girl, this intriguing orderly who cleaned his sores and was not only possessed of an education but also something he had never encountered—culture.

As for Miriam, far from being afraid of this young criminal, she was ever more curious and wanted to learn from him. He grilled her about her school very often and told her that in this penal colony he, too, had classes and was studying quite seriously. This was the first time in his life, he explained, that he had ever applied himself in this way.

"The teachers have obviously noticed your intelligence," said Miriam with a slight smile. "They want to encourage you."

He smiled broadly. "But it's difficult," he said reluctantly, after a moment's thought, "very difficult!" Then he added a little conceitedly, pulling himself up a bit, as was his habit, "I've been a leader, a leader of thieves in the Caucasus mountains."

Then, without being asked, he began to tell his story. It was clear that he was, indeed, the leader, and that the younger men submitted to him because of his force of will, cleverness, and confidence. His gang was very successful, he said, and "only a piece of very bad luck" had led to their arrest. "Or I'd still be free, climbing those beautiful mountains, like a great Russian wolf," he said unashamedly.

His reference to the Caucasus made Miriam think of her own time in the Carpathians, but he interrupted this thought by saying, "I began to study, but it was not easy, because to accept instruction from anyone was to lose respect."

"Lose respect?" asked Miriam, sincerely perplexed.

"Yes."

"How?"

"Of my comrades; a leader can never be seen to submit to another, and to study is to please," he explained. "Dog-like submission would destroy my pride. A wolf can never cower. It's always better to die than be someone's cur."

"I see," said Miriam quietly.

"But here, I'm the leader, too," he added, exchanging his frown for a smile, "just like when I was in the mountains."

Miriam said what she could in Russian, complimenting again his leadership and success. Then she added carefully, "But you need to study. It's an opportunity you must not miss."

He digested this without comment, but it obviously made an impression.

She continued, "You could be a teacher; you're teaching me Russian, you know?"

This pleased him. He grinned childishly, surprised at the idea that he could be anything other than a brigand.

Two months passed. Then the nurse told Miriam she would be moving.

"Where? Am I still staying here?"

"Yes, but in a new job, a new place. You have done well in the clinic; everyone is very pleased. I shall miss you, but you're still losing weight, and it was thought best that you be given some other work."

"What will I be doing?" Miriam asked tentatively.

"You'll be helping with the bookkeeping and living with a cafeteria worker. It will be better for you."

"Bookkeeping? But I know nothing about bookkeeping."

"You can learn. Now pack your things, and I'll take you there," said the nurse with a disappointed smile.

The accountant, a thin, shy, punctilious woman, showed her around her modest office, whose only window revealed the factory yard. Miriam glanced out. She saw inmates working on the army's winter sledges, *volokushas*. *Funny*, she thought, *watching this work, winter seems so far away.*

"Miriam?" interrupted the woman after a moment, her hands folded primly across her waist.

"Yes, ma'am?" Miriam said, averting her gaze from the window.

"You need not concern yourself much with the yard, my dear; your job is much easier. You only have to note the time that everyone works, how much, and what they've produced."

Then the accountant turned, picked up some papers from her desk, and handed them to Miriam, saying, "These charts have to be tallied, a daily report made, and an inventory conducted, all according to regulations."

"Yes, ma'am," Miriam said, as she followed the woman around, trying to remember everything.

The accounting was tedious, yet it was better than sore cleaning. Too, the bookkeeper was a kindly woman, not quite the motherly figure of the nurse but good enough. She was unattractive and obviously very lonely, and Miriam befriended her to her own great benefit. But she missed her chats with Tkachenko. He was by far the most intriguing person she had met since Czernowitz, and she wondered what had become of him.

While she worked with the bookkeeper, she lived with Zinoida, the cafeteria manager, another overly reserved spinster who possessed the greatest luxury—a private room, a small kitchen, plus a modest yard with a flower and vegetable garden. As a kind of rent, Miriam was expected to tend the garden and keep the woodbin filled. After work, she would run home to chore and clean, and she tried very hard to keep things spotless.

As for meals, the two took breakfast and lunch together in the cafeteria but always had a modest supper at home. Then they sat almost too quietly, but Miriam rather liked the silence, and since the food was spiced with their own vegetables, dinner was a very great pleasure, indeed.

Then one evening, just as she was stepping onto the porch, Miriam heard Tkachenko's deep voice.

"Hi!" he said in his uniquely proud but charming way. "It's me, Tkachenko. How've you been?"

She turned to find him standing cross-armed in the road. He was smiling with obvious self-pleasure. He sat beside her on the top step, and they chatted until dark, catching up on things in a flood of questions and answers. He told her the war was going badly and it would not be long before they had to leave. Then, almost without warning, he stood, said goodbye, and disappeared as strangely as he had come.

The next day, Miriam returned to find the buckets of water waiting and the depleted woodbin refilled to overflowing. Zinoida asked about this, but Miriam could only say she did not know how it happened, adding with a wry smile, "Someone likes you very much and simply wants to repay your kindness."

It was a harmless lie, but it worked. The old lady was deeply flattered.

Tkachenko was slowly asserting himself throughout the camp. When the game was repeated, and Miriam came home to find the water and the woodbin filled, it was obvious that Tkachenko took great pleasure in pulling these distance strings. Then one day Miriam returned to find even the flowerbed weeded and the garden watered.

"What miracles of kindness this clever bandit can work!" she said out loud. *How strange that my protector should be a thief! How strangely things happen!* she mused. Here she was living among criminals in Russia, and yet she felt respected, indeed, even guarded by the friendly hand of the master of them all, the mighty Tkachenko, who was gradually taking control of everything.

In this way Miriam passed the winter of 1941-'42, but, alas, nothing, not even the wire and guards, could hold the war away. Spring brought with it not just a resurgence of life but of death as well.

"The Germans are coming! The Germans are coming!" everyone said, and abruptly Tkachenko's carefully orchestrated world fell into ruin. Fate had other plans, and Miriam Kellerman had to flee yet again, ever deeper yet into the Eurasian abyss, south and east, into Tkachenko's Caucasus.

17

Another Farewell

"Get up, Miriam! Get up! Hurry! The signal has sounded! The Germans are coming![16] We're leaving! You must hurry!" a voice shouted into her sleep, forcing her awake.

Zinoida gave her a hard nudge, repeated what she had said, and went to finish packing. Miriam was dressed in hardly a minute. She knew the Nazis must be very near. For the past two days there had been a strange excitement in the air, and Miriam knew why. She thought: *They're young and hate the camp; this is a kind of liberation, an adventure, but if they only knew.... Ah, well, they'll find out. I must go again, God knows where. Keep moving and don't speak German.*

They grabbed their things and went outside to find Tkachenko waiting.

"I'll carry it, thank you, I can manage," Miriam said, trying hard to sound forceful.

Tkachenko laughed and took her bag, then, turning to Zinoida, said, "Miss Zinoida, your bags, please, I'll take them."

Zinoida, without protest, let them go with a shaking hand. Tkachenko carried them, walking ahead, while Miriam, feeling rather foolish with only her little pack on her back, fell behind as they trudged through gates.

As they approached the trucks, Miriam noticed Zinoida was becoming agitated. Before she could speak to her, she was diverted by Tkachenko, who, setting down their luggage, said, "See you at the station." Then he left in that mysterious way he had of coming and going.

"Goodbye, Tkachenko, thank you," Miriam shouted, waving, uncertain he had heard as he quickly disappeared in the crowd.

"How very singular he is," she said, turning back to Zinoida, who now was very pale and increasingly agitated.

"What's wrong?" Miriam asked.

A pause.

"I'm not going, Miriam," Zinoida stammered out, tears coming in a flood.

"Not going!? What do you mean!?"

"No, I can't, Miriam. This is my home, I can't leave it," she said, making a desperate gesture.

"But the Germans, Zinoida, the Germans!"

"I'll take my chances. They won't bother me. I'm not pretty, I know that well enough—never have been, and now I'm too old anyway. They won't bother me, I'm nothing to them. I'm going to stay here in my little place with my garden. I'll be all right, dear, don't worry about me."

"Zinoida!"

"No, this is goodbye," she said with a breaking voice. "I thought I could leave, I really did, but now, standing here, I know that I can't. I must stay here, Miriam. I'm sorry."

What's Zinoida saying? Is she mad? Does she have any idea what she's in for? She can't have any idea at all!

"Zinoida, you can't stay; you don't understand what they're like, the Nazis. I do. You must come with us while there's still time, really, you must!"

"No, no. See, I've never left Belorechenskaya, and I cannot leave it now. You'll be all right. I know that. You can take care of yourself, I can see that, but for me, I must remain. It's my home, the only one, so please don't worry, please don't, and please, please, don't say anything else. I know now that I can't leave."

Miriam began to weep.

Zinoida said, "Don't be silly, dear, please don't cry, I'm not afraid. I'll be all right. And see, some day this terrible war will be over, and you will come back to me, my dear, Miriam. Please, please, return, and find your dear old friend Zinoida here, alive and well. Promise you will come back? Will you? Do you promise?"

"Yes, yes, of course, I promise. I'll come back."

"Good, thank you, but for now it's goodbye," she said as matter of factly as she could manage. She hugged Miriam long and hard, as if trying to keep her forever, then lifted her bags, turned, and walked stiffly away.

"Goodbye! Goodbye! Zinoida, goodbye!" Miriam yelled, waving and sobbing.

"This way! Hurry up!" a guard shouted, interrupting from nearby, pushing everyone forward to load. "You must load now, Miss, it's time to load," he said, giving Miriam a slight nudge toward the nearest truck.

They convoyed to the station, dismounted, and were stuffed into waiting passenger cars. Passenger cars! Not cattle cars! There was none of the desperation of before; things were organized and orderly. They were getting the hang of it; the Germans advanced, and the Russians loaded up and moved away. There was a long wait, and then the process was repeated. There was no reason to panic; just load up and go. Eventually the Germans would tire, like Napoleon, Miriam remembered from *War and Peace*. Like him, they seemed invincible but weren't.

They were divided by sexes. The boys were put into two cars, and the girls were in a third. It was crowded, but Miriam found a seat by a window where she watched the empty trucks pull away. Then she noticed something else: adult male prisoners from the Mykop prison were loading into a fourth car. Her heart began to gallop as if trying to escape. Afraid of fainting, she closed her eyes and tried hard to think of something else. *I must think of something else, anything else* was a repeated thought that was finally interrupted by their jerking forward.

My bag! Where's my bag?! came to her, as now she nervously looked for her little bag. Her pack was in her lap, and the bag, borrowed from Zinoida, was right there on the floor, just where she left it. She wore her only jacket, a brown skirt of light, thin wool, and a pink linen blouse— her uniform at the prison. In the bag and pack she had stuffed a pair of shoes, a cotton dress Zinoida had "found for her," some tins of food, and a small Russian dictionary swapped with the bookkeeper for several large baskets of fresh vegetables.

Leaning back into the seat, the fear left her as abruptly as it had come, and she fell asleep to the easy rocking of the train. Later, she wasn't sure how long, she awoke to find herself trying to recall a famous line she had read with Deborah about the conscious and the unconscious, waking and sleeping, but she could not recall it. *I will remember it eventually. Now I'm just too sleepy*, she decided before dropping off again.

They rode all day, due south from Belorechenskaya, into the evening, finally arriving at Batumi, a popular Georgian resort on the Black Sea, not that far from the Turkish border. Guards came in and gruffly ordered them out.

"Get out! We have a long walk! We're staying here for the night!" they yelled. "Get out!"

Jumping free, they slogged in a ragged line, until after about a mile of walking a large gate loomed ahead. Its large ornate red and gold sign said something in Russian Miriam couldn't make out. Someone translated: "Botanical Garden."

Botanical Garden!? How queer! How wonderful! How absurd!

Then a guard yelled and pointed, "Juvenile inmates to the right. Employees to the left." Everyone shuffled into groups, then stood in mute anticipation.

Where is Tkachenko? Miriam wondered. *He doesn't seem to be among us. He said he'd meet us. Where is he?* She very much wanted to find him, but, of course, he would thrive, whatever happened, she knew that. But she felt sad. *How terrible it is to say goodbye to a friend, but to not say it at all, how much worse!*

"Follow me!" shouted a guard and marched them into the garden. He then told them to remain within the place until further notice and left. Miriam set down her luggage and took a few steps among the plants. *How very peculiar that I should find myself among flowers growing in such a wild kind of beauty! Of course, it has all gone to seed, but still there is a kind of order; nature always has its own arrangement, an inner structure of chaos and order, wound together in a mad fantasy!*

Someone said something about her bag being in the way, so she lifted it and strolled silently along the path. Finally, wearily, she set it back down, took off her pack, and picked a yellow flower. *I wonder what I look like*, she thought, wishing for a mirror, pinning the stem in her hair. Then she lay on the ground, pillowing her head on her pack, and searching for sleep until she found it in a half distortion somewhere between a thought about Isaac and a delicious dream of home.

The sun seemed to rise faster than it really wished, hesitating to fade the garden flowers into a morning wilt. But eventually, in that slow but methodical way she had come to expect, the Russians came with the full light of day to herd them to the station and onto yet another passenger train that carried them through a very dark and monotonous night till she awoke at a place the station sign proclaimed as TBILISI.[17]

The train stopped, cars were unhitched, reconnected, and in minutes Miriam Kellerman was rocking and chugging out of Europe.

For the first time, she realized, she was in the Caucasus. But she felt no excitement and simply fell back in her window seat, sleeping comfortably to the steady clicking and rolling. Of course, they were running away from the Germans' advance. *How far will I have to go this time?* she mused in a half-sleep. *Maybe I have really escaped? My God! Have I really done it?! Can I let myself believe it at last? After all, I am now in Georgia and officially out of the Russian Republic. Surely the Germans can never get this far!*

Another dawn came, and they stopped. A rasping voice on a loud speaker awoke her. It repeated itself, but she could not quite make it out. "Where are we?" the person next to her asked.

"Baku,"[18] someone behind them said.

"Baku?" Miriam said, sitting up and staring out.

"Yes," the same person advised rather officially, "it's an industrial city on the Caspian Sea."

"The Caspian Sea? How could we have come so far?!" Miriam asked. They got off and found themselves marched to a pier where water spread out before them like a smooth blue eternity.

The Caspian Sea?! I've never dreamed of being in such an exotic place, she thought, staring at a horizon that was drawn over a line of greenish water touching white clouds in a conflation of two infinities.

"Miriam!" a girl screamed. "Miriam Kellerman!"

Miriam whirled about.

"Becky!" she screamed. "My God! Becky! Oh my God! Where've you been?! How did you get here?! I don't believe it!"

They fell into each other's arms, crying and asking endless questions.

"What happened? Where's Isaac?!" Miriam cried. "Is Isaac with you?!"

"We got separated, you know, after the bombing at Proskurov. Where were you, Miriam?! My God, did we look everywhere for you, everywhere! Where were you?! How did you get so lost from us?!"

"I was hiding under a building, I don't know for how long. I think I must have been in shock."

"Well, we looked and looked, but we couldn't wait, then we all got separated by the Russians, and I wound up on a collective, you know, toiling as a slave, a maid on a small farm."

"So did I!"

"Ha! Well, I hope it wasn't as awful as mine was!"

"What happened to everyone else? Where is Isaac, Becky?! Please, tell me what has happened to him!"

She said she had tried to find out about him and everyone, but no one knew very much for sure. They thought that it was almost certain that he and the other boys were drafted.

"After all," Becky added, "the Soviets are desperate. They don't care, they take everyone into the army, anybody at all."

"Yes," Miriam said, "but that means he's alive!"

"Yes, yes, dear, yes, as far as I know, but he'll be at the front, Miriam, you must realize that."

"Yes, of course."

"Well," said Becky, unsure of what else to say.

"Oh, thank God, he's alive. I had feared the worst!" Miriam cried, tears flowing. Then, turning a little pale, she said as much to herself as to Becky, "It makes sense for him to be in the army, I guess, but I can't see how he'd be any good. I mean he's a lawyer and not a soldier."

Becky interrupted, "Oh, Miriam, they need officers. They'll make one out of him in a hurry, train him on the spot, and put him in a uniform with shoulder boards with only two days' instruction."

"Two days' instruction?!"

"Yes, two days', and then send him right to the front straight off. Believe me, that's the way they do it. It's crazy, but they're starved for young men. By now he'll be one of the *frontoviki*."

"*Frontoviki?*"

"My, my, Miriam, you have been hidden away, my dear—he'll be a veteran."

"But what've you heard of the fighting, how is it really going? We don't believe a thing they tell us. They're always saying things're going well in one breath, but we had to pull back in the next. You know the line, 'heavy defensive battles against superior forces,' which, as you know, always means yet another retreat."

Becky said she'd heard of the fight for Kharkov.[19] It had fallen "along with Sebastopol,[20] and the Germans keep advancing after their usual brilliant victory over the stolid but brave boys, fed into the machine like sheep," she added solemnly, but wished she hadn't.

Miriam looked down into the water rolling against the rocks, *like those waves being thrown forward and breaking up.* Fresh tears welled up, and she turned away.

Becky touched her gently, asked about what had happened after Proskurov. Miriam told her quickly, leaving out the rape. Then they sat on their bags, chatting madly, until a ferry-like boat chugged up to the quay. A sailor yelled, "Miss, come on! We're loading! Loading now! Hurry, there's not a moment to lose!"

"They're loading all the people from the colony," someone shouted.

Miriam and Becky scrambled up. They hugged, scooped up their belongings, and ran toward it. Then Becky hesitated and said, "I'm not going. I forgot that I can't go with you."

"Not going?"

"Yes, I'm to remain, take other transportation. I'll catch up with you, but don't worry, I'll see you later, I'm sure of it."

"Where're we going?" someone interrupted before Miriam could reply.

"I don't know."

"Krasnovodsk,[21] I think," someone else said excitedly.

"Krasnovodsk?" Miriam asked. "Where's that?"

"In Turkmenistan, across the Caspian."

"Across the Caspian?! We are going across the Caspian Sea?" Miriam asked in amazement.

"So it seems," the person said nonchalantly and turned away.

"Gosh! Becky," Miriam said facing her, "did you hear that? We're crossing the Caspian!"

"Yes, I heard. I wish I were going with you," Becky said with obvious disappointment, adding with a sad look, "but this is goodbye now, I'm afraid."

"Yes, goodbye, my dear," Miriam said, hugging Becky. "See you soon!"

"Yes, it won't be long," Becky said, "but bye for now."

They hugged quickly, kissed, and then Miriam darted away, stepping aboard to find a nook near the wheelhouse. Underway, the unfamiliar undulation of the swells charmed her as the air and rushing water were a great relief from the infernal click, click, clicking of endless steel meeting steel. But soon a stinking salt-excrement-and-oil odor wafted up from the fetid hole below where, she was told, some "chained criminals crouched like galley slaves."

She stepped to the rail for the freshness of a sea breeze. Concentrating upon the unbroken eastern horizon, she tried to remember pleasant thoughts of home, but in a slight shift of wind, the stench caught her again. Now she could think only of the Jews of Czernowitz, whom she imagined were crammed into train or truck or cell not unlike those poor creatures huddling in the darkness beneath her feet. There was a sudden forward pitch, followed by a backing yawl, and she grabbed the rail, held on, then shuffled to the wheelhouse, where she leaned her bag to steady herself against the up-and-down and side-to-side rolling of the boat.

The ferry eased ever eastward, over slightly moderate swells, its bow nosing out a hissing white wake until, within an hour, she lost the gray line of land on either side, and her good mood returned to her. *How delicious to be suspended between two eternities? Such a wonder is this water! What splendor is the sky kissing unblemished upon its delicate surface! Why can't we just keep going till we disappear where the two embrace? Yes, that must be it! Where sky and sea touch we might all vanish into a perpetual loving softness. Let's away! Going and going and going and going, never to see land again! Oh why can't we just sail away forever and ever into the sweet nothingness of this delicious sea and sky?*

This euphoria was broken by nearby laughter at a vulgar joke. "We'll be there before dark," someone added, but Miriam wormed away as far as she could and sat again upon her bag to pass the time. She slept a little, off and on, and then awoke to ask the hour, which no one seemed to know. She stared eastward again in hopes of regaining the trance-like bliss of before, and it was then she saw it. She did not want to see it, but there could be no doubt—a dirty brown edge poking its way up, intruding along the far horizon. Miriam watched as it very slowly, imperceptibly, grew larger and more menacing.

It's ugly, Miriam thought, turning, lifting up her bag, and working back to the stern to spend the remaining time sitting and staring westward, until, approaching a shore she could no longer ignore, she stood reluctantly, removed the little yellow flower from her hair, and cast it on the water. She watched it float up on a rising swell; not once but twice did it ride up. *Will it make a third?* she wondered. *If it does, I'll find Isaac.* It rose again, hesitated, and then vanished.

Drab buildings, warehouses, and a train station loomed up, as everyone began to jump from the boat to a crowded dock.

"Free and prison bound," a soldier said, dividing them into two groups. A guard stopped her, asked her name, checked her papers, and then motioned her toward the "free group."

A young man mumbled as he was pushed the other way. "They know they can't keep us, so we're going to the army! That's how they'll finally get rid of us."

Miriam kept walking, thinking, *But what's the difference? Which of us is truly free?*

A line of green passenger cars waited for them, nicer than before. "We'll be traveling in style," she said out loud with a bitter laugh.

But people were packed in, stuffed, and pushed by the guards in a great crush. Miriam eyed a space near the first bench, but there were more people than seats, and it was quickly taken.

"Let's stand," Miriam said to a girl next to her. "That way no one will fall on us. We'll stand and prop up each other."

So she stood in a corner, traveling all night without sitting.

At last, they boarded a different train in a tiny, dingy, sad little rail station where the only paint was on a sign saying "SEMIPALATINSK."[22] This train was very dark, no lights at all. It was as if they were in a long, dark, rolling prison. *This is the worst, worse than any box or flatcar,* Miriam thought, as she was shoved, suffocating against a wall. *In one I at least had my little corner and in the other I could breathe.* But on and on they went to the infernal, nerve splitting, rattling and clicking with curses and cries in the dark. The train stopped and started, filling with ever more evacuees from places unnamed. Once it lurched sharply around a curve, flinging a body into her, knocking her bag away. In horror, she reached down and squatted slightly, searching her hand cautiously but instead touched a man's leg. He kicked her with an oath. She fell against the wall in a half faint.

I'll find it in the morning; it'll be where I dropped it, but I just can't touch him again. I'll be fine; it'll be there in the morning, she kept repeating. *But I never want to touch a man's leg again as long as I live, not ever!*

The next morning the man and her suitcase were gone.

18

Kazakhstan

The train stopped at Ust-Kamenogorsk[23] on the northeastern border of the Soviet Republic of Kazakhstan. Without her suitcase, Miriam, along with the rest of her comrades, got out and lined up along the platform.

"What's today?" someone asked.

"The 13th, I think. Yes, the 13th of July," someone else mumbled.

July 13, 1942! My God! It's my birthday! I'm 18! Eighteen! Celebrating in Kazakhstan of all the crazy places, in Asia! I left my home more than a year ago, a child, when I was 16! I can't remember my 17th birthday! Where was I?! What happened to 17? But now I feel very, very old. I have nothing except what's on my back, in my trusty pack, bless my faithful old pack.

Bags come and go, but it remains! Everything except my pack has been taken from me, either robbed, ravished, ruined. Am I ruined now at the ancient age of 18?

Then she was jostled before she could answer her own question and distracted by someone asking her something about the next train.

"I don't know," she said, turning away.

How can this miserable country take care of us when it can't begin to care for itself? Other trains will come soon, no doubt, but to what purpose? Won't it just be to some other place to starve? To freeze? What's to become of us? she thought, looking around at the mob milling around this squalid little station squatting in the nowhere of Central Asia, not far from China. Her belly cramped. She stared around, *Alone, save my pack and this wretched, worn-out dress! My God, what am I going to do?*

She said, laughing a little madly, "Happy birthday, Miriam Kellerman, happy birthday to you!"

Then she heard Yiddish. It was a couple nearby, huddled behind her. She approached and introduced herself in German. They stared, then broke into smiles and chatter—German with a Baltic accent—

Fanya and Irene, they said, introducing themselves. "We'll help you, you can stay with us."

But in mid-sentence she doubled over. Diarrhea! A cold sweat, a chill, and a knife stabbed her bowels. She ran away, asking until she found something imitating a lavatory.

When she returned, Fanya and Irene were gone. She wandered, looking, but they had vanished, and she was struck by the terror of how easily people could come and go. Here, then gone forever. *How can it be? It's too uncertain, too like waves breaking over a rock.*

In her despair something came, took over for her again, and Miriam remembered very little except mumbling to a faceless official. Then, without her understanding it, the Thing (she could not remember quite how) found her a room with a married couple; their in-town, two-bedroom flat with living room and kitchen was luxurious beyond all hope.

The woman was a Volga German, Hilda, blond with deep eyes like bluest arctic ice. *She must have been quite beautiful in her youth,* Miriam thought. But her husband, Boris, was a brute and made Miriam sleep on the floor between the stove and wall, with three slats of wood slid under an old mattress.

"What work will I do?" she had asked Hilda.

"Work at the courier office. It's not much, but it's something," she had said.

The office director was an elderly man, bespectacled, kindly and good enough to give Miriam bits of food.

"Here's some wood," she told Hilda, as she squatted, stacking it by the stove and then standing to produce a newspaper wrap of a little bread and a morsel of cheese fished from an interior pocket.

"Wood?! Where?! Where did you find it?!'

"I can't tell you."

"Come on, where?"

"At the warehouse, they always have plenty of scraps."

"How do you get out with it, past the guard?"

"Well, see, there's big new pile every day, over by the fence. At the end of work everyone rushes out, and I always hang back a bit, you know, to be the last to leave. I go to the pile and throw a few pieces over into the ditch on the other side. The guard always looks the other way, bless him. I pick it up when I come along the road after going through the gate."

"Don't get caught, my dear, it's a very serious offense."

"Yes, I know, but freezing to death is a very serious offense, too."

Miriam joined Hilda in a good laugh.

"Things are better now," Hilda said. "Boris is less cruel since you've brought food and fuel," she added. "You've saved me."

"I've saved us," Miriam corrected with a slight smile.

Then after a month, the ubiquitous eye of Soviet bureaucracy, never forgetting her, sent word that she was to take her documents to the city Communist committee "for review." On the way, she saw Fanya.

"Fanya! Gosh! It's you!" she cried. "What's happened to you?! I looked everywhere!"

Fanya was an Estonian Jew. She also was a Communist who was middle-level in the local hierarchy. Her brother worked in the meat plant. He had moved up, was now its director, and had also joined the Party.

"He's brought us all together, can you believe it? Our entire family!" Fanya said. "Imagine, a whole Jewish family actually living together, and prospering, too! Such things simply never happen anymore!"

She offered to take Miriam in.

"No, no," she said shaking her head, "I can't accept, thank you. You are very kind, but I cannot," Miriam said with just a whiff of pride.

"Why not?"

She told her about Hilda and Boris.

"I'm very grateful to her. I can't leave her. She'll die without me. Hilda saved me, and I cannot leave her now; it would be wrong."

"Why would she die?" Fanya asked. "What did she do before you came? Huh? Tell me that?"

"She was slowly starving," Miriam said matter-of-factly. "Without me, she's lost, really, Fanya, but thank you so much. You're very good, but thank you."

Miriam couldn't bring herself to say she had no clothes and could not make the daily trip from Fanya's country house into town and back without freezing.

Fanya did not insist but arranged for her to come on Saturdays. "You can spend the night and return on Sunday afternoon," she said. "Wash your clothes and rest."

"I don't have any."

"Don't have any? What do you mean, 'don't have any'?"

"Don't have any clothes, not really. I lost them when my bag was stolen on the train. Fanya, I have nothing."

"You poor dear, I'll give you some blouses and undergarments."

"Really..."

"No, don't be silly; you need them, Miriam."

Miriam wanted to say, *What I really need are boots and a coat, not to mention a* ushanka, *or I don't know how I'll make it through the winter*, but her pride prevented her. It was October and she was already having problems staying warm.

"The Irtysh is freezing," Miriam said instead.

"Yes, in a few days it'll be solid," Fanya said. "I'll see you on Saturday, OK?"

"Yes, of course, thank you, I'll see you then, goodbye," Miriam said with a wistful smile and a little wave.

"Until then, my dear, be well," Fanya replied and walked away.

The winter of 1942–43 deepened—the worst anyone could remember. Miriam had never known such cold. But still she began to volunteer for various "war-effort" projects on weekends. Her first was to raise money for the Soviet Army Tank Corps. This took her door to door, asking for things, so her feet were almost frostbitten and her arms and legs turned blue.

"Why don't you volunteer at the plant, Ust-Kamenogorsk, being built on the river?" someone suggested. "The town has doubled since the war and they need volunteers."

"Volunteers?"

"Yes, volunteers to help build a jetty for the dam, jutting out into the water."

She volunteered, working on weekends when not at the courier office. A large area of ice had been removed from the river, and sleds carrying stones were driven out and dumped as huge contingents of volunteers shoved these great rocks into the water. The work was frantic so there was little time to notice her ice-soaked shoes and frozen stockings as she worked through the night. She did this for several weeks until she was promoted to being a runner carrying messages. But she had no overcoat, just a jacket, and not even a fur hat or boots, no *ushanka* or *valenki*, and only one pair of "mules" and "mud shoes." Gradually, her legs turned bluer and stayed that way, even when she was indoors and warmed by a fire. Still she didn't complain and did nothing but work and struggle.

Finally, in December, she collapsed. Lying in the street, she remembered watching the washed-out sky permit a slice of sun to shine on her as from a broken and very dirty window. She did not move or speak as she watched the flakes falling, while the pain of one leg doubled underneath her throbbed in a dull, painful competition with the snow tickling her cheeks. She managed to raise a hand to brush her face, only to feel something hot trickle on her lips—it was blood. *It's all over me. I am covered in blood, snow, and ice.*

She lowered her hand and gazed from the sky to the river—from heaven to earth. She knew the sun would not help her any more than it had that summer day in the green wheat. She knew she was dying. She was afraid and yet not afraid, fearful and yet serene. Her mind was alive, but her body was relaxing into oblivion. It was quite peaceful, and she embraced it with a certain delicious pleasure.

I don't care, it doesn't matter anymore. Let death come now, it's my friend, more friendly than the sun or the earth who have never really been my friends. Death is my friend, has always been at my side waiting, waiting to take me away.

Then she thought of her mother. She heard her laughter. "Miriam, you silly child," she said, "get up and brush yourself off! You're an excellent skater; don't lie in the snow like that, you'll catch your death. Get up! Skate to the music! Get up! It's not yet time to die. That time will come but it is not now."

Then Miriam heard a waltz—Strauss—the same she had heard her parents play on the scratchy phonograph when they would have a drink and dance together as they had done in Vienna, and the same she had skated to as she twirled a perfect *pas de deux* with Isaac watching. She smiled now as she listened, thought of them and of him, forgetting the pain, twirling again in the happiest moment of her life as the snow kissed her cheeks and lips like he had once done so gently.

"Get up, dear, get up! You have things to do, get up, you must live," Deborah said. "It's not time to die, Miriam, you must get up and dance to the wonderful music, my dear. Get up!"

There was nothing sweeter than her mother's voice, but she could not obey, not anymore. She wanted to but couldn't.

"What have you done, Miriam?! Look at the crystal lying broken all over the walk. Look how you've broken the vase across the snow! Look how it glistens, so many sharp jagged pieces. How sad, Miriam, to have broken that marvelous vase. It was so beautiful, and now it's shattered. How did it happen?! How could such a vase have been broken into so many pieces?"

Then Miriam said sweetly, "Mama, I am the broken vase, and like it, I'm broken into a thousand pieces and am lying in the snow. I'll never be put back together. No, no one can ever glue me back together again; I am broken forever."

The sun moved languidly behind a heavy cloud, the music stopped, and then Miriam closed her eyes and went to sleep. She dreamed, seeing herself in her room, sitting on the floor reading a French novel. Then the door opened, and Hans trotted in. He bounded over and sniffed and licked her all over with his wet pink tongue. How delicious and innocent were those sweet kisses! She petted him softly. He looked into her eyes, speaking to her as only he could. He told her to relax, to endure; that someone would come soon. "Someone will save you; don't give up," he said. "Wake up!"

She opened her eyes. *I am dying for what purpose, I can't think. I am young, and there's no reason for me to die before I have ever really lived.* Yet she lay motionless, slipping away, while the flakes caressed her and the frigid sun reappeared, seeming to glance down as with a second thought, then hid itself from shame, if not from grief.

It'd be easy to die but I am not going to, no, not yet, it's not time to die. Mother's right, Hans is right, I must get up.

She tried to move her leg but couldn't—it was agonizing, so she stopped trying, closed her eyes again, and fell into a deep, dreamless sleep, more than half wishing never to awake.

But she did awaken. It was light and warm. *I'm in bed?! Bed?! How ever did I get into a bed?!* She looked around. It was a hospital. She never found out who found her or how she was moved. *It was the Thing. Hans had awakened it and Deborah had brought it by the hand to save me. Why does it keep saving me? Why can't it just leave me alone?*

Then she had three visitors—her boss, a Jewish lady from Kharkov; a young gentleman, the secretary of Komsomol, the young Communist League; and the Party's secretary of the "food and clothing" office, Kozlova. Surprisingly a reporter from the local Party paper also came, but Miriam wouldn't talk to him. He seemed ghoulishly hungry to fill a propaganda page about a hero's sacrifice, dying for "socialist construction." *He's the devil's lackey. Why in the midst of so much death could people have satisfaction in one more? I will not make propaganda for the devil or one of his minions,* chyortoo all.

Then food appeared on her tray, and new boots and clothes at the foot of her bed. And, she learned, it was Kozlova, the secretary, who brought the apples, oranges, and chocolates. But she could not eat, so she gave them away to the doctors and nurses, orderlies, and volunteers. They had not stolen it, so now she gave it to them, thanking them quietly for helping her. *What's food to me anyway? What's anything? I have no use for it. Like on the train, it's better to give it away. Then there is nothing to take from me. I want nothing I have to watch or guard.*

A Ukrainian-Jewish refugee saw that the cold food was not helping Miriam, and she managed for her to have something hot. It was better. She could eat a little, had not the burden of keeping it from others, and could not give it away. It stayed down and saved her.

Then the doctors came. Feigning sleep, she listened to their loud whispering; she knew they would not tell her the truth—doctors never do.

"Her left hand and left foot must be amputated," one of them muttered. "There's no other hope!"

"You're right, of course," replied the other quietly, "but she's so young. I think there's something, we must try something else. Perhaps if we can arrest the infection, there's a chance!"

"But we have no way of controlling it. She has no real hope at all," the other said a little too loudly.

"Well," the softer-spoken one said, "it's a risk. I think we can save the hands, but she'll die if she loses a foot or leg. An amputation is a death sentence; we must do something else."

"Yes, but what?"

"I've an idea, unorthodox, but what'd you think if...," he said, his voice trailing off.

The "unorthodox" treatment, it turned out, was so bad that Miriam sometimes wished they had taken the limb. First, the toe and fingernails were pulled without anesthesia. Then they treated each toe by using her urine as disinfectant, followed with "Vishnevsky ointment," a hideously black, malodorous substance spread over her frostbite.

Then Kozlova came in one day and stood by her bed. "You're going to be discharged tomorrow," she said.

"Discharged?"

"Yes, you're healed. I've talked to the doctor."

"Where will I live? I mean, I don't want to go back to that apartment."

"I know. I have made arrangements."

"What arrangements?"

"You must remain with Hilda and Ivan, but you'll spend lots of time with us. We've plenty of food, vegetables, even a sauna. Things'll be lots better, and with your new clothes you'll be warm."

"Thank you," said Miriam quietly.

"And I have you a new job inside a warehouse, doing office work; it'll be easy, and you won't freeze."

Miriam didn't quite know what to say and so could manage only an amazed, questioning look.

"Also, I've made arrangements for you to spend a few days with us at first. You'll come tomorrow, as part of your recovery, doctor's orders," she said with a perky smile. "You know, being a Party apparatchik has its advantages!"

Miriam laughed quietly, took her hand, and said, "You've saved my life. You know that? Thank you."

She, of course, soon learned more about her friend: that she lived with her sister and father, an intellectual who wrote children's books, and that before the war Kozlova had a husband and son. The husband had been arrested in a "purge" and sent to the camps in 1937, and the son had been taken away as well to a "boarding school" and, like his father, had never been heard from. Kozlova hardly spoke of them. People rarely returned from such places, everyone said. Best to think them dead and buried; best to bury them forever. If they came back it was a resurrection, a *Voskresenye*. But "don't expect it," people said in hushed tones.

The Kozlov family lived in a large wooden house, luxurious for Ust-Kamenogorsk, with seven rooms and enough land for a few pigs and even some goats. More importantly, it was warm, and for the first time, Miriam felt she was actually thawing out.

"My God!" she cried, "a sauna, a vegetable garden! Am I dreaming?!"

To her regret, she no longer saw Fanya as much. It was the Kozlovs now who sustained her. With their serenity of woods and garden and, most of all, their friendship, Miriam allowed herself to think, at least for a moment, that perhaps in crossing the Caspian Sea, she finally had escaped.

19

Fedya's Chat

On January 31, 1943, the tenth anniversary of Hitler's Reich (on which he declined to make a speech), Lieutenant Fyodor Mikhailovich Yelchenko was leading his unit in the center of Stalingrad when he learned from three captured German officers that Field Marshal Friedrich Paulus, commander of the glorious Sixth Army[24]—the crème de la crème of the mighty Wehrmacht—was hiding in the Univermag department store that they had just surrounded.

Lieutenant Yelchenko, called "Fedya" by his friends, recounted the story a few days later[25]:

"We then began to shell the building (my unit was occupying the other side of the street, just opposite the side entrance of the Univermag), and as the shells began to hit it, a representative of Major-General Raske popped out of the door and waved at me. It was taking a big risk, but I crossed the street and went up to him. The German officer then called for an interpreter, and he said to me: 'Our big chief wants to talk to your big chief.'

"I said to him: 'Look here, our big chief has other things to do. He isn't available. You'll just have to deal with me.' All this was going on while, from the other side of the square, they were still sending shells into the building. I called for some of my men, and they joined me—twelve men and two other officers. They were all armed, of course, and the German officer said, 'No, our chief asks that only one or two of you come in.' So I said, 'Nuts to that. I am not going by myself.' However, in the end, we agreed on three.

"So the three of us went into the basement. It is empty now, but you should have seen it then. It was packed with soldiers, hundreds of them, worse than any tramcar. They were dirty and hungry, and they stank. And they looked scared! They all fled down here to get away from the mortar fire outside.

"I was then led into the presence of two German generals, who explained rather mysteriously that they were going to negotiate the surrender on the Field Marshal's behalf since he 'no longer answered for anything.' It was not

clear who was in charge, but I insisted on seeing the commander. There was some discussion; still I insisted and so was led into General Paulus' little room.

"He was lying on his iron bed, wearing his uniform. He looked unshaved, and you wouldn't say he felt jolly. 'Well, that finishes it,' I remarked to him. He gave me a miserable look and nodded."[26]

Fedya then arranged for the field marshal to be taken by staff car to surrender formally to Marshal Rokossovsky.[27]

Thus surrendered Adolf Hitler's elite Sixth Army at Stalingrad, victor of the Low Countries, of Paris, and the Kiev encirclement. With Fedya's chat, the turning point had at last been reached, and everyone knew it. Wehrmacht prisoners soon appeared as never before: disheveled, wounded, often lame, young men and boys, who were jeered through the streets of Ust-Kamenogorsk just as they had been in Moscow. Some also appeared in the capital, Alma-Ata,[28] a center for Soviet wounded, as the town boomed, becoming something of a backwater refuge from the war.

German-speakers were in great demand, and one day at the warehouse Miriam was summoned to the supervisor's office. "An officer is here to see you," said her boss from behind her little brown desk.

"An officer? Here to see me?" said Miriam, astonished.

"Yes, a lieutenant from the army. He says he wants to ask you about your German," the woman said with a hint of jealousy.

"My German?"

"Yes, Fanya told them about you; you'll be a translator it seems. It's your ticket out, Miriam. You're very lucky, you know?"

"But I don't want to be a translator."

The woman laughed and said, "You have no choice, my dear."

The officer laughed, too, as he gave her some papers to fill out. "Comrade Stalin'll put you to better use than being a flunky in this place," he said, watching her scribble out the forms in her neat hand.

"When will I know?" asked Miriam, handing them back.

He shrugged and laughed again. "One never knows these things, Comrade Kellerman; haven't you learned that by now?" he said, leaving without waiting for an answer.

In late February, the office phone rang. A gruff male voice said, "Report to the military office to pick up your ticket and orders for the train to Alma-Ata. You're being transferred there immediately. Do you have any questions?"

"No," she said softly. "I have no questions."

"Good," said the voice. "Don't be late."

In less than 48 hours she had said her goodbyes to her boss, Fanya, Kozlova, Hilda, and even Ivan, who was quite sentimental in the way that only Russians can be, crying and hugging almost endlessly, then taking her and her things to the station, where the ceremony was repeated.

Compared to her other trips, this one was luxurious, yet oddly and for perhaps this very reason, it was strangely boring. As was her habit on trains, she slept most of the way. At Alma-Ata she found herself meandering in a cacophony of cars, trucks, jeeps, refugees, and what seemed a million moiling civilians and soldiers. She strolled around until she found a brown uniform sitting behind a desk who took her papers, stamped them, and gave them back along with another ticket. No one seemed impressed, but the papers propelled her along with a silent and inexorable power.

"Where will I live?" she asked quietly as she took them.

There was a shrug.

"Where shall I report?" she insisted in her best and most polite Russian. The uniform looked up in irritation but still said nothing. It was as if her questions were absurd. It mumbled and waved her toward a long bench where she sat for an hour until a kindly looking gentleman appeared to examine her documents, hand them back, take her ticket, and put her in a rickety van that dropped her off at a brick building near an oil mill. Here her papers were looked at again, noted, scratched on, stamped, and new ones given for filling out.

"Wait there," said the official, a stern thin woman in a uniform that was a size too large, who pointed to yet another empty bench in the corner.

"Where?"

"There," she said gruffly, "on that bench; stay there till you're sent for."

Miriam waited, sitting in a long hall, watching people pass as if she were invisible.

Eventually, after several hours of unspeakable boredom, another uniformed official came and told her to take her papers to a nearby building, a women's dormitory.

Here she presented them yet again. Another unsmiling uniform nodded, read, and handed them back. It was the same old story, a frown, a stupid bureaucratic thumbing of documents, a moment of anxiety, but the stamps, signatures, and shuffling always worked their magic, and she was propelled along, as if by an invisible hand.

Eventually, a fat not unpleasant middle-aged woman fingering a long set of keys unlocked a cell-like space with a narrow bed filling almost every inch of it.

"Here's your room," she said, turning on a dim little light. "It's not much, but at least it's yours."

"Yes, thank you," Miriam said, quietly agreeing that it was better to have something of your own, however meager, than to share something better with a stranger.

"The toilet is down the hall," the woman said.

Miriam nodded and then asked about her work.

"You'll have to wait at least a week to begin that," said the manager.

"A week?!"

"Yes, at least that long, maybe much longer."

"But I can start now!"

"Of course you can, but it cannot," the woman said with a slight smile.

"It?"

"Yes, the Party. It does these things in its own good time. You must wait for it. Surely you've figured that out, my dear Comrade Kellerman?"

"Yes, of course, but what shall I do?"

Why have I been rushed here if I have to wait so long? Why not start immediately? Why the delay? I'm ready, she told herself. *It's all so ridiculous. Why can't they just give me something to do right now?*

"Be patient, my dear," the woman said with a more indulgent smile, revealing a mouth full of golden teeth. "It will all come in good time. Try to make use of it."

This Miriam did, settling in her room that was hardly large enough to move between the bed and a modest wooden table. She organized what she had, studied Russian with her little dictionary, and went for frequent walks. Still it was not enough, and restless and forever hungry from the sparse food allowance, she had to do something.

She resolved to learn the city in detail. So her walks got longer and longer and more ambitious till she felt she knew Alma-Ata intricately. Then, in hope of finding German-speakers, she developed the habit of listening to conversations of educated people. This eventually became a kind of sport. *I'll pretend that I am a spy. After all, the Russians think everyone is a spy so I'll oblige them. I'll appear charming and polite to everyone but listen to everything, observe everything.*

She developed the art of tailing prospects without being noticed, of feigning sleep on park benches, of listening behind a copy of *Pravda*, or eavesdropping in street crowds. To her astonishment, she had achieved something she had never had before, a certain freedom. She answered to no one and none noticed. *How delicious it is to be alone, responsible to no one!* she thought. *In fact, it's fun!*

"Excuse me, Madame, do you know of anyone who might wish to learn German?" she would intrude sweetly. "Your child perhaps? Do you know a young person seeking a skill that's in great demand? I speak German perfectly and would like to teach your children."

She repeated this over and over. Not everyone was interested, of course, but gradually she recruited a small number of paying students. Miriam had always suspected that she had a talent for teaching, and this was confirmed as she amazed her students (and herself) with their progress. She worked relentlessly on their lessons, and she knew that one successful student with a pleased father or mother would lead eventually to another. Now that she knew the city, she could make friends easily and, most importantly, would not starve or die of tedium. And, to her great surprise, for the first time in her life she began to make a little money—even bought herself a new dress, ate better from tins, and purchased a fairly interesting German novel from a student's older brother, who was happy to sell it.

For six weeks she was so busy she almost forgot about her assignment. Then, at last, after that inevitable inertia of all things bureaucratic, another gruff male voice summoned her. She was told, "You'll be moving out of the oil refinery dormitory and into quarters at the foot of Mount Alataw. It's reserved for translators. You'll go by shuttle to the city center to the translation office. They have made all the arrangements."

Miriam moved into her new room, which was comfortable beyond all possible dreams. What a delight it was to look at the small iron bed, a tiny table, a simple wooden chair, and a small wood-burning stove. All her own! *How has this miracle happened?! How far I have come!* she thought as she stepped over to her small window, revealing a park with the mountain rising behind as in a painting.

The building, it turned out, was on the site of a former Czarist resort. There were even fruit trees in spring bloom, and early flowers, and clear mountain air that put her in mind of the Carpathians!

So the screw has finally turned. The Germans are in retreat, and I have a room of my own overlooking apple blossoms at the edge of a great and famous snow-capped mountain. How is this possible? How have I achieved this? I have not frozen or starved or been shot. Maybe I can stay here the rest of the war and then go home. Maybe, just maybe, my parents have somehow survived and I can find them, and Karl and Isaac, and all will be well. Maybe all of this then will pass as a bad dream, and we'll be together again in Czernowitz!

She looked at the apple blossoms and the splendid mountain until her reverie was interrupted by a young woman sticking her head through the door and saying, "Hello, hello."

"Why, hello," Miriam startled, turning.

"Good day to you and welcome," the woman beamed out with a great smile, stepping in without waiting for an invitation. "My name is Aljona Maximovna. I live next door with my son, Doto; he's 6."

Miriam quickly introduced herself.

"Nice to meet you, Miriam. No doubt we'll be seeing lots of each other, I'm sure."

"I'm sure," Miriam said quietly.

"The community kitchen is at the end of the hall, down near the bath on this floor. We even have some hot water once a week, if you can believe that. Of course, it's not quite luxurious, but we're all really fortunate. See you later," Aljona said with a cute wave and, without expecting a reply, left as quickly as she had come.

"Hot water?!" "Not quite luxurious?!" "Community kitchen?!" For Miriam, it was luxurious indeed—it was downright posh! It was wonderful to have such a friendly neighbor, a room, a kitchen, an occasional hot bath, a good job! Gone were the terrors of the outhouse! The tyranny of the collective farm! The dreadful chores! The retreats! The bridge! The Stukas! The explosions! The burning towns! The burning people! The hellish trains! The Germans! The heat! The cold! The frostbite! The starvation! The terror! The fear! *Not quite luxurious, did she say?*

Miriam laughed out loud, laughed an almost hysterical, mad laugh, and threw herself on her bed, making it bounce—laughing at the ceiling, laughing at everything.

Apparently, my dear Aljona Maximovna, you have never been in a boxcar fleeing the Wehrmacht. Nor have you been raped or lay freezing in the snow or cleaned the sores of naked criminals or been bombed or starved or frozen half to death! No, my dear, it is not quite "luxurious," but believe me, I shan't complain.

After settling in, Miriam took a walk in the park. Among the shrubs she ran into a thirtyish-looking lady who stopped and introduced herself as "Marina Eitelbaum from the Ukraine," who quickly added, "I work in the little apartment building store, you know, that doesn't really have anything," she said with a laugh. "My husband's an officer in the army, serving on the front."

"Yes, well, nice to make your acquaintance," Miriam said, managing to say her name, which Mrs. Eitelbaum didn't seem to hear.

"You should come see me. The store has little, but I usually can find what you might need—well, everything but coupons," she said with a wink.

Miriam laughed back and promised she would drop by "for a sociable visit" and, eager to continue her walk, made a polite goodbye.

Everyone is so friendly here, she thought as she explored her way through the trees and reflected upon the irony of this good fortune. *How very strange that the German nation should drive me, lashed, as it were, under pain of impending death, and then the German language should save me from the Germans!*

Returning, she ran into Aljona again. "Let me show you around," she said, not waiting for a reply, but taking Miriam by the hand, pointing out things while introducing her along the way. She was very beautiful, almost beyond description, poised, and refined.

After a few days there, Miriam decided it would be safe to conjure Deborah for an up-to-date chat. *Mama, dear, well, it looks like I've survived and am here in Alma-Ata, of all places, where the fruit trees are so beautiful and I can look out my very own window and see the most spectacular, wonderful mountain in the whole world. It seems just too good to be true, and the sun is growing warmer by the day, and spring is really here. And, my God, Mama, we're actually winning the war! Can you believe it?! Everyone says so after Stalingrad! We have retaken Kursk and Rostov. The invincible Germans are in retreat. Even the Americans are helping in the west, and Hitler will be defeated, there is no doubt. He is fighting a war he just cannot win! It's hard to believe, I know, but it's true!*

You mustn't worry, I feel much stronger now, am eating again, have gained a little weight even, and my work is very interesting. I work at a very large desk with several translators. They're all very friendly, and we get along famously. They all are girls like myself, no men, and we work hard but have lots of fun together. They welcomed me warmly, right from the start. The material is routine, official documents and the like, but I enjoy it still. I wouldn't tell anybody but you, but while my Russian is still not too good, I know enough to do the work and am improving all the time. The important thing, of course, is the German, and I'm the best in the office. But I'm careful about that and don't show off; it would make people jealous. I help without being proud, you know what I mean? "Help but not with pride" is my motto.

Still, in the evenings I've found time to keep tutoring. I love that most. If I could concentrate on that, I think I'd teach everyone in Alma-Ata to speak perfect German! Ha! Too, I have done some babysitting as a favor to friends: Aljona, who has been so wonderful to me, has a sweet little boy named Doto, and I sit with him and also with Marina's child. Marina is not quite as pretty as Aljona, but affable, plump, and energetic—you know, with that wonderful peaches-and-cream complexion one sees in the Slavs so often but with unusual wavy, jet-black hair. She's good to me, too, and I enjoy her and her 9-year-old daughter, Anna.

Both of these women have husbands at the front, but I'm afraid there are some perfectly awful suspicions about Aljona; her husband is an air force officer, rather famous and something of a hero, but she works for a high-ranking army officer here who takes very good care of her, perhaps too good, with jewelry and other unheard of things, and people have started to talk. But I try not to think about that. She is such a friend; we have almost become like cousins.

My only problem, Mother, is my fingers; they are so ugly, black, and painful. I still have no nails from the terrible frostbite. Aljona saw my horrible old gloves that I wore all the time, even while working, and she took pity on me and gave me some nice new ones. She is such a dear. I am very fond of her. I guess I have to go for now. I really am getting sleepy. But we will talk again tomorrow, about this time. I love you and Papa so much it hurts, and maybe I'll be home soon, and we will all be together again.

Bye for now; forgive me but I'm very, very tired and think I'm going to take a short nap in my wonderful room. Then I can get up, fix some tea, and go for a walk among the spring flowers.

With this, Miriam rolled over and fell into a very rare dreamless sleep.

20

Engagement

In September 1939 Hitler invaded Poland.[29] Fifteen-year-old Miriam had tried her best to ignore this, but after July 1940, this last illusion was crushed under the treads of Stalin's tanks rumbling through Czernowitz. North Bukovina was now part of the Soviet Union.[30]

The air waves electrified them in a continuous current of propaganda that crackled out that the Ukrainians were "rejoicing that Romanian rule had at last come to an end;" that the Moldavians in Bessarabia were "ecstatic" about their "good fortune of being reunited with their brothers in the Soviet Republic of Moldavia;" that the "working classes could celebrate the end of the slavery of capitalism," and on and on.

Many people (mostly the Ukrainian peasants) hoped that the Communist occupation indeed would mean a better life, but Miriam soon got an economics lesson she never forgot: under capitalism one pays high prices for things that are available, while under socialism one pays low prices for things that are not. Shelves emptied as by magic, while lines formed for what little remained. Queuing was epidemic.

"What happened to all the food, Mother? To the shoes, the fabrics, everything? Where has it all gone?" she asked. "The Russians are sending everything east? People are hoarding the rest."

The Soviets themselves seemed at a loss. The collectivization that was to end selfishness and exploitation only made it worse. Everyone gave way now to extreme self-centeredness; no one considered themselves any longer to be a neighbor. No one trusted anyone beyond the first circle of family and the second of closest friends. Suspicion soon threw an ugly veil over the city. It weighed particularly heavily upon Miriam, who unburdened herself to Hans as she always did, alone in her room.

"I need to talk to someone, Hans, who knows, who understands. Mother doesn't want to discuss what this all means. I think she is afraid. Everyone is afraid now, and Papa is always gone. When he is home, he says nothing about anything. Of course, I talk to you, but I know you don't understand it either. Isaac is in Lvov,[31] at the university. That leaves Abraham; maybe I can talk to him."

But Abraham had vanished. "Where's Abraham?" she asked Deborah. "I can't find him. I've spoken to everyone. People say nothing, even act strange when I ask. Where is Abraham, Mother? I want to know. I can't find him anywhere."

"Abraham has disappeared," Deborah said with a look of quiet despair.

"Disappeared?!"

"He has been arrested."

Miriam gasped. "Arrested?! For what?!"

"Zionism."

"Zionism?!"

"Yes, they see Zionists as enemies of the people."

"Enemies of the people!? That's ridiculous! We are the people! Jews are people, too!"

"Silence! You are not to say such things!" Deborah said in a heavy whisper as she jumped up out of her chair.

Miriam hesitated, then quietly asked, "What will become of him?"

Deborah sat back, brooded through a very long pause, then, looking at her with troubled eyes, replied, "I don't know, but they are shooting Zionists, Miriam."

"Shooting Zionists?! How can that be, Mother?!" Miriam screamed. "Shot?! Dead?! That can't be true! Abraham is just a boy!"

"Maybe it isn't true, no one knows for sure. He may be released; let's hope so, dear."

"I will find him! I won't rest until I find Abrasha!" Miriam said, pacing the room.

"No! No, you won't, Miriam!" Deborah cried, standing again, losing control. "No! You will do nothing! You will say nothing! Nothing! Miriam, do you understand?! Nothing at all! There's absolutely nothing you can do but get us all into trouble! Do you understand?! They will murder all of us!"

She caught her breath, then in a quieter tone said, "We're all in very great danger, my dear, you must understand this, you must. Everything you just said is considered counterrevolutionary. You are not ever to say that again, do you understand?"

The next day Miriam was walking quietly along the streets of Czernowitz. She would obey her mother, of course; she always did. She would say nothing. But she could find out with her eyes. She could still see. They couldn't stop her from that.

Quickly she noticed strangers, strangers everywhere, unknown sullen men whom everyone whispered were the secret police, the NKVD.[32] These sullen gray men watched, as people watched back, then quickly turned away, averting their eyes.

The sullen gray men watched as people walked; watched as they talked; watched as they went to work, went home; always they were watching! Watching and listening. Soon people pretended they weren't there, but they were. The sullen gray men were everywhere, and yet no one wanted to see them—soon they were invisible.

Miriam saw them clearly. "We are all under arrest!" she shouted in the living room. "All of us, under arrest!! All of Czernowitz is under arrest! Hands up!" she shouted, raising her hands up.

"Silence!" Deborah shouted. "Silence!"

"Czernowitz, put up your hands!" Miriam said, ignoring her mother and walking in a circle with her hands in the air. "You are under arrest! You, you there! You Jew there, you are a Zionist! Hands up!" she said, pointing. "You! You are an enemy of the people! Hands up!"

"Miriam, stop!"

"No," she pointed again like aiming a gun, "you must be shot! You, you're a capitalist wrecker, a counter-revolutionary! You will be shot!"

"Be quiet, I say!" Deborah yelled, lunging, trying to pull Miriam's arms down.

"Why, Mother? Why be quiet? We're all going to die anyway; it's hopeless. They're going to kill all of us...."

"Hush, my dear," she said in a loud, rasping whisper, "control yourself! You mustn't say such things! We're not going to be shot; we're going to survive, you hear me?! It is a bad time, truly, but we will survive. I promise. You have to believe that. Miriam, whatever happens, you must never stop believing that, do you understand?"

"Yes," Miriam said, lowering her hands. "I'll try hard to believe that. I'll try hard to have faith that we are all going to find a way to survive."

Soon Miriam was thrown into a special Jewish school, separated from the Gentiles and taught the "evils" of Zionism and capitalism, which were said to be the same. It was interesting to her how the Jews got blamed for everything: the Nazis said they were all Communists, and the Communists said they were all capitalists. Ironically, they were taught the horrors of Zionism in Yiddish, and she started falling behind, despite its cognition with German.

Very much against her will, she was forced to start her long, hard journey of learning Russian, a much more difficult tongue. Studying Russian, she concluded, was like climbing a great Carpathian mountain: you could look down and gladly see how far you had come, but then you only had to look up to sadly see how far you must go. She despaired of ever reaching the summit, but still she climbed daily, wondering if she would ever be able to negotiate around the grammar, a system "written by the very devil," a friend whispered one day as they walked home.

"*Chyort!*" Miriam said, using the Russian word for the devil with as diabolical a laugh as she was capable.

"Hush!" her friend hissed, looking around. "You'll get us arrested!"

"It doesn't matter; we're going to be arrested anyway. We're Jews, aren't we? They'll eventually get around to arresting all of us, that's plain enough."

Stalin was, indeed, the devil, and he spoke such arcane languages: Russian, Yiddish, Marxism, mathematics! Her head was going to explode! What happened to French? German? Poetry? Music? Fiction? Schiller? Goethe? Philosophy?

And Isaac? He presented yet another challenge. "My education is totally inadequate for the new public language of Leninism," he said during one of his infrequent visits, "its dialectics, its turgid absolutes of class struggle, economic determination, and the end of history. I must learn a new idiom now, get a new education, Miriam, if we are to survive. And it means I won't be able to see you very much."

"I hardly see you now."

"I know, I'm sorry."

"What are you studying?"

"Leninism and Marx. I had already read *Das Kapital*, but lately we have been studying dialectics."

"I don't understand dialectics."

Isaac laughed. "No one does, and I'm struggling with *State and Revolution*, Lenin's great work, they insist, written when he was in Finland, during the revolution, in exile."

"And what does Comrade Lenin tell us, my dear Isaac?"

He sighed and said as if by rote: "In order to create our great Utopia, heaven on earth in some distant and glorious future, we must murder lots and lots of people. In other words, institute a reign of Red Terror."

"How can Red Terror, any terror, ever bring about heaven on earth?"

"It doesn't, that's just it. We can't imagine heaven, not really; try as we might, it's always fanciful and vague, and I don't think we can ever realize in fact something we can't truly imagine. Only hell—that we can visualize quite easily, so we can always create hell on earth when we really wish it, which is what Lenin has done. And Hitler. And Stalin; they are essentially the same—devils really, their hells easily conceptualized, easily brought about. But never heaven; that we can never realize because we don't even know what it is in our most fanciful dreams."

"Heaven is always later and hell now," Miriam said quietly.

"Yes, I'm afraid so."

"Why couldn't someone as clever as Lenin realize this?"

"Because he didn't want to. I think Schopenhauer is right, 'we can do what we will but we cannot will what we do.' Lenin did not will it. He willed power, that was his great passion. He cared little for sex, just power over others. I think at heart he was a nihilist, an unconscious nihilistic terrorist. In this sense he was not a classical Marxist."

"Lenin not a Marxist?"

"Not really; for him Marxism was merely a useful intellectual tool in the service of his subconscious impulses, a justification for this obsessive will to power. But I'm heartily sick of his lucubrations that are little more than elaborate rationalizations for revenge."

"You sound like our old friend Dr. Freud."

"Yes, my dear, Miriam, I do, don't I?"

"You are so smart, Isaac, and I love you so much," she said, leaning softly into his arms.

"I hope I'm smart enough to save us from this hell," he said wistfully, embracing her.

"What're we going to do?" she asked, after a tender pause.

"Well, we always turn to the task at hand, don't we? The urgent will forever overwhelm the important, so right now I'm going to learn the Soviet legal code, about which I know very little. I must return to Lvov."

"I had hoped you could stay here."

"No, it's back to Lvov for a crash course in that wretched system that is nothing more than a facade for the lawlessness of the police station, the wall, and the camp."

"When will I see you again, Isaac?"

"I don't know. I'm here for only for a few days more. I'll pick you up tomorrow after class, and we'll go to the park; it's more secure."

Of course he knew about Abraham. Everybody knew about Abraham, everyone thought about him, but his name was never spoken; it remained an unuttered name on everyone's lips. The lesson of Abraham had not been lost. They would go to the park, not just for the usual hoped-for secrecy of lovers but so no one would think they were anything else.

The next day, Isaac sat Miriam down on a bench and said in a low voice that it was "time to talk seriously."

"I thought we had been," she said, puzzled.

"Not intellectually, personally."

Miriam froze.

"Relax," he said with a smile, while touching her arm gently. "We must talk, that's all. You know that I am desperately in love with you," he said matter-of-factly, with a glance around. "I have been from the first day I saw you, a silly but very wise and precocious 14-year-old."

"A lot has happened since then besides birthdays, you know?"

"Yes, of course, I understand; people grow up quickly now, but still for your parents' sake and for yours, I regret that there are so many years between us. But I think that if you look deeply into your heart and mine, you'll agree that those years make little real difference. We're obviously meant for each other; in fact, we're perfect, and I want to marry you."

Miriam gasped.

"And I will not wait until you have graduated from the university. I suspect your parents won't agree, but that's what I want now. We can't wait; these are not normal times."

Miriam moved her lip between her teeth in a brooding, thoughtful silence. He waited for a response, but, getting none, he added, "Even if your parents won't agree, which of course we must expect, you must be ready."

In the face of her silence, he hesitated and then asked, "Tell me that you love me. Can you promise that I'll be the one you'll marry?"

Still Miriam remained quiet. She was quite unprepared. "Well," she said at last, glancing down into her folded hands for the answer, then looking up, "I don't know what to say."

"I understand, of course it is..."

"I'm only 16, you know; that's too young, Isaac, even in these times."

"I've thought of that and..."

"Isaac!" she said abruptly, surprising herself by raising both hands. "Please, don't say anything more. Don't, please, not another word," she cried before he spoke again, putting a finger softly to his lips.

Then, lowering her hands, unexpectedly, she began to sob uncontrollably. Isaac wound his arms around her without speaking. They sat hushed for a time, but gradually she gathered herself, wiped her eyes, leapt to her feet, and ran down the half-lit path toward the fountain. He caught up, put his arm through hers, and side by side they skirted the dripping water, making a loop through the park, until this circling course returned to their empty bench.

Isaac stopped, stepped back, looked around again quickly, an unconscious habit, and then faced her. "Well?" he said, folding his arms with mock sternness, "What are you going to do, my dear?"

Miriam began to weep again.

"Miriam, please, darling," he muttered as he hugged her desperately, regretting what had been said as maybe rash, a mistake, perhaps even wrong. "You don't have to decide now. Think about what I have said for a time. I'll be back soon, at the winter break; we'll talk then."

He waited for a long time, holding her, then in a resigned tone, "Come on, I'll take you back. We don't want your mother wondering, do we?" he said, escorting her through the almost empty park past a previously unseen man, sitting on a bench and affecting to read in the dim light.

By the time they talked again in December, Miriam knew for sure she wanted to marry Isaac. But when? She thought of what little she knew about men, life, and marriage. She thought about everything she had seen, heard, and read, but it was not very much to sort through. In fact, she knew nothing, she realized.

Every path took her back to the same place—like walking around the fountain to their bench—Isaac was to be her life-partner. That much was certain. She was convinced that the future with him would be exciting, interesting, stimulating, and beautiful. She found that even her most mundane moments were "colored by his presence and imbued with meaning," she mused to Hans. "I am hopelessly bored without him; other people and other places bore me, everything bores me but him."

"But there's such a gulf between us. I mean, I'm still just a schoolgirl, struggling with mathematics, that difficult Russian, and Yiddish that I can hardly understand. I don't even have a high school diploma. I feel like such a child compared with him. I mean, Isaac is already an attorney. But Hans, I do love Isaac, and life would be unbearable without him, so it's not a matter of whether at all, just when, and my parents must decide that."

She wrote Isaac her answer, knowing he wouldn't be pleased. Yet she knew he would understand it was the beginning, the first step; she had accepted. When his reply shot back immediately, he said he would talk to her parents. The machinery was in motion. There was no stopping it. It was out of her hands, and she had no choice but to exist in a state of anxiety mixed with relief until that big day finally came at last.

"Without you, Miriam," Isaac said.

Miriam caught her breath. "What do you mean, without me?! You are going to talk about my life without me? You can't do such a thing!"

Isaac said with soft condescension, "Your parents and I care deeply, about the timing, I mean; you said to leave the question to us. Don't worry, I will argue my case passionately, and they'll argue theirs just as passionately. Just wish me luck! But you can't be there; it would change the chemistry in their favor."

Miriam wasn't at all sure how the "chemistry" would be in their favor if she were there, but she could discover no means or reason to contradict him, so she simply turned and walked silently away.

It was a terrible battle. Miriam heard its rumble unfold blow-by-blow from the other room like a poor slave awaiting news of her sale to the victor.

"Don't be absurd!" snapped David, joining in with surprising self-assertion.

"She's only a child!" Deborah yelled.

"Not really, she's precocious and mature for her age," shot back Isaac.

So it went.

But Isaac was the more tenacious: "True, she's young, but she's an early developer, bright and level-headed, and she's definitely the woman I want to marry. You'll never find anyone who could love her more than I. It would be nice, of course, if our ages were closer, and, sure, it'd be great to have more time, you know, to satisfy you. Under normal circumstances, you'd be quite right, but I don't have to tell you, these are not normal times. We don't have the luxury peace affords. So I readily accept the age difference. Miriam accepts it as well. I only ask that you accept it."

For once they seemed to be listening, and he spoke to that. "These are horrible days. We cannot wait. Time is increasingly compressed by events, and things, God forbid, may only get worse, will get worse. It's clear to anyone who has eyes to see that Hitler is planning his war in the East, his real goal. He will eventually invade the Soviet Union, I'm sure of it."

"Nonsense!" said David. "Stalin is his best ally; they have a pact, a treaty."[33]

"A worthless piece of paper," Isaac snapped.

"Hitler'd be mad to attack Russia! He'd be fighting on two fronts. That's the same idiotic mistake Germany made in the last war, and it cost us victory."

"That's just it, Mr. Kellerman; he is quite mad, a lunatic bent on world domination. His ambition is insatiable; it will consume everything till it finally consumes itself. There'll never be peace until Hitler is destroyed, but it will take the whole world to do it."

"I don't see what that has to do with you and Miriam," said Deborah lamely.

"It has everything to do with us, Mrs. Kellerman. Bukovina is on the front line; we could all be thrown into the flames of Hitler's war just to make it blaze. So we must think differently, live for the here and now, without illusions, not for some wonderful, far-off future. Every second, every hour, every day is precious to us. We must live with ever greater intensity. Look what's happened to Abraham! Where is he?! Where is Abrasha?! How do we know we won't be next? How do we know?! Tell me that, Mrs. Kellerman!"

Deborah shook her head as if struck, stepped back, looking away for the first time, then down at the floor. There was a very long pause. Out of this silence she at last raised her hand. "David," she said turning to her husband, speaking quietly and with slow deliberation, "I've seen this coming. It's no surprise. I knew, we knew that these young people...well, we could do nothing to prevent it. It is beyond human power, ours or theirs, that's plain enough. It's bigger than all of us, and I have thought long and hard about what I'd say when this day came at last, which I knew it surely would."

"It's inevitable?" David asked meekly.

"Yes, I'm afraid so, quite inevitable."

Both men stared at Deborah and waited. The climax had come.

"David," she continued with the same deliberation, "I believe we should give them permission to marry, but only on one condition," she said holding up one finger before Isaac's face. "I don't know how to put this, Isaac," she said, now wagging the finger, "but you must promise there'll be no children—not yet. Miriam won't be able to finish her education if she must raise small children. You're a university-educated man, and your wife must be also. Otherwise there will gradually, inexorably develop a separation, a gulf between you, of culture and education that is always fatal to a marriage. Believe me, I've seen it; it is hard enough even when there is much in common, but without it, well, believe me, it's quite impossible," she said with a wave of her right hand. She finished by adding, "She must get her degree before you have children."

Deborah then dropped her hand, only to shake her head forcefully with a silent but very powerful, "No!"

Isaac started to protest, but Deborah shook her head once more, interrupting rudely. "No children, Isaac!" she growled, wagging her finger again. "I will not have my daughter having children this young. She's still but a child herself and will remain so until her education is completed. Then you may have children, of course, with our blessings," she added, dropping her hand and walking away, sitting down.

It was over, finished. The men were speechless. But who had really won? Was it a draw? What had happened? It was final, but what was it? Was she giving permission for an engagement or a marriage? They both were thinking the same question but could not bring themselves to ask it. Finally, they stood, shook hands, and Isaac, having gained this victory, returned to the loneliness of Lvov, while Miriam returned to the drudgery of studying in Czernowitz.

Then the other shoe dropped, as Miriam knew it would. She was summoned and told by David, with a long-faced Deborah standing at his elbow, that they "must wait a year to be married, a year after the engagement."

Her protest went nowhere; a year it would be.

Alone with Hans she said, "I feel like Natasha in *War and Peace*: 'yes' but 'no.' A whole year! How can I wait so long? An eternity! It will ruin everything! It's just like when poor wretched Natasha had to wait a year to marry her Andrey. Everything was spoiled, and he went off to fight the evil invader of Russia! It cost him his life in the end, because if he had Natasha to live for, he would have not have been killed. Hans, I'm afraid. I don't know what's going to happen to us. I really don't; things are so terribly uncertain."

Then, within a few days, Deborah came and sat by her bed as Miriam lay staring at the ceiling. "I've been to see Isaac's mother," she announced officially.

Miriam hesitated, then asked, "And what did Mrs. Blumenthal say, Mama?"

It was Deborah's turn to hesitate. She frowned, waited, obviously considering her words, and said, "Well, many things. She said she likes you very much; she thinks of you already as a daughter, and she is delighted you and Isaac will marry. She was very gracious."

"And what else?" Miriam asked, sensing there was more.

"Well, she and I talked about when you would marry, when you would become publicly engaged."

"Wait, Mama!" Miriam said, sitting straight up. "What did you decide upon, an engagement or marriage? There's a difference, you know! I mean, I'm engaged already, aren't I?"

"Miriam dear, I'm well aware there's a difference!" Deborah said with stern defensiveness. "Of course you are engaged, but it hasn't been announced yet, to the world, I mean. That's what we are talking about."

Miriam apologized.

"The Blumenthals are pleased Isaac wants to marry, and they're going to help him get a nice apartment for you to live in the best part of town, then help him set up an office. They have money and connections, you know."

"Mama! I know about the Blumenthals," blurted out Miriam, "but what does that really mean for me? Me! What's going to become of me in the meantime?!" she said, pointing to her breast with her right hand while her left propped her up. "We have to wait to be publicly engaged, then we have to wait a year to be married."

"Miriam!" Deborah said interrupting, then in a softer voice said, "It means, Miriam, dear, well, what it means is, if he becomes officially, publicly engaged to you, it means he'll wait; that's what it means. He'll wait a year or longer, and it'll give him time to get established."

"I don't understand," Miriam said, shaking her head dramatically. "No one wants me to know anything. I'm always the last to be told. No one ever asks me what I want; it's my life, you know? I'm not a child anymore!"

"Miriam, please. This is difficult, my dear, very difficult for us. Please try to understand that," Deborah said, embracing her. "It simply means that Isaac is promised, spoken for, that he's engaged to you, that you and he are betrothed. But, wait, I'm not finished," she said, letting go of her and wiggling a finger gently when she thought Miriam might interrupt.

Miriam waited in impatient silence.

"Mrs. Blumenthal and I talked about the engagement, when it would take place. Your father and I are concerned about you, concerned about your reputation."

"My reputation?!"

"Please, dear. We just don't want people to get the wrong impression is all. The Blumenthals have planned a small dinner party at the end of the school year, after you have graduated and have your diploma. After that, if you and Isaac still feel the same, you'll eventually be publicly engaged."

"Feel the same? What do you mean, 'feel the same'? Don't you understand how much we love each other? We will always feel the same!" Miriam cried.

"Of course you will, we all know that," Deborah said with a slightly ironic smile.

Miriam caught her breath, hesitated, made a false start at speaking but could not, so lay back on her pillow and stared at the ceiling.

Deborah waited, but seeing that Miriam was not going to speak, said, "You'll be privately engaged, but your public betrothal will not be announced, not yet."

At this Miriam turned her head and stared with a long, questioning look.

Deborah continued: "It simply won't do, not yet. It'd be improper for a young girl, a student no less, to be promised to a man Isaac's age. The age difference will be less of a problem once you are at the university, and, as you grow older, it may well be an advantage—over time, I mean, but not now. Later it'll be different; then, everything is different," she added with a sigh.

Here Miriam tried to interpose a question, but Deborah pressed on. "Your engagement will be formally announced after you have finished at least one year at the university," Deborah said, holding up one finger as if she were teaching her to count.

Miriam could no longer contain herself. "But that's more than a year. I thought we were already engaged; now you say we are not and must wait even longer to marry! That's forever, Mama! Forever! And so when will we marry? When? When? When?! Mama, I need to know!" she shouted, sitting up again.

"Miriam, dear," Deborah said, holding her by the arms, "after the first year, after the engagement, then. However, I strongly recommend that you wait until you finish the university. It's the wisest course, the best time. If you interrupt your education to marry, well, you will probably never be able to complete your education. Over that I have no control. I rely on your good judgment and Isaac's integrity," she said, letting go of Miriam in a gesture of resignation.

Miriam wondered why all this had to be so grim and serious. If marriage was something you put off as long as possible, why would poets and movie stars always make it all seem so full of life and romance? Deborah seemed to be saying that she had been forced to face down an attack at the Blumenthals' and returned with all she could salvage— consent in return for endless delay.

Perhaps, Miriam decided, staring into her mother's eyes, despite all the adult interference, nothing could alter the importance of what had just happened. Isaac's family had accepted her—from this they could not retreat. But still she felt more and more like Tolstoy's sad little Princess Natasha Rostova, with Isaac her dashing but very much older Prince Andrey, and that some otherwise wonderful something had been drained of all its beauty by others. The world and its stupid conventions had done it, and now her betrothal had been replaced with something else, something much less wonderful—something too much like business.

But she accepted it, for the moment. She had no choice and she loved Isaac too much not to. So she lay back on her pillow and, staring intently at the ceiling, told Deborah, without looking at her, in a very quiet voice that she would do as Deborah wished. But, of course, she did not tell her what she was thinking, that someday she and Isaac would simply run away, into the Ukraine if necessary, or even into deepest Russia. After all, they were now all citizens of the Soviet Union, and Isaac was going to be a very successful lawyer; he was learning their system. Maybe they would even go on to Moscow, be like Natasha and Andrey, divided by the world but reunited by love.

The spring term crept along at a dreary pace. Miriam visited the Blumenthals twice, each time coming away feeling she knew Isaac better for having met them. They were quite wealthy, refined, and gracious. More importantly, to her own great surprise, *she* was accepted. Dr. Blumenthal treated her with a courtly respect that made her feel very grown up, and she loved him for it.

At long last, in May of '41, the Blumenthal dinner party arrived. Isaac sat across from Miriam, sending a broad smile beaming at her like a great kiss. She tried to catch every instant in her waiting hands, to be grasped forever. Everyone chatted on about almost everything: writers, movies, music, even a little gossip. Everything, that is, except Adolf Hitler. For the Kellermans and the Blumenthals, Hitler and his war simply didn't exist. It was as though they were picnicking in the final rays of peaceful sunlight while a blackening war-storm gathered around them from the west. Everyone knew it was there—Poland in '39, France and the Low Countries in '40, and now Britain was under siege and alone—but few wanted to look up and see it coming—at least not yet. After all, Bukovina was now part of the Soviet Union, and Stalin, for all his evil, was going to save them from Hitler.

Then Mr. Blumenthal, prompted by some unseen hand it seemed, at last stood and spoke, "Isaac, you and Miriam know that we both love you. We're prepared to help you achieve the life you want. I am confident that you know that."

Then he turned to Mr. and Mrs. Kellerman. "We thank you for having such a fine daughter as Miriam and will cherish her as our own. It's been very special, indeed, a wonder, truly it has," he said a little too stiffly, then made a toast, raising his glass of wine, "To the newly engaged couple!" Everyone followed in ragged unison, drinking down the toast. Then Mr. Blumenthal, nodding to Isaac, said like a poor actor anticipating a line, "Son, was there something you wanted to add?"

Isaac stood facing his father and then, with a shy grace, turned to Miriam. She returned his smile with embarrassed pleasure. He paused, looked at her parents, saying, "Mr. and Mrs. Kellerman, I solemnly promise that I'll take care of Miriam as if she were my other self. I'll cherish her, never will I leave her, and, if need be, gladly sacrifice myself for her, and will give her the kind of life you've always dreamed of for her."

"Miriam, I ..." he spoke softly, fumbling in his coat pocket. "I have something for you. A gift...small but a symbol of our being betrothed," he said more forcefully as he leaned over to Miriam. He offered her a tiny box and with trembling fingers opened it. A bracelet of small diamonds was liberated to sparkle and dance in the candlelight. Isaac lifted it slowly and delicately fastened it around her wrist. For some reason he hesitated.

She worried that he might kiss her then and there, but instead, he took her hands and folded them in his as he transfixed her eyes with a tender look that said, *I would kiss you if I could, but now is not the time, my dear.* There was uneasy laughter as Miriam cast back a smile of greatest joy, with a glint of happy tears flickering like distant stars in her eyes.

On the ride home everyone was quiet. Miriam set the mood as she sat silently staring into the night, partially illuminated by passing lights. Gently she let a finger caress the bracelet, freeing her reverie to chase the dots of radiance that flew from the diamonds like shards of a broken vase sparkling in the snow.

"Life could be so wonderful," she muttered to no one in particular, "if only..." But she didn't finish the thought as they overtook an army truck stopping ahead. It braked, hesitated, and pulled forward—car and truck accelerating together, as a Soviet soldier frowned at Miriam from his rear seat. His stare was unpleasant; he was blinded by the headlights, but she didn't know it and so averted her eyes back to

Isaac's bracelet. Then the truck turned and the street lights vanished, enveloping her once again in darkness, her dreams fleeing from her, running away, as into the deepest woods to hide.

21

June 1941

On the morning of a lovely spring day in 1941, Miriam awoke to the loud voices of her parents chattering in the kitchen. Deborah's was the more urgent, while David's was soothing and agreeable. Miriam quickly dressed and ran in.

"It's terrible! All of Czernowitz is awake! What can we do? What will happen!?" her mother's voice cracked off these questions, directed less to anyone in particular than to some unknown higher power.

Only a little earlier that morning whispers had been heard saying the secret police had arrested hundreds of "rich capitalists" as "enemies of the people."

"Luckily, I'm unemployed and don't own a business," said David Kellerman with a shrug and an odd laugh. "How can I be an exploiter without a job or money?"

They had, indeed, escaped arrest, and for the moment, they were safe. David at last had drawn a lucky card; his losses at gambling had paid off, he had hit the jackpot.

Those "capitalists" (both Gentile and Jew, it was not a pogrom) were now locked away in freight cars "destined for Siberia," someone had said.

"We must collect money for bribes to release these people, or at least buy them some food," Deborah said, crossing the room back and forth.

"How?" asked David.

"David, we must do something!" she cried. "We can't stand by idly, become accomplices. We can't let them do that to them; we must help. We have no choice—it could be us in those freight cars. I refuse to be an accomplice! I would rather die than be that!"

"I wish Karl and Isaac were here," Miriam said. "They'd know what to do."

But Karl had settled in at the polytechnic institute in Odessa, and Isaac was still in Lvov.

Clearly, Deborah was determined. She organized food and clothing and had them loaded into trucks "loaned" from a rich Gentile who somehow had avoided the roundup. Then she called a meeting of everyone willing to help.

"We'll drive to the station."

"What do we tell the guards?" a boy asked.

"We'll have to bribe them."

"With what?"

"Money?" a girl wanted to know. "Will that do the trick?"

"No, it does them no good; there's little for them to buy. We must give them things they need or crave, such as expensive cigarettes, good vodka, and the like."

"It might work," somebody said.

"It might not," someone else countered.

"It must," Deborah insisted, "but we will have to go higher than the guards."

Later that night, some teenagers met at a prominent Catholic's home.

"Two boys are missing," someone said with a quiet sadness.

"Arrested," another said.

"We better wait," said another.

"What?"

"Yes, wait until we can bribe a guard. It's the only way. Like your mother said, the soldiers have nothing; they're easily seduced, and they love foreign cigarettes."

"How about vodka?" Miriam asked.

"They live on it," said a boy she had just met from the Catholic family. "It's like their engine oil, only they change it every day, but they never have enough. It's rationed and never the best; you know it tastes like gasoline."

There was laughter.

"No, you really can't turn their head with that; the army gives them too much. Foreign cigarettes are the thing."

"Or chocolate," someone offered.

"Ha, yes, chocolate will do wonders—it'll buy you a field marshal's cap," said the boy with a clap of his hands.

There was more laughter, then silence.

The next night they met again, a few blocks from the station. Miriam hung back in the darkness, then someone whispered a guard had been bribed and even some higher-ups.

"It was easy: cigarettes and hard black chocolate did the trick; he thought it was pure gold," said the Catholic boy proudly. "I even used my Russian."

"Any language can express a bribe," Miriam ventured with a chuckle. While no one laughed, in the half-light she noticed that the Catholic boy smiled. He obviously liked a good joke, even a lame one. In fact, he seemed to be enjoying himself as if the whole thing were a school prank.

"Let's get going," he said, "before they change the guard."

Soon Miriam found herself in a group shadowing along the freight cars, poking food through the slats like children secretly feeding zoo creatures. She would never forget those whispering voices: "Oh, thank you, thank you, God bless you, God bless all of you, thank you, you have saved us, please come again, don't forget us, please tell my...oh, thank you, bless you everyone, I'm so and so, please, thank you, God bless you, please tell..."

Now weeping herself, Miriam hastily stuffed the little parcels into the cars, the stricken faces just out of sight, immured but partially unhidden behind the wooden walls, close yet so very far in the darkness of a rolling prison on iron wheels—between everything accomplished and everything so easily undone—out of reach but not yet out of touch. She felt those cold fingers caressing her own, squeezing her hand like a blind beggar stumbled upon in the dim lamp light of a night corner.

Dinner the next evening was excruciatingly quiet.

"They are still there," Deborah said at last. "The train has gone nowhere; it just sits. Those poor people are trapped like cattle or worse, but they will leave and no one will ever see them again. Like Abraham, they'll just vanish and never be seen, not ever, just vanish as if they never existed."

"We at least tried to help them, Mother, if only a little," said Miriam. David nodded.

"I'm afraid, though," Deborah said, almost to herself, "that soon we may find ourselves in their place."

"Why?!" Miriam asked, looking up in shock. "We're not rich capitalists!"

"Neither are they, not really, but we are Jews—never forget the scapegoat—and soon they'll need more people to arrest. They will always need more, you see, there'll never be enough, then it'll be our turn. They won't forget us, rest assured," Deborah said morosely.

Miriam, never seeing Deborah like this, wanted to debate, but before she could, several loud knocks exploded against the door.

Everyone flinched but David, who said, "I'll go," calmly getting up.

The knocks came again, only louder and more urgent. There were men's voices mingling with David's.

"It's the police!" Miriam said, going pale.

"No, I don't think so, dear, be calm. The police would rush in; these men are staying at the threshold," Deborah said with a reassuring look.

David sauntered back and sat with more than his usual disinclination to speak.

"Well?" Deborah asked with a questioning look.

"Everyone stuck to their story."

"Who? Who stuck to their story? Was someone arrested?"

"Yes," he said, eating nonchalantly, "The boys, remember? The Russians let them go. Remember the Catholic boys who disappeared that everyone was so worried about? They let them go, they're free."

"Hurrah!" yelled Miriam, jumping up and raising her hands. "Hurrah!" She shouted as she danced around the table.

There was more excited, happy chatter, and then Miriam, sitting, asked, "What are we going to do now? Should we try again? It's so easy; all it takes is some cigarettes, chocolate, and a touch of courage."

"And you have all three," David said with a rare smile.

Deborah, turning to Miriam, said, "You're going to go to bed and get some rest. That's what we're all going to do now; then we'll get through tomorrow, but only tomorrow. Each day, one at a time, each day as it comes, that's exactly what we're going to do. Now off with you, my dear, shoo, go to bed, shoo," she said happily.

The next day Miriam, alone, sneaked down to the station to find the train gone. Walking bravely up to a soldier, she inquired in her bad Russian.

"East," he said under his breath, "they went east, early this morning."

"Where east?" Miriam said, pressing him with a frown.

"You need to be off," he replied and turned away. Another soldier sauntered up, and they shared a cigarette that Miriam noticed was foreign.

Day by day the Red Terror slowly tightened, as Deborah had said it would. Under its pressure everyone tried to find their own individual but ever diminishing space, their own way of breathing and living. Nothing could be done, as she had said, but to try and live as normally as possible, "taking each day as it came."

"How can we live normally, Mother?" Miriam pleaded. "I'm tired of trying to live normally. It's like we are being gradually squeezed to death; soon we will all suffocate and die, so how can we live normally, Mother? Please, tell me that!"

"Just do the best you can, that's all we can do, have faith it will get better," Deborah said half-convincingly. "You think about it too much, my dear. We have been very fortunate."

"How can I think of anything else?! We're in the coils of this creature, this hideous monster, and you ask me not to think about it. Our lives have become a waking nightmare. I just want to have it be over. I want things to be like they used to be, Mama!"

But "living normally" became the slogan of the day. Everyone seemed to be trying it. Miriam's new teacher and counselor, a biology instructor, a Russian Jew, decided on a "normal" field trip for the graduates of the Jewish High School. They would all go out into the woods "for in nature they might find a momentary release from the folly of man," he announced with a feeble smile. He knew just the spot, and so everyone looked forward to an evening of campfires with stories and peaceful sleep in small tents.

What a marvelous escape from the anxious misery of the Terror. Everyone caught the spirit, and even their parents came to the campsite to see if they were behaving. So, for a moment, everything did seem normal again, and all tried hard to wear normal faces and tried even harder to say nice, normal, day-to-day things. It was June 21, 1941.

22

German Class

Oh, Mama, you just won't believe this! In March of this year I began studying at a university! Can you believe it! You always were concerned about that, and now I am a student at the University of Alma-Ata, part time, of course, in the evenings. I have to work hard during the day, but they have given me permission to study languages. So I have enrolled in a German class. Only problem is that I know German better than the teacher! Ha! Of course, I have tried not to be too obvious about that, but it didn't take her long to realize it.

She is such a dear. Her name is Natasha; she is very charming and lovely, about 35. Like everyone else she has two jobs, a daytime teacher and translator who spends evenings teaching us German at the university. Everyone adores her. She is not at all jealous of me because of my German but proud and very pleased to have me in her class—brags on me all the time.

She has given me permission to work on my Russian, and so she is really helping me more with that, and I have learned so much from her. She makes it such fun, organizes things for us to do, like having food parties where everyone comes and brings a little something and chatters away in German. Her classes are a delight, full of spontaneity and new ways of learning. She is truly a born teacher. She calls me her "Little Romanian." Ha!

Mama, she has suffered so much. She is from Leningrad and survived the siege there.[34] The 900 days of hell when the Nazis surrounded the city and slowly starved them. The only food they could get was when Lake Ladoga— you know, the big lake between the city and Finland to the northeast—froze during the winter and they could drive trucks across the ice. Some trucks plunged into the frozen water, but still they kept coming; it was the only relief they got but not ever enough.

She told us horrid little stories of her family living with several families in an apartment, which used to belong to an aristocrat, without any heat and having to eat birds and dogs and cats and finally being forced to make a kind *of soup from weeds and ground-up furniture. They would boil it all, but the resin remained. She says the doctors now tell her that's how she injured herself so badly, so she has to eat standing up. Yes, standing up! It did something terrible to her insides, and even now she is still much too frail and thin from malnourishment. Though people are always giving her food, she hardly eats a thing.*

She says that she was finally able to escape and was sent first to Tashkent, then here to spend three months in the hospital to recover. She has not mentioned it, but one student told me that all Natasha's family perished at Leningrad—she was the only one to escape. But she never mentions that. She is always cheerful and not the least bit bitter, though she is very determined like everyone else to defeat Hitler, whatever it takes. Nothing made her happier than the news of our great victory at Stalingrad; she wept when she heard it. I was pleased and jumped for joy, but Natasha wept like a child. I have never seen such tears of happiness when she heard the news.

I have to confess to you, Mama, that Natasha is the only person I have met who has suffered even more than I have, and what impresses me is her courage and her spirit. She is indomitable! A real inspiration to us all! When I begin to feel sorry for myself, I only have to think of Natasha and I am inspired again. No matter what happens to me, I will always think of her. I cannot tell you how much I love her and how important she has become to me here in Alma-Ata, indeed, to all of her students who feel as I do.

Not that I don't have any other friends because I certainly do. There is Marina, who I have already mentioned who works in the store. She is such a sweetheart and has even given me a bolt of gauze to help decorate my room. She seemed to know that I had been thinking about that and had been saving my coupons and hoarding bread just to trade for some gauze, you know, to get on the black market. I don't like going there, but the black market is the only place to get certain things, and here Marina just gives it to me! They use the gauze for bandages, but people also paint it and make curtains and all sorts of things with it. Marina even came by my little room and helped me fashion the curtains. Then she helped me to make a bedspread.

A bedspread?! It was only yesterday I had nowhere to sleep and then could only sleep on a dirty mat behind a stove like a dog, and now I have my own room with curtains and even a bedspread! Can you believe it, Mama? I hope so, because I cannot. Why, you might ask, has Marina helped me? It's really just her sweet nature and compassion that explains it, though she says it's because I helped her with her "dear Anyuta."

Then there is Aljona of course. When she dropped by one day and saw my new curtains and bedspread she said, "That gives me an idea, Miriam. Come next door, I want to show you something." Mama, she then took me to her apartment and got down on her knees and pulled out a box from under her bed. What did she have in that box, you ask? Rugs! Wonderful rugs from her time in Tbilisi, extra ones that she wanted to give to me "in gratitude for taking care of Doto." I said I couldn't, but she insisted and, can you believe it, Mother, I now have a nice rug covering that horrible ugly stove!

That is not all. Within a few days little Doto comes by and brings me six picture postcards he has sewn together into a kind of collage, kind of like a cardboard vase. It was a gift he wanted me very much to have. He was so dear and proud giving me that. I display it very prominently on my table.

So, see, Mama, I have lots of new and wonderful friends here in Alma-Ata. I have been very fortunate indeed. It's amazing! We're having fun, waging a campaign against ignorance, poverty, ugliness, and drabness in the middle of a world at war.

Miriam's hands and feet gradually became less painful and seemed to thaw with the warming weather. She was even able to work at the translation office without gloves as the ugly, purplish color of her hands slowly faded and people took less notice.

She was also sleeping better and gaining weight, and, thankfully, she knew that with Marina's apartment nearby, the park in early spring bloom, and all her new friends, she could check her grief. At night she would fantasize about everyone she missed, imagining Deborah and David struggling but surviving and dreaming that Karl had found meaningful and productive work and would eventually rescue them. She also imagined that her Isaac had escaped the killing machine at Kharkov, even while she feared that it was too terrible and powerful and would keep grinding on until it crushed him.

Her thoughts, no matter how pleasant, always ended painfully, as she tried to place Isaac in a special category but could not. Somehow he got all mixed up in the general phantasmagoria of war and was lost to her forever.

But Miriam's work remained a great pleasure, and occasionally she would invite the German class to her newly spruced-up room. Here she met an unusual Kazakh girl named Zakti. She was from a village not far from Alma-Ata, and she was one of the more interesting, attractive, and vivacious of Natasha's students. Zakti was also quite intelligent, good at German, and possessed of an enthusiastic, if naïve, charm, of which she seemed completely unaware, making her even more attractive. One evening Miriam's class went with her to a place that was crowded, dirty, and filled with noisy children. Zakti was oblivious and acted as if it were a luxurious apartment with a marvelous view.

Everyone was impressed. Then one day Zakti confided to Miriam that an executive of the local Communist Party had begun to show her serious attention. Zakti was so young, so innocently beautiful, and Miriam was alarmed that she seemed much too pleased with this attention. *You are being taken in*, Miriam wanted to say, *be careful! Besides, he's too old for you, is the father of children—beware, my dear.* But Miriam, who thought all this in a flash, merely made a frown that Zakti pretended not to notice.

"Will you be my study partner?" Zakti asked a few days later, as if to make it up to Miriam.

Delighted, Miriam replied, "Yes, I'd love to," and both passed the first translation exam easily. Zakti was particularly proud of her certificate and announced to everyone that she was "coming to work in the same office with Miriam." Of course, Miriam was glad but a little surprised. *Zakti's German's not quite as good as it should be. I'm not even sure she should've been awarded a certificate, but I'll help her, and she'll do well with more practice. Who knows? Perhaps strings have been pulled by her new friend. She's no doubt working under his protection, a very influential member of the Party, everyone says. Sure, it's how things are done. I should accept it. It's none of my business.*

From the very start, Miriam developed a discreet system of correcting Zakti's errors, but she was a quick study, never resentful, and expressed only gratitude. "Miriam, what would I do without you? It's a good feeling," she said, "having such a wonderful friend."

Miriam replied, "Well, what're friends for? Besides, we're only students, and we help each other with German. It's the only way to learn."

Of course, it was Miriam who was helping Zakti, and Zakti knew it and so smiled ironically. But for Miriam it was nice to have someone to help, nice to have such friends as Zakti, Natasha, Marina, and Aljona.

After all, Miriam thought, *many ordinary people have cared for me, and without them I'd long since be dead. It's simply my chance to care for someone else.* To help Zakti was to help the "Little Romanian," and so she did it with pleasure.

23

Voskresenye

The translators were constantly being asked to "volunteer." In fact, Aljona was in charge of the "volunteers" for the local hospitals, and she asked Miriam to help at the old one in Alma-Ata. Her boss encouraged her. "The men's injuries aren't so devastating. You're obviously not a nurse, but you might be asked to read to them," he said with a patronizing smile.

Miriam briefly conjured a fantasy of reading bedside stories to wounded heroes of Russia's defense of the Motherland, but such jobs were never so romantic, this she knew. She had to prepare herself for much worse—it all reminded her too much of the past hell of sore cleaning. *No more illusions and naïve dreams*, she resolved. *I must steel myself for the worst; it's less painful that way. As vast as Russia is, in a strange way, it's a very small place, and Becky said in Baku that men from the front are often sent to rear hospitals such as the ones in Alma-Ata. Who knows what'll happen! Maybe I'll find someone from home!*

The reality presented itself, as it always seemed to, in the most unexpected way. Miriam was introduced to the trinity of all war hospitals: bedpans, bandages, and blood. "This way!" commanded a stout nurse as she led Miriam into the 20-bed head-injury floor. Its bedfast men were in various states of consciousness, their linens soiled and bandages smelly, blood-soaked, and filthy. Their moans and screams echoed off the walls like lost souls trapped in some forgotten basement of hell.

Miriam's stomach turned and her mind raced back to sore cleaning. One soldier mumbled about his family, telling Miriam about scenes from childhood. Another whispered urgent messages, "They're coming! They're coming! Oh, my God, oh, my God, they're coming!" he kept shouting. "Shoot! Shoot!" he screamed. "Hurry! Hurry up! Shoot! Shoot!"

A nurse poked a mop and bucket at her. "What's that awful smell?" Miriam asked, dropping the mop into the bucket.

"Chloroform, you'll get used to it," said the nurse. "The first day is the hardest; then it gets easier. Just keep busy."

Miriam staggered to her bed.

Put wood in the stove, Deborah said softly, *or you'll freeze.*

Miriam obeyed, stoked the fire to a roar, crawled in bed, then turned over only to find it was dawn. *Oh, my God! Don't let it be dawn!*

Within a few days the staff seemed not so bad, merely harassed. After a week, she caught a nod of encouragement from a doctor and a word of thanks from a nurse as she changed a bleeding man's sheets, helped with a bandage, and emptied a bedpan. *One can get used to anything. If you can clean sores, you can change a dirty sheet or a bloody bandage or even empty a bedpan. What's the difference?* Then a hand patted her as she removed a pan from a chair. The patient was thanking her. Thanking her!

She soon learned there even was a rhythm to the screams and came to expect them: "They're coming! They're coming! My God, they're coming!" was always followed by a cry of agony, then some few minutes of moans and tears, and finally a fitful sleep. Miriam caught herself listening more carefully to the hallucinations. She began to get used to them and somehow forgot the smell and the horror that gradually became bearable under the anesthesia of routine. *You can get used to anything,* she repeated over and over. *Just do it long enough, you'll be amazed. Habit is the strongest thing in the world.*

Now she walked casually to the bus and fell asleep against the window until the driver nudged her gently awake. In her room, without waiting to be told by Deborah, she automatically stoked the fire before collapsing, and in this way the days slowly melted into the shapelessness of a waking dream.

"Miriam, Miriam, are you all right, Miriam?" a voice asked, as she slumped over her mop, in a trance.

Miriam apologized. The floor nurse asked if she'd had any sleep.

"Yes, I'm fine," she said. "I'm fine," she repeated wearily.

"What's your daytime job, dear?"

"I'm a translator."

"I see," she said, impressed. "You're exhausted, that's plain enough."

Then a muffled, somewhat distant voice interrupted. "Miriam! Miriam! Miriam!" it said. "Miriam, Miriam," it intruded over and over.

The voice came from a bed very near the door. Miriam listened, startled.

"Miriam, Miriam," it said in a rasping desperation just above a whisper.

Miriam lurched toward it. The floor nurse missed her sleeve as Miriam ran to this voice, saying, "Please, let me see who this is, please, I must! He seems to know me! But how does he know me?!" she said to no one in particular as she stood there, breathlessly staring down at the bandaged head that had raised up, forming the syllables of her name behind a tiny slice of white.

Who is this that knows me and how does he know me? I see it in the eyes. There is recognition. He knows me. Who is this person, who, who?!

"Miriam," he gasped.

"Yes? Yes, who are you?" she said, taking his hand with both of hers and squeezing it gently.

"Miriam…"

"Yes."

"Miriam, don't you recognize me? Miriam, it's me, Isaac!"

"Isaac!" Miriam cried out. "Isaac! Isaac! My God! It's Isaac!"

"Isaac" reverberated through the hall as a name released by something inhuman. "Isaac! Isaac! Isaac!" the name echoed in a stream of screams as no other scream had ever done before, even in the head-injury ward.

Miriam sobbed, dropped his hand, and flung herself across his chest. Isaac lifted his other arm over her just as she broke into heaving sobs, weeping over his hands, kissing his bandaged face, then holding him, mingling together a mixture of tears, cries, and desperate kisses.

"Miriam! Get up! Tell me what's going on! Who's this?" gasped the floor nurse.

Miriam ignored her. A doctor came. The nurse restrained Miriam, but she broke away and lay across Isaac again, as if protecting him.

More people came—the concerned and the curious—doctors, nurses, orderlies, and volunteers. "Miriam, you're making yourself ill. Come on. Take these valerian drops," the nurse said. "You'll feel better. You must calm down, get hold of yourself!"

A group circled around her, and the valerian was stuffed inside her mouth. She bit and tried to swallow, then choked but managed to get it down. It did no good.

"Go to the director's office!" ordered a doctor.

"Why?" she asked, raising up, gasping. "Why must I leave?"

"Who is this person, Isaac?" the doctor asked.

Why did they care? Why is it any of their business? With so many such stories, why did they care about another? About her or Isaac or who he was or what he was to her? What right do they have to know anything? Why must I answer anyone's questions? But in a few short sentences she told who Isaac was and something of what had happened.

"You must go to the director's office," the doctor said, pointing.

"Why?"

"It's not for you to ask such questions! Go at once!" he said.

In the office, with the doctor at her elbow, Miriam told of her family, the flight, the bridge, the separation, almost everything except the rape, all coming in a great rush until at last she fell silent, awaiting the director's reply, as if she had unburdened herself of a great crime. The director glanced at the doctor and then back at Miriam, sighed, thanked her, and quietly asked her to wait outside.

Another doctor sauntered up, then a nurse. The door closed behind them with a loud click. Miriam sat on a bench and waited. After a time the door opened with another, even louder, click, and the doctors walked past and disappeared. Then a nurse came out, closing the door. Miriam stood up as she approached.

"It's been decided that you'll be excused as a volunteer."

"Excused?"

"Yes, for the time being; you'll be Isaac's attendant, at least until he's recovered. He's an officer with a good record; he's been decorated. And you're a translator," she said with an air of stern kindness. "We need you both to recover; it's for the war effort."

Miriam realized it was really something else, something that could not be officially admitted—it was an act of faith. She, indeed, became Isaac's "attendant," in fact, did little else. It was soon apparent that everyone was touched by this miracle as if it were their own. Each evening she was allowed to sit beside Isaac. As she could not see his face, she imagined his features, remembering him as before. She would stroke his hand and talk and sleep beside him. After a time he told her about his battles and how he had been wounded. Soon their story became a kind of popular legend, a curiosity, and people came by to look, nod, and smile.

Then Isaac, who was improving, took her hand one day and whispered gruffly, "Miriam, you must help me. When I was at the front, my orderly, Vanya, came to see me, asking that if something happened to him, would I deliver a letter to his mother. He told me that she was from here, Alma-Ata, and that I must find her. I cannot rest till I do. Please help me, please, we must find her."

"Where's the letter?" Miriam asked softly.

"There," he said, pointing, "in my bag."

Miriam learned as much as she could about this orderly, this boy who had a premonition that he would be killed and had written his mother a letter, then had given it to Isaac, his platoon commander, to deliver in Alma-Ata. But the mother's name, Anna, was such a common one, and they knew little else since the address was smeared into illegibility by dirt and dried blood.

"How can we ever find her?" Miriam asked.

"I don't know, but we must," Isaac said. "It was why I was allowed to come here, to find her. Without that letter I might have never been sent here at all, and you would never have found me. Isn't that strange? That I found you while trying to find her, that I begged to come when I heard some wounded were coming to Alma-Ata, so they sent them, and I came, too. How very peculiar."

Miriam resolved to find this "Mrs. Anna." Searching, she inquired of everyone. At last, after several days someone emerged who claimed to know a Mrs. Anna. "Perhaps she's the one," she said. "Go see her. She's lost a son, an orderly."

This Mrs. Anna appeared small, old, wrinkled, and much too thin as she extended a bony hand to Miriam before showing off her modest house, so well arranged, so well tended. On one side of the tiny hall was a place for a goat whose stall was kept "as clean as a Finn," as the Russians say. The living room's earthen floor was hidden by a homemade rag rug, and on the stove in the middle sat several large gleaming pots fronting a simple, rude table with circling chairs. There was no sofa. Miriam was charmed by Mrs. Anna, who kept a small bowl of sweet-smelling herbs that permeated everything.

What a marvelous relief! Miriam rejoiced. *How wonderful in its clean simplicity! What a haven!*

Soon Mrs. Anna began to tell interesting things about her son, Ivan ("Vanya" as she always called him), and Miriam was touched to hear how he had written about Isaac, how much he admired him, and how he felt he was so fortunate to serve under such a kind and intelligent young lieutenant. He had said Isaac took a genuine interest in his men, teaching them useful things, and that they all loved him for his compassion and his courage.

Miriam finally said, "Mrs. Anna, I…"

Mrs. Anna interrupted quietly, "I know, dear. I've known it for some time. I knew it when it happened. I've carried here the knowledge of my Vanya's death since that very moment," she said, pointing to her heart with her forefinger, her eyes welling up.

Miriam hesitated and then spoke softly: "Mrs. Anna, I have a letter from Vanya. He wrote it his next to last day. He shared his premonition with Isaac, who gave his sacred word that it would find its way here to you in Alma-Ata. He asked to come here just to find you and deliver Vanya's letter. Isaac kept his promise. And because he did, we, Isaac and I, found each other."

"Yes, that was God's reward," she said, taking it gently as if it were a sacred relic. "In keeping his promise to my dear Vanya, God granted that he should also find you. It is a miracle," Mrs. Anna said with a sweet smile. "In looking for me, he found you. Sometimes in looking for one thing, we find another. It's indeed divine, truly God's gift, a *Voskresenye*."

With her eyes closed, Mrs. Anna pressed the letter to her heart and began to weep. Miriam rose and went into the garden. There she sat for a very long time under a clear summer sky adorned by millions of stars set like diamonds upon the softest black silk. Then a bird began to sing from the trees, so she remained until she thought she heard movement inside. Miriam found the old woman slumped in silence, the letter open on her lap. She sat beside her, taking her hand, holding it between her own, while they listened to the goat eating his oats and the bird singing softly nearby.

24

Sitting in the Sun

That night alone in her apartment, Miriam sat on her bed, huddled under her blanket, sipping tea. *Do the dead rule the world, while we, the living, merely serve in their name?* Mrs. Anna had spoken of her lost son with the agony of one living yet surrounded by the dead. Deborah was never far away, always calling to Miriam, crying out to be remembered. Mrs. Anna, forever thinking of Ivan, had Miriam recalling, as she did every day, what almost certainly were her lost parents. *Remember everything,* she thought, *and everyone—never forget. It is in remembrance that they reign.*

Deborah's farewell sounded once again as it had done over and over like a broken and distant echo. Then Miriam saw her father, waving his pathetic little gesture before dissolving into an old man huddled in a corner with his wife, fearfully trying to retain some measure of dignity. Too, Miriam often thought of the child drowning in the Dniester, and the pathetic children at the collective, standing beside the stove begging for food.

Her thoughts of Mrs. Anna took her back to Isaac, imagining herself sitting on the edge of his bed, seeing the blood-soaked bandages around his skull. The words "While we live, yet we're in death," read in a novel somewhere, came to her, and she now knew, really for the first time, what they meant. These words and scenes blended together until they were too much. She needed to sleep, yet as she finished the tea and pulled the cover over her head, she could only find sleep adorned with fitful fantasies of both the living and the lost, merging without distinction into one painful, almost unacceptable world that she could not live without.

The next evening she told Isaac everything about her visit to Mrs. Anna. He made her repeat it carefully, every detail. Like everyone they knew, they were aware of being caught in an existence hovering precariously between life and extinction. There they sat, engaged to be married but burdened already with a tragic past and a present suffering in a strange, even enigmatic, country with an unknown future. They had slipped death's grasp, but Isaac's wounds still threatened. Nevertheless, somehow they implicitly resolved to live. *They would simply live*, she decided. *Live! Someone must live!*

"We must live, Isaac. We must live," she said desperately one night as she sat on his bed talking to him in a loud whisper.

Then one day soon after that resolution, Isaac told her that Mrs. Anna had come, bringing fresh vegetables and goat's milk, enough for him to share with the others. She had said, "Lieutenant Blumenthal, you cannot die. You must not die. You must get well."

"Mrs. Anna agrees with you that we must survive, live," Isaac said matter-of-factly, adding, "and so must I, and so I will."

Mrs. Anna did not stop; she kept coming with more food to nurse Isaac and to help the other men. Finally, it was decided that he could change wards. Isaac was slowly healing. Mrs. Anna, the nurse, and Miriam replaced his bandages regularly, cleaned and fed him. Then it was decided, after Mrs. Anna told the doctor that she was prepared to devote herself, that Isaac could move to her house for fresh food and rest, far removed from the horrors of the head-injury ward. Within a week Isaac was moved. The nurse and orderlies lifted him to the gurney and wheeled him out to a wagon with Miriam walking alongside. Wrapped in blankets, Isaac was thin, ashen, and frail, but he was weakly smiling, and Miriam thought he might yet live.

The wagon ride itself was agony, and Miriam held Isaac in her lap to soften the shock. Arriving, they laid him in a room where the light found his face, as if streaming from the sun just for him. Near his bed was a little table with a bouquet of flowers sitting upon white linen, "to erase the stench of chloroform from our memory forever," Miriam said.

For weeks Miriam came to Mrs. Anna's every Sunday. Isaac was clearly improving, and thanks to Mrs. Anna, his room was spotlessly unburdened of any hint of infection or illness. His hand grew firmer, his voice more certain, and Miriam studied his eyes each time she came, searching for the usual signs of exhaustion but they were brightening by the return of life.

"You're a wonder," Miriam told Mrs. Anna. "The change is quite miraculous."

Without speaking, the older woman handed her a bowl of soup with fresh vegetables and sent her back to attend him. Finally, when Isaac would fall asleep, Miriam helped Mrs. Anna, learning her routine, taking over chores, helping in the house and garden.

Each weekend saw more improvement. A nurse appeared every day and the doctor once a week. Their story was soon famous—they had become a legend, so the nurses took turns with obvious delight. "I think he can remove the bandages now," one of them announced, touching Isaac's skull gently, as if admiring her work.

"Wonderful!" said Miriam, clapping her hands with uncontained joy.

"I'll send the doctor," the nurse said. "I'm sure he'll approve."

This would be a great event, this coming of the doctor. So they cooked fresh food and milked the goat. Isaac wanted to sit up and look as well as possible, so Miriam stuffed cushions behind his head and shoulders and pulled him up into a semi-sitting position. He looked much better; his thick black hair was growing back, which Miriam now combed despite it being short and stubby and rather thick.

The doctor finally came and said with false gravity, "Most of the bandages can be removed, and if it's warm, he can go outside for about an hour, mind, no more."

When that happy day came, two neighbor men helped lift Isaac into the garden. Sitting in a wooden chair he closed his eyes, soaking in the sun's warmth. Within a short time, Miriam noticed a tear edging down his nose in search of his upper lip. She wanted to inquire but did not. Isaac, as if reading her thoughts, said softly, "The sun is like music."

"Music?" she asked, surprised.

"Yes, music."

It was an image she had never thought of and paused to reflect upon. *The sun as music…only Isaac could think of that. There is in him the touch of the poet—lawyer, soldier, and poet—what a man!*

Of course, as is always the case with such things, they had fallen into a routine, but over the next two weeks an unspoken thought seemed to emerge and hover over them. *What was it that Isaac wanted to say but could not?* Miriam wondered. *There is something unspoken, something he wants to speak about but dares not. What is it? He will tell me in his good time, when the moment is right. I must be patient.*

Gradually, Isaac was taking his meals at the table. The doctor came again and even spoke of his trying to walk, so a neighbor thoughtfully built a frame for him to lean on as a kind of primitive support. By the end of June, they enjoyed sitting in the garden, and he could even shuffle slightly without the use of the walker. Then, with increasing strength and confidence, he began to help with chores. One day he interrupted his work of snapping beans into a bowl and stared at the faraway mountains. They were alone, and as Miriam got up to empty her bowl, he made a nervous gesture. *He wants to say something*, she thought, *the moment has come at last; he's now going to speak of the thing unspoken.*

He tried again, "Don't leave, Miriam," he said, reaching for her and taking her hand as she sat back down. "I've been thinking. I'm almost well now, I mean I have a ways to go, of course, but I am getting stronger every day. I must prepare, think of the future, of what I'm going to do eventually, and I've decided to return to the front."

"Return to the front?!" Miriam cried, standing up, spilling her bowl, the beans going everywhere. "Isaac, that's impossible; don't even imagine such a thing!" she said so fast her words stumbled over each other.

"No," said Isaac, "It's not impossible. In time, I mean, when I am well, stronger, of course, but it's what I must do."

"Isaac, you've done your duty. Besides, you're in no condition to go back to the front, you can't. Besides, they won't let you. It's absurd to even suggest such a horrible thing, perfectly absurd."

And so they argued. Finally, Miriam tried to stop thinking about it. *It's too preposterous even to consider. It's a kind of crazy fantasy of his*, she decided, *a dream that could never come true.* But then it came up again, and so she said, "A soldier with a head wound like yours would never be sent back. You'll be excused. I know that much. They'll give you a desk job, especially with your German and your education. They won't waste you as cannon fodder at the front. Isaac, dearest, you've done your duty, been decorated and terribly wounded. You can hold your head up with the bravest. It's all very honorable. No one will force you back, or even think of such a thing. Believe me, I know how the Party works, and it'll put you where you are most valuable—using your wonderful brain behind a desk. Of course, the Party will be right; there, you can do the most good."

He was silent. He was thinking of his duty and the comrades he had left behind. She knew that without having to ask. It was no longer just a matter of politics or anything of that sort; it was personal loyalty, pure and simple, no matter how he might dress it up intellectually, she decided. What she never knew, and Isaac could never quite bring himself to mention, was what the *frontoviki* said about the wounded that recovered but managed not to return—they were beneath contempt.

"I feel guilty," he admitted one day, coming as close as he could to the truth.

"Guilty?!"

"Yes, for leaving them."

"Don't be silly!" she said. "That's perfectly ridiculous."

Then he added quietly, becoming more animated as he spoke, "What future will we have if Hitler wins? Where would any Jewish couple be if Hitler prevails? We cannot let him win. I must do what I have to do, we all must, until the beast is finally dead and his evil kingdom destroyed. He must be erased from the face of the earth, no matter what it costs!"

"Of course, of course, we all agree, with all our souls we agree, but don't you understand? You are more valuable in the struggle doing something else now. You have been to the front, fought bravely, are a true hero; now you can help in another way that truly uses your talents."

"You don't understand, Miriam, and I can't explain it to you."

Though she never said it, she did, at least in part, understand. Still she cried, argued, and fought with him until they were exhausted. Finally, after one of their arguments, Isaac reached for her gently. "Come here and kiss me," he said, pointing to his cheek. "I don't have to go today; come give me a sweet kiss."

She lay down and cried, saying, "Isaac, I can't imagine a future without you. What's the point of recovering? Why struggle to live if you only have death waiting for you?"

"Miriam, one can say that about life itself, all of it, not just war. What's life worth if it's nothing but a flash of light between eternity and oblivion? We must find a way to give that flash of light meaning, that's our greatest task."

"Oh, that's too philosophical, Isaac! I'm here right now, alive, and so are you, right now! We're young, we have each other and all our lives before us, together, if you wish. You have the power now to make it so, but if you go back, you'll surely be killed. I just know it. Don't tempt fate! You must not go back, Isaac, please, I beg you! I won't let you. I can never accept the point of life as death. No, you must not go!"

Isaac said nothing. "No more words," he said after a time, patting her hand. "No more words, my love."

The morning embraced them as they lay together, holding each other desperately, until at last he fell asleep dreaming of war and she dreamed of all her disappeared ones, now numbering Isaac among the missing yet again.

25

A Trip to the Doctor

Isaac was gone. The month before his leaving had been spent as much in the past as the present. Indeed, speaking of the past between Isaac and Miriam had been a way of holding onto the present. There had been longer walks, stolen moments alone, endless talk of childhood memories, their first meeting, their love affair in Czernowitz, and their escape. They told each other things they had never mentioned. Miriam even told of the trips to the mountains and her fear of the bear. He spoke of his ambitions, philosophy, theology, friends, professors, but most of all, he spoke of his family. It all seemed now to be such another time and place, as if it had never really happened. Other things, the things that had once been so very important: their differences in politics, the discussion of the "future of the Jews," Zionism, the first kiss, the separation in age—all of these somehow seemed a little ridiculous. The reality of war was much too powerful, and although rarely mentioned, it hovered like a great, brooding presence.

"It's strange," Isaac said. "Wars are about politics, sure, we all know that, but during the fighting—at the front, I mean—almost no one ever mentions it, and when they do, it sounds rather silly and self-conscious, the kind of thing that people talk about who don't know what they're talking about."

Then, finally, after they had discussed everything possible, Miriam, surprising herself, summoned the courage to tell him about the rape. *I can't keep it a secret; he must know, must be the only one, but he must know. There can be no secrets between us, none.*

They wept together. He spoke of trying to comfort dying friends, of his helpless rage when they were separated, and his despair about ever seeing her again. They examined each other's hands lovingly: he for her blue frostbite and stiffness, and she for the evidence of clutching a weapon or pressing the wounds of a comrade or digging in the earth for refuge—a foxhole or a grave.

With the tears drying away, she shifted her mood. "What kind of hands do you think our babies will have?" she asked with a quiet, pensive joy, rubbing her eyes.

Isaac laughed nervously. He tried to speak but could not. He was so stubborn in his resolution to return that it was clear even Miriam's having a child someday could not hold him. Nothing could prevent his going, that was certain, and though Miriam did not understand, she had finally accepted it.

Alas, he was indeed gone, despite all her efforts to hold him, had slipped her grasp once again. Miriam was alone once more. She wondered about the point of trying to save him, finding him only to send him back to that demon they had only just managed to escape.

How singular, she reflected, *that our story has paralleled Tolstoy's of Natasha and Andrey: the long engagement, the age difference, the war, the sexual violation—although Natasha's was metaphorical, it was in a sense the same—and the miracle of finding her prince barely alive among the wounded. But there was one great difference; Andrey had died and Isaac survived.*

Miriam decided to cling to this difference while fearing that, maybe, it also was the same. After all, she realized to her horror, Andrey[35] had survived the wounds of his first battle only to die from those of the second. Yet, too, she could not escape the feeling that the prince had wanted to die. Why? There was an essential distinction when she considered this; that he seemed possessed of an underlying despair that nothing could quite remedy, and though he had everything else, lacked the essential thing, a belief in life itself. *Maybe rationality is the enemy of life and vice versa. Andrey had too much rationality. Maybe like Tolstoy himself—a nihilist at war with his own nihilism—Andrey grew weary of the struggle. But with Isaac it isn't true; he wants very much to live, does not seek death out of despair of living. His rationality is not the enemy of vitality at all but sustains it. Maybe he is not rational enough, and that is why he does not see the folly of going back to the front.*

In the deepest possible despair after their parting, she returned to Mrs. Anna's. They now shared the mutuality of loss, and without her, Miriam was quite certain she would have gone mad. Of course she expected letters from Isaac, but none came. This was so distressing that she refused even to speak of him. When people asked, she simply turned away. She would chat about quotas, food coupons, distribution problems, housing, and the like, but never of Isaac or of the war.

Life with its usual irrational tenacity went on, but Miriam's health deteriorated. She was gradually losing ground, tormented by her ubiquitous visions of death and Isaac's second disappearance and, worse, his cruel and unreasoning silence. Time, weeks, months, passed, yet she still heard nothing. She quit eating. *I have no wish to live,* she thought; *without Isaac there is nothing for me in this world.*

Her friends complained so much that, as an act of appeasement, she went to a physician, Dr. Irina Nikolayevna Kasparova, a Jew. Miriam trusted her in a glance and surprised herself by gushing out her entire story. Then the good doctor, waiting patiently for her new patient to finish, informed Miriam of something.

"I'm afraid you have a more pressing problem, my dear."

"More pressing problem?"

"Yes."

"What's that?"

"You're pregnant."

There was a very long silence.

"Pregnant?" Miriam finally asked in something above a whisper.

"Yes, without a doubt."

Miriam absorbed this, turning white as she did. Then after a moment, she asked, "But how can that be?"

Dr. Kasparova gave a slight laugh and said, "Well, my dear, the way it always is."

Miriam began to cry. The doctor waited, then smoothed a hand gently over her forehead, saying with a deep sigh, "There's much we can do, my child, but first you must eat—you are wasting away—and rest. You're exhausted. Most of all, you must begin to plan."

Miriam lifted her head. "Plan?"

"Yes, plan. You cannot give up. You have a child to live for. I will write everything down for you, so you'll not forget," Dr. Kasparova said, reaching into a drawer for paper and scribbling rapidly as if she were writing a prescription. "Can you find fruit, vegetables, and some milk?"

Miriam nodded. The doctor scratched some more.

"Do you work an evening job, as well as in the day?"

Miriam nodded and said, "I do both."

The physician shook her head and said, "That's too much; you're obviously wearing yourself out." Then she wrote on another sheet of paper. "Here," she said, "take this letter to the volunteer supervisor. She'll readily see the effects of malnutrition, so don't worry. I am recommending that your volunteer activities be suspended, that your weekly day off is not to be usurped. That is, if the army hopes to retain you as a translator. You are important to them; they won't find many German speakers of your caliber, and they know it, so they won't make a fuss. Do you have any clothing?"

Miriam looked down at her patchy dress, sewn into discordant colors because it had been repaired so many times.

"I have this one, but I think it might disintegrate at any moment," Miriam said with half a laugh.

"I'll take care of the clothing," the doctor said. "We'll get you some new ones."

Then she escorted Miriam out, handing her the papers, telling her to return for monthly checkups. Then, stepping outside her professional role, she embraced Miriam, looked her in the eye and said quietly, "You must not give up, you must fight on, someone must. You now have another human being to care for. Children are the future, you know. We must nurture them; without them there is no hope."

Miriam clutched the papers as the door closed softly behind. Arriving home, she tossed them on the table and crawled into bed, wetting her pillow with tears.

"Live? Live? There is no life for me! There is no life without Isaac! Isaac! Come back! Please, Isaac, come back! Why have you left me?! Why?!" she screamed, then rolled on the bed and sobbed herself to sleep.

During the next week she staggered to work each day and occasionally rode out to Mrs. Anna's in the evenings. There Mrs. Anna gave her food, tea, and what comfort she could. One day she asked, "My dear, you are pregnant, aren't you?"

Miriam nodded with an embarrassed smile.

"My poor darling, I thought so! My poor, poor darling!" Mrs. Anna said, gently taking her hand. "Don't worry, your Anna will take care of you. Come, come, my dear, come this way," leading her into Isaac's room, where she tucked her into bed, sat beside her, stroked her head, and assured her quietly that all would be well.

Miriam surprised herself by falling immediately to sleep and was surprised again when she was awakened by Mrs. Anna handing her hot soup, saying, "Sit up child. You must eat, then we'll talk."

Miriam wanted to mention Andrey and Natasha to Mrs. Anna, to say how crazily similar their stories were, but something held her back; it seemed silly somehow. Anyway, Natasha had never gotten pregnant by her prince. She had married Pierre in the end and lived happily ever after. *I need to forget the novel and its fantasies and think only of my reality with Mrs. Anna. Art is never a substitute for life—at best, a comment upon it, nothing more. And it's a comment that Mrs. Anna won't understand, and it will only make her uncomfortable.*

Of course, Miriam did tell Mrs. Anna what the doctor said. Mrs. Anna assured her that they could get all the necessary food. In fact, she would get fresh vegetables for her every weekend and as much dairy products as she could, and Miriam could eat it at Mrs. Anna's. Then she would send food back with Miriam in a basket; she would go home with plenty of apples, nuts, carrots, and potatoes; she would have all she could possibly need.

For the next doctor's appointment, Mrs. Anna went with Miriam. Dr. Kasparova seemed quite delighted to have "Aunt" Anna's assistance, as she called her. "Now together," the doctor said, "we can get Miriam through this and have a fine, healthy, wonderful baby."

The doctor then gave Miriam a skirt and two new blouses. "Wear them loosely so you won't show quite as easily," she said with a wink and little tap on the knee.

But Miriam was too focused on disaster—not only those that had happened but those to come. The wink and the tap were lost on her.

Though she never told the doctor or Mrs. Anna, at times she thought she was truly going insane. She did things more and more by rote, automatically, like a sleepwalker. Her old standby, her mother, she conjured again to tell her all about the pregnancy, the rape-fear, everything: how this had poisoned her life and that she had survived only from a sense of duty. Deborah, when she would appear for those sessions, would stay and advise her. It was Miriam's mental salvation. She enveloped herself in this new world as a substitute for the real one that was so cruel, but she knew it was abnormal and worried that someday she might just stay there once and for all, never to return.

Miriam explained to Deborah one day: *When I found Isaac, Mama, I felt that God had finally taken pity on us. It was such a miracle. Isaac was all I had, and God had intervened. You and God gave him to me. You were actually the one who gave him to me, and you gave me to him. You placed me under his protection, and I lost him but got him back again. Now I have my life, but Isaac is gone once more. How cruel that he has been taken from me yet again! He was my only connection to life, and now he has been stolen. It's not fair; why is God so cruel? It all seems like a terrible joke sometimes. How can it make any sense to live? Why do we live, Mama? What was the point of God's miracle if He was going to annul it?*

Sometimes she even tried to conjure a shadowy image of David. Yet his face never quite came into focus. Sometimes she would even speak to them both together! *Mama, Papa, Isaac and I were married—in my mind, that is. We have done nothing wrong. We had your blessings to live together. I know it's not really a marriage in the state's eyes, but I'm not sure I really believe in the state or even know what it is; it's a fiction, but we are married, Mama, married, in the only way that really matters. I mean, where is the state? What country are Isaac and I really citizens of? Where are we recognized? We are Jews! Where is our home?! If God were really taking any notice of his Jews as He promised, I'd say that we were wed under God. But who represents God in the world of Stalin, in his world of death and destruction? Who blesses life in Stalin's world? The political commissar with a pistol on his belt and his Prussian boots? Who sanctions marriage? The atheist apparatchiks? Do they wave a revolver over our heads? Is that sacred? The source of our blessing? What spiritual authority do they represent? How can atheism sanctify anything? Life or marriage? And marriage must have a spiritual sanction to have any real meaning.*

No, there was no meaningful way of marrying, except to marry ourselves, and this we have done. We promised ourselves in spirit, in the only way that matters. We asked God's blessings on us, not the state's, and He gave it, or if He didn't, then there is no God and it simply doesn't matter. We reached out to each other in the only gesture strong enough to bind us together forever. I'm not ashamed. But I am devastated to have lost him anyway. He has been taken away by Stalin. Is Stalin really God now? Does he, as Lenin did, give people something to believe in, to sacrifice for? Is that why men die with Stalin's name on their lips? Is that the secret of History, however terrible? Maybe I should be grateful Isaac was given back at all, that I had the miracle of his ever being found. Of course, I cannot expect another; there are never two miracles.

But I fear that Isaac will die twice! I just know it will happen! Stalin is God in our world now, because History is God. Maybe it is all we have and Stalin is the personification of History so he is God, and he is so very cruel because History is cruel. History is our collective consciousness struggling to manifest itself over matter. It is the force of the Great Will, the Will of Nature, no matter how ruthless, to someday overcome the slavery of all necessity. Man kills in order to overcome death in the hopes that, if he kills enough, it will happen. This is the new faith. Isaac is right; we must have faith in something or go mad. We have nothing else. Hitler is part of the same thing. Stalin and Hitler are History and, therefore, are the only gods at work in our world.

Then Deborah interrupted: *No, you are wrong, Miriam; Hitler and Stalin are Satan's angels, not God's. Together they have taken Isaac from you; he went because of them. But you have the miracle of the child; this is God's doing, that is His real gift to you, your child. God did all that he could. He gave you each other and now the child. Evil took Isaac away, not God.*

No! This is not a miracle. What chance does this child or I have if God is powerless over evil? Miriam retorted bitterly, turning away, the image of Deborah evaporating into the reality of her tiny room like an exiting ghost, her mother's marvelous face giving way to the infinite nothingness that surrounded her in that small space, which in an instant seemed to be the consequence of all godless existence.

Staring at the wall, she thought yet again of God, as she had been taught to think of Him. Her parents had always seemed much more real than God. They had been her god. She could only believe in God because her parents had. In her childhood, she could count on them, and now she could count on no one, and what was God going to do now? Her parents were almost certainly dead. As weak as she was, did she have any power to coerce God into being merciful toward Isaac or helping save her helpless unborn child? She would plead with God to save them, but she was not certain of His response.

It was difficult not to be angry with God and to argue with Him, but she was no metaphysical rebel, and she wearily gave it all up and returned to the ordinary life of an automaton, trusting in Mrs. Anna and Dr. Kasparova, while sustained by some inner will that never had or ever would quite desert her. It was the Thing that had always saved her, that she could always count on it seemed.

But if it's a boy and Isaac lives, I will name him Jacob, she decided by way of propitiation, shifting her thoughts. *Maybe that will please God enough to save them both. God would save him as he saved Jacob, the son of Isaac.*

26

A Second Life

Miriam found herself so gradually imprisoned in her own mind as to have become almost emotionally paralyzed, but she resolved to save herself. She knew she could do this only with application and the anodyne of routine. After all, many people were withdrawn, and one more person was hardly remarkable. Indeed, nothing about her seemed to elicit comment at all as she struggled to go about her life in something approaching a normal manner.

She continued her work and classes, convincing the world and herself that things were, in fact, well, that language study and translation were her future. The best study sessions, the "nourishing ones" as she called them, were those held at Zakti's new apartment. Here, Zakti unselfishly shared her life, which was very fortunate, in a comfortable flat. Zakti offered everyone black tea, cigarettes, chocolates, oranges, and Aport apples. Each night as she walked home with fruit wrapped in a little cloth, Miriam became increasingly convinced, with a vague inner embarrassment, that she was Zakti's favorite.

Meantime, Miriam paid routine calls on the good doctor. In October, she was admonished, "Miriam, you must begin to slow down, look after yourself. You are in your fifth month. More and more care must be taken for your child."

Miriam nodded mechanically.

"Are you still teaching German?"

"Yes."

"You'll need an excuse. Take more rest, do you understand? It's critical."

Of course, the pregnancy, like the rape, was another burning secret. Her life seemed full of them. The first class she missed was explained away as illness, but the truth was she could not get warm and had to stay home by the fire. The winter, as though allied with the god of war, had become exceptionally brutal, as if its frigidity represented the breath of death in yet another disguise.

At last, the university could shiver no more and classes were cancelled. Zakti spoke about the cancellation. "It's not the end of the world, Miriam," she said, brightening. "We'll get together soon, don't worry, my dear. But have I told you? I'm getting married! All of you must come to help celebrate my second life."

Miriam gasped. She had never expected such a thing. *A second life?* she said to herself with an inward irony. She started to say she, too, was also starting a second life but didn't. Her own new life was hidden, while her friend's was open—Zakti had no burning secrets. No one seemed to have those but Miriam Kellerman.

It was difficult for Miriam not to be jealous. She had chosen Isaac as her life's love—there would never be another. He was hers forever, even if he didn't write. *But he seemed now to prefer war to peace. He had gone because he wanted to go! He did not have to, just as Andrey did not have to. Why had they gone?* The question kept coming obsessively to her mind. *Was I wrong before in thinking them different; were they in fact as one in being in love with death more than in love with life? Did they embrace it out of impatience of its ever coming?*

Miriam, when she had read the novel, had talked to Deborah about that. It was always the most troubling thing to her, this unnecessary death. And now Isaac's silence followed his return to war so cruelly. The silence was the worst of all; it was like a kind of living annihilation, just as senseless and even crueler.

The two who knew Miriam best, her friends Mrs. Anna and Dr. Kasparova, continued to fret over her like old hens. They knew what childbirth was like, and Miriam did not. They insisted that her baby could not be born at her apartment, that Dr. Kasparova would have to deliver Miriam's secret somewhere else. The Russians have a saying: "All things will be known," but Miriam now tried hard to be the exception. She wanted to save her reputation, along with the life of her child—unrealizable, perhaps, she knew only too well, but she could not bear the thought of scandal.

At Mrs. Anna's almost daily insistence, Miriam had written Isaac, in the face of his continued silence, and told him everything. This did it. Embarrassed, he apologized, wrote page after page about their "bright future" and how he was going "to work hard to see what a good world our child will grow up in"—win the war, defeat Fascism, come home, start over. How glorious! What hope! What joy! "Miriam, I don't know how I could have found the strength and time to deal with the bureaucracy, but I should have used all my energy to find a way to marry you. Yet, it might be easier for you to carry on with your new life, should I not survive, if you had never been married. But how foolish of me! We are already married! Please forgive me, Miriam. I love you very much and would rather die than hurt you!"

A new life?! A new life, indeed! she thought.

He would "rather die than hurt you," he had said. What did all that mean? He had already hurt her by going away, and worse by not writing. To be sure, that was the only real way he now could hurt her—by dying. His idealism, he had said, was "not going to die but create a new and better world for our child, for everyone, the whole world." *How could he remain so idealistic in the middle of such suffering?* He himself had said such things always seemed rather silly at the front. *Then why were they serious enough to die for?*

But her problems, here, in the domestic world, were far more immediate. She had to find a place for her confinement. For this she relied on Mrs. Anna and Dr. Kasparova. And, too, they had begun to talk about something quite new. "A seventh-month baby is easier to have," the doctor had said. It could survive "because it's smaller and easier to deliver." In some ways "it has a better chance than the eighth-month baby or even the ninth-month baby," she had explained a little too deliberately. This was all very unfamiliar, and Miriam was more than a little shocked. She had never heard of a seventh-month baby. She knew nothing, in fact, of having babies at all.

Then in November, Mrs. Anna began to ask Miriam what she would need for the child. What clothes? Where and how to store the child's things? How about a crib? Blankets? Diapers?

Miriam simply just stared at the wall. She could think only of wrapping up her baby and handing it to Isaac, so she said nothing at all to such questions. "I will do as you think best," she said quietly.

December 31, 1943, was very cold and clear. Dr. Kasparova had scheduled an appointment for the afternoon; then she would drive them out to Mrs. Anna's for the New Year's holiday and stay till

Monday. "You will have an easy delivery," she had said, avoiding the word "premature" but adding, "but this baby might come a little early, my dear."

Miriam felt the all too familiar surge of panic. *Obviously, I'm not being told everything. Doctors never do. I know that much.*

Dr. Kasparova's examination that day not only took longer but was more painful than normal. Afterward, closing her clinic, she bundled Miriam up for the journey to Mrs. Anna's. She easily chattered on, but Miriam huddled in the corner of the car, silent. *I just can't bring myself to think of this as some kind of holiday. Of course, everyone acts as if everything is normal and routine. How ridiculous!*

Once there, it seemed that both Mrs. Anna and Dr. Kasparova were constantly carrying on a subdued conversation just out of earshot. Mrs. Anna's neighbor, Pjotr, a doctor's assistant, had already arrived and was proudly waiting with several loaves of bread cradled in his arms like kindling for the fire. Soon the little house filled with several more mutual friends, who, after finishing the baking, at last sat down to a holiday meal. There was a festive air that included everyone, Miriam decided, but herself; indeed, she felt more and more like the "person who wasn't there," as she picked perfunctorily through her food while watching others eat with such great but exclusive joy.

It is readily apparent, she wanted to say, *that I'm being treated with studied neglect, like a stranger among friends. I might as well be invisible.*

Finishing his dessert, Pjotr scooted back noisily and announced, "Miriam, you look as tired as I feel; you probably should go to bed and rest."

They all said goodnight to Miriam, and, following her into the bedroom, Dr. Kasparova performed a cursory examination and purred, patting Miriam's hand patronizingly, "You will be fine, dear, just fine. Don't worry."

But patronizing Miriam never did any good. Angry, and fearful, she tossed and turned around the edges of sleep, while the party continued with garbled chatter and bursts of laughter heard through a wall and the closed door, irritating her in the way it always does those excluded in a vain search for rest.

Miriam did not hear the furniture scoot back when she screamed or the door slam open or the hubbub of concerned confusion hovering around her. But they were right about seventh-month babies because soon a little red creature entered her life on the very last day of '43—a girl.

"Your daughter," Dr. Kasparova said, handing her carefully to Miriam. Pjotr stood in the doorway, smiling, as the bundle was placed into the crook of Miriam's waiting arm. Her daughter had big, dark-gray eyes that stared into her own. They were obviously Isaac's, and her little fist thrust out and touched Miriam as if she knew her. Then, as a kind of greeting, she wrapped her tiny finger around her mother's forefinger, gripping tighter and tighter.

"Wait! Wait, baby. Hold on, we're waiting for your father," Miriam whispered sweetly. "He'll come soon to see his beautiful daughter."

Miriam embraced her. The new life had been born, a true second life. Something for Isaac to fight for—and *me to live for*, she decided, cuddling her child.

Miriam then noticed a rather faint morning sunlight slipping through the window. It was the very first sun of 1944. In July she would be 20. A teenager, she was already a mother. *How far I've come from that frightened little schoolgirl fleeing down a road away from Bukovina!*

She placed her baby in the nearby cradle, her reddish black hair nestling among the soft sheets and her sweet eyes watching with a questioning look while she curled and then uncurled a miniature fist near her pink cheek. At the foot of the bed was a white, wooden, two-shelf bench with new stacks of clean linen.

Miriam looked at the linen, the bench, and the new baby—a New Year, a new beginning, and, perhaps, a new world: Nazi Germany was slowly collapsing under the allied vise that was squeezing it cruelly from east and west, cracking Hitler's "Thousand Years Reich" like a giant fist slowly crushing a rotten and very evil egg.

Miriam did not know it, but another girl, not much younger than herself, was greeting the New Year with similar hopes, as she wrote a question in her diary that same day. "Could we be granted victory this year, 1944?" Anne Frank asked from her hiding hole in a Holland attic and then answered, "We don't know yet, but hope is revived within me: it gives us fresh courage and makes us strong again."[36]

The next 48 hours were befogged to all memory for the first time in a very long while as Miriam, feeling a burden lifted, actually slept and awoke rested rather than restless. It was almost a novel feeling, to be revived and serene after rising, rather than exhausted, nor did she remember any bad dreams. How odd not to have been visited by hideous visions; they had been her companions for so long that she could not imagine a night without them.

"Try to nurse the baby, Miriam. Try again. It's important," the doctor insisted rather too gravely.

"What shall I name her?" Miriam asked of no one in particular. No name came easily. She tried to imagine Deborah holding her grandchild but found she could not. Were they all truly dead? It was the custom for Jews to name their children after relatives who had been killed or were missing; she must do the same. *Am I burying my mother, replacing her with this child by naming her Ruth? Will Deborah be supplanted by Ruth and no longer live centrally in my heart in the same way?*

But the doctor's voice intruded, "Miriam, we will register the baby's birth next week. Pjotr will take care of it."

"Do you want to hear what we are going to do?" she heard Mrs. Anna add cheerfully from some distance.

"Yes," Miriam said with a hint of such impatience, such irritation at the interruption of her thoughts that Mrs. Anna walked out, leaving an uncomfortable silence behind.

Alone and exhausted, Miriam slept until daylight, and, awakening, asked with a yawn, "Aunt Anna, what day is it?"

"Monday, I think," came the off-handed, faraway answer. "I'm not sure."

Then Dr. Kasparova sat near the bed, holding Ruth. Without smiling she handed the child to Miriam and said, "Now we're going to talk." Both she and Pjotr would be returning to town, she explained.

"I'll call your supervisor and arrange for indefinite leave for reasons of health," the doctor said. "They never question me on such matters. Pjotr Sergeyevitch will register a baby found on his doorstep. No one will be surprised; they're constantly being left in that way."

Pjotr planned to ask if he and Mrs. Anna could take "joint responsibility" for the child. No doubt the officials would be pleased, and the paperwork would not take long. The phrase "joint responsibility" had a nice bureaucratic ring to it.

To her own surprise, Miriam began to cry, "She reminds me of Mother already."

"You will have to raise her on goat's milk, my dear," interjected Mrs. Anna.

"Why?" Miriam asked, looking up. "Why goat's milk?"

"You're malnourished, and you're not lactating properly."

"Not lactating properly?!"

"Yes, but don't worry, dear, Mrs. Anna will show you how it's done," she added, spryly getting up.

Miriam was not to return to work until January 10, so she had the luxury of remaining with Ruth, helping her drink every drop of goat's milk that Mrs. Anna squirted in the little silver bucket.

At last, Dr. Kasparova returned on the third night. She was joking as she entered the door, acting self-consciously nonchalant. "And who are the parents of this little one?" she asked, pinching Ruth's cheek and making it turn even pinker.

"I think this elderly gentleman and this beautiful woman are," said Mrs. Anna, pointing to Pjotr and herself with a shy smile. Then adding with a laugh, "and the goat."

"Yes, definitely the happy couple and the wet nurse," said Dr. Kasparova with a laugh that everyone joined in but Miriam.

At work, Miriam was teased endlessly until she explained, "Mrs. Anna has already found her next patient, don't you know? A little baby girl, I'm told, a newborn, was left on Pjotr Sergeyevitch's doorstep, and he has asked Mrs. Anna if she'd look after her. Unless the parents show up to claim the poor thing, they'll be the foster parents. They've even asked me to help. It'll be such fun! I plan to spend lots of my weekends there now. I mean, I must pay back the kindness done to me and Isaac somehow," she said to everyone as her cover story.

Such a romantic and beautiful tale, it was readily believed. For a moment Miriam's cynicism was obliterated. To her surprise, it was a relief to begin translating once again; language work once again came to her rescue from the pages of the most mundane material imaginable.

Then one weekend Mrs. Anna generously said, "Now that she is three weeks old, we're going to have a picture of the baby made and mail it to Isaac. He needs to see his daughter, don't you agree?"

"What a wonderful idea! I will fill a letter with details of Ruth to go along with the photograph," Miriam said. "How delighted he will be to find a picture of the female version of himself!"

These weekends at Mrs. Anna's were halcyon days for Miriam, indeed. Dr. Kasparova often joined them for short visits. She could readily see that Ruth was still quite small, but everyone agreed she seemed to be doing well and was filling out every day. Her Isaac eyes were growing ever larger and larger, with lashes fringing them with a soft fuzz of hair, and she began to develop a personality that flashed out from those eyes with that unique charm of all laughing babies. She would smile and coo when Miriam looked into those eyes, seeing Isaac there, telling her about him and what a hero he was. While Ruth stared back, Miriam's face would sometimes switch to a frown as she thought of the future, of how long she would have either of them, wondering when God or Stalin or Hitler or the Thing or whatever it was that was in control of her life and history would snatch everything away again.

27

Zakti's Wedding

Zakti's wedding plans were progressing, and Miriam, the underground mother, listened with not a little envy about the upcoming parties, the extended family, and the fiancé's political friends that Zakti would be obliged to entertain. Zakti appeared quite undaunted by the trifling vexations of a wedding. She met it all with great joy, and in the end, her effervescent personality transformed Miriam's mild jealousy into an unfeigned enthusiasm.

Still, it was quite obvious that Zakti's version of a new life was entering a realm quite remote from Miriam's. When, before the great day, Zakti assumed command of her new house, she took possession of this incomparable luxury without the least pretense or superciliousness. She seemed completely unaware of her enhanced status and wealth—the Iranian rugs and other luxuries—and because she shared it with everyone unselfishly, she dissolved resentment like wet sugar.

Zakti's family lived nearby, and soon Miriam was introduced to her numerous brothers and sisters. Most attended the university, but those who did not had very good jobs, and it was becoming increasingly difficult to imagine any hardship whatsoever attaching to Zakti's life. Everyone accepted the wedding as an exciting juxtaposition to the drudgery of suffering—an ecumenical ceremony of delight and pleasure.

To her great surprise, Miriam found herself involved in every phase of wedding preparation, and this soon became an addictive fantasy of reunion with her own Isaac and the wedding she feared she would never have. Afterward there was to be a great reception, but because it would supplant her time with Ruth, Miriam hesitated and then decided, *I must go. How can I not? I will go for the pleasure of going, for the vicarious thrill of it…and I'll go for Mrs. Anna, too, because she'll almost certainly be at my own wedding, such as it might be—that of her surrogate child, Miriam Kellerman—and I will come home and share with her, and maybe someday we will plan one just as grand.*

The reception found Miriam shyly wearing her very best dress and looking as glamorous as ever she could. After greetings, she warily circled the hors d'oeuvres only to find the national dish of Kazakhstan, *beshbarmak*—a quivering concoction of noodles laced with fatty lamb packed down into an enormously deep, bottomless bowl—staring maliciously up at her. The custom was to dip in and fish out the dripping goop and then swallow it in a great slobbering gulp. This custom was not optional. *What am I going to do? I'll be sick, I just know it, but I have to. Better to do it quickly.*

She enlisted a friend as a witness, then took a very modest handful and cautiously raised it to her lips. She had dipped down almost to the very bottom, right up to her wrists, hoping the fat would flow over her cupped hands, and now, careful not to offend Kazakh pride or Zakti, she bravely sucked in a tiny bite.

"Excuse me," she said to her friend, as she ran toward the door.

"Where are you going?" the friend asked.

"To vomit," replied Miriam, disappearing.

Outside she did not vomit but instead sucked in fresh air as an antiemetic, breathing deeply, rapidly, waiting for the diaphoresis and nausea to pass. She even took a little stroll under the stars, walking among the hedges, then returned to find Zakti in search of her.

"How did you like the beshbarmak?" she asked pertly.

"Oh, it was wonderful," Miriam said with a tortured smile. "Zakti, how beautiful you look!" she quickly added. Zakti, adorned in jewelry and an alluring dress, covered as she was with that irresistible aura of a young, beautiful, first-time bride, was positively captivating. Before Zakti could respond, as if planned, her husband entered, bowed, and was introduced by Zakti to everyone, including Miriam. Like some great official, party chief, or politician, he quickly worked the crowd, shaking hands and smiling unctuously before leaving the room with the same studied manner as he had entered, "to make arrangements," someone said in a knowing, confidential aside.

It was incredible to Miriam. Here they were in Alma-Ata, behind the most violent front of the most terrible war in history, and they were bowing and smiling at a wedding reception, quibbling over the unnecessary troubles of dining, dress, and decorum.

Miriam watched with an increasingly ironic eye, trying to absorb the meaning of it all. Zakti had a normal home and family; in fact, she had everything that Miriam did not. All the coveted things seemed so easily granted, and she tried to console herself that perhaps Zakti and her husband, the handsome if somewhat smug Party bureaucrat, did not have the intensity of love that she shared with Isaac. *I, we, will just have to wait for another, better day, made sweeter by such early bitterness. Zakti'll never know what we know, feel what we have felt,* Miriam thought, watching Zakti's triumph unfold.

The rest soon became a haze as Miriam withdrew into the loneliness that only such a crowd can bring. Then a young girl surprised her with an ornately knitted little bag of food: coffee, chocolates, sweets, nuts, fruit, and a can of caviar.

"Thank you," Miriam whispered in surprise. Such a treasure! But she cradled it in shock, thinking of the pathetic little food bag dropped in her lap on the train—*click, click, click* went the train, *click, click, click* pounded again in her ears, *click, click, click,* as Miriam hovered again in her little corner of the boxcar, her heart racing, her breast heaving. She gasped, suffocated, hesitated, then rushed over and embraced Zakti with a soft thank you, and ran for the door.

"Miriam!" she cried. "Miriam, where are you going? Come back!"

But Miriam could not come back, not ever. She heard the sirens of the Stukas—the *Jericho-Trompeten*—screaming at her as she ran and ran and ran. Zakti had never known a noise like that, a pain like that remembrance, and Miriam could never explain. The lurid flashback—the smell and sounds of such fear—had come over her in a great wave, conceived so sweetly by Zakti's thoughtfully innocent gift that had exploded like a bomb on a road.

Miriam raced into the street, breaking into a run. She ran faster and faster until she stumbled, could not catch herself, and fell, dropping the little bag that she had forgotten she even had. A stout *babushka* in a scarf and coat walking nearby came over, mumbling words of concern, and lifted up her little body with stout hands. Miriam recovered her wits, thanked her, stooped over, fumbled up the bag, and shoved it into the astonished woman's grasp, then fled—not caring, just running, thinking only of getting "home" to Mrs. Anna's and holding Ruth again, the only treasure she cared to embrace.

"You are my life now," she said, picking up Ruth and kissing her with a feverish desperation. There seemed to be something faintly wrong. Perhaps it was her guilt and anxiety, she decided, and resolved to ask Mrs. Anna in the morning.

Sunday morning arrived routinely with the usual fuss of child caring, yet she listened carefully to Ruth's breathing. *There's something wrong! It's not my imagination or guilt or foolish fear after all. No, there's something really wrong!*

"Aunt Anna," Miriam said, "I think Ruth's getting a cold!"

Mrs. Anna seemed oblivious, saying, "Oh, well, let's change her linens." And so they put on fresh linens and quickly fed Ruth some more warm goat's milk, then placed her in Miriam's arms for rocking by the hot stove.

Later, with Ruth asleep, Miriam asked Mrs. Anna again if she thought there was anything wrong.

"Yes, well, she doesn't seem quite right, dear."

Perhaps it was the wedding reception. By going there, Miriam had destroyed the rhythm of her visits, she feared, as remorse fell upon her like a great stone. She told Mrs. Anna this.

Mrs. Anna said, "No, dear, that's not fair. It's just the war; it poisons everything, causes so much suffering. I only wish it could end. It has taken my dear Vanya and so many sons like him. How terrible it all is," she said, putting her hand to her forehead. "Oh, how I wish to God it would end. I pray for that every day. I worry so much."

"Isaac? You worry about Isaac?"

"Yes, of course, I worry about Isaac. I worry about them all, each and every one. We're sacrificing a generation, a whole generation," Mrs. Anna said quietly, dropping her right hand into her lap, where the left grasped it in a concerned and agitated double-fist.

Life for Miriam turned increasingly bitter as the anxiety worked incessantly like a venomous yeast in her soul, giving rise to a whole host of horrid misgivings that had only been briefly buried by Zakti's betrothal. By the next weekend Ruth had developed a stubborn cold. She would not eat and could just barely breathe. The nurse was summoned and then the doctor. Miriam was assured that everything was being done—that all would be well. "All that can be done will be done," said the doctor with reassurances that were by no means reassuring.

When the third weekend came, things were a little better. Ruth ate and was breathing more easily. Then a few days passed, and she quit eating again. Dr. Kasparova muttered something about "diarrhea." She proved correct. It came quickly, in a brown flood, like a hemorrhage of darkest blood from a fatal wound.

"Yes, I'm very worried about Ruth, my dear," Mrs. Anna said with an exasperated sigh, leaning over the cradle opposite Miriam. "I worry about everyone. You. Me. Yes, I worry. I worry about Isaac and Ruth, and most of all I worry about you, my dear, precious Miriam. I worry about us all," she said, reaching out and pulling Miriam into her breast like her other self.

28

A Letter

Suddenly the world appeared strangely inside out and upside down. Things had improved, yet somehow seemed very much worse. The Allies were clearly winning the war but now were stymied. Ruth seemed to be developing yet losing weight. Her eyelashes were long and beautiful on her pale cheeks, and her eyes were evermore luminous and searching, while her body had shrunk. Miriam gained Isaac then lost him—gained Ruth and now seemed to be losing her. It seemed to Miriam that her efforts always came to nothing. Now she and Mrs. Anna rarely spoke—words were too painful—so they gradually retreated into silence.

Dr. Kasparova, previously so reassuring, now was always solemn. She said, "We can only hope and pray, my friends. Little Ruth is seven weeks old, but she is growing weaker. We are doing everything we can. Ruth is doing everything she can. Poor thing, she's fighting. But it is not good, not good at all, my dear. You must be brave."

That Sunday Miriam could not tear herself away from Ruth. She studied her sleeping face, stroked her cheeks, hands, and head, and whispered into her ear as if she could understand every word. For her part, Mrs. Anna moved softly and unobtrusively around the house, cleaning, stirring, trying to bring brightness and order without intruding.

Pjotr found everyone weeping when he came to take Miriam to town in the evening. He tried very hard to be stronger than he really was. "My dear Mrs. Anna, don't worry," he said bravely. "Darling Miriam, please, please, all will be well. You'll see. Yes. All will be well. It'll come right in the end. Please, come now, don't worry," he said, trying to expiate the grief of their parting.

The next day Miriam received a note to come at once to the doctor's clinic. Breathless, she bounded up the stairs, bursting in, to find a very glum Dr. Kasparova waiting at her desk. "The diarrhea is back, worse than before," she said without a greeting or attempting a smile. "I've ordered that she be brought to the hospital. Of course, we are very worried."

"Worried?" asked Miriam, knowing full well that Dr. Kasparova had never stopped worrying.

"Yes, dear, worried about dehydration. It's a serious concern with diarrhea." Then in the teeth of Miriam's silence, she stood and said, reaching out for her, touching her elbow, "Come, my dear, come home with me now for a quick dinner. Then we'll go to the hospital. But you must be strong," she said, turning away with a certain nervous abruptness while pretending to busy herself with a file.

Miriam had been at Dr. Kasparova's house before. The Kasparovs were indeed a mystery. Jews from Leningrad, Miriam knew this but little else. There was a Mr. Kasparov working at the film studio, someone said, and Miriam wondered if this was her friend's husband. Was he making propaganda, "Soviet realism," as someone would tag it? They also had a married son whose name never arose, but there was a photograph of a young man on a table. *Perhaps yet again I'm a substitute for a lost child*, Miriam thought. There was clearly an absence present, an unspoken something that Miriam dared not tread upon, so she said nothing.

That particular day at Dr. Kasparova's house, the two of them ate quietly. In this wintry silence her friend saw the unanswerable questions writ large upon Miriam's face. Then they went to the hospital, where Ruth lay sleeping in a white basket with Mrs. Anna sitting grave-faced at her side.

"She can't eat, Miriam. They're feeding her through tubes. Just look! What can we do?" Mrs. Anna said, then with an anxious hesitation, reached out for Miriam.

Dr. Kasparova sat Miriam down, lifted Ruth from the basket, and placed her in Miriam's lap. "Let her know you're here, Miriam. Believe me, she'll know it," she said, touching the child's head with a kiss before leaving.

Miriam returned each night that week. The three of them—Mrs. Anna, Dr. Kasparova, and Miriam—sat with Ruth every evening. Together they watched through the long nights. Exhausted, Miriam would crawl into bed in search of some brief, haunted, ever-fitful sleep—the kind she was so used to, upon which she had subsisted since Czernowitz.

But she could not be excused from work and so arrived each morning to translate German into Russian and Russian again into

German—back and forth, back and forth. She didn't mind; in fact it was a kind of balm. Greedily she grabbed each document like an addict and wrote feverishly, her mind racing between the two languages. All of her worries, all of her frightful imaginings were hidden behind a mental door, as it were, locked out securely for a moment as language turned the key and closed off a threatening world behind her by creating a special refuge among words.

Each evening she would return and lift Ruth from her basket, comfort Mrs. Anna, and receive comfort in turn. It all had long since moved past comment. She'd pull up her chair next to Mrs. Anna and sit beside her quietly, their knees touching, near Ruth's basket, their arms linked. Then one Saturday night after midnight, Dr. Kasparova entered and whispered in a tone of quiet authority, "Miriam, I'm sending Mrs. Anna home tomorrow. She must sleep. She's exhausted. You'll stay here until Monday morning, till Pjotr comes. He'll drive Mrs. Anna back here early. Then you'll get to work on time. I'll bring you blankets and food so that you can stay. You both must stay strong; you must sit in shifts to spell your strength."

The next morning, Sunday, Mrs. Anna roused herself to leave and then sat back down and choked out a sob. "Oh, Miriam!" she gasped, as they embraced again. "I can't leave. I must remain with you!"

"No, you must leave," Miriam insisted. "Dr. Kasparova has ordered it. You have no choice. You're worn out. You must go home and rest, please, you must, please, please."

Mrs. Anna nodded, stood unsteadily, and exited slowly without speaking.

That Sunday Miriam alone held Ruth, nurturing and touching her. Incredibly, Miriam, sleepless, arrived the next morning at work and began her frantic translations. Everyone cautioned her about becoming ill again, but she shrugged them off. They wanted to know what was happening, but she again brushed this aside, saying, "Mrs. Anna's infant is gravely ill. The poor dear that was left on the steps, very premature," she added. She must help her, she said, and they seemed to believe her.

"Don't take it so hard," one of them offered. "It's not yours; such children are dying every day all over Russia, it'll be just one more. After all, what's one more dead child in this war?"

Miriam stared back in dismay but said nothing, turned, and quickly began to devour her work like a famished animal.

That night she returned to the hospital and stayed until dawn, but at the office she was so tired that she fell asleep over her work before she was sent home. Instead, she ran back to Ruth, where she found Mrs. Anna sitting in abject silence. She took Miriam's hand and sat her down by the little basket. Now Miriam had a fantasy of retreating into her daughter's body and lending her own strength. Maybe she could sacrifice herself, just as her mother had done for her, save Ruth in the same way she had been saved.

Then she felt Isaac in the room. He was there, she knew it. But Miriam felt so terribly helpless. She could not help Isaac, David, Deborah, Ruth, nor anyone at all. She could hardly help herself. She was useless. She stared down at Ruth with a hypnotic intensity, trying to match her own breathing with the shallow breaths of the child, inhaling each one as though into Ruth's lungs—filling them, up and down, with her own life. She was transferring all of her vitality into Ruth's little body through this concentration of power. Then she noticed that people had stopped coming. There were no more consultations, nurses, doctors, visitors, or changing of linens or IVs.

They were left alone.

Finally, Dr. Kasparova came in very quietly. She touched Miriam softly and spoke to her. Ruth was again laid softly in her lap. Then Ruth opened her eyes and stared deeply into Miriam's, as if to say, "Hold me, remember me, memorize my face. Emblazon me into your mind. Burn me deep into your soul forever and ever. Never forget me. I love you," she said finally with her eyes and then closed them. She shuddered, and the breathing stopped. The room was strangely cold. It was February 29, 1944.

Miriam remembered nothing afterward. She could not tell how long it had been without remembering. She did not know what had happened, where she had gone, or what had been said. Unexpectedly, she found herself at work, translating. She awoke and was still translating. It was always the same in such moments. They or it or God or the Thing or whatever it was had done for her what she could not do for herself. There was a voice that woke her and whispered gently, "It's time to quit, Miriam. You've done enough. Your work is finished today. There's someone outside for you."

Miriam raised her eyes to see her boss standing across from her. "Thank you," she said softly and went out to find Dr. Kasparova waiting by a black automobile. In silence, they rode to Mrs. Anna's. Pjotr and Mrs. Anna came and led her from the car. They walked slowly back to the winter garden, where waiting for her was a mound of frozen ground beside a dark hole that seemed larger than it really was. Next to it Isaac's old blanket lay folded over a tiny wooden box like a flag of honor. Without speaking, Pjotr lowered the box into the earth with a pair of ropes, paused, slipped free and laid aside the ropes, then handed the blanket to Miriam. She clutched it to her breast as she released a quick sob and then was silent while clods of dirt were shoveled over her daughter's coffin.

Mrs. Anna crossed herself and embraced Miriam. She led her to Isaac's bed and then covered her with the blanket that had once covered Isaac and Ruth. Miriam remembered nothing and awoke thinking, *I need to go back to work. I must work.*

"You must rest," said Mrs. Anna.

"No, I must work. What day is it?"

"A Thursday it seems, but who knows? I certainly don't."

She worked non-stop for three days. She remembered nothing except the mania of translation—German to Russian, Russian to German—and again, over and over. Like a chess player gone mad within the world of the 64 squares, she went mad within the walls of words. Her mind labored in quick shifts back and forth between the two languages, the translations piling up all neat and perfect without mistakes, written in her beautiful, precise hand, each word exuding a kind of exquisite solace for her as she treasured each one, putting them in just their right place, with just the right syntax, giving them their right meaning. They were her friends and the only thing she had left— the only thing she could control. She did not have Deborah or David or Isaac or Ruth or anyone. She only had words, these beautiful Russian and German words, which now she caressed delicately with the greatest of care, sliding them into their proper place like a grandmaster moving his pieces adroitly over the board.

A few days later, Sunday, she returned to the grave. Someone had placed flowers in the snow that peeked up bravely as if spring struggled to be born. *Where did they get such flowers?* Then she realized they were artificial. People came, neighbors offering comfort, bringing gifts of food for the table. And Pjotr was there, surveying the house and garden, doing unbidden jobs for Mrs. Anna, placing more faux flowers upon the little mound of frozen earth.

In time Miriam began to eat, again nibbling, swallowing without difficulty, gradually recovering. Then she found herself at her translation desk, thinking again of Romania and Czernowitz—home— images of her parents with the little princess, her dog, the ice rinks, the trips to the Carpathians and the bear that had chased her into Deborah's arms. She saw her parents returning to their apartment, arranging things like before, and even wrote them a letter asking that they send for her so she could come home, too. She placed it into an envelope and then into a dispatch stack. "Make it so. Make it so," she said. "Deliver this to Deborah and David Kellerman in Czernowitz, Bukovina, so I can go home," she said, rather like a prayer.

Then she hurriedly wrote other letters, scratching out one to Isaac's parents at their old address and to their family friend, Herr Oberlander, at his old house, and, of course, one to Peppi. She wrote everyone, chattering on about gossip as if it were a normal, friendly letter from a relative. She asked them, "Have my parents returned? Have you seen or heard of my mother, or cousins, or my father's brothers? Please write back by return post," she said.

Incredibly she even got an answer. Herr Oberlander wrote from somewhere in the Soviet Union—he had escaped! "My dearest Miriam, I have heard nothing of your parents. Some have escaped from the Ghetto. I've made several inquiries of those few who returned. They do not know your parents' fate. You know, of course, that many have died; many were sent farther east and were never heard from again. Still, without any definite word, I understand you will want to search for any information. Please come see me. If you can arrange it, I will assist you in any way I can. You'll be like a daughter to me, and my new home will be at your disposal. Yours truly."

The door closed once more; she imagined herself leaving her parents' apartment in Czernowitz, again she saw Isaac leaving Mrs. Anna's house, yet again she saw the nurse leaving Ruth lying lifeless in her little white basket, and still again she saw the earth falling on the wooden box, filling up the hole in the garden.

In May, Mrs. Anna came for her. She found herself at her door again, Mrs. Anna reaching out to her, she thought, to take her to visit the grave. But she took her to a table where a letter on official army stationery lay, which screamed at her as she sat. Mrs. Anna picked it up in a trembling hand, opened it, and nervously laid it on her lap. Miriam stared at the wall, her heart fluttering and pounding in such dizzying circles as to admit no breath. She could not read it. She let the thing lie on her lap and then finally fall to the floor. She did not pick it up. They both knew what it said.

The next day Miriam requested to be sent away, and her wish was granted. In a few days she left Alma-Ata as an army junior lieutenant determined to fight, to kill those who had killed Isaac and Ruth and maybe Deborah and David. She was no longer sad; she was angry; she wanted revenge. Peace was impossible—the only place to go now was to the front.

29

The Front

In a small, shot-up stone house, Junior Lieutenant Miriam Kellerman squatted below a shattered window. A German automatic chattered in the near distance; somewhat closer, a Soviet answered. This quarrel continued off and on but hushed after distant artillery seemed to grumble them into silence.

A stillness fell over the little battlefield until Junior Lieutenant Kellerman lifted her megaphone to the windowsill and spoke clearly and distinctly, her words echoing oddly around her: "Give up your arms! The German army is facing certain defeat. You have fought bravely, but the war is lost for you. Everyone sees it. It makes no sense to continue to fight and die anymore. Don't you want to see your loved ones again? Surrender now before it's too late, before you are killed. Everywhere your comrades are surrendering; you can join them and live to go home. You'll not be harmed, you'll not be mistreated. Surrender immediately! Do not throw your life away for nothing. Surrender now! It is the only sensible course! Throw down your arms, and you will not be harmed."

Hunkering beneath the window, she lowered the speaker, shocked as always by the reverberating sound of her own voice. She hesitated, turned, and looked at the officer kneeling nearby. The effect of her own words, of a young woman's, embracing men at war like a caress, was always very strange. *It must seem incongruous to the Germans, she thought, to hear such a soft, youthful, feminine sound. Perhaps it brings to mind a lover or a sister or a wife speaking sweetly in perfect German.* But she could not tell from their own soldiers dug in nearby that it had any effect; they seemed to expect nothing from it at all.

Yesterday she had been taken to a log bunker forward of the regimental headquarters. There she had spent the night, then after a quick breakfast of hot tea, hard rye bread, and a cigarette, she was led quietly along a communication trench to this building on the edge of a forest. Her guide, a lance corporal, handed her off silently to Captain Antonov. He was waiting by this clearing, which now, with the coming of first light, revealed itself as nothing but a patch of black mud and dirty snow breaking up a stand of *beryoza* trees. Together they stood in the darkness, shivering till the sun, gradually, unwillingly it seemed, lifted itself above the forest, illuminating the setting like a stage light on a new act of an old tragedy.

Antonov had whispered to her. "The bastards pulled back a bit, but they're still here, I'm sure of it, camouflaged over there, in that tree line," he said, pointing, "laying low, hoping we'll think they're gone."

It was clear the Germans had been in a hurry, leaving helmets, packs, empty cans, and the corpse of a comrade lying only a few feet in front of the house, its lower half covered by the mud and snow. Now Miriam looked more closely at the body with its torso twisted over, appearing to awaken and greet the sun. It was a boy about her age, staring in frozen amazement at the light lifting warmly over the trees. She averted her gaze.

"We had better get down now," the captain had said as it brightened. They had hunkered down and shared a cigarette until he told her to speak to the enemy.

Miriam was truly a soldier now, but her job was to shoot words and not bullets. At first, it had been the Germans who spoke on loudspeakers, asking the Russians to surrender; but after Stalingrad, the languages had reversed, the losers' voices going silent. The Germans were retreating. The balance had shifted.

"Never surrender to the Germans, better to die," everyone had said. But the Germans were surrendering more and more.

For Miriam, one day was much like another. She would come to the front during a lull and repeat the propaganda over and over, then move on and do it again, shooting her words into Nazi morale. In fact, Junior Lieutenant Kellerman had quickly become an enthusiastic soldier of the Red Army. She was fighting the war that Isaac had died in, and like Isaac, she had found purpose in it. She was no longer a pitiful, helpless, Romanian evacuee but a willing part of the Soviet Union's victorious army. *It sometimes seems as if my entire life has been a preparation for this,* she sometimes found herself thinking.

Today, as she listened to the heavy silence, she heard a bird singing somewhere. *How could there be a bird? How could it have survived? And why is it singing?* she wondered as she listened until Captain Antonov interrupted her thoughts by growling in an undertone.

"Sorry?" she asked quietly.

"Let's go," he said louder, turned and dipped out, dropping into a little trench that let them disappear into the forest floor like a pair of moles. Lugging the megaphone, she followed for about a mile until they reached a shallow trench that twisted them back to the front line again—another break in the trees—to direct more wonderful German at the Wehrmacht. She did this for the remainder of the morning.

In the afternoon she returned to headquarters to interrogate prisoners. Except for the dead boy, these were the first Germans she had seen all day. The attitudes were always the same: the boys were afraid and knew little, whereas the officers were arrogant and knew more than they wanted to admit. She had been instructed exactly what to say and what to reply, and, of course, her interpretation must be done without editing or changes. She did this coldly, without sympathy, maintaining a certain hardness; she never wanted to know them or think about them.

Be ruthless. They're all going to die anyway in slave labor; few will survive. Think how they have treated us—the villages, the millions. Don't sympathize, they are Nazis, never forget! Don't look into the frightened, questioning eyes of the young ones, don't think of their mothers and fathers. They are all killers, they deserve no sympathy or mercy, she told herself over and over. She could see the Stukas, her rapist, her parents' tormentors in these men, whose words she funneled back through herself to the Russians with a kind of bitter diligence. And, always, despite being surrounded by people, she felt totally alone, waging a solitary, personal war. She never complained or spoke the names of her dead to anyone, but nothing else really mattered. *Death was the simplest thing in the world, like the dead boy in the clearing covered in fresh snow and old mud, as if placed there by some dark hand whose fingers of light and palm of shadow slowly lifted away to reveal his dead face.*

Most of the Germans she interrogated were common soldiers like the dead boy. They were faceless, interchangeable. They came in a blur and seemed to be all of a piece. The Germans had been told what to say to the predictable questions, so the same questions and same answers were asked repeatedly thousands of times. People were numb. Her superiors were benumbed from sheer repetition, but they were told that this is what they had to do, and so they did it. While senseless, the effort of questioning and answering, like killing and dying, was done without real complaint. Everyone, especially the most intelligent and sensitive, knew it was not so much a necessary evil as a necessary absurdity.

The Red Army interrogators were really on a big fishing expedition, seeking a bit here and a bit there. "One story is anecdote; several anecdotes are data," went the joke. The more interesting prisoners—officers and high members of the SS—were sent immediately to Army headquarters or Moscow Center for "special" interrogation. Those who were foolish enough to admit fighting the partisans or citizens were eventually shot, especially the SS or Gestapo. But no special questions were permitted about the Jews.[37] The few times that Miriam questioned officers were invariably disdainful because she truly hated them, but she could never hate those like the dead boy. It was only the "special" ones she loathed; they alone were responsible. As for the common soldiers, few saw Germany again. They knew and always had that same pitiful look of exhausted despair. But she couldn't help thinking that the dead boy, lying as in expectation that the sun might thaw out his tears, was somehow better off—better than those living, breathing, and suffering in a disappointed and ever deferred hope of going home.

When in Alma-Ata, Miriam mostly slept, but her place at the translators' table was kept waiting, and she would go there and work until ordered back to the front again. Too, she found time on Sundays for Mrs. Anna. She noticed that time was doing strange things to her; she would go to Ruth's grave and find it seemed both older and almost as new as the day they had covered her with dirt and false flowers. She went to lay fresh spring flowers over those that Mrs. Anna had planted there.

She and Mrs. Anna spoke two languages now. There was the silent one that required no words and a stranger one that spoke of the future, whatever that was. After the war, that dream-like time that must come, one supposed, they would become different. The war had brought them together, and, of course, it would separate them forever.

"You must go on, Miriam. You are young; you'll love again, live again. You must go on. You're not the first to lose a child," Mrs. Anna said with more than a hint of irony. "Think of the future," she said. "Some do not; they give up. Don't despair, you're too young for that, my dear. Never despair; we have a duty never to despair."

Miriam would nod, realizing that Mrs. Anna's situation was far worse than her own. *I must not give in to self-pity*, insisted an inner voice. *Mrs. Anna is right. I must not despair, not ever.*

"Do not shut the door on people, Miriam. Don't be a recluse. Listen. Help those around you," she would say. "In that way you change the world. It's the only way to change anything."

Too, there was always the good Dr. Kasparova. *Another mother figure*, she would laugh with self-mockery. She would ask Miriam what only a mother would ask. "Where do you go in the evening? Whom do you see? What did you talk about? What friends have you made?" and so on, just like Deborah.

Miriam would fill in as best she could, but she was an army officer now. She was no longer a child, much less a substitute for a lost one. Following Mrs. Anna's advice, sometimes she would spend time with Marina's daughter or listen patiently to her other friends at the translator office. She would even visit her German students. But somehow these old friendships were unsustainable. Her nerves were too raw—she was not the same.

Miriam Kellerman quite simply was not good company, for her mind often wandered and her conversation was discursive. To her embarrassment she sometimes would ask questions only to realize she had not been listening, and often she would have to force her mind back to the chatter of ordinary conversation in which she had no real interest. Her mind remained at the front with her new comrades, her new friends.

One evening, she found Aljona's son, Doto, alone, playing on his bed. She read to him several stories and spoke about his future. He made her promise that she would not go away until he was fast asleep, so she sat in his room, reading to him as Deborah had done so many times to her. At last, he fell into that innocent, death-like sleep that she had ever envied since Czernowitz; only then was she free to leave.

While in Alma-Ata, she went to visit an extended family called the Schulmans, whose children she had tutored. She found that Estelle Ambramovna, the grandmother, was its sheet anchor, a short but graceful woman in her seventies. Estelle lived with her daughter, Carla Mikhailovna, and Carla's husband, Isaac Schulman, in a fine, spacious cottage on the grounds of the oil refinery. Their daughter, Alina, also lived in the cottage with her Russian husband, Pavel Andrejevich, and their little daughter, Natasha.

Pavel was the reason for their prosperity. He was a tall, handsome, capable chemical engineer working as the mill manager, with his father-in-law as its director. Alina was a chemist, and she and Carla, teachers, now also worked at the mill. The family enjoyed a high status, indeed.

On her first leave Miriam was invited to dinner, so she put on her best uniform, shined her boots, and polished her few medals to appear a fine-looking soldier, even though, of course, she had somewhat long hair and still managed to wear some lipstick. Miriam Kellerman, officer in the Red Army! Quite a figure she was! Everywhere people respected her; she was a veteran, a *frontovik* to them, a step up in the hierarchy of the Soviet state, and the uniform worked wonders. Outwardly, at least, she was no longer an outsider, no longer a pitiful creature fleeing for its life. *No one wants to be pitied, only respected*, she told herself. *To hell with pity!*

"You must come to Natasha's fourth birthday dinner," Ambramovna had insisted. The family had greeted her not just as a hero in the "war against fascism" but as a long-lost daughter. There was an air of excitement that reminded her of the Blumenthals. It was overwhelming. She tried hard not to think of Ruth, of how she had literally vanished before her eyes like Isaac, nor about her parents. She tried not to envy the health of Natasha, who looked so well, living happily with such loving parents and family, all well-fed, all quite optimistic.

My loved ones are all corpses, have come to nothing, like Ruth or the boy in the clearing, staring at a sun that seemed loath to look on yet another such face, turning to welcome its warm touching of the trees. By force of will she banished these thoughts, and under the warmth of the wine and candlelight found a smile, as if she had never thought of anything unpleasant at all. Resentment soon reasserted itself so powerfully that she was disgusted at her disloyalty to this beautiful family who had paid her the great compliment of sharing this moment. *How terrible to poison her soul with jealously! How ungrateful! How petty! How very wrong!*

But it was a struggle, and she politely excused herself and returned to her apartment. The experience had been searingly painful. "I must get back to the front!" she said out loud, striding about her room like a wild creature locked in a cage.

It was shocking to realize, but Miriam simply could not endure happy families anymore. Indeed, she hated them. She was more comfortable with her army comrades, more comfortable with war than with peace. Bourgeois happiness was unbearable. Speaking inwardly she said, *I know I'm a prisoner of my own regrets. Yes, I understand now why Isaac had to return. It's the honesty of it: the front is straightforward, it's without any illusions of hope and happiness in an unhappy world. The front is my only reality, my family, my life! I have nothing else! I am nothing else! I must return to my home! There at the front, with its living and its walking dead, are my truest comrades and friends!*

But the front was changing, moving ever westward, and Miriam was to be transferred to a unit almost in Berlin. Things were marching rapidly to a conclusion; Germany was finished. With new orders, she returned once more to Alma-Ata for 48 hours, enough to close her apartment and say her goodbyes.

Zakti was the first friend to greet her. She did not look quite well; she was pregnant. Zakti pregnant! Miriam congratulated her with hugs and tears. Zakti complimented Miriam on going to Berlin. "What a great honor! You are a hero!" she said, then gave her an extra clothing coupon and insisted on taking her to a special shop for ladies' clothes. Miriam knew she should not go into such a store, reserved as it was for wives of commissars, apparatchiks, and high-ranking officers. Zakti was undeterred and took her anyway.

Zakti marched in and demanded, "My friend needs a nice silk dress. She'll be traveling to Berlin soon with our army. The dress must be of the finest cloth in the very best style."

Miriam walked out with an order for a new silk dress. She was astounded by how easy it was! To be picked up tomorrow!

The other goodbyes were another matter. She dreaded seeing the Schulmans, but they seemed to understand, even the pain of their happy life. Miriam was embraced and congratulated and sent on her way with all the tearful sentimentality for which Russians are famous.

Surprisingly, Dr. Kasparova's farewell was more awkward, even self-conscious. A kind of settled sorrow showed in her friend when, with a hint of doubt, she asked quietly if Miriam would write.

"Yes, of course," said Miriam, "but I'll be on the move, you know? No one is certain about a new assignment, especially since the war is ending and everything is up in the air so, but, yes, yes, for sure I will write."

"Then all will be well, my dear. You'll see. I will write, too, I promise," said the doctor with a weak smile as she reached out for Miriam.

I'll never see her again, Miriam thought as she hugged Dr. Kasparova. *I have sensed this before. Some friendships go on, some do not, and now we both seem to know this one is ending.*

Miriam, in deepest anguish, turned away for Mrs. Anna's, finding her standing in the doorway already taking refuge in her tears. They embraced as they chatted, walking back to the grave for a moment's grief. Finally, Miriam, in a near delirium, found herself again in Isaac's bedroom. Here they sat, holding hands and silently remembering. Eventually, Pjotr dropped by. He wept, struggled for control, tried to speak but could not. There was nothing anyone could say.

They drank tea, munched a little stale cake, and mumbled a farewell so tearful that for Miriam it almost equaled Czernowitz. Mercifully, her ride came, but they burst out crying again. In leaving Mrs. Anna, Miriam was losing her only real second mother, her daughter, her husband, and everything that was dear.

Mrs. Anna cried out that Miriam was the last of her children, her last tie to a future. "How could this also be taken from me?" she gasped. "I have nothing now—the earth has swallowed up all my hopes! Taken Vanya, Ruth, and now you!"

In the end we have nothing, everything is taken, Miriam wanted to say as she heard these words, but instead said tenderly, "Don't despair, my dearest Mrs. Anna. All will be well. I shall return; we will meet again."

The next morning, after a broken, exhausting sleep, she said sad but very quick goodbyes to Aljona and Doto and the translation office. Then it was off to the station, where thankfully her train was gathering steam. As she boarded, she sensed she would never see Alma-Ata, Mrs. Anna, or any of her friends again. Settling in her seat, the fingers of her memory flipped the pages of her recent past quickly and then closed them like a chapter of a book. She was determined to look forward to the next ones entitled *Moscow* and *Berlin*.

30

My Brother

Junior Lieutenant Kellerman sat on a train re-reading a letter from a friend. His name was Nathan Friedlander. He had good news:

"*Your inquiry about Karl was forwarded to me, Miriam. You're right that all of us from the Odessa Institute ended up in the Technical University here in Tashkent, but Karl is no longer here. You know how particular Karl is. The university here was not up to his standards. He managed to make his way to Moscow and is studying now at the Moscow Polytech Institute for Construction Engineering. I know you will have no difficulty in locating him there.*

"*Now that the war is almost over, I can tell you about our experiences in Tashkent. Karl had a great deal of trouble here, all related to me, I'm sorry to say! The problem started with food stamps. We students were issued food stamps only as long as we were studying and doing well. When I failed some important examinations, my food stamps were cut, and I was thrown out of the dormitory where Karl and I stayed. Your brother, as always, was doing well in his studies, despite working every night at a bakery loading bread in vans. I began sleeping in the streets or on a bench in the railway station, but I had no food. Karl was always able to get a loaf or two from the bakery, so he gave me his ration card for a few weeks until I could get myself reinstated.*

"*I was sleeping at the train station when the militia conducted a raid looking for draft dodgers. They found the identification papers on me saying Nathan Friedlander and a ration card for Karl Kellerman. I was in big trouble! They thought I was a spy! Both of us were arrested. When they questioned him, he explained he had lost the card and had not reported it because it was his fault, and there was only a half-month left on the card, so he could survive without it. When I was interrogated, I explained that I had found the card near the college. We were both released!*

"*Your brother was a straight A student with a night job, but as for me, well, let's just say I was lucky enough to be reinstated soon afterward. I learned my lesson. I have been studying very hard since. I'm now 'living up to my potential,' as they say.*

"Say hello to Karl when you see him. Tell him that my uncle is helping me find an engineering job. I will write to him when I get started. Also tell him that I, too, am planning to marry. Our wives are friends, so we will have to remain friends!

"Yours, Nathan"

Miriam had received Nathan's letter just before getting her orders, but she was still absorbing this about Karl—it was big news for a person with a small family. Maybe they might rebuild everything together.

She dropped the letter and looked out the window at the flat countryside rolling past. It was only then she realized that her post-war life had nearly begun. *A post-war life?! My God! The war is really over! Hitler defeated! Berlin and the Reich in ruins! Is it truly possible? I can't believe it! I can't believe I'm on a train inching via the steppe to Moscow. It's a real passenger train—clean, well-run—and I'm wearing a nice, clean uniform, with medals even and shoulder boards, and I even have a seat with a window to myself. I am an officer in the Soviet Army, with orders and rubles in my pocket, posted to the greatest German city of them all. How can it be?*

Miriam was afraid Karl might still be aloof, still be the great student who had always thought of her as a dunce. *Will he really want to see me?! Shall I tell him about Isaac or Ruth?* Perhaps, like so much else, it would simply stay sealed tightly within her, locked away. After all, they belonged to her exclusively, while Karl now belonged to his wife and to what children he might have. Perhaps she should keep them separate, hidden away as her own private possession.

It was getting late, and she now found the view boring: field after field, crossing after crossing, village after village. She pulled a blanket up to her throat and daydreamed about meeting Karl in Moscow. He would be waiting, so she decided to sleep and dream of him as she approached the fabulous city. She had never been to Moscow or to Berlin; and she had not seen Karl in four years. Four years?! It seemed so much longer! It seemed like four centuries, four millennia!

The train rattled on through the night. She slept. Then some hand seemed to tug at her, and the vague awareness of the hustle and bustle in anticipation of a stop woke her. She sat up, looked around—she was in the environs. She watched buildings, tracks, trains, and backs of factories click steadily by till the train crept slowly into Moscow's Kazan station. *Click, click, click*—slower and slower—*click, click, click.* Now a madhouse pulled into view: people, soldiers, and evacuees were chattering, hugging, saying their goodbyes, swarming in an almost surreal swirl. But it had a different air—one of victory and confidence rather than defeat and panic.

Then there was the rude jolt of a stop. Beneath her window was the pandemonium of the station, a veritable sea of people. She heard the official P.A. voice crackling out various trains and schedules. She scanned the crowd, got up, and wormed her way forward until she stepped down onto the pavement. There he was—Karl, waiting for her, smiling. Karl! Standing there! Waving and smiling! Karl and Miriam Kellerman meeting in Moscow in May 1945! Survivors of the Holocaust![38] Survivors of Hitler's genocide!

Karl saw his little sister standing there in a uniform, and now she saw him, too, smiling as if to say, "We did it, little sister, didn't we, my dear?! We did it!" They positively lunged into each other's arms. They wept, of course. Wept and wept. She had never seen Karl weep so, but he did, sobbing like the child she had never known.

Speechless at first, they were at last able to rattle on as they weaved through the confusion, pushing through until finally freeing themselves by finding an empty bench across the street. Breathless, they sat. Miriam threw down her pack, folded her little army "fore-and-aft" cap away, and gave Karl another great, long hug. He fumbled out sandwiches from somewhere, and they ate, laughing, and talking madly. "Tell me! Tell me! Tell me!" Miriam said. "Karl, how have you been? Nathan wrote me and told me you were married. Tell me all about it. Tell me about your wife. Tell me everything!" she said breathlessly, the words coming in a great gush. There was simply too much to be said, asked, and known, so Miriam chattered on till Karl finally hushed her with two fingers pressed softly to her lips.

"My wife and I are very happy, Miriam. Osya, that's her name, is a top student at the Moscow College of Chemistry. It's internationally accredited, you know. She has a room in the dormitory. You'll be staying with her tonight, but soon we'll have our own apartment. It's difficult, but we'll have it. The strain on the bureaucracy here is incredible. You wouldn't believe it! Everyone needs an apartment! Everyone wants an apartment!" he said, throwing up his hands. "Everyone has to wait; it's terrible."

"I know," said Miriam. "It's the same everywhere."

"How about you? Tell me about you," he asked.

Miriam spoke quickly of her escape, giving him little more than an outline. She talked more about Alma-Ata, being a translator and then an army interpreter, and how fortunate she had been. She had said something about her "other living situations," and Karl politely cross-questioned her. He knew she had suffered. She briefly outlined her escape but said nothing of Isaac, Ruth, Mrs. Anna, Dr. Kasparova, and nothing about the rape. Neither did she mention seeing his train but knew he must know and was relieved he said nothing.

When she spoke of frostbite, Karl examined her hands, taking the one that did not hold the sandwich and looking closely, expertly, like one who knew such things only too well. He saw the discoloration. She could not fool him. She would never be able to fool people about that. Everyone noticed her hands and knew. At least in Russia, everyone knew about frostbite—about that no one was ever deceived.

Then Karl glanced away to see if they were being watched—it reminded Miriam of that moment with Isaac in Czernowitz, sitting furtively in that little park with the fountain and the policeman pretending to read as they spoke of love and hope. She sighed and studied Karl with a fearful look, as he grimaced in that special way he had and said, "Miriam, I will not stay in the Soviet Union long. I must get out. I hate it here! First chance, I'm leaving! I will bide my time, of course. You know me, always cautious. I'll wait, be patient, but I'm determined to leave this damn benighted country." He said this last sentence through clenched teeth in a loud whisper, with the deepest possible feeling.

Miriam looked around, but no one was watching. They appeared to be just another couple of lovers, sitting on a bench like she had once sat in the shadows with Isaac.

Miriam without being told knew that Karl's problems with the Soviet Union were more than just the bureaucracy and its sea of stupidities. His political idealism was disgusted by everything he saw— the lack of freedom, loss of opportunity, and the reactionary nature of a regime that pretended to be so progressive. Karl had no illusions about Marxism or the great workers' state or any of the nonsense. But she had heard no one say it as he had. Everyone was much too afraid.

She remembered Abraham and what had happened to him—she could never forget poor, brilliant Abrasha, shot dead for being a fervent Zionist.

"Then there was Abrasha," he hissed, taking the words from out of her very brain.

"Shot," she whispered.

"No, not shot," said Karl.

"Not shot?! My God! Is he alive?!" Miriam gasped.

"No," Karl said with a sad shake of the head. "He was interrogated and sent to a camp, but he didn't last. They broke him, and he died; pneumonia probably, I'm not sure."

"How do you know this, Karl?" she asked quietly.

"Never mind, I just do. I'll tell you sometime; it's strictly confidential."

She sighed and said softly, "Be careful, Karl, be careful, be very, very careful."

"Oh, yes," he replied. "I'll be careful. I know, I know. I shall be careful, but I shall leave eventually. It's just a matter of time, Miriam; you need to know that."

Miriam knew he meant it. It was not just talk; Karl never just talked. But it was frightening. What would happen to them? Where would they go? What would happen if they failed? Would they be arrested, sent to the camps? Shot? Could they avoid really serious trouble? They were Jews. Everyone in the Soviet Union hung by a thread, but a Jew—every Jew hung by half a thread!

The glow of their rendezvous was suddenly replaced by the chill of fear. It was the same fear that plagued them like a fever—the heat of anxiety and the cold of dread—a disease whose microbes had been burrowed in by Stalin in '40 and Hitler in '41. Fear of the Communists, then fear of the Nazis, fear of everyone but the closest and dearest—fear—fear—fear—fear that would stay with them for the rest of their days and course through their blood like an incurable contagion.

She made a nervous gesture and whispered, "We have to be cautious, dear, very cautious."

He nodded with a distracted look.

"You're all I have now, all I've really got," she said quietly, "you know that?"

Then they spoke of their parents. Karl said he had no hope—that they had perished and that it was foolish to have any illusions.

Miriam said with a trembling voice, "Karl, I know you are probably right, but it's just possible, possible that they have survived,

238

and until I know for sure, a part of me will always cling to that hope, however foolish."

Karl studied her, started to speak but coughed the thought away, and with unconvincing cheerfulness said, "Now, come on, Miriam. Let's go meet Osya."

"Oh, yes," she said, rising. "I have but a few days, then it's off to Berlin."

"Berlin?" he said, turning close to her instead of walking on, obviously surprised.

She quickly outlined her army career as they remained at the bench. He was impressed.

"My little sister has come very far, indeed," he laughed, "from a pampered princess to an officer in the victorious Soviet army with orders to occupied Berlin, no less."

"Are you proud of me then?" she couldn't help asking, swelling up a bit.

"Proud!? Oh, my goodness! What a question! Of course, I am proud of you, my dear, very proud."

Miriam was proud he was proud. *He can see now how much he's underestimated me, the little mathematical dunce, the silly child afraid of imaginary bears. He sees I've changed from the naïve little schoolgirl trying to outrun the Wehrmacht,* she thought, as they crossed the street to the subway station.

The visit with Karl and Osya was limited by a three-day pass and, although Miriam really liked Osya and was excited to see Moscow at last— the Kremlin especially and also a few delightful museums—she found herself thinking, *It's good to feel respected and welcomed, to feel important, but I'm glad to be going.* When it was time, she was shocked by Karl's grief—he was almost paralyzed by it. Finally, after tearful hugs and agonizing smiles, she was off for Berlin, going not as an eager student from Czernowitz but as an occupier of the country that had inflicted so much suffering. *How sweetly bitter my life is now! How unlike anything I've ever dreamed of! How sad! How ironic! How wonderful! How far from that string of pontoons across the Dniester; Proskurov; the girl walking down the track, bleeding out her innocence; the burning towns; the burning people; the boxcars; the farm; the clinic; the starvation; and the cold! Oh, how far, indeed! How so very far I've come!*

Miriam left Moscow's Belyorussia station and proceeded west, following roughly Napoleon's and Hitler's advance and retreat to Smolensk, across the Divina River into Belyorussia itself and hence to Minsk. Here she paused for a few hours, then raced from Brest to Poland, through Warsaw's total ruin, and, finally, at long last, to Berlin. She entered the suburbs. The city was in some ways a summary of the war: some things untouched but others in ruins and rubble—bombed-out buildings standing as shells, rather like Germany's empire. Hitler had invaded her home and ruined her life, but she had survived.

Now he was dead, and his regime lay at her feet as Miriam Kellerman rode into his capital as his conqueror. What a victory! How very just! Such gutted and debased splendor, such hollow success turned to ashes and cinders! Such stupidity! Such greatness had come to nothing!

She came through the Soviet zone with its own peculiar flavor, but while the tension of the war was gone, a new tension had taken its place, that of the uncertainty of the postwar world. *Every ending is a new beginning*, she thought, and certainly the tension in Miriam's life had not abated at all but had merely been transformed.

True enough, she had lived and would go on, and Karl had survived and was making a new life. But no one—Allied, Soviet, or German—seemed quite ready for this peace. War had been such a ubiquitous part of their individual lives and the life of the world that peace had come as a shock, like the war had. Peace? After all, what's that? No one seemed to know. The habit of war was too great, too much a part of daily existence. Could they all now learn the habit of peace after so much habitual war? If so, for how long? Or is it, as Tolstoy implied—*Peace and War, War and Peace*—merely an unending systole and diastole of history, a poignant but perhaps pointless melodrama?

Miriam was 21. She had written Mrs. Anna and Dr. Kasparova from Moscow, sending them gifts with each long letter, but she had heard nothing. Karl was in Moscow, but for how long and then what? When would he escape? Certainly, they would need each other, but it was so hard to stay in touch.

Miriam knew that Karl would try to go to Israel. That was his ultimate destination. He was a Zionist, as he always would be. Other ideas might come and go, but Zionism would remain. She feared that she would lose touch with him. Then, too, if either of them defected, the other would be imperiled. How could they be true to themselves without betraying the other?!

She had not shared her real past with Karl. Not really. She did not tell him for the same reason she did not join him that awful day in the retreat. They were close, but in a sense they would always be alone—separate orphans. Their fate was inexorably linked by an indestructible thread of blood and remembrance, and, like planets, they would always pull at each other from great distances, while struggling and failing to ever be entirely free.

In Berlin she was immediately summoned to headquarters. She was handed orders and shown to modest quarters with some other young women. It was an apartment building with two flats per floor. Their offices were in the same area. Working and living were conveniently close. For Miriam it was luxurious. The young translators in her flat—two from Moscow, one from Leningrad, and the other from Ukraine—did all they could to make do. The largest spaces became bedrooms for two. The third room doubled as a study and a sleeping place for the fifth.

They also had a small kitchen, dining room, and modest living area, which their commanding officer, Lieutenant Colonel Mikhail Andreyevich Golitsyn—a short, unhandsome man possessed of a certain red-faced charm—approved, seeing it as a place for entertainment for the interpreting division. "My command," he called it with obvious self-satisfaction. In fact, he seemed so pleased that he announced they would be getting nicer furniture for "our living area" and for "our dining room." The quality of the new furniture was unlike anything Miriam had ever seen.

She said something about it, and the colonel commented effusively, "Clearly, it once belonged to wealthy but now hapless bourgeois Berliners. When we moved them out and then moved ourselves in, they were sullen but knew enough to count themselves fortunate."

No one around Miriam felt any regret. After all, what would the Germans have done had they won? What had they already done? There was little doubt about that. In any case, losing their apartment and some furniture was the least of the Germans' problems, everyone said.

"To the victors go the spoils," Miriam mumbled, echoing what she had heard so much as to become a daily cliché.

"Exactly!" said Lt. Col. Golitsyn happily.

31

Occupation

In spite of her roommates' glee, the rich apartment with fine furnishings made Miriam a little sad. *Nice things usually bespeak nice people,* an inner voice insisted. *But the Germans started the war and now have to pay the price,* she kept repeating to herself and others, who readily agreed, of course. Another voice said, *Not all Germans supported Hitler. Some were, in fact, his first victims. How do I know these people were Nazis or that they did anything wrong? Maybe they were decent people. How can we be sure?*

"All Germans are guilty," Golitsyn growled as if it were an order. "Treat them all the same, else you'll only be confused. Think what they did in Russia!"

"But who were they really, the family, I mean? And what has become of them?" Miriam replied.

"You think too much," the colonel snapped.

Yet she could not help wondering who the family really was and what had happened to them. However, she did appreciate the comfortable apartment—warm and snug even in the coldest, draftiest weather.

Amazingly, food in post-war Berlin, for the occupiers at least, was abundant, and the translators had a veritable cornucopia from the army store: such unthought-of wonders as black and red caviar, smoked salmon, ham, and cheese—all brought from Moscow. Too, the visitors were plentiful—there were always visitors because the colonel invited all sorts of guests, who in turn brought gifts such as carton upon carton of cigarettes, wine, and chocolates. Miriam loved smoking and drinking strong tea and even stronger coffee, but she was never much of an alcohol drinker and hated vodka, calling it "Russia's national poison."

I feel strangely rich and guilty. Why do I feel so guilty? It must be the apartment. It has been stolen, just as ours was stolen. I know what it's like to have everything taken away, and I have never stolen anything in my life!

Clearly she seemed the only one with these ambivalences, and although they persisted, she rarely gave them voice.

"I hate the Germans," she heard a friend say. "They should all be killed," said another. "Think what they've done!" But these young women, though recently from the trenches of war, thought more of recreation than revenge. They ate food they had never tasted, drank what they had never drunk, and danced as they had never danced before. Yet these pleasures were not quite enough for Miriam, and as their newness wore off, she became increasingly withdrawn.

One day the colonel pulled her aside, saying, "Why are you so quiet? Why do you eat standing up?" Before waiting for an answer, he quickly said, "You don't join in like the others."

Miriam frowned and glanced away without answering.

"The war's over, Miriam. You're young. We've all lost loved ones, all of us. Everyone has suffered; believe me, you're not alone," he lectured. "Get in the swing of things. This is a special time. Things are good for us now. Enjoy yourself, you've earned it! Don't waste yourself moping! Things may never be better than this in your life! Don't always go around waiting for some better and brighter future—that's a great mistake. This, my dear, is the better future! This is yesterday's future right now, and it has gotten as good as it may ever get. My God! You have made it through the worst war in human history! You're alive! You're among friends! You've all you need—food, drink, clothes, a wonderful apartment in a great city at a great time! Enjoy yourself, Miriam! Do you understand? Do your work, of course, but enjoy yourself after it's done! Work hard, play hard. Do you hear me, Junior Lieutenant Kellerman?! Huh? Do you?"

"Is that an order, Comrade Colonel?" she asked with a slight smile.

"Yes, Comrade Junior Lieutenant, indeed, it is! You will cheer up at once, or I will have you shot," he said now with a chuckle. "Now go on with you, and no more moping!" he added with a shooing gesture.

Miriam knew Golitsyn had a point, but, alas, firing squads notwithstanding, *irrational impulses are always impervious to rational objections*, she wanted to tell him. So she remained despondent, although she tried to hide her unhappiness behind a dutiful smile.

Of course, everyone has suffered. Millions have died. Even the Germans have endured terrible things—look at this ruined city! I also know, though he never speaks of it, that his daughter, a nurse, was killed at the front. Does he view me as a daughter? That again?! He's a very sensitive man, too much so for an army colonel. I'm flattered by his concern, and I must say something more to him, so he'll understand, else I'll be in for another lecture.

A few days later she went to him once more and, speaking softly, said, "I was hospitalized twice during the war, sir, once for starvation, another for frostbite. I continue to have pain, and occasionally I'm simply unable to eat very much; at other times, I'm unable to eat at all. Sometimes it's better if I eat standing up, Comrade Colonel, so that's what I do occasionally, I eat standing up; it makes me feel better. And, too, I do it remembering a dear friend who has to eat that way. She has no choice; she ruined her health in the 900 days of the Leningrad siege. In a way, I do it to remember not just her but all those millions who perished there from hunger."

"I see," he said quietly. "I'm sorry."

"Thank you, sir."

"Yes, now I understand you better, and I respect your reasons, even admire them—but you can't eat standing up the rest of your life, now can you, Junior Lieutenant Kellerman?"

"No, sir," she said shyly, glancing away without intending to.

"Then don't do it anymore; that's an order. We have good food now. So I want you to eat more. You have not gained enough weight. I want you to perk up. The war's over," he insisted again. "You must go on living. You've fought; it was your duty to do so. Now it's your duty to live. Your dead would want that; don't let them down, Miriam," he said now wagging a finger as at a naughty student. "Remember and honor the dead, of course, but it's also a duty to go on with one's life. Pay homage to the past, but don't live in it. Besides, that's what they would want, if they were here to speak. So I'm speaking for them, for your dead." Hesitating, he then said, "And my own."

Miriam looked at him with very sad eyes. She had not shared anything with this colonel, and she felt she could not bear to mention Isaac, or Ruth, or her parents. And while he was obviously waiting for an answer, Miriam could see that he was moved by his own words and so she said nothing.

Then he said, speaking into her silence, "I lost my daughter, a nurse, at the front. Everyone has lost someone. Who have you lost?" he insisted with a quiet gentleness.

Miriam hesitated, "Comrade Colonel, my mother, my father, my fiancé." She started to say "my child," but didn't. "My parents were murdered, I think, I'm not sure, anyway disappeared without a trace. My fiancé, an infantry officer, was killed somewhere in the Western Ukraine, I'm told, in '44, trying to cross the Dniester. I shouldn't wonder.[39] He had been seriously wounded in the head, recovered, but volunteered to go back. I nursed him only so that he could be killed. He never returned to me. It would've made more sense if he had died the first time," she said, surprising herself at this thought, which came as if lying in wait for just such a moment.

"No!" he snapped. "You're quite wrong. Then you wouldn't have had that time together."

She paused. She couldn't respond. He was right. She had been too bitter.

He studied her closely for a moment and then continued. "As I have said, Junior Lieutenant Kellerman, you are not alone. There are millions of such stories, millions. Yours is not unique. How many parents have been killed? How many children have perished? How many heroic fiancés have vanished into the mud and blood defending the Motherland? You're not alone, I tell you! But you must move on. You must allow yourself to heal. You're young and healthy. You have your entire life before you. There will be other men. There are even two young men in our division from your own hometown. Did you know that? Huh? Have you met them yet?" he asked, as if trying to match-make.

"No, sir," Miriam said quietly, "I've not met them. I do not recognize their names. I've heard they're quite nice," she conceded, "but..."

"But?" Golitsyn pressed. "But what? What's this but?" A questioning look settled over his face like a very dark cloud. "What happened?" he asked softly. "I know there's something you're not telling me. I can see it. Come on, out with it, my dear. Your colonel demands to know. There are no secrets from Lieutenant Colonel Golitsyn around here. Surely you've learned that much?"

She caught her breath, turned a little pale, and then told him about the rape. She began to sob as she always did when speaking of it. Golitsyn patted her in a fatherly way. After that everything changed. All the visitors who came to their apartment were more polite. No one flirted, no one tried to take advantage, and the men had a different air toward her.

A few days later, Miriam was eating when a Ukrainian friend named Anna, whom everyone called "Anyuta" to her face or "the chatterbox" behind her back, sat her down and said, "I've heard that there are two men from your hometown here, in our department, Miriam. Did you know that? Look," she said, nodding in their direction. "There're over there right now, see?" she said with another little nod and a wink. "I only just met them this morning. They're very nice. They're not really interpreters, just translators. That's why we've not seen them before. They sit in their office and translate documents all day long, like we do. In fact, they live at the other end of the building, on the first floor," she said, pointing. "They're roommates. I think they have no one to talk to but each other. Let's find out. Let's meet them," she insisted with a pert smile. "They must be very lonely, and they'd love to meet someone from home, don't you think? Come on, what would it hurt?"

Miriam shrank back when Anna yelled for them to come over. These two obviously shy and very quiet men, who had been sitting almost surreptitiously at their table eating, stood very uncomfortably, then approached to answer the Ukrainian's questions. They were quite surprised to meet someone from Czernowitz, and their puzzled looks changed to smiles when they were introduced.

"Well, well, from Czernowitz, huh?" Anna asked of the two. "You're both from there, am I right?"

Nodding, one said, "There's another here, too. A man named Gustav Oberlander. In fact, there he comes now," he said, pointing at a strikingly handsome young man descending the stairs.

"Gustav Oberlander?!" Miriam cried. There, indeed, was Gustav. Miriam gasped. She not only knew his family, but his father was the lawyer who had responded so kindly to her letter about her parents. Their only son, Gustav was smart, sophisticated, and very charming. He played the piano and was a good friend of Paul Antschel,[40] the soon-to-be great poet. When Miriam jumped up, Gustav recognized her as she raced into his arms like a lost child.

"You're not dead! You're not dead!" Miriam cried. "I thought everyone was dead!"

"No, dear Miriam, I'm not dead," he said with an embarrassed laugh. "But," he said, looking around at everyone watching them, "perhaps we should go for a walk, huh?"

"What're you doing here in Berlin?" she asked excitedly as they crossed the street.

"Like you, I'm an interpreter. I've been here for over a month now."

"Where do you live?"

"I have an apartment, very comfortable and not far, an easy walk, but I work in the same building as you."

"But I never see you," she said as they entered a little park.

"I'm so busy traveling with my boss; he's a colonel in..." Gustav, who was always so self-assured, hesitated.

"My God, Gustav, you're in counter-intelligence?!"

"No, no, all I do is interpret, pretty routine stuff actually, but I'm rarely here. But don't spread it around—my job, I mean. It's pretty well known, but, like everything, it's supposed to be a great secret and all that."

"My dear Gustav, I don't know a thing," Miriam said with a serious look, putting her fingers to her lips.

"How about you? Tell me about yourself."

Miriam gave him a very quick sketch, the questions coming back and forth in staccato fashion, as they walked deeper in the park, looking for a private place to sit.

"What have you heard from Isaac and Karl?" he asked with a tone of quiet concern.

Miriam stopped short, turning toward him abruptly with a desperate gesture.

"Miriam, what's wrong? Please sit down," he said, taking her by the arm to a bench.

She was silent.

"You must tell me," he said, sitting. "You must," he insisted, caressing her hand.

Miriam exhaled deeply, then found her breath like one standing on the precipice of an all too familiar horror, caught her breath again, and then told him about her flight, separation and reunion with Isaac, his recovery and death, and about Karl in Moscow. She told what she could, still concealing her greatest secret, and because of it thinking of her hero Zweig, as she seemed to do more and more since returning to the German-speaking world.

He started to speak but hesitated into a very long silence.

"Wait, I wrote to your father, Gustav, about my parents," Miriam added. "He was kind enough to write and say that he had not heard anything at all." Then after a half-moment's pause, she asked with a trembling voice, "Has he, Gustav? Has he heard anything of my parents?"

Gustav checked himself, then with a frightful look, sighed and asked quietly what she knew. She told him of their refusal to stay with Isaac's parents and that she believed them dead. "I know that, but still I have hope," she said in almost a whisper, biting her lip into speechlessness.

Gustav waited, studied her closely, leaned forward, and pressed her hands gently. In that moment a pair of arm-in-arm lovers walked by much too close, almost touching them as they strolled past. He watched, waited until they were gone, then turned again to Miriam and stammered out that he'd learned that her parents, in '41, had been separated en route to the Bershad ghetto in Transnistria of Western Ukraine.[41]

"Separated?" Miriam whispered.

"Yes," he said with another, deeper sound that was almost a moan. "They had been taken out of the train, taken out and marched off for, for extermination."

"Out of a train?"

"Yes, they were arrested and loaded, loaded in a train, then they were taken out. I'm not sure where. For some reason Deborah lagged behind, fell back. And when David tried to help, he was shoved aside." Again he hesitated, then spoke quietly, "Deborah collapsed, couldn't go on, and, and, Miriam, your mother was shot."

"Shot?"

"So I understand."

"And David?"

"David was taken to Bershad, the ghetto, where he died of typhus, I think. I'm not sure. There was an outbreak shortly after he arrived."

Gustav waited and watched as Miriam's paralyzed face slowly melted into tears, her heart so filling her chest that she had little breath for the sobs that came in great suffocating waves. He embraced her. Held her a very long time, till she dried her eyes with his handkerchief and sat back, pale and quite silent. Then, without her trying to remember, the words of Schiller's poem came in a flood. She had tried to recall them before, but now they came easily, like an alien but powerful voice:

Empfange meinen Vollmachtsbrief zum Glück!
Ich bring' ihm unerbrochen dir zurucke;
Ich weiss nichts von Glückseligkeit.[42]

She spoke the first line, then faltered and could not finish. But Gustav, of course, knowing the rest, said them for her, stroking her hand.

After what seemed to him a very long time Gustav, with a certain hurried relief, quickly told the remainder of his own story. "Well, my parents were lucky," he said, "they escaped the Nazis. Father knew Ukrainian as well as Russian, as you know, so he made himself useful. The Russians put him to work. They were in Kiev during the encirclement but managed to get out. In this way they survived. They were very fortunate."

Escorting her back to work, he said that Isaac's parents, along with a few other families, had escaped to Palestine and were living there. At the entrance, he waited a moment, gave her a perfunctory hug while promising to meet again, and disappeared. Miriam hesitated, was at a loss, then, unable to face the others, turned and ambled down the street. Somehow all of Berlin seemed warmer that evening as she walked, she knew not how long, thinking about David and Deborah—Schiller's poem echoing in her mind like a dirge.

Take back my permit to happiness!
I bring it back to you unopened.
I know nothing of bliss.[43]

But another thing haunted her. Someone told her and Gustav had confirmed that her hero, Stefan Zweig, had committed suicide in early '42, somewhere in Brazil.[44] *Why had he done such a thing?* Miriam questioned, when she and so many others had struggled so hard to find a reason to keep living. *Why hadn't he done this, too? He should have hung on no matter what it took. His suicide was a betrayal. He should not have given up. He let us down—Europe—the whole world. He, too, had a duty to live for all of us—to keep writing, thinking, and fighting for truth—for David and Deborah, and Isaac and Ruth, and all the millions. He let us all down! He had everything—freedom, fame, money, talent; it would have been so easy for him to press on, to help build a new Europe and new post-war world.*

Then, she thought, taking a few tentative steps and gazing upon the rubble of a bombed-out church, *maybe for just that reason it was harder for him than anyone else. Perhaps, in the end, he had simply despaired because he had been able to do so little with so much, then, like Schiller's poem, had finally handed in his permit to happiness, unopened.*

32

Doctor Polyakov

Miriam and Gustav became closer. For him, she was more of a sister, with the Czernowitz connection making their relationship almost familial. Like most siblings, the differences were at least as important as the similarities. For one thing, Gustav was very much the ladies' man, while Miriam was incurably shy. But there was yet another distinction: Gustav, despite all the attendant gruesomeness of the world's greatest war of extermination, still felt that life was worth living, and Miriam, despite her brave promises to herself, was less convinced. She listened to him but nevertheless remained a skeptic. Indeed, Gustav's faith in life quietly amazed her. And, upon not a little reflection, she at last decided that it was really an act of faith, a turn-of-mind, an inclination or prejudice even, rather than a conclusion of mere reason. Also, he was gregarious, while she continued to live a subdued, reclusive life, with her work paramount, as always.

Somehow Gustav, like Golitsyn, could not accept this. To them it seemed a point of irritation, even an affront. The colonel still sent her specially prepared food and exhorted her to "join the human race," as he put it, but Miriam's despondency only deepened. Gradually she retreated into an increasingly profound malnourishment—it was like quicksand, and she sank into it ever deeper. At last, Golitsyn, with Gustav's agreement, insisted she see a doctor.

"I don't need to see a doctor, Comrade Colonel," she retorted a little too sharply.

"It's an order," Golitsyn replied with such unaccustomed force that she felt rebuked.

To get to this doctor she had to travel a section of unguarded underground. To her shock, defrocked Nazi officials and soldiers were everywhere, but she managed to pass easily among them in civilian clothes. It was then she realized there was an entirely unknown German world running as an undercurrent to the Occupation. Given more time and less illness, she might have found this of great interest, but she was too weak for any serious ratiocination about such a thing. She made two medical trips, an examination and its inevitable follow-up, before she was called in to see Golitsyn.

"Yes, sir, reporting as ordered, Comrade Colonel," she said, standing weakly at attention.

"I have the doctor's findings," he said, rising as she walked in and waving the report at her. "You're completely burned out, my dear. I'm sending you to get some rest at a sanatorium."

"Sanatorium, sir?"

"Yes, in Czechoslovakia, in Karlsbad. It's very exclusive, but I have pulled strings to get you in," he explained proudly, with unconvincing gruffness.

"Sir, I can't go, Comrade Colonel! There's so much work to do. I must..."

Golitsyn interrupted. "True, you're quite right, there's work for you to do here, lots of it. But you won't be able to do it if you're dead." He said this last part while shaking the medical report under her chin. "The doctor makes no bones about that; you simply cannot go on like this. You're wasting away before our very eyes."

"But, sir..."

"Listen, Junior Lieutenant Kellerman, I'm really being selfish, if you want to know the truth. You are my best translator. I simply can't afford to lose you. That is why I am doing this. Meantime the others will take up the slack until you return. Don't worry, everyone will understand."

"Yes, sir, but, too, there's so much more housework. We had to fire our maid; she was a thief, Comrade Colonel."

"It doesn't matter. They'll take care of that as well. In another week or two you will be so sick you can't move. You won't be able to do anything, much less do housework, to say nothing of translating. You will leave the day after tomorrow. I'll send you by car; you're too frail to travel alone by train."

"But..."

"You have no choice. You're dismissed."

The interview was closed, and that was that. She saluted and marched out a little unsteadily.

Within a week Miriam found herself once again entering a sanatorium, not cleaning sores or sweeping and mopping but as a patient. The property consisted of three large buildings set in a spacious and pleasant park with very handsome hardwood trees. Her building was immaculately white with dirty yellow snow in the foreground. She was led in slowly through its front door to a room flooded in light with long, open windows on either side. The floors were polished, the place immaculate—in no way was it like the bed pans, bandages, and blood of the head-injury ward. Politely she was shown to her room "to prepare for a consultation," she was told.

Germans?! How quickly they adjust, she laughed inwardly. *They are already running things!*

She was examined in every conceivable way—poked, stuck, questioned, poked, and stuck again.

"You're undernourished," one doctor said sharply.

"Yes," she said sullenly. "I know. I've been malnourished since June 22, 1941, Herr doctor," she said to the German.

"Your health is delicate since your, your exodus. It has collapsed under the weight of your emotions," he said coldly, ignoring her wit.

Exodus! What a strange word for him to use! Exodus, indeed! The swine!

"We'll bring you gradually back to health," he added curtly, as Miriam continued to turn the word "exodus" over and over like a hot stone.

"Thank you, sir," she said, putting the word "exodus" in the pocket of her mind for a moment.

"The nurse will see to you now," he added, as an unsmiling nurse entered and took her to the "sunrooms."

How ironic! The Germans wear you down, then build you up, destroy and build anew, that's what they do, over and over. The Teutonic melodrama of Europe, the building and destroying by the Germans, building and destroying Europe.

Miriam was made to swallow a small yellow pill and then told to wait for tea as she was left standing at a long window to stare at the sunbeams drifting gracefully around her like delicate impurities in clear water. For the first time since Czernowitz her mind became blissfully empty, and she was surprised by a profound sense of tranquil euphoria that came slowly over her. The empty room seemed ever warmer, all the while filling with bright but very soft light.

She was not the least bit cold, despite the frost that gripped Europe in the first new winter peace since '38, and her flimsy dressing gown, which was next to nothing against the air, kept her warm as a fur coat.

Surprisingly, without conjuring her, Miriam heard Ruth wiggling in her basket and crying. Then she saw Isaac's bandaged face, Mrs. Anna's and Dr. Kasparova's smiles, and Deborah's and David's tears. Quietly she began to weep until someone said in a deep, very masculine voice, "Lieutenant Kellerman?"

Miriam turned around slowly to find a tall, strikingly handsome young man with blue eyes, high cheekbones, and sandy blond hair, who was wearing a military uniform subjacent to his doctor's white coat.

"Lieutenant Kellerman?" he asked again with the greatest possible politeness.

"Yes," Miriam answered almost inaudibly.

"Lieutenant Kellerman, I am Major Alexander Ivanovich Polyakov. I work at this sanatorium, and I want to tell you how glad I am to meet you and to welcome you to our facility," he said in Russian, coming over to her confidently.

"Yes, sir," Miriam said shyly, wiping away her tears with his offered handkerchief, while adding with polite formality that she also was glad to make his acquaintance.

"And to assure you," he continued, as if not hearing her or noticing that she had been weeping, "that all will be done to restore your health that can be done."

This unexpected kindness from a new doctor, a Russian, the light, the warmth, the cleanliness, and his obvious professionalism drained her of all anxiety so that she stopped crying and instead studied this obviously gentle, understanding young man, who seemed to have no interest in anything but her welfare. He quietly gathered two chairs and sat her down across from himself, chatted small talk for a while, assured her again, and, with a pat on the shoulder, got up and left the room.

Almost in the same moment a nurse appeared, took her to her room, and gave her a sedative that immediately erased her consciousness as simply as shutting a door to an unpleasant room, and her mind fell swimming into a current of confused memories that were so often prologue to her deepest sleep.

Slowly she slipped into a kind of eternity, escaping time altogether—*rather like death*, she remembered thinking. In fact, except for very brief periods of fitful wakefulness, she slept for days. Fed with an IV she was awoken for short walks and hot meals. Soon, there were more sessions with the good Dr. Polyakov, more exercise, and still more rest. This regimen continued for several weeks until her fatigue slowly fell from her, like setting down her old valise or letting fall her pack. In fact, she dreamed herself doing just that, setting down her valise and pack somewhere on the road to Kiev with Deborah and David standing there smiling at her on the other side of something. *What was it, the thing they are standing on the other side of?* She couldn't make it out, try as she might, but they were there, waving and smiling for her to join them on the road to Kiev.

For more than a month, her old life scratched itself out in Cyrillic script onto the doctor's little notepad, oozing out all its horror and hope in his neat fine blue ink. She told him everything, all her life's pain: about Ruth, Isaac, and her parents. Once she started she could not stop, telling everything that had happened, even, lastly, the rape. Gradually Dr. Polyakov drained away her sorrow, emptying it through his pen, helping her see that she would never replace the loved ones but she could find others and that "a new life has been given to you—a great gift which you only have to accept to be well again." He smiled slightly at her silence and then said, "It's what Deborah wanted, you know? She lost her life so you might have life. You are her new life now, as well as your own."

Then one day a staff car came. She was scrubbed, washed, and combed into her newly pressed uniform with gold medals and shined shoes and driven back to Berlin. Everyone remarked politely how she had changed and how much better she seemed. Miriam knew what the sanatorium had done for her, that her own dear colonel had saved her by ordering her there, but she said nothing for a while, just smiled and went about her work as before, as if she had never been gone. Finally, she went to him and thanked him by telling him just that.

"You're doing your duty as if you'd never been gone," he replied, trying very hard to accept her thanks professionally but ruining it with a fatherly grin.

"Thank you, Comrade Colonel," she said, saluting, and with a snappy about-face, quick-marched to the door.

It wasn't long before Dr. Polyakov came to see her.

"He's in the colonel's office, waiting for you," said Golitsyn's prim, unattractive secretary with an unintended hint of jealousy.

"Junior Lieutenant Kellerman, you're looking very well," Polyakov said with mock surprise. "I was in Berlin on another matter and thought I'd drop by and see how you're doing. The colonel is very pleased with your work," he said, casually leaning against the front of Golitsyn's desk, smoking a cigarette. "Please sit down."

Miriam sat on a nearby couch. He reached in his tunic and produced a lighter and cigarette pack.

"Would you like one?"

"Yes, thank you, doctor," she said, leaning over, accepting the cigarette and his light and inhaling deeply. "American?" she asked, exhaling as she sat back again. "I've never had one before; it's wonderful."

"Yes, I go to the American zone from time to time."

"Really?" she said, studying the cigarette, not quite looking at him.

"Yes."

"Is it interesting?" she asked, now studying him closely.

"Yes, very."

"What're they like, the Americans? I have never met one."

"I like them. They're open, hospitable, very generous. I prefer them to the British, who're too reserved, cold. You never quite know what they're thinking. The French, as everyone knows, are chattering snobs. But the Americans are like big children, really, more like Russians," he added with a wry smile.

"Interesting," Miriam said, leaning back in the couch, smoking the Lucky Strike with great pleasure. "I've never met an Englishman or a Frenchman either, though, as I told you, we studied French at home. I got quite good at it, and Mother was fluent. She loved French literature, read lots of French novels. I wasn't supposed to read them till I was a certain age, but I sneaked them into my room and read them secretly. I loved Balzac," she said, remembering that they had had this conversation before.

"Balzac?"

"Yes. Do you know him?"

"Of course, though I have only read a few of his things. *Père Goriot* was my favorite." He hesitated, uncertain, then added, "But I remember you saying you liked the Austrian, Zweig."

"Yes, very much. His short stories are his best."

"Oh? Which ones?"

"'The Burning Secret' and 'Letter from an Unknown Woman' are my favorites."

"He was a friend of Freud, you know?"

"Yes, I know," she said with a blank look, almost saying they had talked about it all before at the sanatorium but, out of politeness, did not.

He saw this hesitation, felt the conversation sagging a bit, and so said a little awkwardly, "You know he only wrote one novel?"

"Yes, *Beware of Pity*, a minor masterpiece, I think. I could not stop reading it."

"Yes, I was the same," he agreed.

"There's a foreshadowing of suicide in it, isn't there? If you look at it with hindsight," she said quietly, glancing away at the wall.

Pause.

"You know he committed suicide?" she added, seeing his puzzlement.

"Zweig? Suicide?"

"Yes."

"No, I didn't know that," said Polyakov, surprised.

"In Brazil, Gustav told me. Right before things turned around—in the war, I mean, just before Stalingrad. Gustav says it seems Zweig thought Hitler was going to win the war; he got very depressed."

"He should have hung on," said Polyakov matter-of-factly.

"Of course," said Miriam blankly. "We have all lost those we love," she said, staring blankly at the wall again, without looking at the doctor, "and have hung on, haven't we?" she said, looking at him again.

"Yes, we have," he said, shifting a little nervously, putting a hand in his uniform pants pocket with affected nonchalance. Then the subject was changed to her sanatorium days, and he repeated how pleased the colonel was with her work now.

"Thank you," she said without any real feeling, finishing her cigarette and snubbing it in an ashtray Polyakov handed from off a small table.

Putting it back and standing up, he suggested brightly, "What say you show me around? The whole building is off limits for me, you know. Would you take me on a little tour? I would enjoy that very much."

Miriam laughed and remarked that the place actually was quite dull and everything was classified, even the most routine matters. "The work is very mundane, I have to admit," she said with a forced smile. "There's nothing very exciting about any of it at all. We translate the most ordinary things imaginable. I can't understand why they worry that anyone might know what it is."

Polyakov laughed and said, "Paranoia."

"Yes," she agreed with a quiet chuckle, "I think you are right, Comrade Doctor. But only you can make the diagnosis," she said raising an eyebrow. "I'm not a psychiatrist."

There was a meditative pause as Miriam almost disappeared behind a cloud of smoke; then Polyakov suggested, "Well, Miriam, how about a walk? There's a nice park across the street," he added, pulling his fore-and-aft cap from under his thick belt and straightening it perfectly on his head.

"Walk?" she asked, standing up. "Where?"

"Outside, in the park. It's a nice day."

"I'll have to get permission," she said, rising slowly to her feet.

"I have already seen to that, my dear. Mikhail Andreyevich has already given his permission," he said, his *savoir faire* returning after only a moment's desertion, as he took her by the elbow and escorted her smoothly out.

So began the first of many such outings. Since the good doctor was coming "to check on her," Miriam knew, of course, that he was having long talks with Golitsyn about her, but she said nothing. After all, he was charming, single, and not much older than Isaac. Anyway, Miriam was now 21 and that was less important.

Inexorably, they began to do other things together. On her one Saturday evening off they would go to parties or to the theater in the city center, near the burned-out Reichstag where the Soviet soldiers had raised the hammer-and-sickle in the famous picture "seen 'round the world," as people kept saying. Indeed, the whole world was still rejoicing that the war was over, and even Berlin seemed a little unburdened, as if having exorcised some hypnotic power previously beyond its command.

So Miriam readily went out with this wonderfully cultured doctor who spoke both Russian and German perfectly (one of the few Russians she ever met who did), "the only child of doting parents," as he himself put it, obviously with a very bright future, destined to be part of the highest Soviet society with all the privileges and prestige that would naturally inure to the successful son of powerful Party members.

Their evenings always ended the same, with a meal in a nice restaurant, followed by a slow walk home. To her surprise, she began to feel relaxed among people again. She even met his parents and found them friendly and quite charming. She was reviving and returning to the new life this doctor had promised in their many sanatorium sessions.

One evening at a restaurant, she looked around and found herself saying, "Well, Sasha," (he had rather too quickly insisted on the familiar, but she did it to please him), "it's interesting how soon the bourgeois spirit so quickly reasserts itself, isn't it?"

He laughed nervously, took a sip of wine as if to think about it, and said, "It's eternal, I'm afraid."

Miriam eyed him closely and replied with a little ironic smile, "Well, was the blood of the revolution spilt for nothing then, my dear doctor? Huh? Is it all simply a matter of one bourgeoisie replacing another, is that it?"

Dr. Polyakov made a very poor attempt at a cheerful laugh and said, "No, of course not. A great deal has and continues to be done of a positive nature. But in some respects human nature does not change—remember, Miriam, I'm a doctor."

"Yes, I never forget that. But maybe this is what Lenin meant by the necessity of building the 'New Socialist Man'?"

"Yes, of course, that's exactly what he meant," he said with a small grin and a gesture toward the festive restaurant crowd around them, "but as you can see, we have a way to go."

Miriam laughed quietly into her wine before sipping it and placing it confidently back on its little napkin.

Over the next few days she became increasingly uneasy. It was becoming obvious to everyone that Dr. Alexander Ivanovich Polyakov had fallen madly in love with Junior Lieutenant Miriam Kellerman. Indeed, she had long been certain of it. But she knew with equal certainty that she could never love him in the same way she had loved Isaac. She didn't know why it was so; it just was. Ironically, she was accounted fortunate in this respect by everyone but herself, and the raised eyebrows and nods and winks served only to deepen her consternation. Then, even more alarmingly, he invited her to a New Year's party at his parents' "villa," commandeered from the Nazis.

"I can't come, thank you very much."

"Why not?" asked Polyakov, interrupting a little sternly.

"It's my boss, the colonel, he would not allow me to be away from work, and, too, it wouldn't be proper."

"Oh," said Alexander, relieved, "that's nothing—a phone call will take care of it. You forget that I have great pull in our army hierarchy."

No, I never ever forget that, my dear doctor, she wanted to say but replied with a slight frown instead.

"Don't worry, Miriam, my dear, you'll have your own room, with a key, real privacy. You'll be quite safe," he assured her. "There'll be nothing at all improper. I'll speak to Mikhail Andreyevich. I can arrange everything without any problem whatsoever."

Golitsyn might have appeared a little obtuse, but as an army officer he was not totally devoid of percipience, and of course he suspected that his brilliant translator had a phobia about men. He was concerned about this, but her relationship with Polyakov was much to his advantage and, in the end, he gave Miriam no choice but to accept. After all, this particular man had been her doctor and protector. His family's "pull" in the Party was not to be denied, so Miriam relented with muttered misgivings.

At the villa she found herself the amazed witness to the most extravagant party in her life. There was an orchestra and food and drink beyond all imagining. It was clear that Dr. Polyakov's father was very high up, higher even than she had thought. The New Year's tree dominated the ballroom. Early in the evening, people circled it like some sort of totem, danced, ate, chatted, and enjoyed themselves in a way Miriam had not seen since Romania. In a distinct way, she thought of the ballroom in Czernowitz where she had gone as a young girl and of those American movies she had watched in such wonder in which glamorous people dressed smartly and smoked cigarettes to violin music, embraced and waltzed around. Truly, this was very much like something out of Hollywood—too, remembering Isaac, it was shockingly bourgeois. She saw no sign whatsoever of Lenin's "New Man."

For this, all the revolutionary martyrs have died, she couldn't help thinking with a certain ironic delight of Polyakov's lame defense. But the alcohol slowly began to change things. There was no movie soundtrack, she realized, no sweetly romantic violins at all, but instead the orchestra struggled in ever-rising dissonance against vodka-soaked voices—voices shouting above the saxophone "swing" of a Berlin band "borrowed" from a former Nazi cabaret and driven out in an army lend-lease truck.

To Miriam's sober mind everyone seemed gradually to go slightly mad. Her ears began to hurt, it was too noisy for conversation, and she refused to shout, so she was bored. Polyakov, seated by her in his best civilian suit, urbane, handsome, and red-faced, was busy dashing off glasses of vodka while laughing and chattering with his parents and friends. Then, as if remembering her, he asked her to dance. When she declined, he shuffled around with an attractive married woman sporting a low-cut dress of the latest European fashion. She wore it with a sort of fatuous, self-conscious satisfaction, just like all the others—all these women strutting around, bouncing their bottoms and breasts in a kind of stupid sensuality.

The men were no better, whether fat or thin, florid or pale—in boots and bemedaled like comic opera commissars, they lurched crazily across the floor with an awkward, gawky conceit. No one could dance very well—"the Russians are bears with the gift of speech," Miriam remembered reading somewhere, but tonight she did not think it funny, merely ridiculous. Worse, she felt ridiculous herself.

Indeed, the whole thing was absurd. Here she was, a little Romanian Jew sitting alone amid the lunacy of drunken Russians who were trying to lose themselves in a slightly forced saturnalia. Therein lay its artificiality—*it's imitative*, she decided, *does not arise naturally from Russian spontaneity that can be such a delight. The Russians are never any good at being anything but themselves. But it's a self they cherish and abhor, love and despise, embrace and fear*, she found herself saying out loud since she had no one with which to either listen or speak. *Unleashed, their appetite is bestial, grows upon what it feeds. Under the iron fist lurks a great confusion*, she said, addressing her imaginary interlocutor, but then turned away, could watch no more, wanted to run away just like she had done that night at Zakti's wedding party in Alma-Ata. But where would she go? There at least she had a place to run.

Her heart began to flutter in a kind of all too familiar panic. Abruptly, the music stopped. The shock of this silence was relieved only by an irrepressible murmur of conversation. *How is this happening? Why? Who has the power to order such a thing?*

Then her anxiety succumbed to amazement. Polyakov's father took the microphone into his fat fist and, clearing his throat loudly, shifted nervously, obviously preparing to make a speech. He made a gesture and called for silence. The murmurs nearly died away or were grudgingly suppressed—the beast was momentarily driven into a corner. He thanked the crowd yet again, cleared his throat once more, then, clearly a little drunk, said, "My dear friends, friends and colleagues, my wife and I wish to announce an event that gives us such great joy. Our son, Sasha, has become engaged to a wonderful young lady. Please join us in welcoming this marvelous young woman who has brought such happiness to our family—Miriam Kellerman." He said this with a flourish and almost a bow in her direction. "Miriam, dear, please stand up," he said with a gesture for her to rise.

But she could not stand up. Instead, the ballroom whirled. People cheered and applauded in a surreal tableau of leering faces. She was faint and, gripping her chair, remembered saying something, she knew not what, but finally standing, she began running and found herself alone in her little room.

On her bed she sat gasping, smothering, desperately trying to think and breathe, breathe and think. Did she actually hear what she had in fact heard? Was this real? Or was she just in another episode of an endless nightmare? *How many nightmares can I endure? Perhaps I'm still in the sanatorium sleeping the eternal sleep but dreaming a terrible dream yet again? Running on the burning bridge? Fleeing to Proskurov? Being bombed? Looking for Isaac? Starving? Freezing? Fighting? Or being raped? Yes, by God! That's what is happening to me! I'm being raped again!*

There was a knock on the door. Polyakov's voice spoke sheepishly through it, begging for admittance.

"Miriam, Miriam, please unlock the door. Please, dear, please, let me explain."

"How can you explain!?" Miriam shouted. "Sasha! How can you explain such a thing?!"

"Miriam, my dear," he said stepping in shyly as she unlatched the door and quickly returned to her bed. "We're young," he said, coming over, sitting and taking her hand. "We're attracted to each other. We can find joy together. My parents have approved. I mentioned it casually, and they got carried away, that's all. Father was a little drunk. I'm sorry. He thought you'd be pleased, thrilled. He jumped the gun. Believe me, he surprised me, too. I was shocked. It all went to his head. He is a very powerful man. He's used to having his way. He couldn't imagine anything but pleasure on your part. He doesn't understand. He behaved badly but is truly sorry. He says he'll apologize. But it doesn't really matter. After all, why should you hesitate? I know everything about your life, you know that. We worked through it all—the starvation, Isaac. There are no secrets between us. I know it all, every bit. Only honesty and truth have ever been between us, and I love you dearly, desperately," he said, dropping her hand and taking her into his arms.

Shockingly, his passion seemed to be a living thing, a kind of third person between them as he embraced her. She cried out and struggled, so he reluctantly released her. He fumbled out a small box from a pocket and opened it to reveal a ring centered with three small diamonds interlocking in complementing triangles—"three jewels representing our worlds finally becoming one," he explained. "Jew, Gentile, and Motherland, all merging together in reconciliation," he said sincerely.

She could see he meant it but did not see its impossibility. "My dear Sasha," she said aloud but could say no more, as she was touched. *You do not understand, do not know who I am, do not have my memories.* She could only repeat, "Dearest Sasha," but thought, *You know, of course, but do not remember the evening at Isaac's parents'—his bracelet, the ride, the staring soldier, the escape, once again the bridge, coming to me over and over as if passing from but the previous moment. Oh, poor, dear, naïve Sasha—how can you ever really know? You cannot! You know facts, nothing more. True knowing is impossible! Even for such a doctor as yourself, not really. Your knowing is clinical; it is not true knowing, my dear, not at all. One never truly knows another, not ever! We cannot even completely know ourselves, so how can we ever know another? You know nothing of me, not really! Nothing! How can you know?! How?! I do love you, but not like Isaac; I can never love you like that, not really. And your Motherland? It means even less.*

He looked at her with sad, imploring eyes.

"Thank you, dearest Sasha, thank you," was all she could say, weeping while watching him slip the ring on her finger. Then he took her in his arms and kissed her passionately. She tried to speak, but words were nothing now as his desire quickly took possession of them both.

Miriam accepted him; she could see no alternative, he was so abject, so desperate. She even felt a kind of pity for him as she heard herself saying, "Yes, Sasha, yes," as if he were Isaac. She would do it that way, he would be Isaac, who she had dreamt of and never stopped wanting and would always want so she pretended it was him—was even

afraid she would call out his name and so bit her lip not to utter it—
Isaac! Oh, Isaac, she wanted to cry out, *yes, Isaac!* For a brief, delicious
moment, she was alone with Isaac, made love to him again as she had
done so freely and lovingly and could only really ever do with him and
no one else. Though she knew that Sasha loved her, was tender,
considerate, and sincere, she knew, too, especially now, that she could
never be in love with him as he truly wished.

The next morning she awoke from a disturbed, dreaming sleep to
eye the ring whose discomfort seemed to pinch her awake. She asked to
return to Berlin. A somber, almost chastened, Alexander dropped her
off, and she was met with congratulations from the beaming Golitsyn.
"How lucky you are," he said.

She smiled demurely, all the while knowing that she would never
marry Dr. Polyakov.

33

These Mean Ruins

It was already 1946. The new year was young, and she had no idea what it would bring. She had wanted to be left alone to do her work, recover, and live again, but now this had happened. The world outside her desk and her little room in the ruins of the great city reverted to a great echo chamber of noise and confusion. Outside, there were always rumblings. The world always threatened, was not her friend, this she knew only too well. *Indeed, it is no one's friend. Those who think so are fools.* She could not see how she fit into the brave new post-war world. War she understood; in war everything is simple, and the simplest things very difficult, but it is not hard to understand. Peace was baffling. Who could understand or ever know what to do with it? How could she face peace? She still had not yet accepted the loss of the old and did not truly believe it was really dead, only subsumed into the unconscious of the new.

Perhaps Europe is finished at last, she wondered, *and the rubble of Germany is now its grave? Who can doubt that, if it has such a grave, it is here in these mean German ruins? Oh, sure, it may rebuild and even prosper, but in the only way that matters, Europe is no more.*

Hitler has finished it off. Oh, the Americans will rebuild things, but things are not Europe. America can never rebuild that because it doesn't even know what it is.

Like Europe Miriam Kellerman herself felt like a broken vase. The kind Dr. Polyakov had tried to put her back together again; had put her on his shelf, all glued and new, but she realized now she would never be the same. The seams of her cracks would always be there. And when he could not leave her on the shelf but fondled her with his love and admiration, she knew soon she would only shatter again. He could not leave her alone but had to take her down and show her to others like a prized possession, one that he had found broken and pieced back together for all the world to see, like the Americans were doing with what they thought was Europe.

I must find a place where no one would ever touch me—not ever again. I must flee yet again. It's my only hope. I must run once more. Europe may be finished, but I am not. I must live. I can be reborn, so I must flee Berlin, from all this, from Sasha, like I did from Czernowitz, from the Nazis, and from Alma-Ata. I must flee!

From that point on, she plotted her escape from Sasha's painful love and Hitler's mean ruins.

The Communists were consolidating their power throughout their Zone. The struggle raged all around and throughout Berlin, but especially in the Soviet quarter, Miriam was inundated with its busy political babel. Later that year elections would be held,[45] the first since the war. But the psychology of this struggle was shocking. Anti-Semitism quickly reared its ugly head, and suddenly Miriam was a Jew engaged to a Russian Gentile she did not love as she had loved Isaac. A great schism was now growing between the Jews and the Soviets, a split that would slice the Jews up for swallowing again, she feared. Stalin was an anti-Semite, as everyone knew, little different from Hitler. She debated these things with Alexander, but he did not believe her. He was much too comfortable in his Gentile world, too much a part of it ever to understand what it really meant to be a Jew.

"It doesn't really matter that you're a Jew," he had said.

It doesn't matter to be a Jew?! My God, Sasha! You have no idea what you're saying!

"Once we're married, it'll mean nothing. You'll be my wife. That's the only thing that will matter."

"But I'd have to hide my background, Sasha," she said.

"No, you won't."

"Yes, I would. Once they know you're married to a Jew, you'll be penalized. There's no way around it. I'd have to hide and pretend not to be what I am and to do so would be a dishonor. I can never do that. I am a Jew, and that's all there is to it. I can never disown my past or my parents. I can never hide my background, and I can never hurt you because I love you," she said.

"This is nonsense," he said, growing angry as he always did when they had this conversation.

She knew she could not live with a Gentile as an overt Jew. It simply would not work. She explained to him, "For me, Soviet citizenship, marriage to a Party member, and Jewish identity are impossible contradictions. You will regret it. You love me now, but I know you will grow to hate me, Sasha. Now you love me, I know this, but love is blind, and you are blind. Someday you will see and will regret our marriage. You will grow to resent me in time, and I could never bear that, my dear. I would prefer anything to that."

He would remonstrate but to no avail.

I need to contact Karl, she said to herself. *He's all I really have. I need to know what he's doing, where he is, what he thinks. He's all the family I've got.*

But Alexander became even more importunate. He pursued her relentlessly, always insisting. He grew angry with her again, and the strength of his anger only made it more painful. After a bitter quarrel, she went to Golitsyn and requested a transfer.

He demurred.

Then a few days later, she was reported for helping some Germans. She was guilty, she told Golitsyn, who had called her in. "I no longer hate them," she explained. "I am finished with hate. They were old people, children, women—they were powerless against Hitler, and I gave them food."

"It's against the regulations," he said coldly. "You'll get us all into trouble."

"Yes, well, maybe it's better if they don't hate us so much. Maybe we can free ourselves from the past through forgiveness," said Miriam bravely.

"That's idiotic! You must stop now!" he shouted. "It's an order! No more helping the Germans! Do you understand me, Comrade Lieutenant?!"

"Yes, Comrade Colonel," she said with an edge of sarcasm, saluted, and strutted out.

But things were never the same. Golitsyn was angry with her attitude and her problems with Polyakov, which he thought were foolish, and he became increasingly remote and aloof. He clearly wanted her gone, considered her a nuisance, but in this he unwittingly became her ally.

She knew Gustav had managed a transfer to Vienna. When he wrote, she immediately wrote back, "Please pull strings, dearest Gustav! I absolutely must get out of Berlin! Please! Do everything you can, my dear friend. If ever you are to help me, help me with this! I have no one else to turn to."

He did. The order came quickly, and the door sprung open. She quickly went about saying tearful goodbyes, going in to see Golitsyn, whom she embraced in a most unprofessional, unmilitary, and daughterly manner, breaking down his reserve into his more natural warmth. They cried and embraced.

She was leaving on the night train without saying goodbye to Alexander. She did not really want to depart in this way but thought she had no choice. He might contrive to keep her, even cancel her orders. Just this week he had written her poetry, sent her flowers, come to her and begged her to marry him, met her every objection.

"I understand what you are saying, and I will help you. We can live in Moscow, have lots and lots of Jewish friends. I will dedicate myself to your happiness," he had insisted with the greatest possible sincerity.

She said no but kept his ring, fearing to return it. *I'll send it somehow, by a friend, but now I must go. I cannot see him again, not ever.*

Once more Miriam Kellerman boarded another train, trying to escape. The vase was packed up, free from anyone's touch, and put back in its box to be shipped to Vienna, the city of dreams.

Her Ukrainian roommate, Anna the chatterbox, had gone with her to the Berlin station. Waiting to board in the anonymity of the waiting crowd, Anna felt secure enough to say in a confidential tone, "I know you're too wrapped up with Alexander and everything to think about much else, but you obviously have not heard the news."

"News? What news?" Miriam asked, her friend's question having interrupted a certain mental distraction.

"See? I knew it. You haven't heard?"

"Haven't heard what, Anyuta?"

"Our two Jewish gentlemen from Czernowitz, your friends, well, they seemed to have disappeared."

Miriam gasped. "Disappeared?!!"

"Are you shocked?" Anna asked with obvious pleasure.

"Of course I'm shocked, Anyuta," Miriam said looking away from such a question and back again. "They've defected, is that what you're trying to tell me?"

"Yes, so it seems. As you know, they went out often in the evening. You probably thought nothing of it, Miriam, but the rest of us were sure they were visiting German ladies," Anna said with a very pleased giggle.

"German ladies? Visiting German ladies, did you say?"

"Yes, visiting, if that's what you want to call it."

"Anyuta, I didn't call it anything."

"Yes, well, I, for one, knew their schedule as well as I know my own."

You know everyone's schedule, Miriam wanted to say as Anna prattled on.

"Yesterday we came to work. You were in the colonel's office, having your little chat and all, but I noticed that the Czernowitz men, your friends, were not around, just not anywhere to be found. You know they were always so very precise, punctual almost to a fault. Well, Miriam, I waited for an hour, more than an hour, I really did, then I just couldn't wait any longer, you know. I waited as long as I could, and then I had to report them as missing. I didn't want to, but you know the rules."

"Yes, Anyuta, I do know the rules…," said Miriam, her voice trailing off as she looked away again to see what was happening with the train, which was late in leaving, then turned back again to Anna.

"I found out later," Anna continued, catching her breath. "Sonya, well, she told me everything. Some army officers, intelligence people, knocked at their apartment door, but there was no answer. It was unlocked, the room empty. I mean really empty. There were two uniforms hanging in the wardrobe, but everything else was gone. Poof! Just like that! Into thin air, Miriam," she said with a little gesture toward the sky. "Sonya thinks that they had, well, friends, in West Berlin. That's what she always said, and I agree. We, of course, assumed they were there on other kinds of business, you might say."

Here Anna giggled again and stopped, obviously waiting for Miriam to pick up the thread and tug on it.

"And? What happened, Anyuta?" Miriam obliged.

"Well, she said she had seen them get into a car a few blocks off. No one noticed her. Now what do you think happened? As soon as they got into that car, they started changing their clothes. Quickly changing their clothes! Isn't that a little suspicious, Miriam? Wouldn't you think something was amiss, huh?"

"And?" Miriam asked, ignoring both the stupidity of the question and the rasping loudspeaker that now said her train was leaving.

"Sonya and I both think the men were taking things out, bit by bit, you know, meeting their friends, and all the time we thought they were with the ladies! Ha! Come to think of it, they never bought much. I think they must have squeezed every single kopek they ever had to their name."

Anna continued, "Poor dear Golitsyn was furious, as you might imagine. Positively red faced! I saw him come out of his office after having his little tête-à-tête with the spooks, and I thought he was going to have a stroke or something. Really, now, who can blame him?! After all, he's so good, so trusting of us all. He did all he could for them, and then for them to stab him in the back like that! He'll get into major trouble for it with the big boys, I'm afraid. I mean, they already think he's an old softy heart, which he is for sure, we all know that. So now they're proved right and he's wrong. I shouldn't wonder if they relieve him over it."

"They wouldn't!"

"Why ever not? They can do as they please."

"He does a good job and has too many friends. He'll get chewed out, and then it'll be forgotten."

"Well, Miriam, everybody hopes you're right."

"They must have jumped into the American zone," Miriam said matter-of-factly.

"That's what everyone suspects, you know. 'Jews,' they say, 'Jews can't be trusted; they're loyal only to themselves.'"

"Anyuta, I am a Jew," Miriam said as sternly as she could manage.

"Yes, sure, but you never talk about it, and still everyone knows. All such things are known, Miriam, you've learned that. All these secrets, and everything known! Ha! What a paradox it all is. But, still, you are not like the others, Miriam, not at all, and everyone loves you because of it. You're one of us, I mean. That old sweetie, Golitsyn, if it were up to him, he would trust you with the Kremlin jewels and not worry a wink, you know that? Sure you do, my dear. Like it or not, you're a good Soviet. You have a wonderful vocabulary in four languages, but the word 'betrayal' is just not in any of them. You're one of us, whether you know it or not."

Am I, my dear Anyuta? Am I really? How can you be so sure? Miriam thought.

Anna went on blithely, saying, "I bet those guys're already in the United States—the land of milk and honey. They gave our stupid spooks the slip. How clever! I'll give them that."

"Yes," Miriam said quietly.

"They can always lay it off on the Jews. In the end, that lets everyone, I guess, even the old softy heart, right off the hook. The Jews are always so convenient, aren't they, Miriam? I mean, if we didn't have the Jews, then we'd just have to invent them, wouldn't we?" Anna said with a wry little laugh.

"Of course," Miriam said sadly, adding, "Perhaps that's why my orders came through so easily. They want to get rid of me—one less Jew to worry over."

"Oh, no," said Anna, "That's not it. Not it at all, my dear. Everyone knows why you're leaving. There's no secret there either, but like I said, everyone trusts you, Miriam. You're different, very different. Everyone loves you," Anna said finally, her eyes welling with tears. She picked up Miriam's valise, "Here you are. You mustn't miss your train."

The station voice squawked again, seemingly with greater urgency. Anna followed her to the step of the car and handed over a bulging suitcase.

"Goodbye, my dear, I'll see you soon," she said tearfully. "We'll meet again somehow, don't worry. I just know it. But goodbye for now, and God bless you!"

Miriam hesitated, then thought, *Now's the moment. I knew it would come, and now it has. I must do it now.*

"Here, here, take this!" she said hurriedly, thrusting Alexander's ring into Anna's hand.

"Oh my God! What's this?!" Anna said, truly shocked as she took the little purple box.

"It's my engagement ring, the one Sasha gave me. I have not quite broken things off, but I must give this back to him. Please take it and give it to him. I beg you, do me this favor," she said, closing Anna's hand around it. "I trust you. You're my dearest friend; please, you must take it to him!"

The loudspeaker rasped for the final call, and people rushed aboard, brushing by Miriam as she stood before the train steps.

"But, Miriam, dear, what am I to say?"

"Tell him I love him dearly," she said, hugging Anna and kissing her, then turned and disappeared up the little steps into the train. Anna, holding the ring in her hand like an offering, shouted out another goodbye, but Miriam was gone. In an instant there was a whistle and a jolt as the train pulled away.

34

The City of Dreams

Miriam kept shuffling down the aisle, all the while trying to dissolve the lump in her throat with thoughts of the future. *I can't believe I'm really going to Vienna. I haven't been there since I was a little girl. My parents met and courted in the city of my new hopes, the cultural capital of Central Europe, the Paris of the German-speaking world, and I'm going there at last! How wonderful it feels to finally be on the way to Vienna! Deborah and David would be so happy for me!*

She found an empty window seat, where she settled with a deep sense of relief, but watching the environs of Berlin, its ruins and wreckage unwinding slowly past, was too much, so she looked around perhaps to catch a familiar face. She did, but not one she relished; it was an office worker with her fat husband sitting nearby. She waved and smiled sweetly at Miriam from across the aisle.

Oh, yes, she thought, waving in return, *the secretary in the translation shop. How absurd she looks, sitting there so chipper in that silly hat with her disheveled little husband squeezing a bag between his knees. I wonder if she is a spy, an informant, sent to follow me because of the defectors. Most secretaries inform on everyone; everyone knows that.*

The woman smiled again. Miriam gave a tentative wave and tried but failed to smile in return.

No, they would never use her; she's much too obvious, too friendly, couldn't keep her mouth shut, Miriam decided, as she said hello and asked where they were going. Soon they were chattering, the fat husband even daring to squeeze a word in here and there.

They made their way to Prague, an old and very beautiful city, outwardly untouched by war, and they stopped in the afternoon. Some unsmiling uniformed officials waddled their way between the rows to tell them they would be staying a few days.

"What's going on?" Miriam asked.

"It's a secret," someone whispered knowingly.

Then a nearby man said quietly, "Czechoslovakia is having its first postwar elections.[46] The Soviets want the people of Czechoslovakia to have a completely free choice. We're all going to nice hotels; we'll remain there in isolation until the voting is over. We do not want to influence them in any way," this person said rather ponderously. "It must be entirely free."

To Miriam this seemed a little too canned, too at-the-ready. *Who is he? How does he know so much?* But it was true. They cabbed to a nice hotel near Wenceslas Square to be told they had three hours to shop before being sequestered.

"Three hours to see Prague!" Miriam said to her acquaintance, the wife and secretary. "Three hours! I want to run down and see good King Wenceslas's statue."

"Do we have time?" her friend asked.

"Sure, if we hurry. There're some shops on the street," Miriam cried as they literally ran from the hotel, entering the square a few blocks away.

Miriam was amazed. In the heart of Europe a great medieval prince still ruled from the back of a stone horse, as, under its legs, pigmy-like crowds proclaimed democracy through a microphone.

"Come on," said her friend, tugging and pointing, "We'll go into those stores over there. Let's go now before it's too late!"

They ducked into several shops, but Miriam wanted to go to the Old Town, the Jewish quarter (Josefov), Charles Bridge, and the famous castle overlooking the Vltava River. There were so many things to see, but she could not. She could only taste it like a sip of rare wine.

But it was difficult to be angry. The merchants refused their rubles; Miriam and her friend paid for nothing. "The Red Army saved us. You won the war. We cannot accept your money. This is a gift," they had said, handing them things they had intended to pay for.

No more frowns of hatred! We're heroes! What joy!

The next day the hoopla marched beneath her feet in a carnival of red and gold, but the outcome was never in doubt. Up came a bouquet of flowers—a smiling Soviet soldier applauded as, catching them, she waved like a damsel in a castle flirting with a knight. *I'm a princess at last! Russian and not Romanian, but does it matter?*

Within two short days, they resumed their journey. At the Austrian frontier, glum officials entered to search everyone. Miriam had burnt her letters for fear of interrogation, so they found nothing, only her passport, which they stamped disappointedly. Then the train was moving again—clicking through the environs and slowly into Vienna, which unlike Prague, though outwardly untouched, seemed exhausted, drained, collapsed into a colorless shell. This great center of culture, art, and music had at last turned a little gray, even despondent.

Miriam was too excited to be put-off, and, besides, Gustav was here. He was always fun; he would meet her and show her everything. *Who knows? Maybe I can even find Karl. I'll have a friend, maybe even a brother!* She told herself that Vienna might still work its famous magic, as the train clicked and clicked into the central station. *Sasha told me I could be reborn.*

Sasha?! My God! What have I done to you, my dear?! What have I done?! What did he say when Anyuta returned the ring? How very good he was to me! How he loved me! And, in my way, I loved him. How terrible I've been! How insensitive! How ungrateful! And after all, Isaac is gone, and who will I ever find to love me as he did? What have I done?!

Then a growl said, "Your papers, please." It was an unhappy boy in a uniform who looked her over and then pointed, telling her where to report. Here, they sent her to another building several blocks away, where a thin young woman opened the door, greeted her warmly, and showed her around.

"We're almost in the city center, across from the French Embassy. With you it makes four of us girls, quite cozy, no?" she said with a sprightly laugh.

Miriam tried to appear pleased, but the accommodations were less satisfying than in Berlin. She felt a wave of remorse as she followed silently down the ever-darker hall.

"This is your room here," the woman said, opening a door to a tiny space barely containing a bed, a dresser, and a closet. "Your view, since we're on the back of the building, is not the best," she said, taking Miriam to the window. "See what I mean?" she asked, making a gesture toward some dilapidated brown buildings on a dingy side street.

Miriam was depressed.

"You can relieve it by closing the shade." She snapped down the shade with a little chuckle of delight. "*Voilà!* But this, as you can see, shuts out the light, so it's sun with drabness or darkness without, that's up to you. The French spy on us when they are in the mood. Really, it's better to keep the window shades closed. Be careful. You don't want to be sent back. We're watched a lot. Everyone watches everyone. Vienna is a nest of intrigue. Have fun and enjoy yourself, but trust no one."

Miriam nodded, "Yes," of course. She did not argue. She knew better than that. Excusing herself, she managed to slip out and wander the neighborhood "to get my bearings," as she liked to say. The post-war bleakness was mitigated by the first flush of the spring of 1946, and she soon found the larger city retained a certain understated charm. In time, she grew fond of it. "Like an acquired taste; it's my first olive," she said one day, pleased with her own wit.

Miriam quickly fell into the routine of going out with Gustav and friends. They took her to concerts, the opera, and to American movies. But late dinners in fine restaurants, done without seeing the same menu twice, were a delight. Fine food remained her real pleasure, her only true indulgence, but Gustav paid for everything. He was good to her with no conditions, no questions, and no demands.

On her own, Miriam walked everywhere, not forbidden, and she never bothered with the expense of cabs. "Walking is the best way to learn a city, anyway," she always insisted when Gustav offered a taxi. "You should walk more, my dear. You miss a lot, hidden away in the luxury of a back seat, as the city flies by in a passing series of shadows, like an unexamined life."

Nevertheless, a little knot of fear always strolled with her down the dark, sometimes narrow streets. She felt she was moving between two worlds without really being part or quite sure of either. Indeed, she caught herself looking over her shoulder, wondering, guarding her tongue, watching, and double-checking everyone and everything.

But Gustav's world, she soon realized, was something quite different from her own. He was a comfortable member of it, with one romance after another, till eventually, quite unexpectedly, he had a wife—a dark-eyed beauty from Moscow, Yelena Andreyevna, with a perfect figure, who wore the latest French clothes naturally, as they should be worn.

Miriam watched her closely, gradually perceiving that her "sophistication" arose, as was the case with a lot of Russian women, from the depths of a profound ignorance. She was in reality a peasant girl, from the soil and not the city, who had rather rapidly become the grand dame made over by her good-looking, suave Gustav. But Yelena was a very quick study and played her Pygmalion role well. Everyone knew her culture was a veneer, but after all, they were the victors and wanted to move with pride among "their European betters," as Miriam put it one night to Gustav after an unaccustomed second glass of very fine Bordeaux had loosened her tongue.

Yet Miriam, for her part, went about more "in the English style," as someone observed, that is, with a certain restrained dignity, having just a little more than she showed, knowing just a little more than she said, affecting a more tailored, "sensible" look, even "hard earned." She let Gustav and his bride be the glamorous ones, worthy of Hollywood with all the violins, smoke, cocktails, and expensive things. She was not cheered by these differences but had thought them through, preferring the safety of an unobtrusive and understated style to one that stood out or, worse, bred envy. In a word, being herself was not only less trouble but very much safer.

As always, Miriam lost herself in work. Her German was so good that she was soon assigned to the Allies' interpreter department, where she found herself working with Mr. Compton from the United Kingdom and Mr. Morton from the United States, plus a very anonymous and usually absent debonair Frenchman. All were fluent German speakers in charge of providing translations and, as always, were suspected by the Soviets of being spies. The truant Frenchman's work was delegated mysteriously to Mr. Compton, who, without ever saying why, did it without complaint. As for Miriam, she was honored as the very hard-working and "diligent little Russian"—a novelty indulged by a patronizing kindness that had about it an implicit air of amusement.

"As the only Russian and a female to boot, I'm forever the odd man out," she once joked to Gustav. "Too," she also explained in the same conversation with a sly smile, "I was educated in Kharkov."

"Is that where you learned your wonderful German?" Mr. Morton asked with a frigid smile.

"Yes, of course, at the institute there," she said, trying hard not to appear uncomfortable.

"It must've been very good, indeed."

"Yes, the best," she added, glancing down and pretending to concentrate on some work.

It was clear she was not what the Allies had expected—a very pleasant surprise—but soon she found herself acting as Mr. Morton's unofficial secretary, working through his appointments and assisting in his very busy sideline "business" with women: buying and selling things, particularly dresses, which he not only sold but gave away and traded, always sending the best designs home to America. Eventually, she and Mr. Morton became good friends.

One evening, in a hotel bar, with Yelena yammering away at a nearby table, Miriam said quietly to Gustav, "You know, in Vienna one is a spy whether one wants to be or not."

He laughed a little too loudly, saying, "Of course, everyone spies on everyone else. We're all spies. We spy on the Allies, they spy on us; we spy on ourselves, the Allies on each other. Round and round it goes, and all is secret, and all is known, and none of it really matters. Things will turn out the same way, no matter what is known or unknown. It's absurd, positively absurd, Miriam. Just remember, don't let it affect you. Don't get into trouble. Trust no one, my dear."

"Trust no one?" she asked with a slight grimace.

"No one."

"No even you, Gustav?"

"Not even me, although I would try to save you. But you never know; they could put the burn on me, and I might have to betray you," he said gravely.

"You would never betray me, Gustav, of that I'm certain."

"Yes, yes, you're right, dear, I would die first. Still, you must be on your guard. We're all watched, but you know that, don't you?"

"Yes, I know it."

"You are debriefed?"

"You know I am."

"Do they ask about me?"

"You know they do; I've told you."

"And you say we are friends, and so on."

"Yes, and they believe me."

"They don't think we are lovers?"

"No," she laughed, a little embarrassed, "of that they are certain. Love is impossible to hide; it's the most obvious thing in the world. You know better than anyone about that, my dear, Gustav," she said with a wink.

"Yes, you're absolutely right," he said, chuckling quietly, "but one can be a lover without being in love, can't one?"

"You should know the answer to that, shouldn't you?" she said with only a hint of a smile.

"You know what a hopeless romantic I am," he responded with an overly loud, rather self-conscious laugh. "But I would never compromise you."

"Oh, of course not," she said, her smile broadening, adding more seriously, "nor I you."

"No, no one thinks you would."

"So, besides, they'll never put the burn on me about you, Gustav."

"Really? Are you certain? You can never be sure what they might ask. They are capable of anything, you know. Have they got Karl somewhere? What if they threatened him? What would you do then?"

"But, Gustav, dearest, you have done nothing, and I love you like a brother."

"Yes, yes, I know. And I love you, too, very much, you know that. But see, they have their ways."

"Yes, sure, I see that, but they don't need me to give them anything about you; they know everything about you already," she said with quick laugh, "and, as for me, they know all worth knowing already, too."

"Yes," he said with a heavy sigh, "I'm afraid you are right again, but they only tolerate us because of our German, you know, nothing more. That's a weak thread to hang from, so be careful with everyone," he said, glancing away to find and light a Lucky Strike, which he exhaled with the greatest of pleasure. "Miriam, forgive me, dear, would you like a cigarette?"

"You know I would, thank you," she said, taking one and leaning over the table to accept his light, then sitting back to exhale and study him with an odd look.

35

The Price of Loyalty

"My dear, everyone knows you're not some half-educated, precocious peasant girl from Kharkov who learned German at some provincial institute because you have the ear of a parrot," Mr. Morton said one day when they were unexpectedly alone. "You must be from the Baltic states," he added. "Am I right, huh?"

Miriam went a little pale.

"Oh, you don't have to answer, but you fool me not," he said, wagging a finger. "Nor is Mr. Compton fooled by your little legend," he added with a chuckle. "But don't worry, no one cares."

Miriam was unsuccessful in disguising her surprise.

"It doesn't matter, really. No one cares at all, Miriam. Tell me, what are you doing tomorrow?" he asked, now leaning over.

"Tomorrow?"

"Yes, tomorrow."

"What do you mean, Mr. Morton?" she asked with a deeply worried expression.

"I mean, would you do me the honor of going with me to have lunch at a nice café and maybe do some shopping?"

"Shopping? Where?"

"In the French sector."

"You know I can't go into the French sector, Mr. Morton. It's strictly forbidden."

"You have nothing to worry about. You'll be perfectly safe. It will be delightful, and you can do some shopping."

"I can't afford the French sector. You know that, Mr. Morton, I have no money for such a thing, none at all."

"It will be on me and easily arranged. You get in the car as always, and we will go in such a way that you have nothing whatsoever to worry about."

"Can you promise me that?" she asked, weakening because she had always wanted to go to the French sector, and the idea of lunch and shopping was very appealing.

"Yes, absolutely."

The afternoon exceeded her hopes, as Mr. Morton had said it would, but also it was a mistake. She was called in at once and interrogated.

"Junior Lieutenant Kellerman, what were you doing in the French sector? You know you are never to go there, of course. Why do you hang around with Mr. Morton all the time? What is your relationship with him? Are you his mistress? Where's the Frenchman? Why does he never come to work? Why does Mr. Compton accept the burden of the Frenchman's work as well as his own? Do you discuss politics?"

She could only say her superior wanted her to know everything and everyone in the section.

"Did you tell him you were going?" he asked.

She had a ready answer. "I hadn't time. It was spur of the moment. I have been instructed to get to know the Allies, to do things with them, get close to them, so I have been cultivating Mr. Morton because it might be useful. He might have information. He asked me to go to the French sector to have lunch, and I thought it would be an excellent way to ingratiate myself. I was simply doing as I was told. How can I learn anything useful from him otherwise? If he doesn't like and trust me?"

"Have you gone to bed with him?"

Miriam blushed.

"Huh, have you?"

"No."

"Would you?"

"If it were necessary," she lied.

The officer seemed half convinced. The implications, to be sure, were enormous. Jews were never to be trusted, and she now found herself lumped in with all the rest. This choice assignment she owed to her German abilities and her pull from Gustav, but there were obvious disadvantages—there was no friendly colonel, no Sasha to protect her, and Gustav could only do so much. *I have to be more careful, be on my guard, be ready for the worst. This is not like Berlin at all, she reminded herself. Was this what Gustav was trying to warn me about but couldn't quite say?*

The next day, to her surprise, she found herself isolated once again with Mr. Morton. Though small, the office usually had lots of traffic, but that day they were alone, and she wondered if it were somehow planned.

Mr. Morton did not hesitate. He said, moving very close to her and speaking in a low voice, "Miriam, as I've mentioned before, you don't fool me or anyone, really, with that silly Kharkov story. You're from the western republics somewhere, perhaps the Baltics. Your German is much too good, much too perfect, my dear, and besides you have a slight Viennese accent that you are not quite able to disguise, try as you might. Where, I wonder, did you pick that up? Huh?"

Miriam blanched.

Mr. Morton did not wait for her to recover. "What I'm going to say will come as a shock. You do not have to go back to the Soviet Union. That'd be suicide. I wanted you to be compromised. I knew we were being tailed when we went to the French sector. I did it on purpose."

Miriam's complexion went from pale to red.

"I did it precisely so you would feel you have no choice. I don't want anything from you, you can give me nothing, but I want to push you out of the Soviet nest, my dear, for your own good. I like you, and you don't belong in that uniform you wear so well. You are not really one of them, and you know it. It shows. The whole thing is an act, I see that plainly enough; everyone does."

"Mr. Morton?!" she gasped.

But he continued, saying quickly, "Believe me when I tell you that my sources say your days now are numbered. You are no longer trusted."

"Mr. Morton, you betrayed me! You lied to me! I thought you were my friend!" she said in a loud whisper.

"Listen, Miriam, you don't understand, I am your friend," he said with a very serious look, leaning over even closer, almost touching her, and whispering, "I am a Jew, and I know you are a Jew, too."

Miriam gasped again. "How did you know that?"

Mr. Morton leaned back and laughed. "My dear, as I have said, you fool no one. You and I are the same, the very same. My family came from Vienna, and we escaped. Now I am trying to help you do just that, that's all. You were really doomed before I took you to the French sector, but I wanted to make it plain to you, that's all, shake you out of that fool's paradise you've been living in ever since you got here."

He continued, "Listen, Miriam, anti-Semitism will only get worse. Stalin hates the Jews as much as Hitler did. There'll be a new purge soon. You won't survive. This, my dear, is your only chance, the only one. I can smuggle you out, get you a job."

Miriam remained silent as her face flushed a deeper, very much hotter, crimson. She was being burned by Mr. Morton.

Since she did not speak, he spoke for her. "Where? You must wonder, 'where will I go?' To America, of course. As you know I'm from New York. I know people there, lots of people. You're smart, young, attractive, single, charming. You'll meet someone in time, marry, have a family, if that's what you want—to start over. Both of us are Jews. You know that about me now, and I know that you're a Jew, too; you've just admitted it. You don't look like a little Kharkov girl, a sweet, half-ignorant, Gentile peasant. Ha! I've told you, everyone saw through you, did from the very first day, my dear. It was all such a charming joke!"

Here he laughed quietly, adding, "But you've no chance whatsoever in the Soviet Union. Don't kid yourself about that, my dear. No chance whatsoever. They won't forget you—they never forget anyone, and they know everything about you, everything. You're useful now, sure, but how about later, when they're done with you? You'll be ground up in their machine and thrown away like a piece of rubbish," he said with a wave of his hand. "It'll be like you never existed."

Now he leaned even closer, as if he were going to kiss her, saying in a loud whisper, "Miriam, dear, you absolutely must flee now while you still have the chance. You'll probably never get another. It's now or never. Now or never! You must understand this. Save yourself, Miriam. Don't hesitate! Save yourself while there's still time!"

Miriam shifted away from him, choking out an unintelligible answer. She tried again to speak but could not. He had spoken to her very heart, exposed her worst fears, set them before her as if on paper. The paranoia, the unease, the knot in her stomach, the mistrust—all fell from his lips, as if he had seen into her very soul.

He sat back a bit and then, speaking into her silence, said matter-of-factly, "You know of course that they watch you all the time. They never stop watching you, ever since you got to Vienna, you and your foolish friend, Gustav. He has high-up friends, sure, but his position is quite precarious. He's on loan, you know, is not really one of them. And Moscow Center hates successful Jews like him. They're no different from the Nazis. Believe me, they're all the same! Come away, please, come away now, before it's too late. I can arrange everything without any difficulty."

Miriam was silent. How did he know about Gustav?! Was he an interpreter for counterintelligence, after all? She had never mentioned him to the Allies. But Mr. Morton knew everything! She knew he must be correct. He did not say anything she had not already known. Now she was being shown a way out, a way that simply would not come again. It was now or never, just like he said.

She tried to think. *I have to think of Karl, refuse because of him. There'd be reprisals. I must not escape till he is safely away. I'm afraid to speak, perhaps the room is bugged. Of course, Karl, somewhere, wherever he is, is planning to defect. If I defect, Karl'll be arrested and sent to a camp or worse. He wouldn't survive. Like poor dear Abrasha! He'd die because of me! Then I'd be alone! I can't have my brother's blood on my hands, even if it costs me my life. Better to die first!*

Finding her voice by clearing her throat, she spoke clearly, not afraid of being overheard, "Thank you, Mr. Morton, but I'm a Soviet officer. I'm loyal, and I have a job to do. If you'll excuse me, please," she said, getting up and going to the door. As she opened it without looking back, she could feel Mr. Morton's eyes fixed upon her, but she did not turn around.

With the door's click she knew she had locked herself tightly inside the Soviet Union, possibly forever. The Iron Curtain had just closed shut behind her with a quiet but solid click, and she might never escape or see freedom, wherever that was, again.

36

The Train to Minsk

The summer of 1946 intruded upon Vienna softly, with the smell of flowers sweetening the air. The city windows sprang open to embrace the warmth and admit the sound of Strauss's waltzes that touched the ear like a benediction. This was the city the Romans had built to keep out the barbarians; the city that, within a thousand years, had defeated the Turks and saved the West; the city of the greatest family in Europe, the Habsburgs, who through marriage and war had built one of its greatest empires; the city of assimilation of the New World as well as the Old of Spanish, Slav, Hungarian, Italian, German, and Jew. Welcoming and hospitable, it was a capital of ease and good living, where people ate the best food, made love, waltzed, read the best books, went to the best theatre, and listened to the world's best music—Haydn, Mozart, Beethoven, Schubert, and Brahms. It cultivated great art and thought great thoughts about culture and the inexhaustible labyrinth of the mind—Freud revealing the subconscious of the one and Jung that of the many—so she knew very well how to change her moods, to discover her truer and better self.

Thus, in the year of '46, Miriam Kellerman found her favorite city struggling again to uncover the old enchantment and charm, to lift her spirit as from a chrysalis into a new post-war world, and, in doing so, to find a second youth. As for Miriam, she went to parties, operas, museums, cafés, and restaurants and once even danced with an American general. Gradually she had the delightful, illusory feeling of actually being Viennese, of finding herself, too, like the city with a new life and wishing she could remain forever—*maybe this is my real home, after all*, she thought, *the only one I'll ever really have. I am being reborn within the bosom of my parents' city.*

One evening she was introduced to a diminutive but quite handsome young Jew with serious eyes that were as dark as olives. He was in the army engineers, well educated but much too introspective to be a true army type. Miriam liked this. She preferred somewhat shy people with whom she could relax and be herself. He was very much a gentleman and, perhaps most importantly, did not ask questions. When they went to parties and she was tired, they quickly left, and when she was in a bad mood, he didn't complain. In a word, he accepted Junior Lieutenant Miriam Kellerman for what she was.

Slowly, inexorably, and to her great surprise, she found herself falling in love, almost against her will. *It was just like in the Marlene Dietrich song, "Falling in love again, couldn't help it,"* she sang inwardly, remembering the sad words Marlene cooed out in her heavy Berlin accent and husky, sensual voice in the famous film.

Miriam and her new beau even did a little research on Vienna. Like detectives, they managed to locate a few important addresses. Freud lived at Berggasse and his coffeehouse was at Dr. Karl Lueger Ring, whereas Trotsky had drunk his coffee and read his endless newspapers around the corner on Herrengasse at Café Central. To their horror, they learned that Hitler had lived on Meldemannstrasse, a few trolley stops down from Freud. It seemed strange that Zweig could walk the same streets as Hitler, breathe the same air. "Did they listen to the same music?" Miriam wondered upon learning that, as an impoverished nobody, Hitler had slept on park benches and starved himself for the cheapest opera tickets. Even more surprising was the discovery that, for a short time, Stalin had lived very close to Schloss Schönbrunn, Emperor Joseph's summer palace. But they did not go there; something held them back.

It was interesting and diverting to do these things, and it was abundantly clear that Gregory Zlotnik could provide Miriam with the kind of emotionally safe harbor that she craved. This was what, she gradually realized, she had been looking for since she lost Isaac.

One evening, after escaping a very loud and drunken party, she found herself sitting on a bench near the Ring Strasse with Gregory asking her to marry him. She was not quite shocked, but neither was she quite prepared. It was another hard bump in the emotional road. *Why does it always seem to come to this?* she thought in a flash, remembering Sasha, who was never far from her thoughts.

Pausing, she said quietly and a little too sternly, "You don't know me."

"I think I do," he said quickly. Then he waited with half a smile for her answer.

"Let me think it over," she replied.

"Of course," he agreed.

But the next day he brought it up again, and this time she said, "No," almost rudely.

Gregory was visibly hurt, and she wished to say something by way of amends, but before she could, he said with a blunt kindness, "Miriam, do you want me to tell you why you don't want to marry?"

"You can't marry me," she said, ignoring what he had just asked.

"Why not?"

Then she told him a great deal about her past but not quite everything. He remained quiet. She thought of the small clump of returned letters to Mrs. Anna and Dr. Kasparova, her best friends who were seemingly gone without a trace—vanished. She thought of Abraham, dead for being a Zionist, and of the new anti-Semitic wave awaiting them in Stalin's "paradise." Getting married seemed to be the worse possible alternative, another complication, another hurt. That was the iron pattern of her life: periods of peace followed by another great pain—*that was it, peace and pain.*

Then she added, "I've suffered too much. I don't think I'd be a very good wife."

Gregory waited a few more days. Then one evening when the sun was bearing down hotly on them, he said, holding out his hand gently, "You must decide, now or never. Nothing you have told me matters or has changed anything. If possible, I love you even more, but you must decide, now or never."

Miriam looked into his eyes then, and, to her own great surprise, accepted him. "Yes," she said, "I will." Perhaps it was the "now or never" that did the trick, she wasn't sure.

He kissed her lightly on the cheek. She put her hand on his shoulder and began to dream that maybe a new life was really possible, knowing too well how many times she had believed that. Still, knowing there always seemed to be a fate waiting for Miriam Kellerman, she was resigned to it and anticipated the next act it had written out for her.

She did not have to wait long, because the very next morning a glum-faced Mr. Morton stepped into her office and said rather portentously, "Miriam, I'm afraid there's a gentleman here to see you."

Miriam arose slowly and walked into the foyer, where the gentleman was waiting. He was NKGB and quickly introduced himself as such. He said gruffly, staring with steel blue eyes, "Junior Lieutenant Kellerman, I'm here to report that your brother, Karl Kellerman, has fled the Soviet Union; he's a traitor. You're to report to Moscow at once! Your ticket for the Moscow train will be at the station. Here are your orders," he said, handing them to her rudely. "I warn you: be on that train!" he growled and left.

Miriam looked at the papers in terror. Mr. Morton, as always, had been right. *My God! I should've run. Karl has! Now it's too late. I'll be watched constantly! There's no escape! Any false move and I'll be arrested, and things'll just be worse. My only hope is to cooperate. But I can't complain. After all, Karl warned me in Moscow. I should've listened. I should have saved myself and let Karl take care of Karl. He has never needed me for that, and I should have not worried about him. Now I am trapped and will never leave the Soviet Union, even if I survive. What a fool I was not to take Mr. Morton's offer! What a fool! How stupid I have been! How very stupid!*

She went immediately to her apartment. It was depressingly empty. Frantically, she threw her things into two suitcases and scribbled out a farewell note: "Dear friends, I'm leaving for Moscow in the morning. Have gone to say goodbye to Gregory. Thank you for everything." She scratched her name, tossed the paper on the table, and hurried out.

There was no point in hiding. She went straight to Gregory. Everyone knew everything but him. She sat him down and bluntly, almost cruelly, told everything in a great flood of words and emotion.

He waited for a very long time, then took her hand and said, "It'll be all right, Miriam. I love you. That's the important thing. All of that is in the past, but it's not the end, only a new beginning. They won't do anything to you now, not with your record. It's immaculate. You've done nothing wrong. The most they'll do is kick you out of the army. Of course, you can't come back here. You'll need a place to stay." He scratched out the address of his family's apartment in Minsk and handed it to her. "As soon as you're able, go there. I'll meet you in Minsk, in our apartment. Here's some money," he said, thrusting a wad of rubles into her hand, folding her fingers tightly over it. "I'll write to them and say you're coming. My stepmother will look after you until I arrive. Of course, I'll put in a request to leave as soon as I can. I'll join you, we'll be together. Don't worry, we'll meet again, my dear. All will yet be well. I'll see you in Minsk."

'We'll meet again.' Oh, how sad are those words! How tragic! How many times had they been nothing but a false hope?! she thought. *'We will meet again.'* The motto of this terrible time! But now, maybe, just maybe, it would all be true, she told herself. Maybe all she had to do was follow his advice and everything would, after all, come right. But she could not stop worrying. *Perhaps Gregory was wrong. Perhaps I'll be sent to the camps or shot. I don't know.*

After a long, clinging, tearful embrace, he took her home. The next morning he picked her up, took her to the station, and she left for Moscow.

Miriam sat alone, looking out again as the monotonous plains of Eastern Europe unrolled sadly past her window. She was going into Russia once more, but there'd be no one to meet her. No brother, no friend, no relative. She was on her own. Everyone had been taken from her. All she had now was this kind young man from Minsk. She always needed someone or something more than herself.

It was a dreadful trip to Moscow. She hardly slept, and when she finally arrived, she was sent to a dormitory that was loud, dirty, and not unlike a prison. The next morning she was ordered to an office where she was curtly directed to present her papers and told to have a seat in a dark little hall. She waited more than an hour till finally a frowning, uniformed frump showed her into a larger office where, surprisingly, she was greeted by a major she had known in Berlin, now posted to Moscow Center.

The major waited until the door snapped quietly shut, leaving them alone, and then said, "Ah, Junior Lieutenant Kellerman," his face lighting up in recognition. "We meet again. May I see your papers, please?" he asked, rising slightly from behind his desk, reaching for the orders and sitting again.

She stood stiffly at attention as he flipped pages and then glanced up. "You know, of course, I'm supposed to give you a dishonorable discharge," he said very matter-of-factly.

"Yes," she said meekly.

"You know, too, what that means?" he asked.

"Yes," she replied almost in a whisper.

"Why has this happened?" he asked, sitting back, making the chair creak.

Miriam explained, but the major had obviously read her file.

"I see," he said with a sad laugh. "My boss is away. He's very strict. The dishonorable discharge gains our country nothing, and if you get that, you will not survive. You know that? You will be arrested sooner or later."

Miriam nodded.

"You'll go to the camps; it's only a matter of time."

"Yes," she said, "I know, Comrade Major."

"But you've served the Motherland well," he said, leaning forward over the desk, looking at her closely. "You've served courageously, without blemish. Your army days are over, but you are very fortunate. I will give you an honorable discharge. You'll have a chance then."

Miriam's eyes flashed. She started to speak, but he interrupted.

"You know, Junior Lieutenant Kellerman, our Motherland has been through the worst ordeal in history. She has suffered beyond imagination; you have suffered; we all have suffered. It is understandable you're confused about your national origin. I'm convinced you're actually Maldavian. Let me put you down as Maldavian, for your nationality, I mean. How would you like that? It's...it's...far better to be anything other than a Jew."

Miriam realized the major was taking a great risk. *He hardly knows me; why is he doing this?* So many people had helped her along the way— the doctor who saved her foot, the guard who let her steal wood, Zinoida, Dr. Kasparova, Mrs. Anna, Golitsyn, Sasha, Gustav—so very many—and now this major whom she hardly knew. Everywhere she had gone she had found people who had helped her. *It's always these, really, in the end, ordinary people who're truly good. Only they are ever really kind,* she decided.

For a moment her pessimism about the world evaporated. The major had no ulterior motive whatsoever, except maybe that of being human. *Maybe that's what the world needs more than anything, to be human. He could lose everything—and gain nothing. His colonel would have been quite different; from him I'd have gotten a death sentence. Of this I am certain.*

"Sir," she said quietly, "Comrade Major, you're very kind, thank you, but I cannot accept. My parents were Jews, and I'm a Jew, too. My mother and father were murdered by Hitler simply because they were Jews. I'm sorry, but I cannot dishonor their memory. It was for them that I chose to live. I had no other reason, not really. I cannot deny them. I thank you for the honorable discharge, but, as to nationality, please write down 'Jew.' I can never be anything else but a Jew from Czernowitz. All my life I'll be that. No matter where I go in this world, I'll just be a Jew trying to get home again, wherever that is. But thank you, sir, thank you a thousand times for your kindness," she said, locking her eyes with his and pulling herself up to attention as best she could, almost clicking her heels.

"Very well," he smiled as he wrote, "I thought you'd say that. Here's your honorable discharge and a ticket for Minsk," he said, offering her a new set of orders with a transportation voucher on top, pressed down with his thumb, "your papers and the ticket for the train tonight; the train to Minsk. Don't fail to be on it."

"Thank you, Comrade Major," she said, saluting smartly, then turned and walked out.

The major watched and saluted as she closed the door very gently. He had not told her that it was a call from Dr. Polyakov, a report from Golitsyn, and, most important, the overheard and duly recorded conversation with Mr. Morton that had saved her. But it was all there, in her file that he signed, closed, and put away—the file of Junior Lieutenant Miriam Kellerman, a Jew from Czernowitz, now honorably discharged and able to start a new life.

Afterword

From 1960 until the 1980s, the world's Jewish organizations started helping Soviet Jews emigrate abroad legally. This opened the gates for all of us. One had the impression that the flood of a big river brought thousands of people upon its waves. However, we, Gregory and I, could not leave the Soviet Union at that time; our daughter was too young; therefore, we had to wait.

I do remember well coming home from an award ceremony, crying bitterly on account of the injustice and anti-Semitism I encountered there. That was the last straw.

It became known in 1976 that part of the 1980 Summer Olympics would be conducted in Minsk. That would be an additional opportunity for Jews residing in the city. We decided to join a line at the visa department to hand in our papers to leave. Finally, in July 1980, we ended up in front of the customs officers. They threw everything in our suitcases on the floor. Worst of all were the cries of our little children, whose clothes were taken off. Our baby was 29 days old and sleeping on a heap of cloth diapers. I was very angry. I put the child on the countertop and told them in a rude tone, "You can check out the child; we have hidden gold and silver in the diapers." They did not touch the child, yet my beautiful custom jewelry with amber, purchased in the museums of the Baltic Republics, was on the floor. I did not crawl at the feet of the officers, instead leaving everything there. The officers were astonished by my unusual behavior, and they let us leave.

In November 1980, a couple of weeks before Thanksgiving, we arrived in Little Rock. To say that I did not want to come to this little place that I could not find on the map was an understatement. I called my brother and told him about my grievances. He calmed me down, promising to pay our moving to any large city where he had friends who could help us with jobs in our professions.

Calmer after that, I looked around the apartment and went out into the yard. The apartment was clean; everything we needed was in it. The refrigerator was stuffed with food by Russian immigrants who prepared Russian meals. Representatives of the organization were with us the whole time, explaining every detail.

I was ashamed of myself for hurting the feelings of everyone who helped us, donated things, even money to welcome us here. I prayed to God asking for forgiveness and thanking Him for His help.

The next day we went grocery shopping at Safeway. We entered the store and I could not move; I was in a wonderland. After having stood in lines for food for 37 years, I could not believe my eyes. The manager offered us a cart to take our purchases home until we acquired a car. While we were going home with our cart full of different things, people stopped to offer us a ride home. We were more than surprised; tears were running along our cheeks. In Russia, nobody would have done that, though we were told the whole time that people are the biggest wealth of a nation and we have to be nice and support one another.

A new feeling overwhelmed me. I understood that Arkansans are as warm as the weather, that I have new friends. People from all over—from companies, synagogues, churches—came to our apartment, offering help, support, money. I fell in love with this small state and its people.

Thanks to the support of the Little Rock community and the JFA, we achieved a lot. The main achievement is personal freedom, religious freedom, equality in everything. We belong to B'Nai Israel, a reformed Jewish congregation. In its sanctuary my daughter, Asya, was married. Her wedding became a community affair because she was the first Jewish immigrant to be married to a born American. In that sanctuary our grandchildren were given their Jewish names and had their bar mitzvahs, and my oldest grandson was married on September 6, 2009.

He had graduated from Central High and went to Washington to meet our president, then Mr. William Clinton. He received his undergraduate degree from Harvard University. Though he could have received his law and business degrees in any Ivy League college, he returned to Little Rock and wanted to work in this state. When I asked him to explain his decision, he answered by asking me some questions: "Grandma, have you not reminded us how much we owe Arkansas and its people for having given us all these possibilities? You personally told us the whole time how grateful we should be for everything we were offered in Arkansas. Haven't you told us about your resolution when you stepped on blessed American soil to never be a burden to the country and its citizens?"

When I took my oath of allegiance to my real Motherland, the USA, I addressed the audience, explaining the meaning of the words written at the foot of the Statue of Liberty: "…I lift the lamp beside the golden door." I told them that the door was golden because it was opened for us to enter the country. It will depend on us to make life golden, silver, or wooden. Gold will never come down from the heavens; we have to work hard and earn it.

I am most thankful for having had the possibility to memorialize my parents, killed brutally in a ghetto, by teaching the lessons of the Holocaust, the meaning of bigotry, faith, violence, and so on.

For all this, I love you, Arkansas—your beautiful forests and lakes, your warmth and friendship, your readiness to help those who were brought to your shores. God bless you and your wonderful people. I will go to my grave hoping that you will always flourish.

Penina Krupitsky
2009

Notes

1. *Czernowitz* is the German, *Cernauti* the Romanian, and *Chernovtsy* the Russian name for the capital of Bukovina, a territory now split between Ukraine and Romania on the northern and northeastern slopes of the Carpathian Mountains. A city today of over a quarter of a million people, it is the capital of the Czernowitz Province of Ukraine. Its history is complex, but in the 18th century it became part of Habsburg Austria and so remained until it was given over to Romania after the 1914–18 war. It was seized by Stalin in 1940 and by Hitler in '41. Always with a large German-speaking Jewish population, at Miriam Kellerman's birth it was about 40% Jewish (45,000). Affectionately nicknamed "Little Vienna," it boasted a 600-year-old synagogue and a great university. Encouraged by Vienna's government, Czernowitz became one of the centers of German culture in Eastern Europe.

2. *Barbarossa* is the German code name for the German invasion of the Soviet Union that occurred on June 22, 1941. It was originally tagged "Plan Fritz," but Hitler changed it to "Operation Barbarossa" in honor of the Holy Roman Emperor Friedrich 1 (1123–1190) known as the "Red Beard." Famous for leading the Third Crusade to the Holy Land, he drowned while attempting to cross a stream in full armor. A legend arose that he had lived on and was residing in a cave in the Kyffhäuser Hills of central Germany, where he was awaiting the call of his Fatherland. Prior to the war it was something of a tradition for schoolchildren to hike to his cave and see the marble statue of this Teutonic hero.

3. The Dniester River, 1,360 km long, is the second-longest river in Ukraine and drains a basin of 72,100 km. It is considered the primary river of Galicia. It begins in the Carpathians, where it is a fast, snow-fed mountain stream; becomes slower, deep, narrow, and winding in its middle; and finally reaches its mouth in the Dniester Estuary above the Black Sea. It was traditionally the border between Ukraine and Romania and, between the wars, marked the Soviet-Romanian boundary.

4. A *Stuka* is a small, two-man German dive-bomber. Known officially as the Junkers Ju 87 *Sturzkampfflugzeug* (diving war plane), it was primarily a close air-support weapon used during the *Blitzkrieg* phase of the war. In this respect it was known for its accuracy in delivering its bombs. Its descent from about 15,000 feet to a release point of about 3,000 feet took only about 30 seconds, flown at a dive angle of 80 degrees with G forces so great that the pilots

frequently vomited or defecated during an attack. It was as much a weapon of terror as anything, and to add to this effect, the *Luftwaffe* fitted a wind-driven siren to the aircraft, earning them the nickname *Jericho-Trompeten* (Trumpets of Jericho). As the war progressed and Germany went over to the defensive with a concomitant loss of air dominance, the Ju 87 became less of a factor because it was vulnerable to air attack. Needless to say, the fate of captured Stuka pilots by either civilians or military was rarely a happy one.

5. *Einsatzgruppen* were mobile killing squads referred to euphemistically as "operational units" organized by Heinrich Himmler under the auspices of the SS for the sole purpose of murdering Jews, partisans, Communist commissars, Gypsies, and other "undesirables" exclusively in Eastern Europe and the Soviet Union. Given "all powers to deal with civilians" by Field Marshal von Brauchitsch, commander and chief of the army, they were to operate under the command of Reinhard Heydrich, who gave orders that "the Jewish population is to be totally exterminated and all Jewish children murdered." This wholesale murder preceded the utilization of the death camps, when it was finally determined that, even though at least a million Jews had been murdered in this way, a more efficient means of extermination had to be employed.

According to John Toland in his biography of Hitler: "To supervise this mass killing, Heydrich and Himmler had been inspired to select officers who, for the most part, were professional men. They included a Protestant pastor, a physician, a professional opera singer, and numerous lawyers. The majority were intellectuals in their early thirties, and it might be supposed such men were unsuited for this work. On the contrary, they brought to the brutal task their considerable skills and training and became, despite qualms, efficient executioners." (Toland, *Adolf Hitler*, Doubleday and Co. Inc., 1976, p. 775.)

On August 10, 1947, Nuremberg Military Tribunal II convicted 20 defendants for their crimes as members of *Einsatzgruppen*, of whom 14 were executed.

6. Proskurov is now known as Khmelnytskyy, a city in Ukraine of some quarter million people and the capital of that province of the same name. Situated on the Southern Buh River, it is a rail and highway terminus. Originally a Polish fortress, it was taken by the Cossacks and later was absorbed by Russia in 1793 during the partition of Poland. In 1919, during the Russian Civil War, many of the Jews, almost half the population, were massacred. And in July 1941 it is reported that 146 Jews were shot by the *Einsatzgruppen*. The name of Proskurov was changed in 1954 to celebrate the 300-year treaty of Russia with the Cossacks.

7. The Carpathian Mountain range begins on the Danube River near Bratislava and sweeps southward, embracing Transylvania and Transcarpathia until ending on the Danube near Orsova in Romania. The range is over 1,500 km in length and varies from 12 to 500 km wide. It rises to as high as 8,705 feet and is the most extensive range of mountains in Europe after the Alps.

8. Stefan Zweig (1881–1942) was born in Vienna to a wealthy Austrian-Jewish family. He quickly acquired a reputation as a writer of fiction, poetry, and biography. He was friends with Freud, Yeats, Gorky, Ravel, Joyce, and Pirandello, to name a few, and was considered one of the leading literary and intellectual figures of his time. In 1934 he fled the Nazis first for England, then the United States, and, finally, to South America. In 1942, Zweig took his own life in Petrópolis, Brazil. His memoir *Die Welt von Gestern* (*The World of Yesterday*) is a tribute to the European culture that he believed was destroyed by the disastrous world wars and Hitlerism.

Harry Zohn, in his introduction to the memoir, refers to Zweig as a "Freudian moralist." He also states that one of Zweig's great themes is "the spiritual superiority of the vanquished."

9. Kazatin, known also as Koziatyn, it is the administrative center of the Koziatyn district of Ukraine. Small in population, it is a railroad hub arising on the Kiev-Baltic railway.

10. Fastov, also known as Fastiv, is a small railroad hub about 100 kilometers to the southwest from Kiev. (Its population today is about 50,000.) This is as close as Miriam got to the Ukrainian capital.

Nuremberg Military Tribunal (NMT) (Vol. 4, p. 19) reports that "In July or August in Fastov, *Sonderkommando* 4a murdered all the Jews between ages of 12 and 60." The *Sonderkommando* ("Special Commando") was a killing group run by the SS. The same NMT document also reports that, down the track a bit from Fastov, "during the period September 7, 1941, to October 5, 1941, in the vicinity of Berdichev, *Einsatzkommando* 5 murdered 8,800 Jews and 207 political officials."

11. *Kolkhoz* is a Soviet collective farm created in Stalin's attempt to socialize agriculture in the 1930s. This policy involved the dispossession and deportation of millions of peasant families, the abolition of private ownership, and the concentration of millions into collectives run by the state. The resulting famine and repression caused the deaths, according to Robert Conquest, of 14.5 million peasants in Ukraine and North Caucasus. (See Conquest, *The Harvest of Sorrow*, Oxford Press, 1986, p. 306.)

12. Rostov, also known as "Rostov on the Don," is a regional capital on the right bank of the Don River only about 30 miles from the Sea of Azov, a large inlet, if you will, of the Black Sea. A seaport, Rostov is famous as the "Gateway to the Caucasus." The Germans took it on Nov. 19, 1941, but the Soviets recaptured it on the 29th; then the Germans took it again on July 28, 1942, but lost it for good again in February 1943 after their defeat at Stalingrad.

13. Lev Davidovich Bronstein Trotsky (1879–1940). Brilliant, erudite, and ruthless, Trotsky was one of the more interesting figures in the Russian Revolution. A Jew born near Kharkov, he became a dedicated Marxist in his youth and was eventually forced into exile, where he met Lenin in London. He did not approve of the latter's authoritarian policies and broke with him in the Menshevik and Bolshevik split of the Social Democratic Party. Later, as a Menshevik, Trotsky returned to Russia to play a leading role in the 1905 Revolution. He was arrested and spent 15 months in prison but was able to escape via Finland. He settled in Vienna with his wife in 1907, where they resided for the next seven years.

With the outbreak of the First World War, he went to Paris but was deported and fled to New York City. With the news of the crises of the Romanov dynasty, he returned to Russia and, reconciled with Lenin and his Bolsheviks, was instrumental in planning the October coup d'etat that overthrew the Kerensky regime. Trotsky was made the Commissar of War and quickly emerged as one of the most important Bolshevik leaders in the Civil War. A bit of a *poseur*, he rode about the various fronts in his armored train that became not only his trademark but, in a sense, that of the Revolution itself. It is one that Boris Pasternak obviously uses in his great novel *Doctor Zhivago*.

Trotsky is credited with founding the Red Army and initiating the commissar system, whereby political officers were assigned joint control of military operations in order to ensure political reliability of the command structure. After the Civil War in which he played such an important part in the Red victory, and the death of Lenin in 1924, he was outmaneuvered by Stalin, purged from the Party, and exiled in 1929.

Believing that Stalinism was a betrayal of the Revolution, Trotsky became the leading anti-Stalinist Marxist of his time. He was assassinated on Stalin's orders in Mexico on August 21, 1940. So, while he did live to see the beginning of the Second World War, he was dead when Miriam Kellerman thinks of him on seeing the train pass at Rostov. Indeed, trains became a symbol in the Russian mind and literature for the iron forces of modernity, representing, it seems, a malefic but inevitable working out of humanity's historical destiny.

14. *Krasnodarsky.* Kronsnodar, located on the Kuban River, is a city in southern Russia and is the administrative center of the Kuban region. Founded in 1793 it was called "Catherine's Gift" in gratitude to Catherine the Great's grant of land in that region to the Black Sea Cossacks. After the Revolution it was renamed Krasnodar. During the Civil War it changed hands many times, even though many of the Kuban Cossacks were Whites. In the Second World War the Germans took the city in August 1942 and relinquished it in February '43 for the final time.

15. *Belorechenskaya.* Down the track a bit from Krasnodar, Belorechensk is a small town in the Krasnador Region of Russia. Unknown to Miriam, it was the site of a rather large Soviet labor camp or what would in time be known as a *gulag*, a term essentially invented by Alexander Solzhenitsyn in his monumental work *The Gulag Archipelago*. Established in the 1930s by Stalin, the system got increasingly larger, reaching its apogee in 1953, the year of his death, with a population of 2,750,000 prisoners in over 500 labor camps. (See *The Black Book of Communism*, Courtois et al., Harvard Press, 1999, p. 238.)

16. "The Germans are coming!" Halted at the gates of Moscow on December 6, 1941, Hitler in 1942 decided not to go against Leningrad or Moscow but to attack in the south. In his Nuremberg testimony, Field Marshal Paulus, former commander of the Sixth Army, testifying for the prosecution, stated that Hitler told him at a conference at Poltava, on June 1, 1942, "If I do not get the oil of Maikop and Grosny, then I must end this war." Both Maikop and Grosny are north of the Caucasia region (NMT, vol. 7, page 259, Feb. 11, 1946).

However, the German generals were dubious about a new offensive anywhere, but, according to Alan Clark, "In reality, Hitler had an absolutely clear idea of what he was going to do. He intended to smash the Russians once and for all by breaking the power of the army in the south, capturing the seat of their economy, and taking the option of either wheeling up behind Moscow or down to the oil fields of Baku" (Clark, *Barbarossa*, Quill, 1965, p. 237). This would involve basically three thrusts: Voronezh in the north, Stalingrad in the middle, and through Rostov into the Caucasus toward Baku on the Caspian Sea. The offensive began on June 28, 1942.

17. Tbilisi, the capital of Georgia on the river Kura, has a population today of over a million. On the Suran Mountain range it is on the watershed between the Black and Caspian seas.

18. Baku, the capital of Azerbaijan, is situated above the half-moon–shaped bay of the Apsheron Peninsula, which fingers out into the

Caspian. At the time, Baku was the oil capital of the USSR, which attracted the petroleum-starved Third Reich.

19. Kharkov, a Ukrainian provincial capital about halfway between Kiev and Rostov, very near the Russian frontier, was the scene of much heavy fighting and fell to the Nazis in October of '41. No doubt Becky is thinking of the Soviet attempt to retake Kharkov in May 1942, which failed.

20. Sebastopol was traditionally a fortified town on the southern tip of the Crimean Peninsula in the Black Sea. It was a redoubt for the White forces in the Civil War and the scene of tenacious defense by the Soviets in the struggle with Hitler. The Germans dropped 50,000 pounds of bombs and thousands of artillery shells on the city over the course of six days as a prelude to the German-Romanian offensive that took three weeks of hard fighting, including two days of house-to-house before the city fell on July 3, 1942. Toward the end, the stench from the bodies was so bad that the defenders had to wear gas masks.

Leo Tolstoy served as a young officer in the Crimean War at the siege of the same place. His *Sebastopol Sketches* expressed his attitudes about war, which became more fully developed in his masterpiece, *War and Peace*.

21. Krasnovodsk, a Russian fort and port built in 1869 on the eastern edge of the Caspian Sea, became a railway junction for the Central Asian railway leading to Tashkent. It has more oil than water.

22. Semipalatinsk, also known as Semey, is the capital of the Semey region of northeastern Kazakhstan on the Irtysh River and the Turkistan-Siberia railroad and today has a population of nearly 400,000. The name means "seven palaces" and derives from a famous Buddhist temple with as many halls. It has traditionally been a hub of trade for Russia with the east, particularly China, and before the railroad was on the caravan route between Europe and Mongolia.

In 1947 Lavrentii Beria (1899–1953), head of the NKVD, chose the site for nuclear testing. Gulag labor built the test facilities on the banks of the Irtysh only about 150 kilometers from the city. The first Soviet atomic bomb was exploded there (called *Joe One* by the Americans), scattering radiation over the entire Semey region.

Dostoyevsky, incarcerated in 1849 for political subversion, was released from a Siberian prison in 1854 to spend the remainder of his sentence of exile as a solider in the 7th Battalion of Siberian Infantry posted at Semipalatinsk. He stayed for more than five years, returning to Russia for the first time on July

2, 1859. Coming to the signpost marking the frontier (a two-headed Romanov eagle on a small obelisk), Dostoyevsky took off his hat, made the sign of the cross, and said, "The Lord has at last permitted me to see once more this promised land." Then he, his wife, and stepson went off into the woods to pick strawberries.

23. Ust-Kamenogorsk, in the Kazakh Soviet Republic, is the end of the line and the easternmost point of Miriam's journey. Here she is literally in a mountain corner, down the Irtysh River from Semipalatinsk between China and Siberia.

24. Field Marshal Friedrich Paulus (1880–1957), commander of the Sixth Army, was born in such modest circumstances that he was rejected by the navy because of poor pedigree. He then joined the army and served as a junior staff officer in the First World War. Despite lack of real command or distinction, he stayed in the army and was promoted to lieutenant general in 1940. In '41 he was promoted to full general and given the Sixth Army in relief of Field Marshal Walthar von Reichenau, who had recommended Paulus for the post. It's not clear why. Clark says of him, "Paulus may have been a good staff officer; as a commander in the field he was slow-witted and unimaginative to the point of stupidity" (Clark, *Barbarossa*, p. 237).

The Sixth Army distinguished itself in the Great War and was reorganized in October 1939 with Reichenau at its head. Though the army saw no action that year, despite guarding against an Allied attack from the west that never came, in 1940 it fought in the Low Countries and then made its famous triumphal march into Paris. In Barbarossa it spearheaded the attack on Kiev in September 1941, and then Reichenau, an ardent Nazi, ordered that the remaining Jews there should be liquidated. Some 33,000 people were murdered at Babi Yar by the *Einsatzgruppen*. (It's estimated that more than 100,000 people were ultimately killed there: Jews, Communists, Gypsies, etc.)

To clarify matters to his army, in October 1941, Reichenau issued his infamous general order that stated: "In the Eastern region, the soldier is not merely a fighter according to the rules of the art of war, but also the bearer of an inexorable national idea and the avenger of bestialities inflicted upon the German people and its racial kin. Therefore, the soldier must have full understanding for the necessity for severe but just atonement on Jewish subhumanity."

Both General von Rundstedt and Erich von Manstein issued similar orders. Using Reichenau's as a model, Manstein's proclaimed: "The Jewish Bolshevik system must be wiped out once and for all and should never again be allowed to invade European living space. The German soldier has therefore not only the task of crushing the military potential of this system, he comes also as the bearer of a racial concept and the avenger of all the crimes which have been perpetrated on him and the German people. The soldier must appreciate the necessity for the harsh punishment of Jewry, the spirit bearer of Bolshevik terror."

Reichenau died of natural causes in early 1942 and so was never brought to justice, but von Manstein, when asked under cross examination at Nuremberg, said that he "had forgotten about" the directive. Manstein was later tried by a British military tribunal and sentenced to 18 years in prison for war crimes but was released after serving only four.

General Paulus, to his credit, rescinded the order. Greatly reinforced he advanced his Sixth Army as the central element of the 1942 offensive described in note 16, leading it eastward to Stalingrad, where it was annihilated in the greatest battle of the war. Of the 284,000 Germans surrounded by the Soviets, 34,000 were evacuated, 160,000 killed, and 90,000 captured. Of these about half died on the march to the camps, with only about 5,000 getting home. The Sixth Army's shuffle through Red Square in 1943 had a decidedly different air from its parade down the Champs Élysées in 1940. A Russian woman related to this writer said that as a girl she had gone down to taunt them as they marched through, but upon seeing them, instead of jeering, she wept.

John Lukacs, in *The Last European War*, makes a compelling case that the real turning point of the war was December 6 and 7, 1941—Moscow and Pearl Harbor. In those two days, he points out, the war swung from a European one that Hitler might have won to a world war that he had no hope of winning (Chapter 9, "Germany Halted," Yale, 1976). Still it is interesting to note that, after Stalingrad, the Germans never again thought of victory, while the Soviets never thought of anything else. If Moscow/Pearl Harbor was the strategic turning point, then Stalingrad was the psychological one.

As for Paulus, promoted to field marshal on the day he surrendered, he survived to make propaganda for the Soviets and to testify at Nuremberg for the prosecution. He lived in East Germany, finding employment as a police inspector until his death in Dresden.

25. This account of Lt. Yelchenko is quoted word for word as reported by Alexander Werth in his book *Russia at War* (Carroll & Graff, 1964, pp. 540–541).

26. "Well, that finishes it" (Werth, p. 541).

27. Marshal Konstantin Rokossovsky (1896–1968) had an unclear background. Polish, he was orphaned at age 14 and forced to work in a factory.

In the Great War he joined the Tsarist Army and served as a non-commissioned officer in a dragoon regiment. In 1917 he joined the Bolshevik Party and became an officer in the Red Army during the Civil War. He distinguished himself and won the Soviets' highest award for bravery, the Order of the Red Banner. Afterward he became an armored specialist.

He clashed with senior officers on the importance of tank warfare and was falsely targeted by Stalin "for having connections with foreign intelligence." He was arrested in 1937 by the NKVD and tortured and imprisoned in a gulag, where he remained at hard labor until 1940, when he was released on Stalin's orders. He was sent to the so-called "Villa of Ecstasy" on the Black Sea to recover and then summoned to meet personally with Stalin, who made him Corps Commander in the Kiev district. He led the 16th Army in the defense of Smolensk in 1941 and played a pivotal role in the defense of Moscow, serving under Zhukov. In a famous encounter he openly argued with Stalin over the tactics of defending the capital. Stalin relented, and Rokossovsky's approach proved successful. At Stalingrad he commanded the northern wing of the army that encircled Paulus.

Rokossovsky served with great distinction at Kursk and later led his forces into Poland and into north Prussia, where he linked up with Montgomery while Zhukov took Berlin. On orders from Stalin he halted his army on the banks of the Vistula River and so did not come to the rescue of the "Warsaw Uprising." It is not clear whether this reflected his personal views or was merely an act of obedience. But as a Pole who spoke Polish with a Russian accent, it is clear he was no Polish nationalist but a faithful servant of Stalin. For this he was made a marshal of the Soviet Union.

28. Alma-Ata is now known as Almaty. In 1929 it became the capital of the Kazakh Republic of the USSR and then of the Republic of Kazakhstan in 1991. In 1998 the capital was moved to Astana. The city is almost 3,000 feet in elevation and lies in a spectacular valley between mountains that are perpetually snowcapped. Traditionally a tourist city because of its beauty, parks, museums, boulevards, and snow sports, it has a harsh winter climate that is particularly daunting.

29. Hitler, after signing a non-aggression pact with Stalin on August 23, 1939, invaded Poland on September 1, thus beginning World War II. Stalin invaded Poland from the east on September 17, and Warsaw surrendered to the Germans on the 28th.

30. On June 27, 1940, Stalin invaded Northern Bukovina and annexed it to the Soviet Union as part of Western Ukraine.

31. Lvov (Lwow) is a Polish city in the southeast part of the country. The Jews there were fortunate to be in the Soviet zone. However, things were difficult under Stalin: he never initiated a policy of outright genocide against them, but little was done by the Soviet regime to warn the Jews or evacuate them from the Nazi threat once it came in 1941, and most of them perished.

32. NKVD—This Soviet political police has gone by various names. Under the czar it was known as the *Okrana*, then under Felix Dzerzhinsky (1917 to 1922) it was known as the *Cheka*. It was "abolished" and replaced by the GPU, after which it was the NKVD from 1934 to 1943, and was changed again to NKGB. This name lasted only until 1946, when it was replaced by the MVD, and then in '54 to the KGB. The more it has changed, the more it has stayed the same.

33. David is referring to the "non-aggression pact" mentioned in note 29.

34. In the Leningrad siege, Hitler's army in the north failed to take the city but laid siege to it on October 30, 1941. This lasted for "900 days." While some supplies got over the frozen Lake Ladoga, between the city and Finland, they were not enough. It's estimated that of the three million people remaining in the city, half either froze to death or died of famine. Leningrad was not finally relieved until January 27, 1944. The best book this writer can find on the subject is Harrison Salisbury's *The 900 Days* (Harper and Row, 1969).

35. In Tolstoy's great novel *War and Peace*, Prince Andrey Bolkonsky, a wealthy nobleman, serves valiantly in the Russian army against Napoleon. He is wounded and presumed dead on the field of Austerlitz. He becomes betrothed to the beautiful but very young Natasha Rostova. The prince's eccentric father insists on a long engagement, and, in frustration, Natasha is indiscrete with another man. Andrey breaks off the relationship. Later, Napoleon invades Russia, and Andrey, declining a safe staff position, insists on leading his regiment and is fatally wounded at the battle of Borodino outside Moscow. He is found among the wounded by Natasha, who nurses him; they are reconciled, but he dies.

36. Anne Frank was a teenage Jewish girl who hid from the Nazis in an attic in Holland. She and her family managed to evade capture until August 1944. They were deported to Birkenau. From there she was sent to Belsen, where she died of typhus at age 15. Needless to say, her *Diary of Anne Frank* is one of the most moving accounts in all of Holocaust literature. She wrote: "Who has inflicted this upon us? Who has made us Jews different to all the

people? Who has allowed us to suffer so terribly up till now? It is God that has made us as we are, but it will be God, too, who will rise us up again. If we bear all this suffering, and if there are still Jews left when it is over, then Jews, instead of being doomed, will be held up as an example. Who knows, it might even be our religion from which the world and all the peoples learn good, and for that reason and that reason only do we have to suffer now. We can never become just Netherlanders, or just English, or representatives of any country for that matter; we will always remain Jews, but we want to, too" (pp. 174–75 as published in Washington Square Press Publication of Pocket Books, Simon and Schuster, 1972).

37. "Questions about the Jews" refers to a Soviet policy, mandated by Stalin, that no distinction was to be made between the Jews as Nazi victims and other groups. Hence, no special questions or inquiries on their behalf were permitted.

38. Although it has become nearly synonymous now, the etymology of *holocaust* does not clearly mean Hitler's systematic destruction of the Jews. According to the *Oxford English Dictionary*, the word was first used in this sense in 1942. But it's clear that by the 1970s, at the latest, the term had come to mean just that. Some credit the present meaning of the word to Elie Wiesel.

As to the number of victims, Martin Gilbert states: "The systematic attempt to destroy all European Jewry—an attempt known as the Holocaust—began in the last week of June 1941 within hours of the German invasion of the Soviet Union. This onslaught upon Jewish life in Europe continued without respite for nearly four years. At its most intense moments, during the autumn of 1941 and again during the summer and autumn of 1942, many thousands of Jews were killed every day. By the time Nazi Germany had been defeated, as many as six million of Europe's eight million Jews had been slaughtered: if the killing had run its course, the horrific figure would have been even higher" (*The Holocaust*, 1985, Preface).

Some scholars think the term should be broadened to include all victims of Nazi crime: Slavs, Gypsies, partisans, dissidents, Russian prisoners of war, etc. Done in this way, these numbers are 3.6 to 6 million Slavic citizens: 1.8-1.9 million Gentile Poles, 2.5 to 4 million Russian POWs, and 1-1.5 million political dissidents. In this calculation it is not difficult to reach 17 million victims. According to Gilbert the total war deaths will never be known, but he puts it at about 46 million. Almost half of these were in the Soviet Union, which lost 20 million, while China lost 6 million to the Japanese (*World War Two*, Henry Holt, Chapter 53, "Unfinished Business").

39. On March 19, 1944, the Soviets crossed the Dniester River against German resistance, and on April 2, they entered Romania.

40. Paul Celan was the *nom de plume* for Paul Antschel (1920–1970); "Celan" is an anagram for the Romanian spelling of his surname. Born in Czernowitz, he was raised by his father to be a Zionist and by his mother to love German literature. He is now considered one of the major poets of the last century. As a youth he left Bukovina to study medicine in Paris, but he returned home the next year determined to dedicate himself to poetry. On his way home he went via Berlin and was there to witness the *Kristallnacht*. Then in 1940 Stalin's invasion of Bukovina deprived him of any lingering illusions about communism. For a time he considered himself a "Trotskyite," but he always remained a Zionist.

When Hitler invaded, Celan witnessed the horrors of the *Einsatzgruppen* as they rounded up Jews for execution and deportation while busying themselves with burning down Czernowitz's 600-year-old Great Synagogue. Eventually Celan was arrested along with his parents, and, for reasons that are not clear, they were separated. Like the Kellermans, his father and mother perished at the Bershad ghetto. But Celan managed to survive in a labor camp that was liberated by the Soviets in February 1944. He returned to Czernowitz for a time but then went to Bucharest until 1947, where he was active in literary circles. His *Todesfuge* (*Death Fugue*) appeared that same year.

Unable to live under communism, he left for Paris, where he settled. Though fluent in French he continued to write in German. He said, "There is nothing in the world for which a poet will give up writing, not even when he is a Jew and the language of his poems is German."

He developed a profound interest in the philosophy of Martin Heidegger, but this relationship was compromised by Heidegger's Nazi past. Many European intellectuals, having lost faith in religion, also lost faith in reason and so were left with little else than faith in the absurd. Hence, Celan's interest in the Existentialist movement of the post-war period, of which Heidegger was considered a prominent member.

Celan took his own life in 1970 by drowning himself in the Seine. Anyone interested in his life should look at *Paul Celan* by John Felstiner (Yale, 1995).

41. Bershad was a ghetto established across the Dniester River in the Western Ukraine region known as Transnistria. Jews were deported there beginning in the autumn of 1941, with about 100,000 dying at that location or en route. Of those that survived the journey (many doing hard labor along the way), most died of disease in the ghetto, particularly from typhus (Michael R. Marrus, *The Holocaust in History*, Brandeis, 1987, pp. 79–80). The trip from Czernowitz took about five days, packed in cattle cars.

SS *Einsatzgruppe* D, under Otto Ohlendorf, reached Czernowitz July 5–6, and aided by Romanian fascists, burned the 600-year-old Great Synagogue and began to murder, torture, and round up Jews for deportation to Transnistria.

42. Schiller's poem "Resignation":
   Take back my permit to happiness!
   I bring it back to you unopened.
   I know nothing of bliss.

43. Ibid.

44. Zweig and his wife, Elizabeth, committed suicide in Petropolis, Brazil, on February 23, 1942. After thanking the people of Brazil, he said: "My love for the country increased from day to day, and nowhere else would I have preferred to build up a new existence, the world of my own language having disappeared for me and my spiritual home, Europe, having destroyed itself."

However, perhaps the best explanation is found in his preface to *The World of Yesterday*, his memoir: "And so I belong to nowhere, and everywhere am a stranger, a guest at best. Europe, the homeland of my heart's choice, is lost to me, since it has torn itself apart suicidally a second time in a war of brother against brother. Against my will I have witnessed the most terrible defeat of reason and the wildest triumph of brutality in the chronicle of the ages. Never—and I say this without pride, but rather with shame—has any generation experienced such a moral retrogression from such spiritual height as our generation has. In the short interval between the time when my beard began to sprout and now, when it is beginning to turn gray, in this half-century more radical changes and transformations have taken place than in ten generations of mankind; and each of it feels: it is almost too much!"

45. On October 20, 1946, the first free elections since 1932 occurred in Berlin, and another was not held until 1990, after the Berlin Wall came down. The last Soviet soldier left Berlin on September 8, 1994.

46. On May 26, 1946, elections to the constituent assembly were held, which gave the Communists 114 of 300 seats. As a result, Communist leader Klement Gottwald formed a new coalition cabinet. On February 25, 1948, under a threat of a coup d'etat, the Communists, under Gottwald's leadership and Moscow's direction, seized control of the country, and Czechoslovakia became a Soviet satellite.

Glossary

Barbarossa. "Red Beard," the code name for the German invasion of the USSR that took place on June 22, 1941.

Babushka. Russian for grandmother.

Beryoza. Russian for birch tree.

Chyort. Russian for the devil. Often used as a curse.

Frontovik. Soviet army slang for a veteran fighter.

Einsatzgruppen. Nazi killing squads used exclusively in the East against Jews, Communists, Gypsies, and "other undesirables" (see note 5).

Izba. Russian for a peasant hut or small house, often with only a room or two.

Komsomol. Acronym for the Soviet Young Communist political organization with the upper age being about 21.

Heinkel. A medium German bomber officially known as the He 111. Used extensively in the Battle of Britain, then shifted to the Eastern Front after Hitler's invasion of the Soviet Union in June 1941.

Kolkhoz. A Russian or Ukrainian collective farm (see note 11).

Muzhik. Russian for a peasant.

NKVD. Soviet secret police. Formerly the *Cheka* (see note 32).

Shabbat dinner. The Jewish Friday evening meal preformed in preparation for the Jewish holy day of Saturday. It was the only religious ceremony regularly observed by the Kellermans.

Stuka. A small German dive-bomber, officially known as the Junkers JU 87. Used almost exclusively in the early phase of the war during the German *Blitzkrieg* or "lightning war" (see note 4).

Treif. Yiddish pejorative for any non-kosher food.

Ushanka. Russian for fur hat.

Valenki. Russian for winter boots.

Voskresenye. Russian for rebirth or resurrection; also the word for Sunday.

Wehrmacht. The German regular army. To be distinguished from the *Luftwaffe* (air force) or the more elite forces like the *Waffen* SS or the murder squads like the *Einsatzgruppen.*

Photographs

Penina Geller Krupitsky, the real-life Miriam Kellerman,
as photographed in Vienna in 1946

*Penina, shown here in Berlin in 1945, emigrated from Russia
to the United States in the 1980s.*

About the Authors

Phillip H. McMath, writer, trial lawyer, and Vietnam veteran, has combined his interests in history, in his native South, and in war to create a unique body of work, his fiction trilogy: *Native Ground* (1984), *Arrival Point* (1991), and *Lost Kingdoms* (2007). The latter novel won the Arkansiana Award for fiction sponsored by the Arkansas Library Association. McMath also is the author of two plays—*Dress Blues* and *The Hanging of David O. Dodd*. He lives in Little Rock, Arkansas, with his wife, Carol, and practices law with McMath Woods PA.

Emily Matson Lewis, a lifelong resident of Little Rock, Arkansas, has always been fascinated by stories of young people who find their lives defined by extraordinarily difficult times. She spent a year interviewing Penina Krupitsky, whose life inspired this book and showed Lewis a story on a larger scale—one encompassing a grand sweep of time, geography, and emotion. Lewis feels honored to have provided the initial notes for *The Broken Vase*.